The Blac

CW00409036

by

Christoph Fischer

Dedicated to the 'children' of my generation:

Hannes, Rupert, Ingrid, Barbara, Margret, Simon, Maria, Susanne, Gabriele, Monika and Michael.

Also with much gratitude to the many people in Germany like my characters Maria and Esat, who are working hard to make the resurrected Germany a modern state that one can be proud of.

www.christophfischerbooks.com

Excerpt of the Hinterberger Family Tree

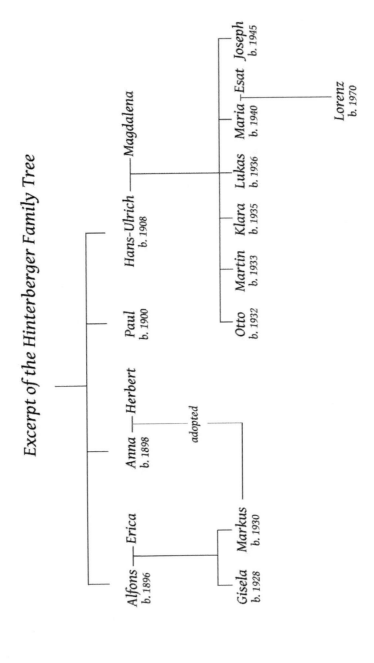

Alfons (b. 1896) — Erica

Anna (b. 1898) — Herbert

Paul (b. 1900)

Hans-Ulrich (b. 1908) — Magdalena

Gisela (b. 1928), Markus (b. 1930) — children of Alfons & Erica

Herbert — adopted — Markus

Otto (b. 1932), Martin (b. 1933), Klara (b. 1935), Lukas (b. 1936), Maria (b. 1940) — Esat Joseph (b. 1945)

Maria — Esat Joseph — Lorenz (b. 1970)

Table of Contents

Prologue: Anna and Hans-Ulrich

Anna Stockmann, nee Hinterberger, and her husband Herbert owned a huge farm with an equally impressive and renowned restaurant and inn, called The Black Eagle Inn, just outside the city limits of Heimkirchen, a sleepy Bavarian town. Their wealth of earthly possessions had made her the undisputed leader of the wider Hinterberger family and everyone who had joined them through marriage. She was a sly tyrant and a cold and hard business woman, but she had a soft spot for her little brother Hans-Ulrich.

The two siblings were part of a gang of eight children and Anna in particular had quickly learnt that it was easy to be forgotten in a crowd as large as that. Her parents were too busy running the farm to care much about individual children. Since the build-up to the Great War, they had more pressing matters at hand and left it to the elder two boys, Gerhard and Alfons, to look after the younger ones. The two boys made a terrible job of it, too young at heart and child-like to rise to the occasion. In an effectively unsupervised world it was the selfish ones who got the most and the fast ones who got some more. Any matter reported to the parents was regarded as only wasting their precious time and was resolved by punishing all involved, regardless of right and wrong.

Through Anna's early years it was a dog eat dog society and she quickly came out on top by studying her rivals and playing them off against each other.

"If you don't tell father what swear words Gerhard used against you and father finds out from someone else, he will be angry with you," she once manipulated her little sister Barbara.

"But father said we mustn't tell on each other," came the reply.

"If I told on him that would be wrong. But Gerhard spoke to you, so you have an obligation to alert father so he can make Gerhard own up and get a fair judgement for what he has done. That is not snitching, it is your holy duty," Anna insisted.

Gerhard and Barbara were both sent to their beds early that night – predictably without food - and Anna got her desired bigger share of her favourite desert, strawberries and cream.

Unaccustomed to such Machiavellian talents her siblings soon gave up on even trying to compete with her. The older boys Gerhard and Alfons remained officially in charge as far as the parents were concerned but by the time Anna was 12 she had already established herself as the actual and natural leader amongst her siblings. That position grew even stronger when the Great War broke out and her older brothers were drafted to fight for their country.

Anna was 16 years old that year and was a beautiful and much admired young woman. It was astonishing to think that someone of her high social standing in the community and who was also blessed with remarkable beauty, should worry herself over material goods in the way that she did.

Gerhard was shot in the first few days of the war and his younger brother Alfons came back soon after, badly wounded and incapable of physical work. As the third born child and eager to be considered a candidate for the running of the farm Anna got engaged to a man named Lothar at the young age of 18 in the middle of the war. Lothar, was a rich farmer's son and the match pleased both families and promised a potential further step up in society for both dynasties.

When Lothar returned in 1918, he was shell shocked and in a dreadfully lethargic way. In a scandalous move that outraged the entire community Anna unilaterally called off the wedding. The offence was irreparable and her reputation suffered from this almost unprecedented measure. Anna didn't care because she felt that she would have no future whatsoever with a dead weight like him around her neck.

Her father had once publicly hinted at the possibility of leaving the family farm to Anna - even though traditionally it should have been handed over to a son; now he was beginning to mention her younger brother Paul as his successor, a simpler but very reliable fellow.

Desperate to be given the reign over the farm herself Anna knew she had to act quickly and so she encouraged one of her admirers and a farmer's son Herbert to propose, and was engaged to him within months of breaking off with Lothar.

By now Paul had also been built up as heir and the family was expecting an announcement to that effect soon. In the brief window of time between her second engagement and a handover of the business to Paul, Anna took her brother aside one evening and had a long and uncomfortable talk with him leaving him convinced that he was not cut out for the responsibilities of a large farm on his own. He succumbed to his already latent feelings of inadequacy and left Germany a few days later, departing without a good bye, a cowardly and broken hearted exit, stealing himself out of the door at night without more than a scribbled note of farewell. He ended up making a new life for himself in America.

The shock over the sudden departure tipped the fragile father over the edge and caused a heart attack from which he never recovered. The old man was confined to his bed, swaying between life and death. Anna made sure to see a lot of him during that time and pointed out his responsibility to the farm and to make a will before it was too late. Although the dying man had his suspicions that Anna was behind Paul's abrupt departure, he realised that as his wife had no sense for business, he had no workable alternative than to leave the Hinterberger Farm and The Black Eagle Inn to his daughter.

At the age of only 23 Anna became the new mistress and married her Herbert a month later, carelessly violating the local custom to observe a year of mourning for her father. At her wedding she wore black in church to show her grief; vicious tongues whispered the black was worn for marrying Herbert rather than for losing her father.

Hans-Ulrich as the youngest boy in the Hinterberger family was the least threatening to Anna. She was ten years old when her mother had him as an afterthought to the other seven children and as the oldest girl she became a surrogate mother to him. Receiving her undivided attention Hans-Ulrich felt singled out and blindly did everything she told him to.

This special bond had lasted long into their adulthood. So much that even before he proposed to his wife Magdalena, Hans-Ulrich first asked for Anna's opinion and consent. Anna was a little jealous of Magdalena's youthful beauty - compared to her own ageing looks. However, Anna immediately recognised the vulnerability of her brother's wife-to-be and happily approved.

"Her family and their music store are nothing special of course," she was quick to point out. "Magdalena won't ever come into money," she added with a sigh.

"I know they struggle a little," Hans-Ulrich admitted, "but her father has managed to turn his musical talent into a business. Besides, he spends all his spare time playing the church organ and directing the church choir. We need to respect him for that. Magdalena has been brought up as a formidable Christian."

Anna hid her eyes which were rolling at that statement but reminded herself that it did not matter. Since Hans-Ulrich had a serious heart problem he could not himself be regarded as a great catch. His physical fragility had forced him to leave the farm and begin a career at the city administration. In the loneliness that his departure from family and farm had caused him, he had started to spend a considerable amount of his spare time at church with the choir and the priest, and the congregation had soon made Hans-Ulrich an integral part of their community. The extent of Hans-Ulrich's religious ambition shocked Anna frequently. However, so far Anna still seemed to be held in higher regard than the priest and the religious maxims.

It had been no surprise to her that Hans-Ulrich would have found his bride amongst the church crowd and if it had to be one of those rather than a farmer's daughter with a generous dowry, then it might as well be someone as easily dominated and persuaded as Magdalena promised to be.

Magdalena, in turn, was in complete awe of the Hinterberger family who was so large and well-connected, and she was hugely intimidated by Hans-Ulrich's bigger sister of whom her future husband had always spoken so highly. She soon grew accustomed to the rules of the Hinterbergers and accepted her low rank in the pecking order humbly.

Chapter 1: Maria (1940)

During the early stages of the new war, a time when victory was certain and - in the view of everyone in Heimkirchen - completely inevitable, the baby Maria Hinterberger was born; it was a Saturday evening in September 1940 and absolutely nothing seemed to be able to stop Hitler and the German nation.

The small Bavarian town – like the rest of the country – had already been thoroughly 'cleansed' of the very few Jews, Communists and other 'subversive' elements that had found their way to this little backward and hidden corner of the world. There was no one left for the enthusiastic supporters of the Fuhrer to focus their hatred on but the Russians, the French and the British.

German troops had made remarkable progress everywhere in Europe and despite what the deeply religious Hinterberger family and some other citizens of Heimkirchen secretly thought of Hitler and his hateful politics, the military success promised a great future for the nation and left the people on the streets with wonderful feelings of optimism and curiosity.

All the posters sent there from Berlin, warning of Communists and Jews, seemed totally out of place and unnecessary. The city was in total harmony with their leadership - at least that was how the population of Heimkirchen would appear to any outsider passing through the town. On this beautiful early autumn day it was easy to forget about the war.

Being the fifth child Maria caused her mother Magdalena comparatively little pain in the way of labour. The first signs of an impending delivery had – rather conveniently - started moments before lunch was being served, leaving just enough time to feed the other four children and send for the midwife before things became more complicated.

Magdalena was a beautiful woman, whose body seemed to have suffered little damage from giving birth four times already. Born herself at the beginning of the Great War Magdalena had learned to keep quiet and not to bother her own worried mother with any demands of her own.

The latest addition to the family arrived with what felt like consideration for the pregnant woman's other duties. Magdalena could not have chosen a better moment for this birth had she been asked to and this gift for convenience and timing made the new child utterly likeable, albeit easily forgettable in the context of the bigger and more dramatic picture.

She had inherited her mother's long and thin nose, her green eyes and dark blonde hair, she was of average size and weight for a new born and had few remarkable physical features and to a mother of five it came as a relief to have at least one child that was so easy to handle.

From the smooth way that Maria had come to her today Magdalena already sensed that this child was special and would not cause her as much grief as her siblings had. Little did Magdalena know how wrong she was.

Magdalena had never really wanted to have that many children. Uneducated and naïve she truly believed for far too long that who had children and who didn't was the Lord's will regardless of their night time activities in the bedroom. Her husband, Hans-Ulrich, told her on their wedding night that every married couple had to perform this act daily, so it would not be the couple's lower urges that dictated reproduction but the Good Lord himself. He himself had only heard this from a friend at school, and Magdalena believed him, just as he had believed his classmate.

Magdalena suffered a miscarriage after her fourth child and her doctor started to explain the biology and physiology of reproduction in more detail to her, recommending that she should 'take a break' for a few months before trying for another child. Being a devout Catholic woman she rejected any type of contraception, even the most natural methods such as abstinence and celibacy. It was a terrible sin that would cost her the reserved place in paradise for sure. The furthest she would be prepared to go would have been a passive acceptance should her husband chose of his own accord not to become intimate. Should however Hans-Ulrich be drawn to the act by his urges or by divine inspiration then she certainly had no right to stand in his way of fulfilling what was the Christian duty of married life.

"Can you believe this impertinent and blasphemous man?" she asked her husband when she got home that day.

11

"You mustn't get angry," Hans-Ulrich replied. "God will punish him for his conduct."

"You should have heard him talk," Magdalena insisted.

"Shush," he interrupted her. "I don't want to hear about it. That is between him, the priest and the Good Lord to judge and deal with. You did well for walking out before he could corrupt you with his sinful ideas."

It was not as if Magdalena would have known any modern ways of contraception. In her own sexually oppressed upbringing she would not even have been able to tell the dangerous from the harmless days of her cycle. Once at school she had overheard one of her comrades talk about ways to satisfy a man 'by other means', but to this day she could not make sense of what the girl had meant and if she had managed to figure it out, she would have been outraged by the mere thought.

The Lord seemed to have mercy on her troubled body and two years went by before she noticed the first signs of Maria's conception.

Since the Nazis had taken official control of the state any expectant woman was admired and complemented even by complete strangers and praised as a symbol of the prosperous future. Populating the world with German offspring was in line with the current politics and had earned Magdalena good will and benevolence wherever she went. Everyone loved a fertile woman and her round belly.

The summer had been very hot and humid and had made the pregnancy quite hard to bear. Being a mother of four was hard work even on a good day. The extra weight was pulling her down and the high temperatures brought on unexpected faints. No longer fascinated by the miracle of life and generally very tired, Magdalena found it an unwelcome ordeal and only her strong faith made her put on a brave face and thank the Lord for it.

Since the miscarriage fear had developed in Magdalena's mind and the more children there were outside of her belly the harder it had become to go through her daily duties with one inside of it but she kept such thoughts quietly to herself and hoped that the Good Lord had not heard her thoughts on that particular occasion.

The actual day of Maria's birth was surprisingly warm, especially for September, leaving Magdalena doubly relieved when the child was finally pushed out of her womb just as the cooling evening temperatures started to make for a much more pleasant environment too.

The child screamed briefly to save the nurse the hassle of slapping it, then it remained quiet and endured the washing and weighing without the slightest signs of rebellion or discomfort. While Magdalena's experienced breasts cushioned the new born child during its well-deserved first rest in the outside world, the mother was already making plans to go to early Mass the following day and then continue with her Sunday duties.

Magdalena was a hard working and devoted mother. Well-meaning and good hearted, she was caring and gentle to her neighbours and her family alike, and always happy to put her needs last. She hated it when she had to be cruel to be kind and force them for their own long term good. She had experienced a strict upbringing herself and since following Catholic principles did not always come naturally to her offspring, an attitude of gentleness sadly was often not the right way to guide the 'lost little souls'.

She also had to spare Hans-Ulrich disappointment with moral failings of his children as well as with herself as their trusted educator. Any punishment she had to give out she regretted deeply.

"Don't let your father see you like this," she would scold the children when they returned dirty from the playground.

"Make sure you say hello to the priest so he knows you were there or else your father will think you disappointed him."

"Don't force me to beat some sense into you, please don't!"

The day of Maria's birth Hans-Ulrich took his four other children to his sister Anna so that they would not be in the way of their mother's impending ordeal.

"Magdalena must have gone into early labour," Anna called out excitedly when she saw Hans-Ulrich and his four little ones walk in the door. "That woman is doing well," she added.

"She is indeed," Hans-Ulrich agreed. "I know I have left the children with you a lot lately and I heard you telling off Alfons for always bringing his children around…"

"Oh, his children are a different matter," Anna interrupted. "They just use this place as an amusement park. Yours, in contrast, do nothing but help. Now go and don't miss the birth of your next child. We can chew the fat when that is over and done with. Don't worry about those four; they'll sort out the hay loft nicely."

Once he had left Anna stopped smiling and abruptly told the children to make themselves useful and then she left them in the hands of her farm staff.

Hans-Ulrich and Magdalena's children were frequently invited to help out at Anna's farm in exchange for a good meal. They were worked very hard in the fields or in the stables but seemed to enjoy it and rarely complained.

One of the servants at the farm, a woman called Helga, had a talent for utilising even the little ones for her work. Magdalena's youngest son, Lukas, was four years old and he followed Helga wherever she went and happily assisted her sweeping the floors, feeding the animals and picking the feathers of dead chicken.

Anna always rewarded hard labour with the most exquisite meals and treats that put their lunches and dinners at home to shame but these were only served if Helga assured her that such privileges had truly been earned.

While Anna was a figure of authority and had little time for the follies of youth, Helga served as buffer between the huge demands and the children's need for release. Under her rule the children were allowed to make noise and have fun as much as they wanted - something that was considered inappropriate in the square between their house and the local church. The stiff reserve that came from living with a civil servant for a father and an obsessive church goer for a mother was already getting to the little children and they cherished the opportunity to let off steam without being reprimanded. Once they had got that out of their system they happily worked hard without the need for any pressure. The prospect of a delicious meal was motivation enough.

Magdalena knew she was lucky that Anna took such an interest in her children. It was noticeable just how much better behaved the little rascals were when they returned from the farm. She was unaware that the reason behind her children's model

14

behaviour was the result of Helga's free rein rather than Anna's strict regime.

Sadly for Anna her own marriage had produced no children. At first she blamed her husband. It had to be Herbert's fault: Anna's family was too fertile to suggest otherwise. She never spoke about it in public but it secretly caused her much pain.

One night Helga walked in on Anna crying and after much probing found out what the source of Anna's sorrow was.

"It isn't God who gives us children," Helga assured her. "You mustn't think that you have done anything wrong or that there is any rhyme or reason for it. It is not a punishment from God. It's just bad luck."

"How can you say such a blasphemous thing?" Anna replied mechanically.

Even in her weakest moments Anna never forgot her responsibility as a public figure.

"I do believe, you know. I am not a heathen," Helga assured her. "But you need to keep your eyes and ears wide open to more than just religion. There is a lot that you and I don't understand. I have heard that the scientists can prove that a long time ago humans used to be like monkeys. God did not make us the way we are now," Helga said animatedly. "We became that way."

"But the garden of Eden and the Bible..." Anna said quickly, eagerly waiting for Helga to continue with her line of reasoning.

"Some say that maybe the writers of the Gospel misunderstood or someone translated it wrongly," Helga elaborated. "Trust me. The Pope is stubborn and refuses to accept the most obvious facts of life. There are new scientific facts and they are widely being accepted in the world. You may not have heard about them here on the farm, but I have."

Protestants in this Catholic heartland of Heimkirchen were already considered heathens and so this radical view that Helga was relating was outrageous to Anna's ears but very appealing and received her full attention. Over the months that followed Helga gradually persuaded Anna that also some other teachings of the Catholic Church were out-dated, superstitious or irrelevant.

15

Anna's childhood experience of an unjust and chaotic world where the fittest triumphed and not the most pious, had not induced much faith in her. For her, regular church attendance was just a matter of appearance; one needed to be perceived as faithful as everyone else in a town like Heimkirchen and she used religion and quotes from the priest or the Bible mainly to manipulate her siblings to comply with her will. Anyone demanding justice could be told to 'turn the other cheek' and anyone challenging her was reminded to be humble and not display the shameful characteristics of the deadly sin of hubris. Anna had an answer for everything, whether it was true to the Bible or not. By the standards of the Catholic teachings Anna had violated many rules and it was much more appealing to believe her servant's logical and liberating modern views than to live in permanent fear of purgatory, even if it left her without anyone to blame for her childless state.

As soon as Hans-Ulrich had his first child, her maternal instincts towards him immediately transferred to his children. Anna had many nieces and nephews but only a few of those were realistic candidates in her eyes to ever become her successor. During harvest time and other busy periods all family offspring were frequently sent to the farm to help. This was a chance for the new generation to prove themselves worthy and attract Anna's attention in an unofficial competition for her favour. Like with her own siblings when they were young, Anna used this to her advantage and ruled her nieces and nephews by dividing and conquering. The ones with potential were the ones that needed to be challenged and forced to succeed against the trying circumstances and heavy obstacles which she readily threw at them. She wanted a survivor like herself, a fighter with determination and a strong power of endurance. Because of her inclination towards Hans-Ulrich, she would have preferred to pick one of his children as successor but so far she was not sure that any of them had what it took. Admittedly they were still young, there were currently few male role models for them, and Hans-Ulrich's offspring seemed naïve and immature for their age.

"They are too young to show what they are going to be like later," Helga often told her. "Let them have a little fun. You have a long time to shape them into how you want them to be. You are still young, you don't need to pick one of them yet."

Anna was not convinced. Her little empire had grown and she felt she could not start training the next generation soon enough to pass on her experience: the sooner she started to challenge them, the deeper it would be ingrained into their very core.

Her war wounded brother Alfons had two healthy and strong children who were both a little older than Hans-Ulrich's offspring and were also frequent visitors to the farm. She liked the boy, Markus. He was clever and whatever he lacked in endurance he made up for by making useful observations and suggestions. There was a lot of potential there, if only he didn't always cling to his little sister Gisela and bring her everywhere with him: the girl was dull and simple. There was something wrong about those two and their close relationship. As the oldest of her nephews and nieces, Anna would have expected Markus to take the lead and become a figure of authority but he seemed only to be interested in Gisela and her company. The boy was unlike any she knew and as much as he intrigued and fascinated her, she also wondered if he would ever be able to run a successful business. She would have considered disciplining the young boy into shape if only he displayed stronger characteristics and so her focus remained desperately on Hans-Ulrich's children with only half an eye directed at Markus.

Markus and Gisela were almost teenagers and needed less careful observation than the little ones. The two often disappeared into the nearby woods and came back with mushrooms or berries or a bunch of wild flowers for Anna and Helga, attention that Anna enjoyed despite her suspicions that she was being played.

Lukas, Hans-Ulrich's youngest son at the age of four, was also the youngest of all the children at the farm. Helga favoured him because despite his young age he displayed enormous discipline and worked very hard.

He had an enquiring mind and Helga had a hard time making sure he did not run into trouble or hurt himself with the farm machinery. She adored his interest and involvement and in her view he was the one whom Anna should be considering as her successor. He seemed to have all the skills necessary for success.

His older brothers Otto and Martin showed little promise. They were irresponsible rascals and needed a lot of play time before they could be usefully employed: Helga did not blame them. She appreciated what a tight regime these children were exposed to daily and how desperate they had to be for freedom and a break from this strict discipline at home. Lukas never had these urges for silliness.

Anna watched Otto and Martin closely. Otto frequently spoilt any good impression he had made on his elders by playing pranks on his siblings or dropping plates and tools. There was carelessness in his character that didn't respond to any attempts to eradicate it. Martin was surprisingly strong and fit but his downfall was a compulsive need to show off and put his other siblings and cousins in the shade. He liked to brag about everything he did, a quality that Anna never had liked in men.

Since Helga was the only person who had ever seen Anna cry she had felt almost motherly towards her mistress and was determined to help her to make the right decision as to who was going to take over the Hinterberger Farm and The Black Eagle Inn.

The evening after Maria's birth Anna surprised the children with a small banquet of fresh cheese and meat. Two of her servants carried in a large table filled with the delicious food. As usual she asked each one of the children present to report what they had done during the day and why they should be granted to participate in the celebrations for Maria's birth.

Martin immediately ran up to his aunt and bragged about how much hay he had shifted all day. Otto told of his hard labour in the stalls and generously mentioned how Lukas had helped him. Klara, Hans-Ulrich's only girl so far, said that she had done the dishes in the restaurant. Helga confirmed how well the four of them had performed their duties, omitting the initial mess the boys had made of their jobs. Satisfied Anna granted the four of them their seat on the table. Of the other children a few were sent away to beg for food at the restaurant since Helga confirmed that their efforts had not been particularly dedicated today; amongst that group were Markus and Gisela.

While his sister was turning away with a sunken head and sad eyes, Markus, in a theatrical gesture, bowed in front of Anna.

"I sincerely apologise for my shortcomings today," he said with comical exaggeration. "Dear auntie, please forgive my youthful foibles. May I make it up to you by staying and serving food to the more deserving of my family?"

Anna could not help but smile. Who had taught the boy to speak like this? What a silly billy, she thought. The other children all laughed out loud at his speech and she found herself caught up in it.

"Fine. Since we have a new addition to the family today everyone will be allowed to share the banquet," she ruled. "Gisela, get the other wastrels back here, too, and tell them to thank your brother for their good luck today. Next time they won't be as fortunate."

Helga was the only one who was not amused by Markus. She resented that all day he had been day dreaming and wasting time in the woods and now he would get the same rewards as the hard working children.

"Thank you Aunt Anna," Markus said with a more serious note. "You shouldn't have. I really have been useless today. Do you want to know why?" he asked.

Anna was intrigued. The little boy certainly had a way with words.

"Go on, surprise me!" she encouraged him.

"I am more of a people person," he said. "Working in the stalls or the fields just isn't for me."

"You should consider yourself lucky to be able to earn your keep, young man," Anna said dryly.

"I know. You are absolutely right, dear aunt. What I mean is that I would be much more useful if I could work in the restaurant. I would like to help where I can talk to people and have company all day. Couldn't you let me try to earn my keep that way?" he asked with his best sad puppy eyes.

Helga who had overheard the conversation liked the idea. She knew from her own experience that waiting was anything but an easy job. The clown would soon learn how demanding this line of work could be.

"That is a great idea," she said before Anna could dismiss the suggestion. "He can't be any worse than he is here."

Instead of taking offence Markus looked at her gratefully. "Thank you Helga, that is exactly how I feel about it."

19

"Fine," Anna said after a short pause. "We can certainly give it a try Markus, but if you break any dishes you are back in the stalls."

Helga was delighted that Markus was being taken out of her sight. She was convinced that this evening had also taken this boy out of the running to become heir to the farm and her favourite Lukas was one step closer to coming out on top.

Martin and Otto showed Anna how well they could climb up the beams of the loft and how Martin could stand on Otto's shoulders but such childish circus acts were not for her. Klara showed Anna her latest knitting project but her efforts were pale in comparison to the cardigan that Gisela could present as her latest achievement.

When Markus produced a multi-coloured striped scarf he claimed to have knitted himself the two women were speechless. At first, they were silent because of his admission of performing such a womanly task but as soon as they saw the finished product they were silent in awe of its perfection and beauty.

"You can't possibly have done that by yourself!" Anna exclaimed. "That is ridiculous."

"He certainly has!" Gisela confirmed proudly. She was the one who had taught him to knit. As his older sibling, she wanted to take credit for his achievement even if it outshone her own cardigan currently on display.

"I am very impressed," Anna admitted, "but you know, a man cannot do a woman's work. You can't be seen knitting things. What will people think!"

"I made this for you!" Markus said.

Anna could not deny that she liked the scarf and would love to wear it but she couldn't tell people that her nephew had made it for her.

"That is very nice of you but I cannot accept that. Give it to your own mother, I am sure she will be grateful for it."

With that she stood up and walked towards the door.

"Have fun kids but don't stay up too long. Milking the cows can't wait until you have slept in."

Chapter 2: Magdalena (1932-40)

When Hans-Ulrich returned from the farm at a rather leisurely pace, the midwife presented him with his new daughter, whose arrival into the world did not amaze him too much if he was being honest with himself.

"Isn't she beautiful?" the midwife said excitedly.

"Of course," he replied mechanically but his mind was elsewhere.

He clumsily picked up the child and half-heartedly smiled. Magdalena had been asleep but woke up when she heard the door. As besotted with their new daughter as she was, she doubted that her husband shared much of her enthusiastic sentiments. Even on a good day Hans-Ulrich was of a more melancholic nature and his heart murmur often caused him weariness and pain. Luckily that had excused him from military duties for which she thanked God every day but it didn't seem likely that the Germans would lose the war and it wasn't that she feared for his life. As devout Christian he would have found it very hard to comply with an order to kill, so much that at any other time he would have become a conscientious objector but in the current fascist climate such whimsical and cowardly escapades were taken care of by the firing squad. How opportune that the Good Lord had helped the Hinterbergers by blessing him with this ailment.

Hans-Ulrich had to take care not to exhaust himself and the resulting lack of exercise had lately translated into an ever growing belly. He possessed small and narrow shoulders, thin arms and legs and looked permanently sad and weary. His slumped posture when he was at home and out of the public eye gave away that he did not share the current spirit of optimism with the rest of the Nation. Instead he worried continuously about the future. Despite their sheltered life in Heimkirchen they were surrounded by unchristian ideology, their souls exposed to temptation and tainting influences and so their salvation by the Good Lord was in grave danger.

Magdalena got up and went through the open door to the living room where she saw Hans-Ulrich holding this new child in his arms and she could tell this baby was just one more worry he would rather do without. She recognised this helpless look only too well. Her mother had looked like that during the Great War and all Magdalena could do then was to try and please her silent mother with good behaviour and pious deeds. She quietly moved backwards and began to tidy up the mess that was the kitchen. Hans-Ulrich heard the noise and immediately came after her.

"For the love of God Magdalena, leave the housework for one day and have a rest. You're not the youngest mother in the world," he scolded her.

"I don't mind, Hans-Ulrich," she replied calmly. "After the long walk to Anna's you must be exhausted. You with your heart. What a day it must have been for you."

"Look at yourself. A few hours after giving birth you are standing in the kitchen!" he said and shook his head.

"What if there are people coming to congratulate us? I don't want the place to be a mess," she justified.

"There is not going to be anyone to congratulate us for a girl," he said coldly. "Now stop, for the love of God."

Magdalena obeyed her husband and went over to the living room to check on her baby which Hans-Ulrich had left with the midwife.

"She is asleep," the midwife said in a hushed voice. "I will be on my way now that Herr Hinterberger is home," she added, grabbed her small bag and rushed out of the door.

"Wait!" Magdalena called out to her. "Will you come to church with me and pray?"

"You don't need me for that," was the curt reply. "I am late cooking for my bunch at home."

And so Magdalena put on her street clothes and went across to the church by herself. Sitting in the almost darkness of the church she remembered how she had met Hans-Ulrich in this very building.

There had been fancier men than Hans-Ulrich in the church choir led by her late father. Many of whom had attempted to court her but her heart had instantly taken a liking to this serious and devoted Christian man when she first saw him. Because of her father's strict regime, Magdalena was very serious about life and had never really learned to enjoy herself like other girls had. Her life was purposefully led and was a constant attempt to please her parents and to obey their many rules. Some men only wanted to flirt with her and they disgusted her. None of them sang with as much passion and conviction as Hans-Ulrich; he enunciated every syllable clearly and lost himself in the words of the Lord.

"What a show off," she heard one of the women whisper but in Magdalena's eyes he was just the type of man she was longing for. Her own religious education had been vague and so her beliefs were often inconsistent. For example, she was very confused but too scared to even ask: if she confessed her sins was she home free or did she still have to go to purgatory for them after her death? The one thing that she did know for sure was that going to church and trusting your priest was all you needed to do to become a good person, but would that ever be enough in the eyes of the Good Lord and her father?

In Hans-Ulrich she seemed to have found a man who would be knowledgeable enough to guide her through life: someone who knew how to stay on the path of righteousness. He never ran after other women as so many men at the choir did. He had come to church to worship God alone which made him even more appealing. As word spread through the tenor section that Magdalena had turned down all the men who had asked her out he too started to notice her and thought he recognised a kindred spirit.

One evening he struck up a conversation with her after church about the sermon which she seemed to know surprisingly little about.

"I can't say that I always understand what the priest means," she admitted shyly. "Sometimes he talks so quickly and uses words I have never heard before. But I know a good man when I see one and I always feel so elated after his speeches."

"Yes I agree. Our priest can get carried away and talk quickly, but tell me, which words did you not understand?" he asked and when she could not remember he repeated the entire sermon for her. He seemed to know better than to ask her if she had understood after he had finished, yet she kept nodding and agreeing with him with such a flattering admiration that he decided there and then that she was the one for him. They were as inseparable as the morals of the time allowed them to be, became engaged as soon as his career with the local

23

administration had been secured and got married a year before Hitler became the German Chancellor.

The couple noticed little of the changing politics and the hateful propaganda because in the sleepy town of Heimkirchen there was little that the Nazis needed to 'put right'.

Magdalena had one child every year: Otto in the week of Hitler's inauguration, Martin the year after, then Klara and then Lukas. Hans-Ulrich's job at the city administration was stable and because of the many children that his wife bore the Fuhrer, he was well regarded and most likely earmarked for promotion.

When Magdalena came back from church Hans-Ulrich sat by the table reading the paper, next to the sleeping baby.

"Isn't she beautiful?" Magdalena asked proudly.

Unable to fake much excitement and happiness Hans-Ulrich kissed his wife and instead of congratulating her he brought up the issue of naming the child. Uninspired the two looked at the little bundle in her arm and searched their minds.

"How about we just call her something biblical?" suggested Magdalena. "I don't want to name the child after some forgotten great aunt that Anna wants to be honoured. I bet that is what she wants you to do, isn't it?"

"What else could we expect?" Hans-Ulrich conceded.

"I am sorry but Vinzenzia and Ottilie, those are like swear words on a children's playground," Magdalena replied. "No, I think a simple religious name would be the best."

"Well that would be Eva, like Eva Braun. I don't want that. Names from the Bible sound Jewish," he pointed out.

"How about Maria, like the mother of god," Magdalena suggested.

"Fine," he agreed.

A biblical name was the perfect way out of this dilemma, a token of Christian protection against the sinful times.

Magdalena loved her new child. It was not Maria that woke her up asking to be fed; no, the new mother woke up naturally and when she offered her breast the infant took to it without any problems at all. Mother and daughter were in perfect harmony.

Hans-Ulrich had slept in the children's bedroom so he would not to be disturbed by the baby during the night. He had

24

agreed to look after Maria in the morning so Magdalena could go to early Mass but the child seemed so calm and peaceful that the mother decided to let the poor man rest and took the little one with her. Maria did not disappoint and made not one sound during the service.

On her return it was time for nursing again and then the infant fell back to sleep, during which Magdalena managed to tackle a few chores in the house. She once had heard in church that one should not work on the Sunday but when she had mentioned this to her husband he had told her that Christian love for your family and your neighbour demanded that one did at least what was necessary for others. When it came to interpret this maxim he was rather liberal as far as housework was concerned. She did not mind, as long as Hans-Ulrich cleared her of any wrong doings and she acted in good faith, God could not be angry with her for it, could he?

"How long before we need to collect our little rascals from the farm?" she asked her husband when he got up.

"I better go and get them this afternoon. That way I can have a little chat with Anna about the name and maybe the children can get an early tea before coming home with me," he replied.

"I thought now would be a good time to get the dust off the carpets. What do you think?" she asked him.

"What are the neighbours going to say if we do that on a Sunday?" he pointed out. "They are not too dusty. Try to rest."

"I don't feel like I need rest," Magdalena declared. "If anything I feel lighter now that she is out of my body. You know how much there is to do. My work is never done, Hans-Ulrich, or else I'd do some more praying and bible study."

"The way you are always rushing around, that is no good," he said with sudden concern in his voice. "And I hope Maria is all there in her head if she is so quiet."

"Now don't be ridiculous, Hans-Ulrich!" Magdalena exclaimed, dismissing his fears.

He put on his Sunday clothes and crossed the square to attend the main Sunday morning service himself. An hour before the service commenced the priest and some monks were available to take people's confessions and he was in the habit of taking this opportunity every week. He wanted to make sure that his mind

25

and body were completely pure before he took part in the Holy Communion later during Mass. Traditionally this had been the normal behaviour for Catholic churchgoers but gradually people were being more cavalier about it. He knew for a fact that some people even had breakfast or a drink of coffee and still went to share the body of Christ, even though the Pope had clearly ruled that no one who had consumed food or drink was allowed to do so.

He felt a lot of guilt this morning. Instead of being grateful to the Lord for his latest child he felt unhappy to have yet another mouth to feed. The biggest sin he would have to confess was that his mind had lately been full of impure thoughts about a woman he saw regularly at church. He was ashamed of himself and hoped the priest would give him a good talking to and make him pay a heavy penance for his sins.

Strengthened by the absolution that followed and the forgiveness that he had been granted, he passionately prayed as he had been ordered all the way through the service, then he returned home. He decided to forego lunch as an additional and voluntary sacrifice to Him and made his way to Anna's farm. The walk there took a good two hours normally but he decided to take a different path through the forest which would take much longer but he would have the opportunity to pray in front of some crucifixes that had been put up on the way.

As he approached the farm he saw his children amongst a large group of workers raking in the hay from the large fields adjacent to the main building.

He found Anna in the stalls, overseeing the calving of a cow.

"Look familiar?" Anna said jokingly when she recognised Hans-Ulrich.

"Yes, it certainly does," he lied; he had not been present at any of the births of his children.

"Boy or a girl?" Anna asked business like. She hoped it was a boy. After yesterday's showcase of talent she desperately needed a new glimmer of hope.

"A girl. We decided to name her Maria Magdalena or Maria Vinzenzia. What do you think?" Hans-Ulrich almost stammered as he said the names out loud.

Anna just raised her eyebrows. "Maria as the first name?"

"Yes, I know it is not what we agreed to..." he started but Anna interrupted him.

"...but it is what Magdalena wants. Well, she has chosen wisely. You can't argue with a biblical name, can you?" she said defeated. "Let her have this one. Who really cares about the girls' names anyway."

"Is everything going well with this birth?" he asked, pointing at the cow.

"Should be," Anna replied.

"How have my children been?" he asked.

"Your kids have been behaving well. They had a big feast last night as a thank you for their hard work."

"Thank you. We appreciate you taking so much time to teach them," Hans-Ulrich said humbly.

"That Markus makes me laugh. You know he knits? Yesterday he showed me a scarf he had made by himself. It looked really good. It is such a shame I can't wear it, coming from a boy. Well, we decided to take him off the farm work and try him as a waiter in the restaurant for a while. That is what he wants to do now, work with people."

He was surprised at the ease with which Anna told him all this. Her otherwise so harsh and judgemental demeanour had taken on an amused and rather playful tone that he was unfamiliar with.

"Well, good luck to him," was all he could think of to say.

"You should bring your boys more often," she suggested. "Klara is a great help in the kitchen but there is no shortage of girls here so maybe you could keep her at home to help Magdalena."

"We wouldn't dream of it. The more help you get the better," he insisted. "Magdalena would never take her away from you and frankly we don't need her."

Chapter 3: Joseph (1945)

The Good Lord looked kindly on the Hinterberger family during the next five years. While all over Germany bombs rained from heaven and destroyed entire cities, Heimkirchen was too small a target to get such attention from the Allied forces. Maria never suffered the trauma of sirens and the whistling sound of falling missiles. Until the American tanks peacefully rolled into the market square after the German surrender there were very few signs of the war that a child would have noticed.

The children had all joined the Hitler Youth years ago but in the Catholic environment of Heimkirchen even the group leaders themselves had joined out of obligation rather than enthusiasm for the Nazi cause. Instead of wasting their energy on futile resistance, they chose to comply, particularly as the character of their meetings and activities was much more comparable to the Boy Scouts than to that of a politically motivated organisation; after their meetings they would frequently see each other at church.

For adults the political threat was much more obvious, although this was nothing compared to the big cities or the areas of Germany where the Allied troops approached.

Families in Heimkirchen of course also received letters from the war ministry informing them that men were dead or missing; wounded soldiers were transported to surrounding hospitals and refugees from the eastern parts of the Reich streamed into Heimkirchen. The war had come to the city but everything really happened on a minor and less violent scale.

Food was scarce and there was a dire shortage of oil and most consumer goods; among the refugees were many Nazis on the run who tainted the peaceful atmosphere somewhat with their full-on propaganda about miracle weapons which would save the day. There were also some last minute desperate recruitment campaigns in town for children to join the army, the character of which contradicted the previous assurances that a victory was still possible for Germany. The people of Heimkirchen responded by trying to keep their heads stuck in their prayer (or party) books and generally ignored what was going on as much as they could.

Hans-Ulrich had strangely benefited from the war by quickly climbing up the career ladder and had become head of the administration of Heimkirchen. He hated this work that had brought him face to face with the hated Nazis but Anna had drilled him to be diplomatic.

"No need to play the hero or to burn bridges," she warned him time and time again and so he obeyed her orders by doing what his superiors in Munich and Berlin told him to do.

He managed to keep relatively unnoticed and without being identified as a religious person, which was yet another sign of how unimportant the town of Heimkirchen really was to the rest of the country and the party leaders. Nazis here did not have the same momentum as elsewhere; the most ambitious ones had left for Munich and other cities a long time ago anyway. Most of those didn't like to mention their humble origins and rarely came back.

Hans-Ulrich was spared the nasty work of dealing with the 'subversive elements' of society. He only delegated and knew how to turn a blind eye, followed by frequent visits to the confession box to clear his conscience. He felt helpless when alleged enemies of the state were denounced and deported or when party members amongst the refugees were given preferential treatment and he was very grateful that the priest absolved him every time.

The biggest task was organising accommodation for the many war refugees that came from all parts of the country. He applied his usual pragmatism to the work since he found it of neighbourly Christian value and therefore a rewarding use of his time - even if it meant that he had to give priority to party members and check that the refugees were neither Jewish nor Communists.

The Good Lord had not thought it timely to bless him with yet another child, despite his frequent passionate night-time activities with Magdalena. Then, in what would be the last year of the war, his wife displayed the all too familiar morning sickness once again.

Apart from Herbert nobody of the Hinterberger/Stockmann family had been drafted, all of the next generation being just that little bit too young to be considered fit for the war.

Since the landing of the Allied forces in France, Herbert had not been heard off.

"No news is good news," Helga had told Anna but given the loveless state of her mistress' marriage she was not sure if that was precisely true. If Anna felt distressed about him she did a good job of hiding it.

Like many other farms outside the war zones, Anna had been assigned quite a few Ukrainian and Polish workers to ensure continuous productivity, but she did not trust them as far as she could throw them and whatever they did had to be supervised and checked closely.

Without ever having to compromise herself by associating with or using the Nazis in town, Anna had profiteered from the war more than could have been expected. The only time she accommodated a request it concerned The Black Eagle Inn. There used to be a sign outside the entrance to the restaurant with a black eagle on it, but on ordered by the Gauleiter, who often came to drink there, it had been replaced by the Nazi flag. The sign had been rusty anyway and so the sacrifice was small and it kept everyone happy. Smaller farms struggled to survive and Anna swallowed them up for a pittance when war widows decided to give up and sell.

The Black Eagle Inn had suffered due to the food shortages but it still drew in more business than other inns and Markus had proved himself an amazing asset with his charms and impeccable manners which worked wonders. There was no doubt in Anna's mind that one day he would be running that entire section of her empire and she had gradually transferred all of her maternal feelings from Hans-Ulrich and his children towards Markus alone. She could not leave him all of her fortune, she knew that; the farm would have to be given to someone much more capable, but she had still not decided to whom.

Her husband had been a formidable worker and in that respect she certainly missed him. He had never been her equal but then again no one ever had. She certainly had never loved him passionately but he had been her partner in crime and now she felt lonely at the top of the pecking order.

In her new sense of loneliness, the evenings were the hardest for Anna.

A few weeks before the arrival of the American troops she sat forlornly at her desk trying to focus on the numbers in the book when Lukas knocked on her door.

"Where on earth have you come from?" she asked him. It was the middle of the week and he was not supposed to be here until Friday.

"Mum is having the baby but it is not going so well," the little boy said matter of factly. "Otto and Martin are taking her to the hospital and father sent us here." Behind him she could make out Klara and Maria in the door frame.

"Well, don't just stand there like idiots," Anna said grumpily. "Come in and have a seat. Maybe Klara can make some tea or lemonade." she suggested. It had been a long time since the hardened old woman had felt so happy to see someone else but Markus.

Klara naturally did as she was told right away and Maria followed her, leaving Lukas in the room alone with Anna.

"What do they teach you in maths these days?" she asked the little boy but as usual she did not wait for an answer and carried on right away.

"Do you think you can help me with some of these equations here? They are terribly boring and it would be good if you could see if I made a mistake."

"Of course I can," Lukas said confidently and sat down next to her. The boy had a sharp mind and immediately found several careless errors in Anna's sums.

"How can you be so young and be better at this than me?" she asked in disbelief. "Try these ones," she said and made him go over older receipts which he easily corrected. It was amazing how diligent this boy was. To anyone else she wouldn't have admitted her sloppy mistakes but since the boy was so young she didn't feel threatened. From that evening on Anna requested that Lukas assist her whenever she balanced the books but in effect he never left her side in the evenings and soon it was really his company she wanted and not just his mathematical skills.

Anna's youngest nephew Joseph Hinterberger was born after the longest labour Magdalena had ever had the misfortune to experience. His head was enormous and would not pass until it ruptured his poor mother. Lately the hospital had harboured too

31

many wounded soldiers so medical supplies and staff were extremely short. She had arrived at the hospital on advice of the midwife early in the afternoon after a dreadful morning of agony and no sign of progress. By the time she was seen to at all it was late at night and Magdalena had been left completely unattended for hours during which she felt that she was going to die. The contrast to Maria's birth could not have been greater and she hated this new child that she never had wanted in the first place.

Of course all was forgiven a minute after she had finally pushed Joseph out of her body. Once on the outside he behaved as well as Maria had and stopped making any more unreasonable demands on his mother and her body. The birth left an injured mother who was ordered by her doctor to rest, an order she was very distressed about but given how poorly she felt for the first time in her life she considered following it.

The only urge on Magdalena's mind was that she desperately wanted to go to church or at least see a hospital priest and confess her unchristian thoughts and words during labour.

"What if the labour has damaged me and I die before my confessions. I need to see a priest!" she insisted.

Hans-Ulrich had been surprised at her outbursts and her sinful utterings during labour.

"I will get one right away," he promised. "In the meantime pray for your salvation and I will do the same," he added but by the time he got home it was late and he didn't dare to disturb the priest; he was too concerned that he might make a mistake at work the following day if he did not get at least a few hours bed rest.

First thing in the morning he sent Otto to the priest who rushed to his most faithful church member immediately. Otto returned to find his father already gone. Proud of his success he decided to see his father at the office. None of them had ever been inside that building: Hans-Ulrich always kept his work life separate from his family.

When Otto arrived Hans-Ulrich was furious at first despite the good news. Being overheard speaking about confessions and priests in front of his co-workers seemed dangerous. He felt less secure and more challenged in his position than he used to be since so many new people with Nazi convictions had arrived in town. In what was clearly the last days of the Reich, it would be imprudent to expose himself and be demoted just before the war finished. Fortunately the reason for Otto's visit remained unnoticed.

The Prussian woman who showed Otto in had lost two of her sons on the Russian front years ago and made a huge fuss about the boy, admiring his beautiful Aryan looks.

"Look at Herrn Hinterberger's son!" she called to the women in the post office next door. "Come and have a look. Who would have thought that our dutiful boss even had children. I thought he was married to the office. And such a handsome young man too."

Hans-Ulrich was taken completely off guard and had no idea how to handle this situation. He was saved by a comment from one of the post office girls to Otto.

"You must be pleased finally to get to see where your father works. Are you going to follow in his footsteps and become a civil servant yourself?"

Otto looked questioningly at his father, whose anger he did not want to incite. Hans-Ulrich nodded encouragingly, having decided that this line of reasoning was the perfect way out.

"Oh yes," said Otto. "When I grow up I want to become just like my father."

"Well then come and stay with us at the post office," the girl suggested. "Do you know the alphabet? Because if you do you can help me with the sorting of letters and documents. We could see how clever you are."

Hans-Ulrich nodded and so Otto got started and agreed to come again and help out after school from now on to learn the ropes of administration.

Martin in the meantime had been sent to Anna. He used to love school but during the war all male teachers had been drafted - even the really old and really young ones. Another favourite of his, a female teacher, had lost her husband and left to live with her sister in Berlin and soon Martin lost interest in his studies completely.

The new head teacher was yet another stranger from East Prussia who continuously talked about Germany's enemies and their evil nature. None of the children liked to hear this and most were scared more of her than of the Russians themselves. Martin would have preferred a teacher who stuck to the syllabus.

He had high hopes that Helga might make him some sort of breakfast for having come all this way. Otto had ended up with the short straw as visiting the priest often went hand in hand with long lectures on Christianity and family values. As if their parents did not expose their children to enough of those. He found Anna in the restaurant having breakfast and she cordially invited him to join her.

"I guess your mother needs to be very careful with her health now," Anna said after Martin had told her the news. "You know what, tell your father that all of you can come and stay with me, well, at least the boys. Maybe he wants the girls to help him in the house - that is up to him."

Martin was delighted. Compared to the serious atmosphere at home, he preferred the physical work and the banter that they were often allowed here. Although life under Anna was far from liberated and free of discipline, it was much simpler and, in his view, a much more natural way of life.

"That would be great," he called out loud.

"What would be great?" asked Markus who had just approached the table to serve some dry bread and butter.

"Us coming to live here while mother recovers." Martin answered excitedly.

"Oh," Markus said with a slight sneer on his face.

"Watch your manners!" Anna scolded him. "Aren't you happy for the company of your cousins?"

"Oh, I didn't mean it like that," Markus said hastily. "I was just concerned for Magdalena. Is she alright?"

Martin could sense that this concern was fake but Anna seemed to buy in to it.

"Oh, you are so considerate, Markus. No wonder everyone adores you. Don't you worry your pretty head," she assured him. "Magdalena will be fine. This kind of thing happens all the time. She'll recover soon, trust me, I have seen my share of women giving birth."

Markus beamed his broadest smile at her and went back to the kitchen and Martin made his way back home to convey Anna's agreement.

Later that day Hans-Ulrich wrote a note to excuse his children from school because of the family emergency and sent the boys on their way, then returned to the rehousing of a new batch of recently arrived refugees from the Sudetenland.

Otto and Martin went straight to the farm. If they were quick enough they might even be there in time for dinner.

"That Markus is really weird," Martin told his brother.

"I don't care," Otto replied unmoved. "We never really see him, do we?"

"That is just it. When he heard this morning that we were coming he pulled a long face as if he really did not like it," Martin reported. "I don't understand why it would bother him so much."

"Maybe you misunderstood." dismissed Otto. "I hope this is all over soon so I can go back to town. I am going to be an administrator with father."

"Are you now?" Martin said disinterested.

"Yes, apparently I am very good at it."

"Good for you but you have to help me watch Markus while you are here. I am telling you, there is something not right here," Martin insisted.

Otto mumbled some undistinguishable words and shrugged his shoulders.

Later that night Martin told Lukas about his suspicions.

"Of course," agreed his little brother. "I once heard Helga and Aunt Anna talk about who will inherit the business. He thinks we are competition for him."

"No," said Otto even more dismissively. He could not understand his brother's obsession with the material world. Admittedly his father was at the other end of the spectrum with his religious fanaticism but this idea of fighting Markus seemed a plain waste of time to him.

"She can't be thinking of that already. That is years in the future and it would never be a silly billy like him," Otto pointed out, hoping they would start to see sense.

"Just watch your back!" Martin said warningly. "If his attitude is not about inheritance then we better find out what it is about."

Over the following week the issue seemed to be forgotten. The fields needed to be ploughed and all three boys were exhausted in the evenings. Lukas was excused from the work in the afternoons so he could help Anna with the accounts and none of the three ever even saw Markus.

The restaurant had seen a dramatic increase in business. With Allied troops slowly approaching from the south, west and the east, the wealthier of the refugees chose to remain at The Black Eagle Inn in this peaceful little town until a clearer picture of the invasion could be formed. Markus was kept very busy and rarely set foot outside.

The increased business meant that there was less food for the family and staff. Martin found this new situation very hard to accept. He worked like an ox and felt that it was only fair to be given adequate food rations. He found himself unable to sleep at night because of his empty stomach and started to break into the restaurant larder at night to have at least a little relief from his agony.

He knew that stealing was wrong and so he only took very little, just enough to help him sleep. He had seen where Anna kept the keys and found it no problem sneaking out of the loft and getting what he wanted without being noticed.

The modesty of his portions meant that in the mornings no one suspected anything either: his little secret was safe. After about a week Otto saw him leave the hay loft and when the little brother had not returned after a few minutes he decided to follow Martin and so uncovered the ritual of theft and demanded to join in. Now there were two hungry mouths that raided the larder every night.

Their initial luck made the two boys complacent and careless. One night as they were tip toeing through the dark kitchen Otto noisily dropped the large key ring and when he bent down to pick them up his back pushed against one of the work benches, making another loud noise. Mortified the two thieves stood still and held their breath trying to hear over their drumming heart beats if there was any reaction to the sounds they had just made.

After a few seconds they heard an unmistakable rumbling from one of the nearby guest rooms, the opening of a door and footsteps on the stairs.

Otto pulled Martin by the sleeve and dragged him into the corner of the kitchen where they nervously remained in hiding.

The kitchen door opened and Markus came in with a candle light. He walked around the centre table and called "Hello?" a few times, but when there was no answer he shrugged

36

his shoulders and left the room without having discovered the intruders.

Otto and Martin waited for several minutes before moving. They heard Markus going back up the stairs, opening and closing a door, and then there were muffled voices until everything became quiet again.

After what felt an eternity, Otto gestured to Martin to get out.

"Aren't we going to have at least a little snack?" Martin whispered disappointedly.

"Not tonight. It is too dangerous." Otto replied. "Now shush!"

They returned the keys to the drawer in Anna's house and went back to their beds in the hay loft.

"We will have to wait for a few days before we can do that again!" Otto said the next day when they were alone and out of anyone's earshot. "We were lucky we got away with it for so long. Last night was a close call, that should be a lesson to us."

"But I am so hungry!" Martin said whiningly.

"Tough luck," his brother replied coldly.

"You know what really puzzles me? It was that Markus was coming from a guest room. The staff quarters are towards the top of the building, are they not?"

"Do you think he's allowed to sleep there now to guard the kitchen?" Otto asked, suddenly worried.

"No, if that were the case he would have been more thorough when he checked the kitchen last night. Maybe he is allowed to sleep there as a special favour," Martin said.

"As a special favour?" Otto asked provocatively. "So you think it is a sign that he will be the heir already? You are seeing ghosts, Martin."

"Well I am certainly going to find out about it." Martin swore.

"No you are not!" Otto ordered him abruptly. "We mustn't draw any attention to ourselves at the moment, do you understand? We can't just show a sudden interest in the restaurant and the inn now that we made that noise in the kitchen. If Markus has noticed that someone is helping themselves to food we have to lie as low as we possibly can."

37

"If there were any such suspicions Markus would have found us last night," Martin reiterated.

"Regardless," Otto insisted, "we had better stay clear of the kitchen for a while."

Martin was not convinced that his discovery had no meaning at all but he didn't bother arguing with his brother any further. He decided to remain alert and try to find out on his own what exactly it was that didn't add up.

The two boys went hungry for a few more nights before Otto suggested that they could try again. The first night they had another go the drawer where Anna kept her key was empty: frustrated and hungry they returned back to the loft. The next time they were lucky and found the key back in its place, which seemed a sign that no extra security measures had been taken by Markus or the restaurant staff and that nobody suspected anything.

Otto still insisted that Martin wait outside the kitchen door to keep watch as a precaution. Nothing stirred and Otto came back with a small ham for each of them – a big treat in those days.

However, the brothers never got to raid the larder again and would not be able to solve the so called mystery around Markus and the guest room. By the end of that week Magdalena sent Hans-Ulrich to the farm to collect her children. Since the war was finally coming close to their sleepy town, she worried about them and wanted to have the entire family around her; she had had nightmare visions of what the soldiers might do to them out in the fields.

Current accommodation policy – conscientiously implemented by her faithful husband – meant that the family living room had been given to a group of German refugees from the east. This had been easy and comfortable while the children had been staying at the farm, but now the flat was hugely overcrowded. Hans-Ulrich could have registered their own increased need once the children were back, but that would have been against his Christian principles and he wanted to lead his fellow citizens by setting a shining example.

The two refugees were sisters and they spoke little to anyone. They were quite timid and behaved as if they did not want to be in the way; Hans-Ulrich had chosen wisely. It was so much easier giving charity to unassuming and kind people. He received frequent complaints about ungrateful and demanding refugees who were nothing but a pain in the neck to their landlords and benefactors.

Once his family was reunited, he took all three of his sons with him to work. School happened to be on term break and he wanted to give Magdalena a little space in the flat. He also had come to enjoy bathing in the glory of the admiration his sons got at work. Lukas was as talented and useful as Anna had suggested. He was fast and accurate with numbers, far beyond the capabilities of any of his elder brothers.

Growing up, Hans-Ulrich had seen how children could be neglected by their parents. Had it not been for Anna teaching him a thing or two, he would have ended up just a number in the large Hinterberger clan. He saw this new situation as a great opportunity to educate his sons in more practical matters than the purely theoretical instruction in religion and ethics, to which he had previously limited his contact with the children.

Otto shone at repetitive and simple tasks like filing and putting things in order, whereas Martin found the work in an office tedious and frequently begged his parents to let him go back to the farm and earn his keep there. After all, the farm needed strong men and someone had to protect the women from the enemy soldiers – once they arrived.

Lukas seemed to be enjoying the education and work experience the most. Everyone was amazed at the intelligence of this little boy and his grasp of such abstract principles as housing policy and administration legislation.

"What you learn as a child you'll never forget," one of the post office girls once said to him. "Much better to learn something that you can use in your later life than the silly baby stuff they teach you at school," she added.

Hans-Ulrich agreed even though he made a mental note that he would have to remember this once the war was over. Then he would gather his flock at the living room table again and hold his own bible classes.

With the final surrender of Germany to the Allies a few weeks later came the American tanks, the chewing gum and the chocolate. Some initial arrests of war criminals were made in town in the process of de-nazification but Hans-Ulrich, endorsed by the priest for his integrity to the occupying forces, proved essential in protecting the good reputation of Heimkirchen. Against clear instructions from Berlin he had kept some records of deportations of Jews and Communists but had made sure that only some of those documents made it in to the hands of the new prosecutors. He gave up those people's names which were too publicly known for their deeds to ever stand a chance to be cleared in court and also gave out some names of people who had died. The total number of war criminals imprisoned in the Heimkirchen area was well beneath the national average thanks to his discretion, but the Allied inspectors trusted him and he was able to protect many more who had actually been involved.

He was shocked that newspapers, radio announcements and cinema news reels were showing proof of the horrors that had been going on, all of which had been so easily dismissed as rumours when concrete evidence was not available in Heimkirchen. A small part of him was angry and wanted to give out the complete list of the men and women who had reported Jews and Communists in the early days of the Nazi regime or had incriminated themselves in other ways as spies or hangmen. Only his deep sense of Christian charity made him stop in his tracks. He felt that he could neither be the judge nor the executioner of these criminals. In Hans-Ulrich's view, the Allies and the war tribunals could not take on such a role either; it was only the Good Lord who had the right to judge and punish.

His destruction and falsification of files and documents to protect the guilty from tribunals, imprisonment or death brought him a lot of unexpected friends within the city.

Soon after almost the entire population was forced to testify and vouch for one another to clear their names of anything more than a casual connection with the Nazis. Too many official documents in the Reich administration, such as party lists and execution orders, had been destroyed; the Nazi party head offices had been set aflame at the last minute so that blatant lying and hoping for the best was a valid option for anyone who had something to hide.

Some of the worst offenders chose Hans-Ulrich as the reputable man of the hour to give his credentials to their name, knowing full well that he already had saved them once by destroying hard evidence. Once again the local priest reminded him in a private conversation that no human being should cast the first stone and that it was time to look forward, forgive and bring the lost sheep back into the protection of the Christian faith and spirit of forgiveness. Thanks to this de facto absolution by the priest Hans-Ulrich found the so called "Persil"- letters (that whitened one's name) much easier to write.

Apart from the Nazi big wigs, most of the accused either denied all of their evil doings or asserted that they were tricked and forced into those deeds against their better will and judgement, which at least some of them truly had been. Since the worst committed war crimes had almost exclusively been committed outside the city limits of Heimkirchen, it was easy to forget about them and try to leave the past behind.

As law and order were restored throughout Germany, Hans-Ulrich was praised by the new law enforcement and appreciated by the former Nazis alike. Calls were made for him to go into politics as his name was associated with formal integrity and a Christian purity of the soul. A clear forerunner in the new forming political scene was a Christian orientated conservative party who recruited him through the priest.

Anna, of course, encouraged such a career path for her little brother, less so because she thought of him as particularly capable but more so as it might aid her own prospects in the future to have a brother in a useful political position.

Anna still had not heard anything about her husband Herbert and whether he had survived the war. Although the Red Cross was working overtime to establish its files and lists of all missing persons and prisoners, there was no word about him as yet. A few years ago she still would have given anything to have him back by her side but as time had moved on she had largely made her peace with the fact that he was probably dead by now. His qualities were of purely physical nature, in the farm and in the marriage. She could easily replace him in the former and had long lost her appetite for the latter. Essentially she felt alone but she no longer thought that getting her Herbert back would be of any use in the matter at all.

"If he is a prisoner somewhere in those camps you'll hear about him soon," Helga once said, when she saw her mistress with a sad look on her face. "You'll find out eventually. I bet he is fine."

Anna took a moment to realise what Helga meant, she had been thinking about Lukas and how she missed his company in the evenings.

"It was lucky that Herbert was on the Western front," Helga continued, still in the false belief that Anna's sentiment was to do with her husband, although she should have known better than that. She knew that their marriage had not been the rosiest and had doubted Anna's love many times during the war. Now that that was over what else could Anna possibly be so sad about if not her missing husband?

"They say that the soldiers are being treated much better in the west. The conditions in those camps are meant to be much more humane."

Anna still didn't reply. The thought of Herbert returning as a shell shocked shadow of his former self hit her just as badly and she almost started to cry over it.

"Don't cry," Helga said and put her hand on Anna's shoulder for comfort. "We lost the war. Our prisoners now can be used in forced labour in France and Britain. We might not see him for years, it is just the way it is."

"I know," Anna said, having composed herself again. Herbert may never come home, she thought, an idea much more comforting than a second 'Lothar' coming home to her.

"Now there is no need to sit around waiting and biting your fingernails in anticipation," Helga continued. She sensed that the best way out of this misery for her mistress was to focus all of her affections on the future generations and the capable boys in waiting: Markus and Lukas.

"You should get Lukas back here," Helga suggested and Anna could not agree more.

It did not take much persuasion to get Lukas back now that the war was over. Magdalena made a token effort of resistance when Anna suggested that he attend a school closer to the farm instead of the one in town but the headstrong matriarch only needed to remind her sister-in-law how the farm had supported the family during the war and all objections were retracted.

Martin begged everyone to be allowed the same privilege. The thought of having to help his father in the office after school was unbearable to him and of all the children he seemed to have had the least inclination to worship the Good Lord three times a day and receive lectures from his father about the Bible at the end of each day. Anna jumped at the opportunity to have another strong pair of hands at her disposal.

Many of the abducted labourers from the Ukraine and Poland longed to stay in Germany rather than going home to their newly Communist home countries. Despite such desires most of them were returned on the expressed wish of the Soviet regime. With no German prisoners being released just yet to replace them, the only available workforce was a surplus of female refugees from the Sudetenland and Silesia; Anna childishly would not employ any of them. She had a deep distrust towards most of them, especially those from Czechoslovakia. The 'so-called' Germans coming from there had lived with and been affected by a nation of 'lazy bones and under-achievers', she thought and she said so frequently. These refugees had never really been Germans; in her opinion they had belonged to the Austrian Empire, another group she had a personal dislike of. Living relatively close to the Austrian border she had always considered them inferior, had ridiculed their accent and enjoyed their political decline after the Great War in comparison to the great German nation. She hoped that Hans-Ulrich would become a politician and a leading figure in their town so that he could help her get rid of anyone assigned to help at her farm.

"Even if you are right, you can't dismiss them all," Helga tried to persuade her. "We need more working hands on the farm. I am sure the Germans in Czechoslovakia never mingled with the Czechs or the Slovaks and are just as hard working as the next German person."

"Those people are Austrians and not Germans," Anna said, suddenly full of unexpected rage. "All they share with us is a language. Their entire nation is a disgrace. Do you not remember the First World War? They started it out of stupid pride and then they could not manage by themselves. If it had not been for Germany they would have been overrun within a month. We paid a big price for the war in the end: reparations, inflation and all. Austria just said sorry and split their pathetic Empire into smaller new nations who all pretended that none of them ever had

43

anything to do with it. I have no respect for them whatsoever and I shall be damned if I employ even only one of them."

Helga knew better than to argue. It seemed to have conveniently slipped Anna's mind that her Lothar had had a mother from Austria, a family she had nearly married into.

Now that Hans-Ulrich's political career seemed set out for him, he was only too happy to have his sons taken off his hands. He was concerned that his ideas for personal intense religious instructions would be neglected and urged Anna to make sure his sons went to church regularly and pray three times a day. She reassured him of it even though she had no intention to supervise the boys in that department. He was too busy to check up on her, so lying and assuring him was the easiest option. He regretted depriving his children of his moral instructions but it was for the greater good of everyone to have someone as religious and conscientious as himself in the town hall: a talent that he could not limit to just his own offspring anymore. In politics he would be able to do more good and reach more people with the word of God and his spirit of charity and well meaning.

Many of Hans-Ulrich's social evening engagements during the time that saw the formation of the Christian Party and the writing of a new constitution for Germany and were for party members or for men only, but he urged his wife to join the party herself, attend their women's meetings and to get involved in charity work.

"Do I really have to go?" she asked annoyed. "I am not one for big spectacles and speeches I don't understand the first thing about. Oh Hans-Ulrich, please!"

"I know it is inconvenient but you must see it from a long term perspective and see the bigger picture. The Nation needs a new Christian government for this New Germany. It is essential to bring the country back on track and to make the people repent for their sins. Why else would the Lord have put me in such a promising and powerful position?"

"Well if you put it like that, Hans-Ulrich, of course I will do as you say. I am just hoping I won't make a dog's dinner of it," she replied.

The parents regretted that Joseph would become the first child in whose upbringing they would be so little involved. Maybe it was a fair punishment for her harsh words and hostile feelings during his birth. The Good Lord was right in doing so: her behaviour and thoughts had been shameful and unforgivable.

Now that her husband was staying out late many times during the week and still went to work early - to make sure no one could accuse him of neglecting his current administrative duties in favour of his political ambitions – she noticed how the rule of daily love making to please the Good Lord seemed to have slipped his mind completely. Not that she minded much, she was usually too tired and worn out to be in the mood. All she longed for in her life was more time to spend in church but she was a good wife and co-founded the women's group associated with the new Christian party and did everything Hans-Ulrich asked her to do in order to support his aspiring political career and ambitions.

Chapter 4: The Adoption (1947-48)

Eighteen months after the end of the war Anna finally received notification from the Red Cross that her husband Herbert was alive and well in a prisoner-of-war camp in England. Her joy over the news was moderate.

She did not give much to reading the newspaper or to listening to the local gossip but no one could escape the horror stories about the way the German prisoners-of-war were treated abroad. She knew she should feel relief and happiness over the good news that he was alive - even if it was under bitter and harsh conditions but all the cheer left her shockingly cold.

Many women in Heimkirchen shared Anna's status of waiting for their husband. They usually took a greater interest in finding out about what those poor men went through than Anna did. Rumours circulated about German soldiers being used to clear minefields and dying in hundreds every day. For every article that exposed the cruel and inhumane treatment of Jews in the German Concentration Camps there was one that accused the Allies of the same kind of behaviour towards the prisoners they had taken.

While this outraged the large parts of the nation, other parts of the population wallowed in loud proclamations of self-loathing and nation shaming; these voices took every opportunity to demand that everyone involved with the Nazis in any discriminatory way should be brought to justice. When in October 1946 the Nuremberg trials came to an end, public opinion seemed to swing towards an orientation to the future instead of a continued shameful look back onto the past. The culprits had been dealt with and now it was time to stop the repetitive self-condemnation and 'Nestbeschmutzung', the smearing of one's nest.

Anna cared little about the past. It sounded truly horrific what she heard had happened but, as her little corner of the world had hardly been touched by the war, she felt as if it had nothing to do with her anyway.

Despite all efforts by the Red Cross in that regard, very few women had knowledge of where their husbands were. Many women had been waiting for years without ever finding out if their husbands were alive in Siberia or dead in an anonymous field somewhere. Anna did not appreciate her fortunate position of knowing.

If these newspapers were right, then those prisoners-of-war abroad who were exempt from mine duties were used as slave labour on French and British farms and kept under harsh conditions in detention camps. Wild debates were taking place in both of those countries about the morality of such a treatment.

As pragmatic a businesswoman as she was, Anna refused to get drawn into the panic and hunger for more news that the women who shared her fate were party to. She did not want anything to do with it. Especially since so many of the prisoners were reported to die in the camps or in the mine fields there was no reason for it to affect one's hopes.

All she could really do was to build the farm up and wait and see if her Herbert was strong enough to survive life in the prisoner-of-war camps. In that respect her future was just as uncertain as it had been before. Worrying about him did not help anyone and it would not change the outcome and so she put it out of her mind and instead focused on the present. She would do better to establish good relations with the occupying forces and the forming future political powers, something she had done consistently and successfully ever since the end of the war.

With his emerging political connections, Hans-Ulrich was one of her big hopes in that regard. His party was one of the stronger voices in the new world of German politics and following the party line, he began calling the citizens of Heimkirchen to stop wasting their time and join the reconstruction of the fatherland on a Christian foundation. Germany had surrendered unconditionally and was occupied territory so it would be some time before the country was to be entrusted with a self-governing authority and before Hans-Ulrich's growing influence would pay off for her and the farm.

It was Markus who turned out to be a much more immediate asset for Anna than Hans-Ulrich and his party. The young man had made some contacts with the key players of the black market, which helped to establish the restaurant as a reliable and luxurious meeting place. Accusations of underhand dealings led to frequent raids and inspections but never to any consequences. Markus seemed to be perfectly able to handle all problems and to conceal the illegal goods from the eyes of the police. Anna was amazed at this young man who could be so cunning and ran the business in such hard and difficult times and still made profits so easily.

She knew he had befriended some of the American soldiers in town and maybe that was what gave him the edge over some of their competitors. Markus seemed to be getting along with everyone, well everyone apart from Lukas and Martin. Anna did not usually waste her time with petty quarrels and personal animosities between staff or family members – just as her parents never had - but even she could not turn a blind eye to the tension that was building between the boys since they had been reunited and she wondered why that was. In Martin's case she could see that it was pure envy of Markus and an uncontrolled and childish personal dislike. She reined him in with draconian measures whenever she found him badmouthing Markus or trying to interfere with his business.

Lukas' feelings had been much more subtle and it took her a long time to find out about them. His complaints about the way Markus conducted business always seemed to have logical points and administrative reasons.

"Sometimes one has to look the other way when a business is going well," she explained to her angry nephew. "You know the odd 'mistake' in bookkeeping and in our accounts is normal and only 'human' and therefore excusable if not even necessary to ensure our survival in times like these."

Lukas said nothing to those justifications but his face betrayed how indignant and disappointed he felt. Anna suspected his high morals to be a product of his upbringing and never paid it much attention. Only eventually did she realise that Lukas was well prepared to let other minor indiscretions slip through without making the same fuss about them and she saw the pattern in his complaints that pointed to Markus alone.

Initial attempts to bring the two 'business men' closer and force them to become friends failed miserably.

"Today I want to have lunch with both of my golden boys," Anna once said during breakfast.

"Fine," Lukas said, remaining his reserved and cold self.

"I would love to," Markus said. "However, the lunch customers keep us so busy, I can't join you just like that, but thank you for the thought."

Anna smiled at his perfect manners.

"Of course, how silly of me to forget how much you have to do," Anna said resigned.

"You should be more grateful, Markus," Helga added with some edge to her remark. "You are not the only one who is busy but Lukas will always make time for his aunt."

"Let him be," Anna defended her golden boy. "He has to entertain our customers. They appreciate his company as much as we do."

Markus did not even notice the frosty tone from Helga and Lukas, too involved in his thoughts to pay any attention to their words.

"Why do you always have to try and blacken his name?" Anna asked Helga and Lukas when Markus was gone. "It is a miracle what that boy achieves when there is virtually no food and aid for Germans. Everyone envies us. He must be able to get hold of some American Care Packets. Only the Displaced People and camp survivors get the goods he gets his hands on. I don't know how he does it but you better not spit in his face like that. It is him that is keeping us all afloat. It wouldn't hurt for you to get over your animosities and try to become friends."

Lukas defended himself: "Don't look at me. I said that I was coming for dinner!"

"Yes but the way you said it you might as well have declined," Anna pointed out.

"I don't have anything against him," Lukas protested.

"Well I am sorry but I think that boy is playing you," Helga now answered back angrily. "I can't help but feeling that you are being too easily led by him and I need to say it once in a while so you remember it."

"If he acts strangely right now then it is because his father is not well. Alfons has been poorly for some weeks now and that is a grave concern for the boy and for us all. Yet Markus still works as hard as ever," Anna reminded her friend. "Don't be so hateful."

Helga said nothing but her face spoke volumes. She felt quite differently however when soon after this discussion

Markus's father Alfons died of consumption, only days before Christmas 1947. Helga felt dreadful for having given the young man such a hard time.

Worse news was that Erica, Alfons' widow, had decided to move back to Munich where the rest of her own family resided. Without Alfons she did not want to stay in Heimkirchen. She intended to take her children with her but Markus begged her passionately to let him stay. Since the mother was already quite estranged from her children she relented without much ado.

"The boy must be feeling awful," Helga said to Anna with sudden and rare compassion. "How can a mother abandon her son like this?"

"Well I don't think he should feel too badly about it," Anna said angrily. "Have I not been more of a mother to him than that miserable Erica? He should be more grateful that I am here for him and always have been. He has not lost any of his family as his family is me."

"Yes, you are his family now, but Erica could call him back at any moment," Helga pointed out. "He is not your son and I doubt he will ever be as reliable and loyal as Hans-Ulrich's children. He has something of that flighty Erica in him after all. Don't count on him."

Helga's words had their effect on Anna and before Erica could abandon her two children Anna decided to take some action and have one of her famous talks with her.

"What kind of mother ups and leaves like that?" Anna scolded her widowed sister-in-law.

"I thought it was you who wanted them to stay?" Erica commented surprised by the sudden outburst.

"It didn't matter what I wanted, Markus was desperate to stay here with us. I told him he could stay if you allowed it. I hear you put up little resistance to the idea and easily gave up trying to take him with you. That is all I am saying. I won't deny that I am pleased about it but you are a heartless mother. You should give up all your rights and let me adopt Markus. The boy just lost his father and you were going to take him away from The Black Eagle, which has been his real home for years. I want to adopt Markus and give him a proper home. We need him and The Black Eagle is all he has," Anna said forcibly.

"Gisela works at the restaurant, too. Will you adopt her?" Erica asked pointedly.

"I'd rather you took her with you," Anna said. "The girl is not much use and she distracts Markus."

"He will need her as much as she needs him," Erica said. "It is both of them or none of them. So do we have a deal?"

Before she left, Erica told her children how much she loved them but with Alfons dead, she had lost everything she cared for in life. In her mind handing over her children to Anna was a last selfless gesture to give the two a future beyond anything she could have given them herself: as far as she was concerned, her life was meaningless now.

She felt bitter that her poor Alfons had survived the war and then had died of natural causes, just after everything was over. She knew that broken like this she would be no role model for her children and moving away was the best she could do for them. It had cost her the last of her strength to fight so that Gisela had been included in the deal and now she was finally free to go her own way. Gisela refused with surprising vehemence to be adopted. She was happy to stay on at the farm for Markus' sake but she did not want to become a Stockmann child.

Soon after his mother left Markus appeared to have made a 'remarkable recovery' as the vicious tongues among the Hinterbergers let it be known. The wounds over his father's passing seemed to have healed quicker than what was considered appropriate. Anna defended him and pointed out that of course he had to be pleased because by adopting him she had given him a new future and restored his lost security.

Helga was the only person to approach Anna directly about the adoption.

"Have you considered making a will?" she asked.

"Why would I do that?" Anna asked surprised.

"That Markus might do wonders in the restaurant business but what about the farmland and the livestock?" Helga stirred.

"Someone with a persuasive smile like him can turn anything into gold, Helga. He will find a way to make it work," Anna assured her.

Lukas found himself surprised at the anger and resentment he came to feel about the adoption. He had always disliked

Markus but mainly because his older brothers were feeling that way. Personally, he wasn't fond of the loud and attention seeking behaviour and he certainly found the joking and flirting that Markus liked to do was common and totally out of place. Yet without being aware of it he had come to assume that he would be heir to the empire himself and imagined Markus would be working for him some day instead of the other way round. It took him some time to adjust to the new prospect. To see the clown-like behaviour rewarded was hurtful and disappointing. The only indication of Anna's favour towards Markus had been her tendency to brush his muddy financial transactions willingly under the carpet. Only now that it was too late did he realise that Markus had in fact been an actual rival.

Lukas had taken pleasure in having Anna's ear and being relied upon for tasks that were way beyond what was appropriate for his age. Would there ever be a reward for his loyalty, he wondered. To miss out to such an unreliable wastrel added insult to injury.

Martin felt exactly the same as Lukas and angry that his hard labour had always been far less valued than anything that Markus or Lukas ever did. He too decided to watch the new 'prince' closely and find his weak spot.

Chapter 5: Herbert (1948-49)

On Martin's fifteenth birthday in 1948 a withered and skinny man entered Anna's living quarters. It took a while before anyone recognised Herbert underneath the bearded face. He was unusually quiet and subdued and not as happy and pleased as one would have expected.

"Oh Herbert!" Anna finally got out, as many conflicting emotions were running wild inside of her. To hide her torn feelings she hugged him tightly so he would not see her lack of joy and her many instant worries about the changes that his return might bring to her life. Holding this skeleton of a man bore nothing familiar for her.

"How are you?" Helga asked him, stepping into the breach for her lost-for-words mistress.

"I've been better," Herbert answered curtly. "Now don't just stand there woman, can I have something to eat or what?" he barked at the servant.

"Of course," Helga said quickly. "I'll bring you the best we have."

She had never known him to be so rude and unkind. He never spoke much, but at least in the past he had always been benign. Well, he had to be exhausted and a hungry man was an angry man.

Over the course of the evening Anna and Helga learned a little about Herbert's ordeal during the last few years. He had been captured soon after the Allied troops landed in France and had been transferred to a prisoner of war camp in Great Britain. The first year of his imprisonment he and his fellow inmates had taken their lot in good faith. Many of them had had enough of the fighting and were pleased to be out of it, particularly those who had no interest in Hitler's fancy ideas about world domination that had started this absurd war. The hard labour they were forced to do seemed somewhat preferable to the grenades and hostile fire on the battlegrounds. The harsh treatment and scarce food rations were only to be expected under the circumstances; there was hope and optimism that these might prove to be only a temporary measure. Herbert and the friends he made were expecting the war to end any day, since the landing of the Allied troops in Europe there could be no doubt about the outcome of the war and its conclusion must be soon. Most inmates were pleased about that prospect and were looking to the future with hope.

However, when the war actually ended the guards revealed that Herbert's ordeal was far from over. Their captors told them about the death camps and what Germans had done to their victims, and treated the prisoners with appalling cruelty in retaliation. Herbert and his fellow inmates were robbed of all hope. As an entire two years went by and nothing changed, an unsettling anxiety gradually took firm hold of the prisoners. How could this war be over for so long without a negotiated release? Were they forgotten, would they never be free again? Were they condemned to die in this camp?

As more time passed without a change to their situation, the dark realisation of such possibilities made them hopeless, depressed and nihilistic. By the time their camp was dissolved late in 1948 – over three years after the end of the war - the prisoners had no spirit left and found it hard to reanimate themselves and their joy of life. It was hard to trust that the ordeal was really over.

"I guess that is how the Jews and Communists must have felt when they were liberated from their camps," Herbert conceded thoughtfully. "I can almost understand why the British bastards did to us what they did."

"I am glad you are home," Anna said with as much conviction as she could muster.

"Are you really?" he replied sarcastically and left the living room abruptly.

Anna looked at him in shock. This was not the same man she had once known and respected, and she began to realise how differently her future might look, with such a miserable and bitter man on the farm.

Memories of Lothar and his nervous and frightful self after the last big war came rushing back to her. She prayed that Herbert might recover soon so she would not be stuck with a hopeless and wrecked madman for a husband. Lothar had at least been happy to be home and to see her. Herbert was just full of gloom and anger.

Over the next few days Anna tried hard to make Herbert feel welcome and to spoil him with food and luxuries; her reasoning being that the way to a man's heart was through his stomach and he needed a lot of love and affection to reassure him of everyone's benign and kind intentions. Herbert had never been a nasty man and this new character trait had to be eliminated as soon as possible by an overwhelming dose of care.

Since he ridiculed all of her efforts however, she soon lost her temper and went on collision course with him. His aggressive and unfriendly behaviour had to be controlled, she could not let him gain the upper hand by giving in to his threatening and nasty outbursts. Who did he think he was, all of a sudden? He had not even once enquired about the war times here in Heimkirchen, so self-involved had he become.

She sat down with him one morning for breakfast to try and tell him all that had happened since he had been gone, but he paid little if any attention to her and interrupted her several times to get more food from the kitchen. Anna had no chance to locate or re-animate any remaining love for her husband: his rude and cold demeanour was killing any such feeling in its infancy.

"I just thought you might want to know," she ended her little speech with a sarcastic undertone. "Although it seems as if you don't care what happened to any of us while you were away?"

"Of course, yes, naturally, all I could think of while I was dragging heavy rocks and metal for 16 hours a day was how my wife is coping in her comfortable bed and how much money The Black Eagle is bringing in," he repaid her sarcasm.

"Fine! Be like that. Since you are so experienced in hard labour find yourself something to do. There is always work for a strong man around here," she told him. "I won't waste my time with burdening your mind with trivial matters about the rest of us. You clearly have a lot of anger to get through. Do it in the fields where it can be useful and leave me alone."

"If you think I am going to get my hands dirty you have another thing coming," he bellowed back at her. "I have done my share of hard labour for more than one lifetime. Why do we have servants? Order them about if you need to, but not me. From now on, I will let others do the running around for me, do you understand? I swore to myself after I was released from the camp that nobody would ever tell me what to do ever again, and that includes you."

"You lazy bastard," she shouted at him. "I have been doing perfectly well without you. I don't need your advice and your lazy bones making an indent in the sofa. All we need here is a strong man who works in the field, leads by example and keeps an eye on what goes on out on the farm. Get up and get on with it!"

"Get Markus to do that!" he replied sharply. "Isn't he 'our son'? He can get his hands dirty and learn the trade the hard way just like we all did. I guess I should be grateful that you didn't have a bastard child while I was away. At least that proves that you are the one with the problem and not me, as you always insisted. If I had known I would have found myself a fertile wife and my life would have been better than this pathetic excuse for a family!"

"Get out!" she screamed hysterically.

"I'm done with being told what to do," he said coldly. "If you don't like it leave yourself! I am not going anywhere."

She gave him the most hateful look of their marriage and said with a voice that was struggling for authority:

"This is my farm! Go ahead and divorce me. Or have the marriage annulled. See if you can charm another woman with your miserable mug! Do you think the ladies are going to fight over a 'catch' like you! No widow is going to trade her lot for a life with you. We were happier without you."

"I am not going anywhere, Anna," he repeated, this time more threatening than before. "I married you when you desperately needed someone and I stuck with you through those years of your dictatorship. Those days are over now and you better get used to it."

"What are you going to do? Hit me? Beat me into submission?" she ridiculed him.

"Why not? Might even do you some good." he laughed nastily. "First I think I am going to reverse the adoption. What were you thinking woman? I am not having that clown for a son."

"Well, there is something you don't know about the country we are living in: the authorities have better things to do then making an adopted boy an orphan again. And Hans-Ulrich is now head of the city administration and will make sure your requests will be denied; you haven't got a chance in hell with that," she said triumphantly.

That silenced him for a little. At first he looked at her with contempt and hatred but then he suddenly smiled and said almost cheerfully:

"Go and bring me 'my son' then so I can lay down some ground rules." he ordered her.

"Meet him after lunch if you really feel such a sudden fatherly impulse," she suggested. "He can't just drop everything for you. This is his busiest time."

"I want to speak to him now." Herbert bellowed. "A 'father' speaks to his son when he says so, not when it is convenient for the little prince. I never even knew I had a son, you always said I couldn't have one. Off you go and get him."

"Come on, Herbert. Let us not be like this," she said in an attempt to pacify him, hoping to bring this row to an end. "We never quarrelled like this before."

Herbert was having none of it.

"Well, maybe we should have. I am going to go over there myself then and see what is what. In the mean time you can go and make yourself useful in the cow shed, how about that. It will do you some good."

With that he left the room but instead of going to the restaurant and making a scene he went to the wine cellar and opened a bottle of sherry.

She wanted to tell him just how many times she had been in the stalls herself and had got her hands dirty, if only he had been interested in her life during the war she could have told him. But he had become egotistical and self-involved and impossible to reason with. Damn her luck, she had been landed with another broken man.

In the days that followed Herbert made a lot of empty threats but mainly he sat at home and ate and drank whatever he could get his hands on. Anna wasted no time in notifying Hans-Ulrich about her husband's ambiguous feelings around the adoption and urged him to make sure that this was taken care of. As it so happened, Markus did not meet his new father until a few days later. Anna told him to wait until Herbert's rage had calmed down. She stayed out of her husband's way during those days and slept in one of the guest rooms, hoping that his temper and foul mood might wear off naturally.

Despite his threats, Herbert took no interest whatsoever in running the farm. He played out famous chess games and sorted through his stamp collection for hours; the rest of the time he wasted being drunk and stuffing his face with all the food he could get from Helga.

Anna felt she could not let him get away with his self-absorbed and gluttonous outrage and hoped by bringing Markus over and showing Herbert his grown up adoptive son, it might be a suitable first step to turn her husband back into a useful and responsible human being. Those sides of him had to be in there somewhere, waiting to be woken up. Markus was a little scared and could only hope that his experience in the restaurant business and its often tricky clients might help him to brave this storm ahead of him.

"I hope you have stopped all your foolery," Herbert said to him dismissively.

Markus knew not to rise to the provocation and smiled.

"Of course I have. I am much older than the last time we saw each other. A little bit of entertainment value of course is necessary in our line of business but I would never put the family name to shame."

"Good!" was the short reply.

Herbert was impressed with the way this boy could talk. Maybe Anna had been right and there was more potential to this clown than he had expected.

"How would you like me to address you, now that you are both my uncle and my new father?" Markus asked humbly.

Another verbal chess move that didn't miss its spot. Herbert had not been spoken to with this much respect for a very long time and Anna could not believe she had overlooked the obvious way to ingratiate oneself with the angry veteran so easily. Watching her 'son' in successful communication she realised her mistake at once. The flattery was right on target and her otherwise grumpy husband suddenly seemed moved.

"Whatever you like, son, whatever you like," he said with a sigh. "Let's not pretend that names make much of a difference. It's what you do that counts. Call me Uncle Herbert or father, both are fine."

Anna was shocked. Was that how she would have to play it from now on? Please her husband and play up to his damaged need for acknowledgement? She was horrified by the thought. That would never come naturally to her.

"If I may, I will stick to Uncle Herbert for now just so that you don't think you owe me anything. I am very grateful that Aunt Anna has let me stay with you in Heimkirchen. I am just glad I did not have to move to Munich to live with people I don't really know. Being your son is too much too soon."

"Now you're overdoing it," Herbert warned his new son with a dismissive hand gesture but Anna could tell that Herbert liked it all the same.

"Do you play chess?" he asked curtly. "I learned how to play and I need a good partner."

"I don't play it yet, but I can always try," Markus replied readily.

Herbert got his old chess set out of the cupboard and started to explain the game to Markus. It was as if Anna was not even in the room any more. Markus picked up the moves and the nature of the game quickly but every time it seemed that he could beat Herbert at the game he made a terrible mistake and gave his opponent back the advantage.

"No, no, no," Herbert screamed a few times. "Now I have to take your queen. How could you not see that?" He became frustrated and irritated that his son seemed to be so careless in the game and let great opportunities slip through his fingers. It never occurred to him that this was done on purpose to flatter Herbert's bruised feelings of self-worth.

Soon Markus excused himself to go back to the restaurant and check that the new rooms had been cleaned properly. Maybe there weren't always many guests in the restaurant but people still travelled and needed somewhere to stay. The Black Eagle was usually fully booked, especially in the summer months.

Herbert ended the day in a much better mood and Anna hoped this might be a sign that he was on his way to recovery and would become his old pleasant self again. Herbert had always worshipped her, why had the war damaged his affection for her? She just couldn't make sense of it.

She went into the kitchen where Helga was preparing her master yet another big plate of food.

"You can't give him that much," Anna scolded her. "There'll be nothing left for anyone else."

"Markus brought all of this," Helga informed her. "He said he saved it especially for his new father. Our larder has not even been touched."

"Oh, what a flatterer Markus can be," Anna said with astonishment. "You have to hand it to the boy, he knows his moves. I hope he can keep Herbert's temper in check. Frankly, I have already had enough of it."

"I know, he is a real bully. Who would have thought he had it in him?" Helga agreed. "He was always so accommodating."

"The question is how we get him to snap out of it? This is not the man I married. I did not agree to such a life or ever to become an obedient wife. I don't know what I'll do if he stays like this."

The following day Herbert demanded to see Lukas to go over the books together.

"You impress me with your sums," Herbert said jovially to the little boy. "You have a real talent for numbers, that is obvious, but I am disappointed that you have let a few things slip in the account books of the restaurant," he added in a more serious tone. "That goes for you too, Anna."

Lukas was just about to justify himself and direct the blame at Markus where he knew it belonged but Anna signed him to be quiet and looked at him imploringly.

"What do you expect?" she said hastily to Herbert, "when Hans-Ulrich asked him to help out at the city council and go to church and pray three times a day. He is bound to make some mistakes: he is only human. He is doing tremendously well for his age. I'll make sure he gets more time to do them properly, what do you say?"

"I say that I am going to personally oversee our little boy wonder here for a while. You can tell Hans-Ulrich that Lukas lives under my roof now and I am making the rules. We are a commercial business and not a monastery. You are his older sister, you should be telling him not to waste so much of his own time with the afterlife anyway. We live in the here and now."

"Fine, I will tell him," Anna replied obediently.

"Now Lukas, do you play chess?" Herbert asked.

"I learnt the moves last year but I have not played it much since," the young man replied.

"Excellent," Herbert said gleefully, "let us see what your master mind is capable of on the chess board."

After a few hours of losing every single game the old man however had enough and grumpily asked Lukas to come to the office with him where they spoke some more about the account books.

"I know you are only covering for Anna and Markus," he said to Lukas. "I am not an idiot. All the alleged mistakes you made were in the restaurant business, I know something is up there. Anna gave the game away when she tried to brush it under the carpet so hastily. Her favouritism for Markus is obvious, I am surprised she bothers to hide it. You are a good lad for not telling on them. Nobody likes a rat. In the camp we were all looking out for each other, one for all and all for one, as they say."

Lukas just stood there and waited for Herbert to continue. He sensed that it was worthwhile waiting to see where the old man was going with this conversation before rushing into making a decision.

"From now on that dubious business has to stop." Herbert said authoritatively. "If there is anything wrong with the accounts again you come and tell me, you understand? Anna and Markus are nothing but naïve little children who think they know it all, but I have spent four years with a group of men who taught me everything. We were so desperate to battle the boredom and emptiness that we taught each other all we knew. I have learnt tricks now that those two have never even heard of. If we leave it up to Markus and my wife we could all end up in jail. I promise if you tell me I will make sure it won't look as if you have told me."

"Of course, Uncle Herbert." Lukas agreed. "Of course I will. It is your money after all."

While Lukas was happy to compile evidence against his arch rival Markus and was eagerly waiting for the next false move, his brother Martin was on a mission of his own to bring the restaurant manager into discredit. He was trying to spend as much time as possible at the restaurant and watched everything that went on there. He was eager to listen in on conversations that Markus had with other staff, and more importantly with the

61

American soldiers that frequently came to see him. Unfortunately he did not speak English well enough and could not gather anything about the nature of their dealings with Markus.

What he did notice was that some of the guests at The Inn seemed to be on very familiar terms with Markus. Martin recognised one of them from previous visits, a middle aged man who regularly travelled here from the Territory occupied by the French. Martin remembered him mainly because of his strange accent that must have been foreign. The man was tall and burly with a moustache, always well dressed and was recently travelling in what appeared to be a brand new car.

The secrecy between those two spurred on Martin's imagination. Was this the man who supplied Markus with the goods from the black market? If so, his father at the city administration could be informed and the police involved. That would be the end of Markus, he envisaged dreamingly. The fact that Hans-Ulrich would never participate in an action against his own family was something Martin had never even considered. He thought of his father as the most proper and incorruptible man, who in the line of duty would never stray from the path of righteousness— even if it did affect his own nephew.

Some evenings Martin hid underneath the main staircase that led towards the guest rooms. He waited for the last guests to finish their drinks and return to their beds for the night, hoping to hear at least some snippets of the alcohol fuelled conversations that may involve Markus and his friend.

One of those evenings Martin had waited a long time until the connecting door between the restaurant and the guest rooms opened one last time, Markus said goodbye to a group of people who had to be from town since they made their way to the front door, then he locked the front door and the connecting door from the inside, the evening ritual that meant that no one but Markus and Gisela were left in the restaurant area. Food had not been served for at least an hour and the kitchen staff had left already. It was only the siblings now tidying up the place before going to bed themselves.

Martin got out from his hiding place and moved towards the kitchen door to see if he could hear anyone else moving about but everything seemed to be quiet. He stole himself inside so he could listen in on their conversation.

"You have got to be careful," he heard Gisela warn her brother. "Herbert is a nasty piece of work."

"Oh, I know that," Markus reassured her.

"I am not sure you do," she contradicted him. "You think you are invincible and immune but from where I am standing you are playing an incredibly dangerous game. I care for you, please promise me you'll be careful, and not just with Herbert."

"Of course I'll be careful, Gisela. You don't have to worry. I think I have Herbert exactly where I need him. I won't take any risks as far as he is concerned. It is more likely that someone working in the kitchen will find out one day."

"Are you totally sure you have to do this? Is there no way you could not live like that?" she asked pleadingly. "It is so dangerous, what if you were caught? They'd kill you."

"Oh calm down Gisela. How would anyone even suspect a thing like that? Him, of all people, a business traveller from the Alsace?"

"I wish I had your confidence. Everyone can tell that you and he know each other well," Gisela kept reasoning.

"Yes, but he has been here so many times, of course I am bound to know him and vice versa. Everyone knows he is a regular visitor passing through the area. It doesn't mean there is anything suspicious about it."

"Well I hope nobody thinks any more about it."

"If it were not for him this place would not be doing well at all. Don't ever forget that. Whatever you think of him, we owe him a lot," Markus said curtly, almost offended.

"I am sure he gets enough out of the deal for himself," Gisela sneered.

"You don't understand these things, and I am off to play some chess. Good night angel."

With that he left while Gisela stayed behind, wiping clean the last tables and clearing away empty glasses on her own. She had grown in to a fine woman herself, almost twenty years old with long blond curly hair that she tied into a not very efficient pony tail behind her head. She spent a lot of her day re-adjusting her unruly hair but refused to listen to Helga's advice to use hair pins, even though it was obvious how much easier her life would be if she did.

Gisela was stubborn in everything she did and had it not been for Markus she would have probably left the farm a long time ago. She had a reputation for being quiet but difficult and completely fixated on her brother. Everyone had been amazed at her refusal of the offer to become a Stockmann daughter by adoption, but as unwise and short sighted as this decision of hers seemed to be, it did fit in with this uncouth side of her character.

She could have made a good marriage on account of her beauty and her reputation as a hard worker. Unfortunately, too many of the men in the age group that would have been her natural hunting ground for a husband were already taken, dead or wounded.

Martin wondered why she had become so attached to Markus, who obviously enjoyed her attention but who rarely showed any interest in Gisela and her life at all. It was so sad to watch her run after him only to find him abandoning her the second something more important came up. Yet her loyalty and persistence seemed unbroken.

Gisela moved angrily around the restaurant, knocking over chairs and noisily moving the tables as if there were no guest rooms above her. She let her anger out uninhibited. She caught Martin off guard when she stormed in to the kitchen to get some water to clean the floor and he only just managed to hide behind one of the large storage cupboards, otherwise she would have seen him. Unfortunately, she had left the big broomstick leaning against the wall by the kitchen door in a way that he could not get past it without giving himself away. He had to wait until she was finished or else she would be able to tell that someone had been here. The next half hour seemed an eternity but finally Gisela was done with her work, left by the kitchen door and then to his surprise locked all restaurant doors from the outside and left him trapped.

Martin waited for her steps to disappear up the stairs and once his eyes had adjusted to the darkness he slowly tip toed his way through the kitchen towards the dining area. He had no other option but to open the window and jump out onto the road. Two of the windows he tried first seemed to be stuck and he could not open them, however hard he pushed. Two others were no use because of bins and other debris on the floor outside: that would make too much noise and draw attention. Just as he was trying the last window, he heard muffled voices again and footsteps coming down the stairs. He slipped under the next table and managed to hide under a corner bench that hid him from view.

Someone opened the door with a key and came into the room with a torch. It was Markus with that man from the Alsace.

"Fine, you can have one more beer but that is the last one," he heard Markus say. "We should not be here at this time and you know it. If anyone sees us together we will have be even more careful than we already are and where is the fun in that?"

"Don't be such a goody two shoes," said the man with the weird accent. "You know the more relaxed I am the less painful it will be."

The two men giggled on their way to the storage room. Markus opened the bottle noisily and handed it to the man.

"I wish I did not have to leave tomorrow," the man said. "This time seemed even shorter than the last."

"I know," Markus agreed. "I have so much more to do now that I am the son of the master. I need to let him win at chess during the day and then feed the greedy bastard like a pig. I don't like the way we always have to rush everything now either."

"I can try and stay longer next time, if that will help?"

"No, Antoine, you would risk being found out. It is too dangerous with that much merchandise. We mustn't get greedy and let our little operation spiral out of control."

"I am done with the beer," Antoine said and slammed the empty bottle on the table. "Let's go upstairs."

Soon Martin was alone again and he was jumping for joy. His spying had paid off at last. He was certain that what he had heard confirmed for him that Antoine was one of the smugglers supplying Markus with black market goods, just as he had suspected. But where was the hiding place for the 'merchandise', and could that man from the Alsace really bring enough black market goods with him on his travels? The more he thought about it, Martin found this didn't add up. How much 'merchandise' could the little car bring across the border from the Alsace? Martin had little but the secrecy and their strange private jokes to base his suspicions on. If there was no black marketing going on, what else could their secret be?

He jumped out of the one window that made for a safe landing and ran to the hay loft where he told Otto and Lukas what he had found out.

"We all know that he has got American soldiers as friends," Otto said unimpressed with the report. "I doubt he would need to get his black market goods from France."

"I totally agree," Lukas said, "With all the control posts between the sectors that is highly unlikely. Their secret has to be something else, maybe they fake documents or passports."

"Whatever it is, they are worried that it could be uncovered. Gisela knows and she is very nervous, too," Martin pointed out. "We have to watch him, all three of us. He could bring the entire family to ruin, I am sure of it."

"You hate him," Otto said calmly. "You would like to see him do something stupid, which I doubt he will. Whatever you think of him, he is very clever. We just don't know what he is doing. For all we know he could be helping us. We should not interfere out of spite and hatred. We might be shooting ourselves in the foot."

"Well, let's find out." Martin said full of fighting spirit.

Lukas kept quiet and wondered what to do. He could not decide whether to trust Uncle Herbert and tell him about their suspicions or to keep it between the three brothers. Honouring the forced promise to the choleric war veteran could bring him enormous credit but it could also be a trap. Herbert had emphasised in the same conversation that he did not like a snitch. Now what would be more important to the veteran, his code of honour or gaining knowledge? It was difficult to tell and so Lukas decided to wait and see if any more details might emerge before speaking to anyone outside the trio about it.

Herbert had taken a decisive liking to Lukas, despite being beaten by him at chess. They rarely played these days but Herbert enjoyed having the little boy around and he made him listen to his war stories and world philosophy.

He had seen how quickly the circumstances had changed in the First World War. From the hyper-inflation of the Reichsmark just a few years after the war's end he had learned that money itself meant nothing. Not compared to what hungry people were willing to sacrifice for a little bit of food in those days. Even a simple egg could bring in a fortune in the right economic climate and the farm had profited largely from its fortunate position in those days. Unable to pay for food with worthless currency, many people had no choice than to trade the few worthwhile possessions for a decent meal here and there. A few years before the Second World War he and Anna had bought the farm next door for a pittance, after the poor man had been arrested by the Gestapo as an alleged Communist.

"Your Aunt Anna was right when she told you that money is nothing. How many currencies have we had this century, and how many of them have been a success? None of them did us any good, they were just tools for the bank to make us little people lose a large part of our fortune. These new coins are only a few months old. I will always remember it because they came into circulation at the same time as I got out of the camp. But do you want to put your trust in them? I'd rather have land and houses, businesses and commodities. Then keep it all in the family and not let anything slip away to outsiders. Always remember that kid, we need to keep it together and we need to keep it big. We could split the land and give every one of you a little but what good would it do you? You'd all struggle on your own and some of you would go under: strength comes from size. Anna and I can feed all of you. The smaller farms can't do that. That is our strength. We don't buy them out straightaway that would be too easy. We buy just a field or two at a time, maybe take over their cattle and let them struggle for a little longer. The banks are asking for interest on their credit but now the farms have less income so they keep running themselves further into debt. We offer to buy a little more, appearing to be the helping hand in need, but all we do is to prolong their struggle until it is all over. Anna understood that. She was the perfect woman but her downfall is her sentiment. Just see how she adopted Markus in her panic to have an heir. She has become so needy and desperate. There was no need for that. There would have been better people for the position," he added with a benevolent look at Lukas.

Lukas listened patiently to these ramblings. His uncle had learned a lot from his companions in the camps, there was no doubt about it, and a lot of what was said made perfect sense. Herbert's years of experience at the farm and his new philosophical streak added up to a much more interesting lecture than one would have thought. Would it be wise to butter him up to get a slice of the pie? The only problem with Herbert was his big mouth and his arrogance. It made him unpredictable, and tempted him to underestimate other people. Lukas was unsure how to handle his uncle and wished he had the cunning nature of Markus.

As far as Aunt Anna was concerned, Lukas had lowered his opinion of her remarkably. Since Herbert had returned she had become a shadow of her former self and had lost her power and confidence. What good was taking advice from a hopeless woman like her now? She seemed almost scared of Herbert and avoided getting into arguments with him. She intercepted information and held clandestine meetings with the staff to have things done her way. When Herbert found out that she had gone behind his back and had failed to consult him he blew up and even hit her occasionally, but Anna feigned surprise and innocence and claimed she had not known he wanted to get involved in 'trivial matters'. They were no longer in a marriage; they were in a cold war in the same way as America and Russia: careful provocations and tactics without actual bloodshed. Lukas was not sure which side he was on.

On May 23 1949 the Federal Republic of Germany was founded by an amalgamation of all of the American and British occupied territories and most parts of the French led zone. In the election for the first post-war government of this new 'West Germany', Hans-Ulrich's party became the main political force in Bavaria and he had even won the direct seat to represent his area in the new federal parliament in Bonn.

While Anna was pleased for her brother, she hated the idea of yet another confidante being taken away. Herbert had already interfered with her relationships with Markus and Lukas. She had only Helga now to confide in and even that was difficult with Herbert being around all day, and being so unpredictable in his movements.

To clear her mind she decided to visit her sister-in-law in town. Maybe Magdalena and her remaining children were feeling alone too, since Hans-Ulrich spent most of his time away from home now.

Magdalena however had made a lot of new friends during the years her husband's political campaigning and was busier than ever. When Anna came to visit she was not too pleased at all.

"Anna, what an unexpected honour," she said with forced enthusiasm. "Klara, brew some coffee for your Aunt."

"I have to take Joseph to church. He has some training with the altar boys," Klara said resentfully.

"Then go and come straight back," Magdalena said impatiently. "That child is so useless sometimes. Hans-Ulrich has asked me to do some work for the Caritas charity and do you think I could rely on my daughter to help me out?"

"She was always a bit difficult," Anna agreed. "But why does Hans-Ulrich want you to work for free?"

"He thinks it will help his political career; all the work that the Caritas did after the war lobbying to get food aid for us on Christian grounds. He says that, without them, the Allies would have given everything to the Displaced People and would have let us Germans starve. His voters will like it if he can associate himself through me with such an organisation."

"Sounds like a waste of effort to me. He has just been elected, no need to please the voters anymore now for a few years. Who will even hear that you are spending your time with this?" Anna asked cynically.

"Plenty of people will. I am also involved in a scheme for Catholic neighbours to help each other with childcare and their sick and elderly. We touch a lot of people's lives and they will remember me and my name and that should help Hans-Ulrich get more votes next time round."

"Well I suppose he knows best, our Hans-Ulrich," said Anna with a hint of disinterest.

"You must be so glad to have your Herbert back, I am not sure what I would do without Hans-Ulrich. Even when he is away for just a few days I feel rather lost," Magdalena said.

"You can't compare the two," Anna insisted. "Hans-Ulrich is a formidable, industrious man whereas since he came back from the war, my Herbert is not much of a help any more. If it were not for the boys I would struggle myself."

"I wish my Klara was more reliable too, if it makes you feel better," Magdalena moaned.

69

"Maybe you need to be stricter with her," Anna offered, wondering why she had ever thought that coming here would bring her relief. Magdalena was so naïve and simple.

"I suppose you are right," Magdalena agreed with her sister-in-law. She did not really dedicate much thought to her oldest daughter but Klara was definitely a disappointment.

"Well at least she looks after Joseph," Magdalena admitted. "He is our pride and joy. He is so devoted to the church. He is the youngest altar boy they ever had."

Again Anna found it hard to fake enthusiasm. Magdalena had taken religious indoctrination almost to the extreme. Still guilty over her outbursts and behaviour during Joseph's birth, and helped by Hans-Ulrich, who believed that Joseph had been given to him by the Good Lord as the last chance to raise a perfect Catholic son, both parents spent more individual time with him than they ever had with their other children, despite their new careers.

Joseph responded in the way all of his instructors were hoping he would and dedicated a large portion of his young life to the church, assisting the priest with the preparations for Mass, running errands for him and attending bible classes and prayer groups. The church had become an extension if not a complete replacement for his home.

Anna was taken back with what she saw as a step back into the dark middle ages of blind faith and dogmatism. Under Hitler at least such ideas had been hidden from sight and she missed those days of rational minds. Instead of getting practical and useful advice for her current predicament, or maybe just a dose of sympathy and female solidarity, Anna was invited to join Magdalena in prayer.

"You can find all answers through prayer," Magdalena promised her cynical sister-in-law. "I often say the Lord's Prayer repetitively for half an hour and that makes me see sense. You should try it. If you want to we could go over to church and do it together. I am sure the priest will let us in. Joseph practically lives there and so we are always treated with special respect."

"No thank you. You can do that for yourself, I don't think that is going to help me," Anna said dismissively.

"Don't you believe in His power? Are you lapsing in your faith?" Magdalena asked, almost panicking. "You, who I have entrusted with my children."

Anna started to panic. She lived for the few moments she got to spend with Lukas and could not let Magdalena take that away from her now.

"Oh I don't mean it like that," she said quickly. "Of course I go to prayer groups at my own church. There is no shortage of that in my life. I came here today because I thought that you as a woman might have some insight in to the mind of a man and could help me get Herbert out of his lazy state."

"If you think that your husband is doing anything unchristian or if you disagree with him about anything else, I suggest you take him to church to have the Lord purify his soul with prayer and faith," Magdalena said, full of conviction, although it sounded a little rehearsed, like a line learnt for a play. "If that does not help him you should ask your priest to come and mediate between you. If you cannot hear God's will directly then get your priest to relay it for you."

Anna felt that there was no arguing with this woman but she needed to placate her in order to keep Lukas and his two brothers at the farm.

"What good advice, you are right of course. If you fail on your own, ask God and his disciples," she said to humour her sister-in-law, and then she turned her attention towards the children.

As always, Klara was cold and unapproachable to Anna. She still bore a grudge for having been sent away from the farm like a useless piece of furniture while her brothers were allowed to stay. She had never been noticed in this environment that favoured the boys.

She was all the more jealous now that Maria, as the baby and younger girl, received the attention and love that Klara had craved, but had always been deprived of. Magdalena praised Maria as the quiet and undemanding child without ever acknowledging those same qualities in Klara, who had been treated as if she were the same noisy rascal as her brothers had been. This afternoon was no different from any other. All the time that the older women were chatting about their lives, Klara had been ordered to set the table, to do this and to do that, but

71

Maria was asked to stay at the table and draw a picture, sit on Anna's lap and braid her hair. When the family went to church all her mother's friends made a huge fuss over Maria, but no one noticed Klara.

If she made an effort to look pretty and wore her good clothes all she reaped for it was criticism from the women for being vain, making a spectacle of herself and looking indecent.

As soon as she could she stole herself away from the flat. Anna's visit only brought up bad feelings. Klara asked to be permitted to do some praying herself but she went to an area by the small river where some of the American soldiers smoked cigarettes and tried to fish. If only she had more confidence she would approach them and hope that one of these men would take her away to America, as she had heard did happen occasionally.

Anna, in the meantime, saw clearly that there was nothing to be gained from a visit to Magdalena. She loved seeing the cute Maria but she was bored of Magdalena's simplicity and most of all she missed her brother Hans-Ulrich badly. As religiously devoted as he was, he had still a foot in the earthly sphere and, unlike the naïve Magdalena, he might have known what to suggest to help her with Herbert. As she sat at the kitchen table and witnessed Magdalena turning her life away from reality and solely towards the church and her religion, Anna could not help feeling a little jealous of this woman who was content with so little, and whose life was so easily fulfilled by blind faith.

If only she herself had such a simple character and an easy-to-please nature. With her tunnel vision, Magdalena cared about nothing but salvation and worship, while Anna wanted so much more: to gain the upper hand over Herbert, achieve success in the business world, enlarge the farm and raise the children of others in a way that they would be able to carry on the family fortune and name with pride and glory.

Anna left without getting any ideas as to how to regain control over her little empire. She thought it was ironic how the two violent and devastating wars had left the farm and her business ventures more or less completely unharmed, but they had more than damaged both men in her life and ruined everything for Anna in such an indirect manner after all.

On her way down the stairs she suddenly felt sad to leave Maria behind. The only comfort during the wasted time here had been to rock that cheerful and sweet child on her legs and watch her play. Maybe now that Herbert was monopolizing the boys at the farm this girl could be the companion and friend that Anna needed. She ran back upstairs and begged Magdalena to let her take the child with her to the farm.

"Of course she can come with you," Magdalena said generously. "If you think she can help, I am more than happy for the two of you."

"Have you noticed that the new flag for Germany has a black eagle on it?" Maria said excitedly. "Everywhere in the whole country there will be the new flag and it will be like an advertising sign for our business. That is good, is it not?"

All the way home, Anna held Maria's hand and smiled at her new acquisition. She swore to herself that Herbert would never be able to take her away. He would not be interested in this little girl. At least Maria was hers and hers alone now.

When Klara came home a little later and heard about the favour bestowed on her little sister she was fuming with rage and jealousy.

While Anna had been in town, her husband Herbert had taken the opportunity to have a word with Helga. He did not like the way his wife seemed to be listening to every word that servant woman said. At first, he had fallen for the obedient manner which Helga had displayed towards her new master, but there was far too much whispering and secrecy going on between the women to trust either of them. They clearly shared secrets and were closer than he felt was appropriate. He had learnt from one of his prison mates that the best friend of a woman often was the downfall for a man. Whoever had the biggest influence on a wife was a threat to the husband, and Herbert would be dealing with this right here and now, before it went any further.

"What is wrong with you?" he asked Helga as she came to clear his latest plate of food away.

"What are you talking about?" she asked calmly, not rising to his provocation.

"Well, you are getting on in years but even now that the men are back from the war you still hang around here every day and night without fail, never taking an evening off or going to town or to a barn dance. All you live for is this farm and keeping my wife company. Something must be wrong with you."

"I think it is a bit late for me to find a husband now," she said dismissively.

"You're not that bad looking," Herbert commented. "You have aged better than my wife has. You could still turn a few heads if you wanted."

"I wish I could have had love and romance when I was younger but it never worked out for me then. Now it is too late for children and my own family. The farm has become my life, I will admit that," Helga said, sounding quite content.

"If you don't want a companion for your life that is your choice and no one will mind that," Herbert said. "I just want to make clear to you that I do not appreciate you focusing all of your attention on my wife. I can hear you two are gossiping and whispering behind my back and I can see that you have too much of an influence on her. She is difficult and stubborn enough as it is, she does not need anyone to encourage her to contradict me and make her own decisions," he added, pointing his finger as a warning gesture towards her.

Helga was not completely surprised at this conversation. It had only been a matter of time before Herbert would turn his attention towards her, his anger and hate were rooted so deeply, they had to come her way at some point. She did not get upset over his ridiculous accusations and paranoia. The difficult bit was to respond in a way that diffused his absurd ideas yet played up to his need to be right.

"Anna does not want my advice on many things," Helga replied eventually. "She sometimes asks me about Markus and Lukas. Since neither of us ever had children of our own she often wants to know what I think about their behaviour and their lives. You should know better to believe that she ever would consult me on anything important. I am just a maid."

That made sense to Herbert but he had taken a hostile approach and he did not want to leave this conversation without a final warning or a threat to prove to her that he was the boss.

"Just make sure you mind your own business. I am on to you, do you understand?"

74

"Of course I do. You have nothing to fear from me," she said humbly.

"Damn right! Now get me some more of that cut meat," he ordered her.

Chapter 6: Helga (1949)

Maria seemed to be a symbol of peace and at least for a short while her arrival brought an end to the hostile relations at the Hinterberger Farm. One day the little girl drew the farm and The Black Eagle Inn and painted a black eagle on the outside of the wall. Anna thought the idea brilliant and commissioned a local artist to make a fresco painting on the outside wall of the restaurant. She dedicated almost her entire time to the little one and her ideas to liven up the place, and in doing so she seemed to let everyone else get on with their work: Markus at the restaurant and Lukas and Herbert with the farm. Anna appeared to have given up the fight and only managed some of the minor daily tasks on the farm, just as her husband thought it should be. Of course, the idle war veteran delegated all heavy work to others and he ridiculed her for her idea with the fresco but let her have her way for once.

"Make sure it does not look exactly like the 'Bundesadler' from the flag, or we will attract the wrong kind of attention," he warned her. "The German flag is still tainted and nothing to be openly proud of and to wave too enthusiastically."

'People do want to be proud of something,' she thought to herself, and secretly she was more than pleased that the dark but somewhat romantic bird associated with her little empire would soon be found on every flag in the country. There had to be some advantage for her in this once the 'shame' had worn off.

Herbert noticed that Helga and his wife had visibly fewer of their intimate moments, which he attributed to the strict warning he had given to the servant. He was most pleased with himself and his new found authority. Before the war he used to work himself stupid in the fields and what for? Why not, for once, enjoy the benefits of being your own boss? All that was needed was for him to keep an eye on things and not become too complacent; the days of hard leg work and back breaking blood, sweat and tears were over for him, and thank God for that.

From what he could see, Markus was making a tremendous success out of The Black Eagle and the restaurant, the amount of people staying and eating there was proof enough, without Herbert having to get involved. There was no need for him to check on the details; his new right hand Lukas was doing that for him.

Beneath the surface however, things were far from peaceful. Helga hated to see her mistress in distress and was not prepared to keep her distance any longer just to placate the paranoid notions of this tyrant of a man. She had just about had enough of this tedious and hateful man, who turned her whole world upside down and added insult to injury by harassing her with threats. She would not endure this by sitting idly and hoping for it to end, the way her mistress Anna seemed to do.

Helga decided to take the initiative herself because after dedicating her entire life to the farm, and working her way to a comfortable position, she was not going to be edged out and driven away by this nuisance of a man. However, without legal rights or any other hold over him, she saw no other way out than to gradually poison him and get rid of him.

Small doses of rat poison and other 'remedies' at her disposal, administered slowly over a long period of time, she hoped, would gradually wear him down to such a poor physical state that he would not be able to interfere with the business any longer and her mistress Anna would be back in full charge.

Talk in town was full of tales of men like Herbert who had returned from the war and had changed in their character and in their health. It was not unheard of that the years of nutritional deprivation finally took their toll on the survivors, years after they had returned home. Even Alfons had succumbed to consumption long after the war and everyone attributed this to his poor diet.

Everyone could see how Herbert stuffed himself with food. He had gained a lot of weight since he had returned and looked bloated and unhealthy. Helga was sure she would get away with her plan if only she was careful and proceeded slowly enough to not raise any suspicion. Besides, no one would suspect her of foul play, she seemingly got on with everyone on the farm and had not as much to lose as some of the family. Suspicion would fall on other people first, none of whom could be implicated by evidence unless she herself planted it.

While Helga was planning her attack on Herbert, Anna had, in fact, not at all given up on her hopes to regain control of her empire. She was only recuperating, resting and temporarily allowing herself to be besotted with Maria. The pure angel seemed to smile continuously and radiated goodness and happiness. Maria's charm made Anna forget the upset that Herbert and his new regime of terror had brought into her life. But this temporary distraction acted only as a band aid on her soul and did not bring a lasting remedy to the situation.

While she could not go directly against her husband, she could try and influence him through Lukas and Markus. Pretending to take Maria for strolls she could escape Herbert's line of sight and meet the two boys secretly: for scheming and finding out what he was up to.

Ideas she had for the farm were now presented to Herbert as coming from the two boys, that way they strangely did not meet with as much resistance from the old man as if it had come from her.

Buying new equipment or hiring new staff was something he categorically objected to whenever she suggested it, always on the grounds that she had an extravagant lifestyle and her ideas were too big for the farm, or that the unstable times might not financially permit them. However, when Lukas brought up the same ideas and spoke of nearby farms who had invested in modern equipment he was all ears and took to visiting said farms to see for himself whether he thought it might be worth his money.

Markus proposed to create more bedrooms as The Black Eagle found itself frequently booked up. He believed that during the years of hardship that were to come for the German Nation, holidays at home would be all people could afford and many would choose the warm and sunny south with its beautiful Alpine scenery. During the war, in line with the Nazi's Heimat ideology, many people from all over Germany had been attracted to holidays at The Black Eagle Inn and they must have returned and told their friends about it. He suggested turning some of the many servants' quarters into large dorms, some into smaller rooms, and to relocate the staff to some of the older barn buildings. In his view, this would widen the choice of accommodation for visitors and utilise a few unused outbuildings.

The idea was, of course, Anna's but she decided to see whether Markus could get this radical idea through. Herbert did consider it for some time, but given that Markus had the reputation of a wild child, he dismissed it for the time being.

Herbert had come from a comparatively small farm and so his leadership style was less experimental and daring: more small minded and tight fisted.

However, he did trust Lukas' advice and authorized the acquisition of some powerful tractors and a second-hand threshing machine. Spending money did not come easily to him and it took him a good deal of deliberation before he agreed to the proposal. He finally decided that he had to demonstrate to everyone that he was capable of making tough choices by himself with dramatic consequences. This investment in machinery would show him to be a man of vision and help feed his fragile ego. Herbert had been watching his wife make the decisions for decades and then it had never bothered him. Since he had been with all those men in the prisoner camp he had learnt that this attitude was considered cowardly and ridiculous. His fellow inmates had been amazed at the extent of her reign and at how little Herbert had actually known and wanted to know about running the farm himself. During the endless days of hard labour they had implored him to take control and taught him how to speak to his staff and his wife to be taken more seriously.

He enjoyed being the big boss now but naturally his experience dated from the economically challenging times of the pre-war era. In the new West Germany the economy was improving and Herbert was unsure how to assess the new circumstances by himself. Were these improvements permanent and was it possible for a beaten nation like Germany to recover economically so unbelievably quickly? Would the investments pay off or was he risking everything for some fancy but unprofitable acquisitions?

Despite this discomfort and uncertainty, he was pleased that his wife was keeping busy with the little girl whom she took everywhere with her. How easy it had been to drive Anna away with his unpleasantness and how odd to find her taking refuge in pseudo motherhood. Bizarrely, he despised Anna's new weak character, although he knew that it was him who had created it with his bullying. He had fallen for Anna because of her ability to take charge and her interest in business and men's things. What he had intended with his new confident stance was for her to take a more humble attitude towards her husband and respect his opinion and authority. The strong and hard-working wife of his had turned in to a fragile and needy mother figure that engaged in all the effeminate pastimes he had resented in women from his childhood onwards. He felt nothing but contempt for her.

It did not take long before Helga's new 'ingredients' to Herbert's food showed its effect. He frequently complained about stomach pains and felt tired and lethargic. Helga always erred on the side of caution and had started with very small doses, and also added other substances to the meals, any left-over medications and even drugs prescribed for sick animals.

The result was that no doctor could make sense of Herbert's many irregular symptoms. He was fit and healthy one day, then low and depressed the next; clear in his head in the morning and drowsy and confused that very evening. Headaches and stomach pain tormented him often but then stayed away for weeks.

His house physician, Dr Alexander Hofer, whom he knew from his school days, drew the most plausible conclusion from it all and decided it was a nervous reaction to his years of imprisonment. He prescribed bed rest and a healthy diet. Herbert did not mind so much about the nausea and the vomiting but he was scared out of his mind about the quickening and slowing down of his heartbeat, courtesy of some nitroglycerin which Helga's aunt had used for her angina and Pervitin, a toxic stimulant with the opposite effect on the heart; a substance the Wehrmacht had used for some of its combatants to improve their performance. Helga had come into possession of a rather large quantity of it from a deserting soldier. Towards the end of the war, she had sheltered the poor man in the hay loft and shared with him what little food she had because she could not bear the idea of him being shot as a deserter. To see another life being wasted so close towards the end of the fighting was idiotic, she thought. When he finally made his way home after the German surrender, she gave him civilian clothes so he would not be arrested and, in return, as thanks for saving him, he had left her everything he had that was worth anything, including these 'life-saving' pills.

In Herbert's years in the camps he had seen many men die of heart related problems due to overwork and poor nutrition and he fell into a state of hysteria whenever symptoms occurred that he thought he recognised as precursors to a heart attack. The fact that no doctor felt they could do anything about his bizarrely changing heart rate and the mood swings left him in a state of intense fear for his life. Dr Hofer could try and calm the patient all he wanted but for Herbert, this was far too alarming to be dismissed as a simple matter of nutrition and rest.

Instead of suspecting foul play and recognising the women around him as the force behind his malaise he suddenly turned less harsh towards them, and sought their counsel and emotional support when he was suffering from either the anxiety that the Pervitin left him with, or from the sudden lethargy following doses of nitroglycerin.

Like a frightened child, he begged Helga to do something to make him feel better: to look after his diet, get him some water or a hot water bottle, use her natural remedies, find a healer, a witch or just about anyone who might be able to help.

Helga had heard of some gypsy woman called Alice who lived in a shed in the woods and to whom superstitious people went for help. Helga personally thought little of Alice's talents of divining, tarot card reading and herbal remedies. Some said that the woman had second sight, something that Helga would under normal circumstances never believe possible, but since she had the poisoning of Herbert to hide, she was not as confident about those doubts any more. What if Alice really could see through her and her scheming?

First, Helga went to see the gypsy woman by herself, to find out what she was capable of. Rumour had it that Alice was prepared to do anything for money.

"I want you to tell me my fortune," Helga said, hoping that such a reading would establish the powers of the gypsy.

"You're from that big farm, aren't you? That will cost you, you lot can afford some, can you not?" the gypsy said, bluntly.

"If you're any good that won't be a problem, but if you are having me on then you won't earn much from me," Helga said confidently.

Alice smiled knowingly and got her tarot cards out without any further ado. She shuffled the cards then pulled a few out and turned them over one by one.

"Death! Well that comes up a lot when people are in turmoil. Everything is falling apart around you. I can see a tough time, a big change and renewal. Let's see what it is that you want:

The World? Now, who doesn't? That is not a bad card. Looks like you're going to get what you want. The cards say you will have to be patient, my dear. Now for what your fear is…The Magician! He is a man that tries to fool you. But sweetheart, the cards say that your fear is not necessary, you can trust me. There is the next card, the Wheel of Fortune! That's good news too, it means more changes of fate. Everything is taken care of. Let me see the next card: The Hermit! Be careful, you need to be very, very careful. And now for the outcome: The Priest: That means help is at hand."

Helga was relieved. This reading was as unspecific and general as it could be; sure proof that Alice had no psychic powers whatsoever.

"The Magician, he is unpredictable and frightening. I know it is your boss, I have heard of him, but the Wheel of Fortune is taking care of him, he has it coming naturally. You don't need to worry," Alice said.

"Well, he wants you to heal him."

"And you would rather I don't succeed?" the gypsy asked with a smirk.

"I wouldn't want any remedy to get in the way of nature's cause, if you catch my drift," Helga admitted vaguely.

"As I said, it will cost you. I don't like that Magician myself," Alice stated. "I could be monetarily persuaded to turn a blind eye but I have to warn you. When people see me they often heal themselves. They have such a strong belief that I can cure them that they get better, even if I don't do anything myself."

"He wants to see someone," Helga said. "You might just be the perfect person for the job."

Together they went to the Hinterberger Farm. Herbert was over the moon that the gypsy had come and was certain she would bring a remedy for his ailments.

She took out her rods and did some divining over his body.

"It is your head that is the problem," she said sharply. "No doctor can help you with your problems there; it is your worries that cause your heart to race and slow down."

"What can I do about that?" Herbert asked eagerly.

"If I were you I would go out and do some regular work. That is what your body is used to. You are not made for sitting inside and pondering about papers and books. Your head is so full of problems it throws everything out of kilter," Alice proclaimed.

"Can't you just give me some herbs to make it better?" he asked, visibly displeased with the answer.

"I can make you some remedies, teas and ointments, anything you like. They will help a little but I am not a miracle worker. The rods do not lie and they tell me where the real problem is."

"Just make me those remedies, money is not an object," he promised.

A few days later Alice came back to him with a self-made tea to drink whenever he was feeling anxious and she gave him a large tub of an ointment to rub in to his temples whenever he felt lethargic. It smelled disgustingly of onions and garlic and the stink permeated the entire room. Lukas and Markus could hardly breathe when they played him at chess.

Chapter 7: The Will (1949-55)

As Alice had predicted Herbert's state improved initially, due to his trust in her ability. He obsessively drank the tea and rubbed the ointment into his forehead and temples, but a few days later Helga increased the doses of nitroglycerin and Pervitin and he was back to his old helpless state of fear and lost the confidence in the remedies as quickly as he had acquired it.

"Call me a notary," he ordered his wife. "I need to make a will. I could die any day now. Oh, I wouldn't wish this on my worst enemy."

Anna was furious to hear about the idea of a notary. It could only mean that he intended to disown her.

"Of course I will call one," she assured him falsely.

"Would you mind doing the books tonight?" he asked her. "I feel dreadful. Maybe that gypsy was right and I should not make every small decision by myself. As long as you check with Lukas wherever possible, you can make the decisions again."

She beamed at the remark, although his arrogance stung. Being bedbound, he had no more control over her now and she had not the slightest inclination to get a notary in the house.

"Of course I will and don't worry; I have relied on Lukas' help for a long time anyway," she said warmly.

Anna re-established herself quickly as the sole mistress of the farm but she continued to play the humble wife and servant for Herbert. It was lucky that she could rely so well on her two boys and had still enough time for her 'parental' joys with Maria. Fortunately the girl was not so little anymore and would happily follow her eldest brothers after school when Anna was busy.

Unaware that Helga was behind the physical symptoms of her husband's illness and could control it like a puppet master, she expected to be a widow before long. Anna postponed calling for the notary as long as she possibly could, but Herbert would not let the matter drop. Additionally, he simply did not seem to get any worse than he was now. She had hoped that he might drift into a vegetative state before he was able to tell that she deliberately kept the notary out of his reach. He was so adamant about his wish that he even urged both Lukas and Markus to call for the official to make his will in an increasingly desperate manner.

Anna successfully persuaded both boys not to fulfil his demands for the time being. She told Markus how unwise it would be to allow Herbert to give away anything that was thus far his sole inheritance. As the only son, Markus was to be given everything by law: a will could only take something away.

She made Lukas comply with her wish by promising to adopt him as soon as her husband had died, so that he could get the farm and Markus the Inn. It did not take much to persuade the ambitious and arrogant maths genius to believe that Anna would never leave her precious farm in the hands of the wild boy Markus. He saw himself as too indispensable already to even think that he might be being played. It had occurred to Lukas that maybe Herbert was planning to leave the farm to him in this will but all the same it seemed safer to trust Anna and her promise than to rely on the whims of a mentally disturbed hypochondriac.

In one of his more violent panic attacks, Herbert got up from his sick bed and screamed the house down.

"Will someone in this forsaken house go and get me a notary or do I have to walk into town to make my will?" he shouted.

"Don't exhaust yourself," Anna tried to calm him down. "I keep calling on the notary. I don't know why he hasn't shown up yet."

"Yes," Helga agreed. "Be careful with your heart. Don't get too excited. Remember the gypsy woman and what she said about your head."

"Oh, rubbish!" he exclaimed loudly. "Lukas! Markus! Where are the boys? I will get the two of them to do it. I can't rely on you women, can I?"

"There is no rush, Herbert," Anna said. "Now calm yourself down."

"You're not taking me seriously," he whined. "Do you know what kind of agony I feel? Get me the boys!"

Lukas and Markus swore on their life to take care of it and that seemed to quieten him down for the day but the next morning he started asking for a notary again.

"I will go into town this afternoon if nobody is here by lunchtime," he threatened, and there was no doubt in anyone's mind that he would see his threat through. Lo and behold, an hour later Markus appeared with a notary who was currently a guest at The Black Eagle.

"This is Herr Etherlinck, a notary from the former Alsace," Markus introduced the man to his uncle. He can make all the arrangements with you."

"Fine, now all of you can get out." Herbert shouted. "This is private."

"Surely your wife can stay?" Herr Etherlinck asked his client.

"I prefer to do all of this by myself."

Lukas, Anna and Helga were sending Markus reproachful looks. How dare he break their pact? They could not believe that Markus could be so obedient to Herbert and foolishly risk losing part of what would legally be his inheritance. Herbert and the notary were left alone for an hour during which Helga and Anna tried desperately to hear what was going on inside the room but to no avail. Suddenly the door opened and Herr Etherlinck asked in his thick accent that two strangers from the Inn might be persuaded to come and sign as witnesses for the completed will.

Helga went over to the restaurant and shortly after Markus brought two men who had kindly agreed to act as such witnesses. Once this had been done the notary and the two men left the farm again.

"What have you decided?" Anna asked her husband as he rested on his sofa with a sorry and long suffering face.

"Mind your own business," he said.

"This is my business," she screamed at him full of rage. "I may be a Stockmann by name but the farm is still known to everyone as the Hinterberger farm. How dare you decide what is going to happen and to do it without even asking me for my opinion?"

"Leave me alone, I am dying," he told her, sounding tired and only a little annoyed. "You'll find out soon enough."

Anna stormed out.

"Helga, get me some more of that cut meat and some buttered bread," Herbert ordered. "And make sure that there is enough butter this time. I hate it when I can see the bread through the butter. Don't be so stingy, do you hear me?"

"Maybe you should have something less fatty to line your stomach first," the servant suggested, but Herbert would have none of it.

"If I am going to die, I might as well enjoy myself the last few days I have on earth," he bellowed and turned his back to her, posing as the dying soldier on the divan.

She angrily prepared his meal, wishing she knew what he had written in his will. If she were to send him over the edge now with a final dose of the Pervitin they would never get a chance to change the will, unless Markus could somehow steal it off that guest of his.

No, she would have to wait a little longer and so she put a large dose of nitroglycerin in his meal, making at least sure that he would be mellow and subdued this evening. The gypsy woman had told her that everything would be taken care of naturally and Helga had come to believe it. Maybe Herbert would die soon and solve all their problems. Maybe the will was just a nasty mind game that he was playing; he was just about capable of everything these days.

She never got to serve him his meal. When she got into the living room he was lying on the floor clenching his chest and neck. She almost dropped her plate but managed to compose herself quickly. She turned on her heels and tip toed back out, leaving him struggling on his own. He could not have seen her and if he were to recover he would never be able to tell for sure that she had been in the room and had failed to help him. If her master should die of natural causes so be it. It dawned on her that now there was no time to waste, she had to get hold of that will and make it disappear. Whatever it contained it could not be good news, without it the estate would simply remain in Anna and Markus's possession, as per current legal procedure.

She hid the plate with the extra nitroglycerine on top of one of the kitchen units, hoping that no one would find it until she had time to dispose of the poison by herself. As fast as she could she ran towards the restaurant to find Markus and Herrn Etherlinck.

Anna had been very upset by her husband's behaviour and could not think of anyone better suited to talk about it with than Lukas, her serious and worldly nephew with his analytical mind.

He was as taken aback by this sudden development with the will as she was, and outraged by Markus' betrayal, but he remained calm and thoughtful

"It does not make sense at all," he said. "Markus is the one who will lose the most if a will is made. He is the only son, the sole heir, why would he of all people help Herbert? He is neither pious nor sincere enough to do it on grounds of moral principles. It makes no sense unless he knows something that we don't. Maybe during their chess games Herbert has let something slip what he intends to do and Markus agrees."

"I doubt that very much," Anna disagreed. "I don't understand why Markus did what he did. What puzzles me much more is what it possibly could be that Herbert so desperately wanted to write into this new will. I didn't think he cared about anything beyond himself. Why would he take an interest after his own death? Who does he want to protect or punish and why? And now that he has made the will, why would he not talk about it either? None of this makes sense."

"You are right. That is bizarre," Lukas agreed. "Well, he seems totally confused. Maybe tomorrow he might demand to make another will."

"What do you think he has decided? Would he favour you or any of your brothers? His sister? Give everything to Markus and leave me empty handed?" she wondered.

"Give him time," Lukas said. "He has had a dramatic day; he might be feeling more at peace tomorrow. He often calms down after a stressful episode."

"I hope so," she said, sceptical. "By then, of course, that notary could be back in the Alsace. What a mess Herbert has made of everything."

Helga reached the restaurant in the middle of the quiet afternoon period. Gisela was half-heartedly tidying up in the kitchen.

"I haven't seen Markus," she told Helga. "Why are you looking for him?"

"Never mind. Where do you think he could be?" the servant asked, trying to sound casual.

"It is hard to tell these days. Maybe at the army barracks meeting his friends?" she suggested slowly.

"You know everything about your brother. You must know where he is?" Helga tried to push her a little harder to get at the information she knew was there.

"Honestly, I don't know," Gisela insisted.

"Fine, I'll go and check his room," Helga said.

"Oh, he won't be in his room," Gisela suddenly said very quickly. "He never stays there. If he is in the house he is usually in the office, but rarely at the beginning of the week and it is Monday today."

Helga closed the restaurant door behind her and walked towards the reception area on the east side of the building. It was clear to her that Gisela was trying to hide something and instead of going to the office, where she was expected to go, she followed her hunch and went back in the opposite direction towards Markus' room in the west wing. She had to cross the restaurant area which was now empty. As she reached the stairs, she could just about make out Gisela's skirt disappearing upwards ahead of her.

Helga followed her slowly so as not to be seen or heard but instead of going all the way up to the staff quarters, Gisela went to one of the nicer guest rooms and knocked on the door. After a long pause the door opened and the Herr Etherlinck, just wearing his trousers and an under shirt, opened the door and pulled Gisela inside the room.

Helga went closer to the door to listen but could not make out anything that was being said. All she could tell was that Gisela seemed very worried but the male voices of the notary and probably Markus were relaxed and calm. Careful not to be exposed as an eavesdropper Helga left her position, went up a flight of stairs and waited there for Gisela to come out of the room again, which didn't take long. The girl had left the restaurant unattended and was bound to go back as soon as she could.

After about twenty minutes the door opened again and Markus came out by himself. Helga carefully tip toed down the stairs and only just caught a quick glimpse of him before he disappeared out of her sight. Through the angles of the staircase she had only seen parts of him since he was moving too fast for her to follow quietly. All she knew for certain was that he was holding something that looked remarkably like the copy of the will with the red seal clearly broken in half.

She was both pleased and shocked. Had this crafty young man bribed the notary into giving up the document? If that were the case she had to seriously reconsider her estimation of Markus. What a cunning little monster he had turned into.

Did this also mean that he had intercepted the will completely or merely gained access to the information? What had Herbert written in his will that could not wait and had to remain a secret? She could not bear to think that Markus already knew. If only she could ask him, then she would know whether to try and rescue the dying man over at the farm building or finish him off with some extra 'medication'.

She waited several minutes before she decided it was safe to move. She quietly walked down the stairs and tried to leave the building unnoticed. Unfortunately, the exit to the outside from this staircase had been locked and that meant that Helga had to cross the restaurant and walk past Gisela on her way out.

"Did you find him?" Gisela asked her as she walked in.

There were a few guests playing cards in the corner which meant that Gisela probably had been too busy to pay attention to Helga's movements. It was safe to assume that she had no idea that Helga had followed her earlier or witnessed anything that went on between the siblings and the man from the Alsace.

"No, never mind," she replied and made her way to Anna's home.

She wondered what had happened to Herbert in the meantime. By now he would have been lying on the floor without help for almost an hour. The way he had offended Anna it was sure she would not return to him for at least a few hours and Lukas was slaving away in the office, which he rarely left. Helga hoped that the old git was dead by now and the nasty atmosphere that had befallen the house of late would come to an end with him.

As she approached the building nothing indicated that he had been found just yet. Helga went straight to the kitchen and cut up some more meat and bread, this time without lacing it with nitroglycerin. Her previous plate was still untouched on top of the kitchen unit and to make sure no one innocent would end up eating it she went to the pig stalls and fed it to them. If any of them died no one would suspect her. The gypsy woman had told her to cover her tracks and so Helga took good care to eliminate all evidence.

Then she returned to the kitchen, picked up the new plate and entered the living room. Herbert was lying on the floor without moving. She quietly slipped inside and put the plate next to him on the floor, making it look like he had just reached for the food when his attack had killed him. She quietly left the room and looked for Lukas and Anna upstairs in the office.

"Aunt Anna has gone out," Lukas informed her. "I think she is looking for Markus to have a word with him. I wouldn't want to be in his shoes right now."

"Wouldn't we all want to have a word with Markus," Helga said, meaningfully. "I am going to see if I can find Anna and calm her down. The poor thing must be quite shocked. How do you feel about this awful business?"

"I don't think I am going to lose anything from a new will," he admitted. "Whoever is gaining from it is bound to keep me on in my position. I am curious to hear what Markus has to say for himself, though. He must know that I might benefit from a will so it is a puzzle to me as to why he did it and how odd for Herbert to say nothing about it either."

"I find that a really surprising, too," she said. "I actually have not heard anything from him for a while. I guess he has nodded off for a snooze. Normally he calls for me every half an hour with something else, all demands and requests."

"Enjoy the break while you can, especially today," Lukas said.

"Do you want anything to eat before I go on my search for Anna?" she offered.

"No, thank you. Maybe later when all of you are back? I am sure Uncle Herbert will have woken up by then and be back demanding food."

"I bet he will," she said and continued her hunt for Anna.

Anna had indeed gone to find her adoptive son and she had been more successful in her search than Helga. She went to the Inn's reception and office area seconds before Markus arrived there himself. Having the opened copy of the will in his hand there was little else he could do but to smile at her and show her

91

the document with the triumph of a co-conspirator rather than a boy caught with his hands in a cookie jar.

"Look what I got," he said smugly.

Anna did not know what she wanted to know first: how he got it or what the will said?

"Give me that!" she ordered.

"You don't have to worry, mother," he said with a broad smile. "Herr Etherlinck is not a notary."

"Isn't he? Then what about the will?" she asked, not understanding the implications immediately.

"This is no valid will," Markus explained.

"Won't your father find out? He has got a copy in his safe." she pointed out.

"Wrong. I have both copies of the will. The envelope that we gave 'father' is empty," Markus said triumphantly.

Anna stared at him for a second in disbelief. What was this young kid capable off, she asked herself. She wanted to grill him about his cunning plan and how he had come to know criminals like that imposter, but then she thought better of it and decided that she would rather hear about the clever deception story later. First of all she wanted to know who her husband wanted to leave his fortune to.

She pulled the pages out as quickly as she could and looked through them. What she saw was an outrage. The man had intended to leave everything to his unmarried sister! She was numb. The entire business, farm lands, livestock, restaurant and Inn was meant to be left to a stupid and incapable woman who would not know what to do with it. Worse: the bastard had tried to swindle her out of everything she had and pass it on to an outsider spinster who did not even work on the farm. Even in his daze and paranoia he could not be that insane and malicious? When was the last time he had seen his sister? She had shown up once after he had returned from England, and that was it. The silly cow would not have a clue how to run the farm or what to do with the money if she sold it. What a waste and what a slap in the face. Herbert was clearly mentally unstable and incompetent, not even the meanest spirit of spite would allow for such a disastrous choice. All of the Hinterbergers would go empty handed unless the sister was prepared to share the responsibilities or at least employ them.

As she read on Anna saw that Herbert had decreed that at least his wife, Lukas and Markus would have a right to live and work in the business. How very generous of him, she thought angrily, to be allowed to become a servant to that cow.

"What a bastard!" she hissed.

"You can say that again, mother," Markus agreed. "Well, we got our own back. This will is not valid, no one is ever going to see it and it will never be acted upon."

"Are you quite sure?" she asked him doubtfully.

"Yes. The best thing is that he thinks he has done his deed now and won't bother us about it again. We just have to pretend we know nothing and continue to ask him about the will so he won't be suspicious."

"How did you do it?" she asked him.

"I can't tell you that, only that I have my own methods and connections. The less you know about this the better, trust me," he replied smugly.

"I won't complain about your methods, son. You have just saved us from a complete nightmare. We would have been ruined. What was he thinking?" she said, getting angry again.

"I guess in his state of anxiety he gave it to the one person he trusts the most, the only person in his life that is actual family by blood. I can understand why he decided that this was his best option. I am not his real family."

Anna cringed at this statement.

"I hope you know that as my brother's son you are just like my own," she tried to assure him. "Do you think of us as your real family?" she asked pleadingly.

"You are my family, of course you are," he said almost too mechanically. "I doubt however that Herbert thinks like that at all, probably not even about you, especially given how emotional and confused he is at the moment. I think you should have him examined, maybe you can have him committed to a lunatic asylum and get rid of him that way?"

"Get rid of him?" she said, with poorly acted contempt at the thought. "He is my husband!"

"You and I no longer have to pretend, mother," Markus said coldly. "He is a pain in the neck and everything would be much easier if he was out of the picture. He has just shown us

93

how little he thinks of us, his family. You and I, we two want the same, don't we?"

"Yes," she admitted finally with a big sigh, "I guess we do. If only Hans-Ulrich was here he could help me with that," she said longingly.

"That goody two shoes holier-than-thou man of God?" Markus said laughingly. "He won't help you with anything. He will tell you that this is yet another ordeal that God has sent us to become better people. If the farm goes down the drain and all of us end up on the street he will see it as a just and fair ruling for any past sins he thinks we may have committed. No, mother, if you want to get this done then let me handle it. I have a few favours to call in. Just promise me to stay out of it. What I have in mind is not going to be pretty."

"I don't want to hurt him!" she claimed half-heartedly. She wanted Herbert out of the way badly, but not at any cost.

"He won't be hurt. I am just saying that it isn't a pleasant sight to have someone committed to a lunatic asylum. The guys are not very gentle when they pick up a mad man. I'll have to make sure I make him angry and agitated before they come so they see the worst of him. I think it would be best if you stayed out of the way when it happens."

Anna was astonished. Markus was only just in his twenties and already he had bypassed her talent for scheming and manipulating people, and in almost criminal ways.

She had been the alpha female amongst her siblings when she was younger and in those days she had been good at getting her way but she felt useless and helpless in this type of battle. Markus had methods she could not command. Maybe this was why Herbert had won the upper hand. Beyond a certain level of childish rivalry she could not compete.

"Who is this Herr Etherlinck anyway?" she asked finally, deliberately leaving their previous conversation about Herbert open, neither telling Markus to go ahead nor stopping him.

"Oh Antoine? He is an old friend of mine, a regular visitor who happens to be in possession of a notary stamp. Etherlinck is a common Belgian name, we thought it sounded right for someone from the Alsace, and it seems to have fooled everyone." He laughed complacently.

Anna was torn between adoration for her beloved Markus and a chilly feeling of fear. Could she control the monster she had created or would he become a threat to her, too? Did he like her or at least feel grateful for all she had done? Could she be next on his hit list? Well, for now it did not matter. They had a common enemy and Markus would help her with it.

When she came out of the restaurant she felt much stronger already. The farm was hers again after all: it was a miracle. She took a long walk from building to building and inspected the estate as if to repossess everything. The servants seemed to have done a good job, she noticed, and things were tidy.

No, there was nothing to fear from Markus at all, she decided. He was content in his little world, however dubious his methods were. He did not need to know that once Herbert had passed away she would adopt Lukas so she could leave him the farm.

Her husband did not have much longer to go in this world. Controlling the farm instead of Herbert had made them both a target for nasty comments. People had looked upon her with part respect, part fear, but also with a hint of bemusement and ridicule for being a mannish woman. This would change once she was a widow. People would then respect her for her strength to carry on, she reckoned, just as they had done during the war. She would be considered a survivor again.

When she returned to the main farm building it was already time for dinner but she found the place empty and quiet. She went to the cow shed where she found Otto and Martin shifting some hay for the evening feed and Maria sitting quietly beside them.

"The house is empty. Where is everyone?" she asked them.

"Who are you looking for?" Otto replied.

"Helga, Lukas, your Uncle Herbert? The house is completely deserted."

"We haven't seen them," Martin told her, bored and disinterested. "Helga was looking for you earlier but that must have been a good few hours ago."

"If I can't find Helga, you will have to eat at the restaurant tonight," she said which seemed to make the boys very happy. "I don't know what is going on today. I had better go and tell

Markus that you are coming. Make sure you dress properly, I don't want you sitting in your rags in front of the customers," she added and walked off, taking Maria with her.

"I can't wait to see Lukas and hear about what has been happening today," Martin said passionately.

"Don't get too excited," Otto said disinterestedly. "You are always expecting some drama. Your fantasy is getting the better of you again. I am sure that everything is in perfect order and completely normal."

"No, today is totally different," his brother insisted. "You just need to look at Anna's face. She never gets this worried or excited. I bet something huge is happening if Herbert and Lukas are missing. That has to be a first? I can feel it."

"Hmmn..." was all Otto uttered and then he returned to the hay.

The two brothers carried on with their duties for a little longer. Once they had cleaned the stables and put hay in the feeding trough for the cows they called it a day. When the cows came in from the field later in the evening everything would be ready for them. The young men went to the hay loft to get changed for their evening meal at the restaurant. They found Lukas lying on the bed, nervously shaking his legs and picking on an old scar on his forearm.

"Look how nervous he is," Martin said to Otto in a triumphant manner, "I told you something is up." He turned to Lukas and asked him: "What is the matter with you? Why are you so fidgety? What is going on today?"

"Uncle Herbert has had a fit. Markus found him on the floor in the living room. He passed out and when he came to he was full of rage, it was so bad that Markus has had him committed to the lunatic asylum," Lukas told them.

"No way is that true. You're making this up. That is terrible," Otto said half-heartedly. "What has happened? Will Herbert be alright?"

"How should I know?" Lukas said.

"Well you were there. Tell us, were they fighting? Why did they row?" Martin asked.

"Uncle Herbert has made a will," Lukas explained. "He has been talking about it for some time but Aunt Anna, Markus and I have been trying to stop him. Today, however, our little

96

innkeeper broke the pact and brought in a notary from the Alsace. If something happens to Herbert now, who knows what will come of us all. Who knows to whom he has left the money? That Markus is an idiot." He looked at his brothers full of gloom. "Uncle Herbert screamed the house down and said that Markus wanted to kill him. Herbert warned him that none of the Hinterbergers would ever see a pfennig once he has died, not even Anna."

"He can't have been serious about that," Otto said calmly. "Was Markus hitting him or something?"

"No, you know he is not the violent type. Markus was almost calm in comparison," Lukas reported. "I only heard them half way through the fight. By the time I came down from the office to see what the drama was about they were already in the middle of it. Markus seemed just as shocked as I was."

"Uncle Herbert has finally lost his marbles then?" Otto summed up.

"Looks that way. It all happened so quickly. I was sent away to cover for Markus at the restaurant and by the time I got back to the house two men in white uniforms were picking Uncle Herbert up with a paddy wagon in a straightjacket."

"Did you speak to the doctor?" Otto asked.

"No, the doctor was gone. Markus showed me a certificate and an admission slip for the asylum," Lukas explained.

"Did it say what is wrong with Herbert and how long they should keep him?" Otto asked.

"I never saw the doctor," Lukas repeated impatiently. "He must have left by the time I got there. I couldn't read the writing on the note and I was shocked by the straightjacket and those men. They were handling Herbert really roughly, not what I would have expected to happen with a man who has heart problems."

"The straightjacket speaks for itself. Did Uncle Herbert try to fight them off?" Otto wondered.

"Yes he did, still screaming like a mad man. They gave him an injection but it didn't seem to hit the spot."

"You said the notary was from the Alsace, not from Heimkirchen?" Martin asked suddenly. "How strange is that? Is it the same man as...?"

"Stop it," Otto interrupted his little brother. "Don't start with your absurd theories about Markus and his friend from the Alsace again."

Helga had gone round in circles all over the farm looking for Anna or Markus but had continuously missed them. Finally she found Markus in his office.

"I saw you and that notary!" she opened the conversation.

Markus's face went pale. "When did you see me doing what?"

"I saw you coming out of his room!" she said with gravity. "I know."

Markus was visibly getting nervous but he kept his head. "You know what?"

"You opened the will, you had it when you left his room this afternoon. What is going on here?"

"Listen Helga," Markus said, visibly relieved. "You are not family, you don't need to concern yourself with this. The less you know about the matter the better for you and everyone else. All is taken care of, just trust me for once."

"Trust you why?"

"I know all you really care about is Anna. She and I are fine. Mother and son, remember? Ask her and she will confirm for you that there is nothing for you to worry about. Just leave it be and go back to your kitchen where you belong."

"We will see what Anna is going to say about it," Helga said, not giving up the threatening undertone in her voice just yet.

"You go ahead," Markus said, sounding tired of her. "When you see her, tell her to come and see me. I have big news about Herbert."

Now it was Helga's turn to flush. Had Herbert died this afternoon after she had left him struggling on his own?

"What news?" she asked, too quickly to sound as casual as she had wanted to.

"I might as well tell you," Markus said hesitantly. "He had a fit this afternoon and we had to commit him to an asylum."

Helga could not make sense of this. Herbert had been having heart troubles, from what she had seen, not a fit of madness. How could the doctors mistake his physical stress for hysterics?

"I thought he was having heart problems?" she asked confused.

"Maybe his madness fuelled his irregular heart patterns, it can happen. The doctor took one look and signed the forms to have him sent away. Herbert was in quite an emotional state. He said we were trying to kill him and he would make us all sorry for it."

This news worried Helga. Had Herbert suspected being poisoned after all? Had he said so to someone? Oh, she had to get rid of her stash of drugs, maybe even plant it on someone else to divert any suspicion from herself, should the need arise. Why did she have to play with fire, she scolded herself. She had felt too sure of herself. Now she might go to prison for it.

"You look a bit flustered," Markus observed. "I'm sorry to have sprung the news on you like this. I thought you did not like Herbert, I had no idea you cared."

"It took me a little bit by surprise that is all. I'd be as glad as everyone else to get rid of that tyrant but I don't like the idea of an asylum and all the official business that comes with it," she explained.

"Nothing to worry about, I am taking care of it all," Markus promised.

At that moment Anna came in to the office.

"Where is Herbert?" she asked without even saying hello. "Where is everyone?"

"Herbert had a fit this afternoon," Markus repeated a little too casually for Helga's idea of breaking such big news to Anna. "He was committed to an asylum."

"Without my consent?" she asked pointedly. She could not believe the cheek of her son. Yes, they had discussed it in principle but not right now. So quickly. That would not look right. The same day as he had made his will.

"Helga, please give us a moment alone, will you?" Markus said with a sigh.

"Of course, I am going to get dinner ready," she said and left as she was told. Markus closed the door and locked it behind her.

"No one knows about the will. The two 'random' witnesses are business associates of Antoine. Whatever Herbert blurts out about it in the asylum is not going to be taken seriously. Do you

99

know what goes on in these asylums? They lock people away and don't take any notice of them. If someone screams too much they pump them full of drugs and leave them alone. We have a doctor's note certifying his state of hysteria. That is more than enough for the staff in the asylum. If there were to be a physician interested in his improvement we'd find out about it. I have paid one of the nurses to give us regular reports."

"You should have told me! I should have been there!" Anna insisted.

"Well you were gone, we couldn't find you," Markus said with casual coldness.

"Did you even look for me?" she asked.

Markus just smirked.

"It seemed the right time for him: he was already so agitated after the notary visit. We needed to do it before he could tell anyone else about the will. Now it is only family that know about it, all trusted friends. I went to see him right away and to try and annoy him; it didn't take much to send him over the edge," he said, amused.

"What did you say to him?" Anna asked, fascinated and intrigued, forgetting her put on outrage.

"He was in a bad state, said that he was having a heart attack and passed out but nobody had been around to look after him. Someone was out to kill him, lots of nonsense. A real doctor might have locked him up as well, the way he was going on: I said that I had seen you talking to the notary, I commented on his poor chess skills, I said Lukas had no idea about the farm equipment he had bought and that I believed that he had just wasted a load of money. Not much at all," he laughed.

"You little devil!" she hissed, back in her assumed role of the indignant wife. "I never wanted any of this. Who gave you the right?"

"You never said no to the plan," Markus replied calmly. "When we discussed it you were not against it. I knew that even though you wanted it to happen as badly as I did, you would never have the guts either to say yes or to do it yourself. I took care of it, as I always do," he explained assertively.

"Where did you get the certificate? Who wrote it? Dr Hofer?" Anna asked nervously. The local doctor had been disinterested in the whole drama surrounding her husband. If he had not even bothered to prescribe any other medication previously, she doubted that he could have been persuaded to commit her husband.

"Antoine wrote one. He is good like that, a man of many talents," Markus said with a wink. "The good thing about it is that if father talks about the notary Etherlinck they will tell him that his doctor was called that name. That way Herbert is even more discredited."

"I hope you know what you are doing," Anna said, still worried.

"I do," he assured her." I signed the papers as his son, so there is nothing for you to worry about. You are in the clear, just don't interfere."

Anna was taken aback by his harsh tone and direct manner of speaking. She felt provoked by it but admitted to herself that her son was right. Why she had this need for pretence she could not understand.

Without talking any further she left him in his office and made her way back via the hay loft to tell the boys the news.

Lukas, Otto and Martin all wanted desperately to hear about Uncle Herbert and the will but when they saw a distraught and thoughtful Anna they could not build up the courage to ask her directly. As they were growing up they were gradually given more responsibilities, but the invisible gap between the generations was still there and rules commanded that news was given to the younger ones, and not asked for. Markus frequently overstepped the mark in that regard, but the three Hinterberger boys had been brought up better than that.

A little later at the farm the three found Helga preparing dinner with the help of Maria. Anna had decided to eat at the restaurant by herself and for once had not taken her little angel with her.

"We'll have a lot of leftovers now that we don't have to feed that pig of a man," Helga said jokingly. "I hope you brought an appetite."

"There is never a problem with that." Otto said excitedly.

"I am probably not supposed to tell you," she said in a low voice, "but I think you should know. That awful will that Herbert made has been destroyed and taken care of."

"How?" Lukas shot out.

"Markus got it off the notary," she answered.

"That man from the Alsace again!" Martin exclaimed out loud. "I knew it. They have been thick as thieves all this time."

"You should be grateful to Markus," Lukas reminded him, unsure whether or not that was, in fact, true.

"Herbert was going to leave everything to his sister," Helga told them. "If it had not been for Markus, this could have been the end for everyone."

"Herbert is such an idiot," Martin shouted. "I am glad he has been committed."

"We are not going to see any money either way," Otto pointed out. "It will all be Markus' now anyway."

"Don't be so sure about that," Helga contradicted him. "Anna has a big heart and she would like to see you all getting your shares: all of Hans-Ulrich's children are like her own."

"She has only adopted Markus," Martin said bitterly. "That says it all. Lukas might stand a chance of getting a share, but never us."

"You have gotten that wrong," Helga corrected him. "You know the circumstances were different then and Anna almost had no choice but to adopt him to keep him here: your Aunt Erica was going to take him to Munich."

"Well, I'll believe it when I see it in black ink on white legal paper," Otto said soberly.

"Something about that notary person is wrong," Martin insisted with his suspicions.

"You are right there," Helga said. "He is no notary, really, he just posed as one."

"Who is he then?" Martin wondered. "We know nothing about him, not even his name and yet he has got more influence on our fortune than all of us put together. We should try and find out a bit more about him; there is something wrong about him."

"I said stop it." Otto tried to rein his brother in.

"How do you mean?" Helga asked undeterred by Otto. She shared Martin's suspicions but could not explain why. The man had saved them all and still she didn't think him trustworthy at all.

"Did you know that there are men who don't like women?" Martin said. "They choose to go with other men instead."

"Jesus," Otto hissed. "Are you completely mad? That doesn't happen here."

"Markus has never chased after a girl," Martin pointed out, "even though he meets so many at The Eagle. He doesn't seem to be interested in any of them and that is not because he is pious or celibate. It is as if he just doesn't care: that is not normal."

"His mind is on the business, that is all it is," Otto explained. "It does not mean he is sick or a pervert. Next thing you will tell us is that he is after his own sister, it is your sick mind that thinks that way."

"I don't know," Helga said suddenly. "He has never been strong, he even knitted when he was younger. I always thought of him as a lesser man compared to you boys. Only a weakling would rather serve tables than plough the land."

"There was something that I could never forget when I heard them talk one night," Martin confessed. "The guy from the Alsace said he wanted to drink a beer so that it would not hurt so much. You see, those men, they sodomise each other."

"Stop it," Otto shouted. "You are disgusting. The lengths you'd go to just to bring Markus down. This has gone too far. You should be ashamed of yourself."

"That is true, though, Otto," Helga confirmed. "I have heard about that, too. The Wimmer Farm had a son like that who went after one of their servants. That was under Hitler and they had him deported in no time. That sort of thing can happen, even in Heimkirchen."

"This is so disgusting, I am going to be sick," Otto said.

"If we could find the two of them together we could get rid of Markus right away," Martin said hopefully.

"You could," Helga said, "but I would not recommend it. I don't like him but he is not our enemy. We need to watch him but we don't know what would happen if he left."

"Yes Helga, you are right," Lukas agreed.

Martin was fuming at this missed opportunity to gain momentum for a group conspiracy against Markus, but he felt at least satisfied that he now knew how to bring Markus down if there should be any need. Finally, he had found his enemy's Achilles heel.

Nothing however came of his plans. Herbert's departure and continued absence from the farm settled matters between everyone. For five years, life at the Hinterberger Farm and The Black Eagle Inn continued in a very stable state with everyone relaxing and in a calm state of mind. Nothing ever came of the hostility between the cousins. Markus kept running The Black Eagle Inn and restaurant successfully and did not interfere with the farm or the lives of Hans-Ulrich's children, who in turn forgot about their rivalry and stuck to their side of the business, which was booming and keeping them busy. They grew older and got lulled into the peaceful atmosphere that seemed to settle in Heimkirchen. After the uncertain and hard times that began immediately after the war for Germany and its people, the new decade promised a better future and a new Heimat romanticism spread over Bavaria and it distracted the Hinterberger boys, too.

In Herbert's absence Lukas became the unofficial but asserted right hand of Anna who delegated more and more responsibilities to the young and capable man. By know he was very experienced with the material world and no one could fool him and the Hinterberger boys felt assured enough in their position not to go after Markus anymore.

The ageing mistress of the farm continued to try and relive her fading youth by clinging on to her niece Maria, who was turning into a teenager and liked listening to the American radio stations. As the boys were often working into the evening, Maria would keep her aunt company and Anna even purchased a modern wireless for her little darling and let her switch it on once in a while to listen to the new music phenomenon, Elvis Presley.

Lukas was a little jealous of his little sister but his self-esteem and ego were growing through his success in business and put these worries aside. At the age of seventeen Lukas had turned into a young man and took great pleasure in the fact that his father was a member of the German Parliament in Bonn. He considered himself quite a catch and so did many young women in the area.

However, he had developed an unfortunate obsession of talking about himself and lecturing others: a trait that only Anna really appreciated. She loved to hear what he had learnt and achieved, seeing it as a result of her teaching. Most of the girls that he was interested in, however, soon shied away from him, few being willing to spend time with such an arrogant man, regardless of his high connections.

Lukas thought that this phenomenon was purely the result of not being the heir to the farm and the old rivalry with Markus occasionally flared up again. Since the latter never even showed up at barn dances and other social activities outside The Black Eagle, the suspicions and rumours amongst the boys about Markus' sexuality grew more believable again.

The German economy was doing better than could have been expected and the farm did really well, too. Lukas started to pressurise Anna about being adopted by her so that he would have a right to the farm in the future.

"I don't want to upset Markus with this, he has done a lot for us" she evaded the subject. "And how would it look if a member of parliament let his son be adopted. With Herbert in the asylum there really is no need to do anything about it now, he is not going to make a new will either. No one is going to take anything away from you. When I make a will I'll make sure it is all taken care of and you will get the farm, I promise. What more can you want?"

Lukas remained unconvinced and suspicious but could hardly admit to her that he did not believe her.

At first, the staff at the asylum had sedated Herbert with a lot of drugs to calm him down but when they considered him to be safe and no harm to himself or others, they gradually reduced his dosage of tranquillizers. As soon as his mind became clearer, less hazy and confused, his argumentative and irate nature resurfaced. He hated to be imprisoned after his years in the camp and his intense anxiety expressed itself in violent outbursts and a desperate drive to escape. His reluctance towards treatment and lack of submission frequently got him into trouble with the nurses. Eventually, it was decided not only to sedate him again but also to ask for permission to try electroconvulsive therapy with a new anaesthetic, succinylcholine, on him, which Markus authorised happily.

This new method of psychiatric treatment was gaining popularity and its reputation had grown rapidly. Very quickly Herbert became much calmer and almost subdued. However, family visits seemed to agitate him and so the medical team stopped everyone but Anna from seeing him. Following another session of shock therapy, he suffered a minor stroke and became withdrawn in an impenetrable world of his own.

Surprisingly the asylum did not discharge him, the official justification being his sensitivity to seeing his family, but Lukas and his brothers were sure it had to do with the fact that the doctor in charge frequently enjoyed free meals at The Black Eagle.

The only radical change that occurred during those quiet years was that Martin decided he could no longer stand life at the farm. Not only did he despise Markus, he knew that there would be no future here for him and that all his efforts would never be rewarded. Additionally, he was fed up with the in-fighting and the injustice. In his desperation he wrote to his uncle in America. Paul, the man manipulated out of his inheritance years earlier by the cunning Anna, had sent the occasional letter or postcard from his new life in Arizona. The pictures and stories of the desert and the heat had instantly fuelled Martin's fantasy about cowboys and Indians and had created a utopian vision of a better life over there. He begged Paul to help him with money so he could come and visit his uncle or even better, let him live with him.

Paul recognised a kindred spirit in Martin and with help from his wife's family they were able to collect enough money to bring Martin over and join their dire but proud existence.

Abandoned by his brother and confronted with his own poor prospects at the farm, Otto also decided to leave this life of intrigues and back stabbing behind him. Of the three brothers living with Anna he had always been truest to his father's religious convictions; his secret inner torment had always been sex. He had unwillingly once witnessed his parents in the act during his youth and had developed a strong sense of disgust and repression around it. When he heard other boys making dirty remarks he always felt disgusted, just as he had been repulsed by the thought about Markus and the man from the Alsace. He wished there were no need for sex and no desire: it was all base. Nothing about his own sexual urges ever left him feeling good about himself and he knew he could never be with a woman and freely enjoy an act that was so shameful.

His own fantasies and longings were too perverted to even mention to a priest and the guilt for not confessing them had caused him a lot of pain.

So, very soon after Martin left for America, Otto joined a monastery where he could live in seclusion and do nothing but pray.

Magdalena and Hans-Ulrich were over the moon to learn that their eldest would spend his life in the service of the Good Lord. Surprised by his sudden decision, they almost felt guilty for having forced him to live on the farm with the mundane and unchristian people there, when deep down his heart had been set on his religious duties and a life of worship.

Lukas regretted losing both allies. However, part of him was relieved that his two older brothers would not be in the way. As unlikely as it was, the thought that either of the hard working, strong men might find favour with Anna had repeatedly occurred to him over the years and frightened him.

Chapter 8: Lukas (1955-57)

Although she had just regained control over her empire, Anna - to everyone's surprise – remained vaguely disinterested in the business and almost turned into an irresponsible child. She still spent most of her time with Maria and Helga; it seemed that with her husband locked away she relaxed completely and, feeling no longer under any threat whatsoever, she was happy for Markus and Lukas to run their parts of the business, with only minimal supervision from her.

The only time she tried to interfere directly was right after Otto and Martin had left the farm in 1955 and Lukas was looking for replacements. Anna surprised the young man with a sudden interest in what he thought was a minor decision. The young nation was lacking numbers of strong men capable of hard physical labour. The government in Bonn had signed an agreement with Italy to let their workforce surplus fill the gaps in Germany. Lukas saw this as a wonderful opportunity for the farm and proposed that Anna should hire some of these labourers, who also happened to be comparatively cheap. This could also enable some of the young men of the Hinterberger family to seek higher education and more prospective employment while the dirty and bone breaking work could be carried out by those foreigners, but Anna would hear none of it. She had never liked having those captured and enslaved Ukrainians and Poles on the farm during the war years. She could not trust those 'unruly' and 'uncivilized' folks who knew little of discipline. This, she claimed, was even worse with the people from the south. As an example she retold the story of the Italian family that had stayed at the Inn and who had kept everyone awake with their loud voices before breaking a lamp in their room. Those people, she claimed, did nothing but talk, eat and spread chaos and would never get anything done.

To come up with a solution, she took Maria with her on a casual tour of the neighbouring farms where she then tried to lure the workers there into her service, but the reputation of the Hinterbergers for their fighting and rivalries kept enthusiasm for her 'generous' offers to a minimum.

Since she had failed to recruit a single person after weeks of trying, Lukas persuaded her to agree to a trial run of recruiting just a few of the immigrant workers to see if it would work out. Soon Marco and Gustavo, two young Sicilians, arrived at the farm and they proved to be as good workers as anyone else. The language barrier, of course, was a big problem at first, especially since the two Italians stuck together, missing out on the opportunity to learn German from the other staff. Lukas bought a dictionary and a book to learn the language so he could make himself understood: his progress however was slow.

The same year, Markus had a similar problem with Anna when Gisela got engaged and left the farm soon after she married one of the regular guests of The Eagle. Nobody had noticed she had been seeing him - that was how little attention was paid to her. The newlyweds moved to the north of the country where he received a respectable promotion in the insurance business.

Markus knew better than to seek a replacement amongst the Gastarbeiter community, given Anna's outspoken sentiment about foreigners, but he still managed to underestimate his 'mother's' xenophobia. He had hired a young and attractive woman who had managed to flee across the protected border from East Germany to the west, scared that she might be permanently stuck under a Soviet regime.

"You want to employ a Prussian woman?" Anna screamed when she heard about it. "Have you lost your mind? Those northern folks are all no good! They know how to order people around, and they might be more disciplined than those gypsies from the Mediterranean, but Prussians are so stiff and formal, they could never serve in a Bavarian Restaurant! What were you thinking? Her accent alone will drive our regulars away. Our customers come here for a traditional Bavarian holiday. How disappointed do you think they will feel when the waitress is from the north? The Prussians always hated Bavaria. You can't hire one of them. Get rid of that woman and find a proper local girl. There are plenty of them around," she insisted.

"She has good credentials mother and a great attitude," he insisted. "She will fit in nicely, it might spice things up having a Prussian. Let's try her."

"Hans-Ulrich won't like it if we take in one of those escapees from the east. He told me that we provoke the Russians and their German puppets in East Berlin if we provide for those who flee from there for a better life in the west," Anna protested.

"They say that to pay lip service to President Pieck in East Berlin but our government is really quite pleased to have them," Markus argued.

"It doesn't matter, there must be someone else."

"You didn't like the woman from the Sudetenland, you said she is not even a proper German and has an accent. You find the most obscure reasons to reject anyone."

"If you cannot find someone who is right for us then I will work in the restaurant myself with Maria," she offered.

"You can't possibly get involved there now," he argued. "Imagine the scandal. It would look desperate to have the mistress of the estate and a young teenage girl working as waitresses, you know that yourself."

"I won't have any outsiders or foreigners, do you understand?" she reiterated.

He did and let the Prussian woman go. Eventually he found a local girl called Luise that Anna could not find any formal fault with. Luise had worked at several restaurants but always only for a short time. Markus was a little suspicious of her frequent job changes but her references were all good. No one really liked her much, she seemed nothing special and was timid and shy but she did have the right accent and they were running out of time before Gisela's big day.

Gisela's wedding reception was held at The Eagle. It was a small celebration with only a handful of relatives of the new husband making the long journey south. Erica, Gisela's widowed mother, declined the invitation due to her weak health. Even a strongly worded letter from Anna trying to guilt the runaway mother into fulfilling her duty (Erica was still Gisela's official mother after all) failed to persuade her. Markus didn't manage to distract his sister from the disappointment by adding small luxuries to the ornaments and decorations.

Hans-Ulrich was also unable to attend due to his parliamentary obligations. Anna oversaw the reception arrangements for her niece and acted with the best of intentions. Compared to other celebrations that had been held at The Eagle, the food, the decorations and the accommodation arrangements for wedding guests however were modest.

"It just shows how unimportant and easily replaceable I am," Gisela said bitterly. "I can't wait to get away from here."

"This is not bad compared to Anna's own wedding," Helga pointed out.

"When was that?" Gisela snapped. "Wasn't that during the war or shortly after? There is more money now; she could spend it if she wanted to."

"Don't be ungrateful to Anna when your own mother won't even as much as show up," Helga said angrily. "Be happy that Anna forks out as much as she does and, more so, that you have found a good husband. You are young and in love. How can you not smile?"

"I am smiling all right, but it is about getting away from here," Gisela hissed with bitterness.

"And I thought the joy and happiness that I see on your face were signs of your love," Helga said. "Your Erwin is such a likeable and sweet man."

"Erwin is a good man," Gisela admitted, "but there is not much passion between us."

"You can't be too choosy in times where marriable men are scarce. He is charming, polite and pays so much interest in you, you have moved on in your life," Helga commented.

"I never planned on staying here forever and live in my brother's shadow," she said thoughtfully, "or to watch Maria being treated so much better than me: she is given so much attention. It was difficult enough to watch Markus being chosen over me, but I always thought it was a boy over girl thing; to see that a girl can actually receive love and affection around here just goes to show how low my position in the clan is. It is clearly personal."

"For what it's worth, Anna has tried to get your mother here and she has paid the bill for the wedding. You mustn't be ungrateful for that," Helga pointed out.

"Yes, but to save money she has also arranged for Erwin's visitors from the north to sleep in the hay loft instead of reserving them proper guest rooms," Gisela said angrily. "Even Markus complained to her about it. He had reserved some of the rooms for the occasion but Anna forced him to release them for paying guests."

"She is already paying for the food," Helga reiterated. "Money does not grow on trees."

"I think I should get a little more for all the hard work I have put in to this family."

"Honestly, I don't understand what you are complaining about? You take everything Anna does for you for granted." Helga said pointedly.

Gisela left Helga standing on her own and went to Markus to seek comfort from him. Markus knew better than to rise to the bait. Of course, Helga would take Anna's side but since Gisela was leaving there was no need to fight her corner.

"Look at Anna," he said to his sister. "Have you noticed that she is doing the rounds with little white envelopes? It is an old tradition that is rarely used. Guests are given the opportunity to contribute financially to the wedding by putting money in those envelopes. Anna has been handing them out to everyone and she is not leaving their side until everyone has put some money in, getting them to dig deep into their wallets. She even got that stingy farmer Wimmer to fill the envelope in front of her."

"I don't think I will ever see that money," Gisela pointed out. "She is going to keep it all to herself."

"I will let you in on a little secret. Lukas was outraged when he saw how much Anna is spending on you," he told her. "It was the nasty little git who is behind her stinginess. I bet you that money is for you."

"You seem very angry at him. Does that mean your old rivalry is back?" she asked.

"It has never really gone away as far as he is concerned. When I tried to persuade Anna to release more money he called me spoilt and demanding; just because he has been brought up in spartan circumstances, he tries to show off his commitment to modesty and humbleness."

To Gisela this was the final nail in the coffin for her. She left the wedding reception for her honeymoon without even saying goodbye, let alone thanking her aunt for everything she had done.

She quickly hugged and kissed her brother and then decisively stepped in to the waiting car next to Erwin. If she had needed confirmation that she had made the right choice for her future today had been exactly that. This would be the happiest day of her life because she knew that she needed to break free and start her own life, where she would be the centre of attention, feel valued and important.

Luise filled the gap that Gisela had left at The Black Eagle perfectly. She was a very hard worker and what she lacked in personality she made up for with her dedication to improve.

Despite her young age, Maria also helped out on the odd busy days in The Black Eagle and she told everyone just how much she enjoyed the work. Her warm and friendly manner, something that Gisela had always been lacking, added to the already welcoming atmosphere that Markus had created. Pretty and elegantly made up by her aunt, Maria enjoyed a lot of attention in the restaurant, much more than the pale and shy Luise. Because of this Markus took a liking to Maria, whom he previously had never really even noticed. Had it not been for Anna's possessive nature he would have asked Maria to help out more often to improve the business. It was such a pleasure to watch the young girl charm the customers.

"Why doesn't he get married and get his wife to work in the restaurant?" Lukas often asked Anna when they were alone. "He is getting on in years and should be thinking of having a family of his own. It can't be that hard to find a suitable bride?"

Anna, however, ignored his frequent caustic remarks directed at her beloved son.

As long as the two rivals stayed out of each other's way there was an unofficial truce between them. The rivalry had always been more intense on the Hinterberger side of the family and he, as a Stockmann, had never felt threatened enough to take action or revenge. Since Lukas had confronted him so openly about Gisela's wedding Markus was angry, and was planning to scheme against his annoying and opinionated cousin.

Thanks to a discovery on the day that Herbert had been taken to the lunatic asylum, Markus already knew how. He had noticed something odd and reserved in Helga's behaviour towards him on the day of Herbert's institutionalisation, but he could not quite figure out what it was. He thought she had been very nervous when she was told about the old man's breakdown. Gisela had told him that only an hour previously Helga had been looking for Markus and that it appeared as if Helga had been spying on him. Markus knew that Helga had never been entirely on his side, and warned by Gisela, he had set his own spies on her. On the evening of Herbert's internment, Antoine had followed Helga and seen her sneaking out of the house and burying two small bottles in the garden. As soon as she had left he had unearthed them: nitroglycerine and Pervitin. Not a stranger to controlled substances in his shady line of business, Antoine knew right away what Helga had done to Herbert and why she was getting rid of it exactly on the day of Herbert's committal.

Markus had kept these two bottles until now. As the hostile atmosphere between him and Lukas grew he decided to make use of his find. One Sunday, when Lukas was at home with his parents, Markus planted the bottles in the office. He knew that Anna was in the habit of looking through the books secretly to check up on Lukas without upsetting him. Markus left the drugs in the same drawer as the books so that Anna would have to see them. She was bound to question what they were and why they were in the drawer. Hopefully it would cause a stir and in the investigation the truth would be found out.

However, Anna happened to ask Helga to go and fetch the big and heavy books from the upstairs office and it was the guilty servant who ended up finding the bottles. She shook with horror when she recognised them. She could not explain why they were there. How had Lukas got hold of them and what was he planning to do with them? Should she just take them, although it might draw attention to herself, or should she ignore them and leave the incriminating evidence in the hands of Lukas? What did Lukas know and what were his intentions with the bottles? Had he kept them to protect her, or to incriminate her? She had felt sure of his affection all that time but now she doubted his friendship.

After a lot of deliberation, during which Anna kept calling for her from the living room downstairs, Helga decided that her main priority was to get rid of the evidence for good, regardless of what the consequences might be later. She took the bottles, even though Lukas would instantly know that someone had been in his drawers. He would also be likely to assume that it was her who had taken them. Well, she consoled herself, he probably

114

knew all along what her game had been. If he had not confronted her about it by now he was unlikely to bring it up at all. Better to have destroyed the evidence in any case. For a little while her fear about it drove a wedge between her and Lukas and made her keep her distance from him, despite the fact that Lukas knew nothing about the entire affair and did not treat her differently. Markus was very disappointed when he realised that his little plot had not worked and had not caused any obvious fraction. He needed a newidea to bring down his rival.

The next time Magdalena came to visit Maria at The Black Eagle Markus had a few private words with the devoted woman. Magdalena was outraged when she heard that her son was not praying three times a day as she had been led to believe, and that he had not been to church other than on a Sunday for months, always too busy with the business.

"You promised you would look after him and make sure he'd grow up to be a good Catholic," she scolded Anna. "You know I can't leave him here if I can't trust your word."

"Lukas has never been better," Anna tried to cut this silly woman short. "He has food and he is learning how to run a business. One day this will all be his."

"None of that matters when it comes to Judgement Day. None of this will count. It is the boys' salvation that I am concerned about. Does that not matter to you heathens? What is wrong with you, Anna, you were brought up in the same family as Hans-Ulrich. Imagine what he would have to say about this," Magdalena carried on. "It is a disgrace to his reputation, too. Maybe you could think at least about that."

Anna looked at her sister-in-law, half with admiration for her passion and half with a sense of ridicule.

"I tell you what I do think about, Magdalena, and that is your cheek in coming in here and preaching about things you do not know the first thing about. You never studied the Bible and you won't convince me that you grasp any of the concepts behind it, to say the least."

"I do too," Magdalena shouted angrily but she knew that Anna had just found her Achilles heel.

"Nowhere in the Bible does it say that you must go to church every day," Anna continued her argument, "nor that you need to say a certain prayer for salvation. That was all made up afterwards. The Pope has changed his tune many times over the years. You are being ridiculous with your obsession and probably quite an embarrassment to Hans-Ulrich as a respectable man with power. Don't you think that maybe that is why he never takes you to Bonn? The boy is brilliant, clever and old enough now to decide how often he wants to go to church. He is free to do as he pleases, I won't force him in the way that you do. Leave us be and concern yourself with the things like your charity work. You are making a great difference to the world there."

Anna thought she had been clever in the way she had undermined her opponent's confidence and yet ended it with a soft note about the Caritas. Magdalena's blind stubbornness however knew no limit.

"Never mind about the age of the boy," Magdalena hissed. "I am taking him with me and I will take Maria. I am not leaving the two of them here with you. When you have come to your senses and have learnt how to live a pious life we can meet again. Until then Hans-Ulrich and I will have nothing to do with you heathens."

"You can go anytime you like," Anna said coolly, "but Lukas and Maria stay here. They are needed and they are happy here now. You have been so obsessed with your church and charity work, you are no longer their mother. I am more of a family to them than you ever were. During the war and ever since, I was good enough to feed and home them. How dare you take them off my hands now that I need them most? Hans-Ulrich would never allow it and you know it."

Magdalena did not have the strength to see her plan through and to go against Anna and thus she left on her own. She was furious but she could not make a decision like this on her own. When she told her husband about the unchristian state of affairs at The Black Eagle he was as displeased as she had been and a week later the couple returned united to claim their children.

"Anna I am so sorry," Hans-Ulrich said to his sister, "but I have a certain reputation to keep now that I am in the government. A Christian party cannot have a member whose religious devotion is questionable. The church won't support me if it became known that my own children are ambiguous in their faith. The people expect us to lead the country by example. How

116

could they trust us if we cannot even keep our own children in good Catholic shape? Please forgive me," he added, "I am so grateful for everything you have done."

Anna had never seen her brother as confident or decisive towards her as on that day. Since he had taken up his political career she knew him to be more eloquent, but she had always thought that she had kept her hold over him.

"After all I have done for you and your family?" she asked with hurt in her voice. "Lukas was going to inherit all of this, did you know that?"

"He still can if you change your ways. I am only doing this for his salvation." Hans-Ulrich insisted.

"If you can take him away from me when I need him the most and all for the sake of your political ambitions and your blind and foolish beliefs, then get out of my sight. We will never be a family again." Anna hissed and stormed off.

Hans-Ulrich and Magdalena stood stunned for a second. The reaction was beyond their worst expectations. They grabbed their children, asked them to collect their belongings and quietly left the farm. As was to be expected Maria accepted her fate stoically even though she had enjoyed the work at the restaurant very much and had become fond of Markus. Yet the scene between Anna and her parents had left her with contempt for the fighting between her family members, who were either too greedy for their own good, or too obsessed with the afterlife to enjoy the here and now.

The war had ended twelve years ago but her family had yet again returned to their characteristic in-fighting. After years of relative freedom out here in the countryside she would find it hard to be with her mother and the strict regime of praying, church going, repentance and charity work. There would be no more barn dances or American music. Her mother had no radio and thought little of Elvis Presley and the likes of him but hopefully it would be more peaceful.

Lukas was outwardly taciturn about the turn of events but underneath the surface he was fuming. He was still a minor and would have to go along with his parent's decision for at least a few more months when he would turn 21.

He did not mean to burn bridges with Anna but her fury was as blind as Magdalena's devotion to the Catholic doctrine.

She stormed out of the room before he had a chance to explain his feelings. He needed to speak to his aunt and assure her of his loyalty before leaving. He managed to sneak out of the building and found his aunt on her way to The Black Eagle.

"You know I do not want to leave you," he whined.

"Then don't go. You are old enough to stand up to your parents!" she snapped.

"If I stay here Hans-Ulrich will call the police to collect me. I am still a minor."

"Let him do that and risk the scandal," Anna replied. "I dare you. That would certainly prove your loyalty."

"You know I cannot do that either to him or to you. What will the people say?" he said, trying to be diplomatic.

"Then you have made your bed. Lie in it. I don't care about the scandal. I care about loyalty. Go home to your monastery of a family. It looks like I misjudged you after all."

Lukas was in turmoil. To keep the peace with his parents he would have to sing from the same hymn sheet and condemn Anna and her unchristian ways until he was old enough to move out but by then Anna might not take him back or forgive him. The thought of losing everything he had worked for over a ridiculous dispute between Anna and his mother about religion seemed unbearable. His worst fears were confirmed when he saw Anna turn away and go straight to Markus at the restaurant.

Although he was busy, Markus could see that Anna was at breaking point and he left Luise alone and took his 'mother' upstairs out of the sight of their customers, where she collapsed into his arms and told him the dreadful news. Markus was delighted but managed to conceal his feelings well.

"Let them take those two town folks," he said to calm Anna. "We have nothing to worry about. You always used to do well with the farm and I am doing well here. My friend Antoine can help you with the bookkeeping and I can always find another girl like Luise to replace Maria. It is a loss but we can control the damage. Don't even let on that it matters to you. Don't give them the satisfaction. How dare they stick their noses up at you when you were always there for them? They owe everything they have to you and everything they are. We don't need them. As a matter of fact, without the pious and conscientious Lukas we can do a lot more with the business than we could before," he added, suggestively.

"What do you mean?" Anna asked, temporarily distracted by his speech.

"There are ways to make a business more efficient, pay less tax and be a little more inventive with the bookkeeping," Markus explained excitedly. "I could never do anything while Mr Goody-two-shoes was in charge but Antoine has a few brilliant ideas that could improve our lives and finances dramatically."

"Wouldn't that be dangerous?" she asked, sounding more intrigued than concerned.

"Not at all," he said dismissively. "There are grey areas in the law. If anyone ever complains we can say that we interpreted the law differently. I am not talking about stealing, just misplacing and reshuffling of money."

Anna liked what she heard but was too emotional to make plans about the inventive bookkeeping. Out of nowhere tears came flooding out of her.

"My own brother!" she cried. "How could he do such a thing?"

"Exactly, this is where you see who your real friends and family are and who aren't, mother," he said and held her while she sobbed uncontrollably.

The following months were hard for Anna and Markus but they managed to replace the apostate family members. Antoine, of course, could only do some of the work because of his travelling and Anna was no longer able to do the bookkeeping by herself, she kept making mistakes and got confused by some of the changes Lukas had made. Markus found another accountant through his business contacts, Lorenz Schrader, a very quiet and introverted man who had something strange and off-putting about him. Lorenz was slightly overweight and pale which came from sitting indoors all day, but he seemed, on closer examination, more secretive and cunning than shy. Anna didn't trust him but from the evidence she could gather he seemed to be working hard.

Twice she took the books over to Markus and queried some of the entries but he assured her that this was exactly the kind of transaction he had talked about. There was nothing to fear, all was totally legal and in the interests of the farm.

Antoine too seemed a sly fellow to Anna. His accent was very off-putting for her pure Bavarian soul and she realised that maybe it was this prejudice that made it hard for her to become friendly with the saviour of the farm and the good, dear friend of her adoptive son. Antoine was closer to her own age than to Markus', he had a sporty physique, wore elegant clothes and had a moustache. She thought he had something dubious and untrustworthy about him, but Markus told her she should stop worrying and enjoy the freedom she was allowed by letting the men take care of the business.

Desperate for company, Anna now more than ever frequented the restaurant to be with her golden boy. She was proud of him and never allowed herself to miss Lukas or Maria. They had made their own bed, as far as Anna was concerned, and now they could lie in it. But Markus, he had come from nothing and had worked hard to make something out of himself that could be respected. He stood by her and she would reward him for it.

Markus was not particularly keen on his 'mother' showing up almost every night. He had guests to entertain and could not spare as much time for her as she needed and demanded.

This oddly desperate phase of hers and her fixation on him turned Markus' feelings against her. So far he had seen his adoptive mother as a role model in many ways, a woman who took what she wanted and who was strong and capable. He was pleased to help her along and thought that the two of them had similar visions of the future, particularly since she had shown herself to be so open to the concept of inventive bookkeeping.

However, when he saw her in the restaurant, sitting at a small table by herself and watching his every move almost every day, he felt overwhelmed by her neediness and felt pity for her. His high opinion of her vanished and began to turn to contempt. He resented her for monopolising him and weighing him down, as if he were the only thing in the world for her. He found her presence daunting and depressing.

At her age, no longer attractive enough to find a lover or a second husband, she would remain a de facto widow with a mad

120

husband in an asylum. He had to get rid of her somehow or get her out of his sight, if only he could think of a way how to.

At least she had long stopped asking him to get married. She was so desperate for his company that she would have seen another woman as a rival for his affection. Yet with her being around all the time it was difficult for him to make his dubious and shady dealings and he had to invent excuses every day to get any privacy or space.

It took Anna a long time to give up wooing for his attention; she could see perfectly well that she was in his way. He was busy and had too much to do and she felt the distance between them that her perseverance had created. Strong enough to see her own fallings and determined to save face, she gradually weaned herself off her unhealthy fixation on the young man but her cravings to fill the void with a purpose and a focus remained and looked for an outlet.

In a moment of temporary confusion she visited Herbert at the asylum and demanded his release. She declared that she would now take care of him herself.

Markus was furious with her when she returned to the farm with the heavily sedated husband of hers. The doctors had only reluctantly let Herbert go but Anna had been very insistent. She pointed out how her husband had been stable in regards to his stroke and he was also physically too weak to be a danger to anyone else. The doctors gave up arguing and released him into her care.

To Markus this was the end of his trust in Anna. How could he rely on her now that she had brought their arch enemy back to the farm?

"What exactly were you thinking?" he asked her when he found out.

"Herbert is completely harmless now, he won't be any trouble," she tried to avert Markus' outburst. "I owe it to him."

"Don't you remember what he did to us both? He wrote us out of his will. Why on earth would you take him out of the asylum? Now we have to watch him every second of the day to make sure he doesn't do the same thing again. What is wrong with you?" he shouted at her.

"He won't be making a will. He thinks his old will is valid and he is too fragile to even get up. They only let him out because he is so weak and harmless," she argued.

"That means physically harmless," Markus corrected her. "They meant that he won't hit you. That does not stop him from harming us in other ways. He could change his mind and make a different will. You cannot take anything for granted when you are dealing with someone as volatile and bad tempered as he is," he warned her.

Anna was convinced that her son was grossly overreacting. Herbert had been so placid and calm when she had visited him at the asylum. She felt pity for him and had been plagued by terrible pangs of guilt about what she had done to her husband.

"Let us just wait and see how it goes. You should see him, he is only a shadow of his former self. Besides, he is not of a sane mind, a new will would not hold in court. He hasn't got any fight left in him," she said hopefully.

"You had better watch him!" Markus said almost threateningly and returned to his work.

Anna walked back to her house to tell Helga, another conversation that she knew would not be easy.

Helga understood her mistress much better than Markus ever had. She knew it was loneliness that had driven Anna to suddenly allow herself to feel guilt and remorse about Herbert.

"Let's hope he is worthy of your kindness," was all Helga could say to the shocking news. She resigned herself to a life of being ordered around again, being made to cook extra meals and having to bear his coarse language and behaviour. Herbert, however, was calm and peaceful: hardly any bother at all.

Unbeknown to Anna, the doctors at the asylum had given him an extra strong last dose of tranquillizers before discharging him to make the transition into his old environment easier. The next morning Herbert was already a little bit more alert and demanding.

"I have been dreaming about a proper breakfast with fresh jam and cut meat," he said to Anna when he woke up. "Go and get that lazy Helga to make me some."

Happy to please him Anna got up in her nightgown and made the breakfast herself. Helga would be in the cow shed at this early hour.

"Where is that useless woman?" he shouted when he realised that Anna had prepared the food herself.

"In the cow shed, milking," Anna defended her servant.

"She used to be able to do more than one thing a day," Herbert bellowed. "Time I returned and got things back on track."

Fortunately for everyone, Herbert was too weak physically to get up by himself and had to stay in bed, from where he could not interfere with the business. He did manage to demand attention and make threats and abusive comments all day but there was no danger of him doing anything without the help of either Anna or Helga and frequently the two women just closed the door on him and let him stew.

Helga endured his outbursts stoically and calmly but she was seriously contemplating poisoning him as soon as she felt that Anna was suffering more than benefiting from the situation.

For now it seemed that her mistress seemed pleased, in some masochistic way, to be bossed around, whether it was the hidden pleasure of being needed or some weird Catholic guilt thing was difficult to tell. All Helga knew was that the times ahead were not going to be easy.

No one had dared to mention Antoine and Lorenz to Herbert since he had returned. It seemed unwise to concern him with business matters and Anna felt it would only cause him unnecessary anxiety to hear that strangers were entrusted with monetary affairs of the family. All office affairs were moved completely to the restaurant building so that Herbert would never even see the two financial assistants.

Markus had enjoyed all the benefits that running a strong business brought with it: the social standing in the community, the wealth and the internal satisfaction of being successful, but he had no intention of spending all of his life under such stress and pressure that the return of Herbert might pose. He had for some time now planned to get away and start a happier life somewhere else, some place far away where the sun always shone and nobody would tell him what to do. During the Nuremburg Trials, he had been fascinated by the reports about some former Nazi leaders who had escaped justice and fled to lead a life of luxury in South American countries on the relatively little money they had managed to take with them from Germany. When Antoine taught him how to forge signatures and how to falsify the books, Markus had immediately begun to salt money away from the business into his own pocket, more than Antoine had recommended him to do. The question was only how much would be enough for a life of luxury in some remote place. Antoine did not want to leave Europe and come with him so he would have to do it all by himself. For that reason he had not pursued these plans any further. Since Herbert had returned, he also started to sell off unused pieces of land and forest to raise more cash for his future private use. The arrival had brought more urgency to his dreams, which now became more concrete again. Anna had become an unknown factor, too. Unsure how she would stand up to Herbert in the long run, the status quo on the farm had been lost.

He had hoped he might be able to stand a few more years and maybe wait until Anna and Herbert died. Then he would be able to sell everything and certainly live very well off the proceeds for the rest of his life. Yet, even the stroke patient Herbert looked like he would be around for some time and to Markus the thought of another twenty years of this life at The Black Eagle Inn was way too much.

Chapter 9: Marco (1957-58)

Markus was tired of hiding his yet undiscovered secret, his love for Antoine. They had been very lucky not to have been found out, but the secrecy and hiding was no longer exciting or entertaining, as it had been at the beginning of their romance. Antoine had been in and out of his life for years because of the travelling and the urgent need for secrecy in a country where homosexuality was illegal. A farewell to The Black Eagle now, however, would also mean the end to their relationship, as Antoine and Markus had different ideas about a future life.

Markus' mind was heavy with all these thoughts and grave decisions and he took long walks in the woods during the day whenever he could. Out there at last he could think clearly. The peace and calm was a huge relief from the madness and hectic life at the farm. He found a clearing not too far away from everything, where he could sit by himself on a forgotten felled tree, relax completely and put the world to rights.

What would it be like to live in a country in the southern hemisphere? He didn't speak any other languages but neither had those Nazis on the run and they had got by until they were found. Possibly quite a few were still living out there in hiding.

Obviously, money would go a lot further there than it did here: he felt a deep contempt for Germany. Heimkirchen had appeared to be a safe haven within the fascist madness under Hitler but still, enough people here had voted for him and had informed on Jews and Communists. He had also learnt what had been done with the men and women of 'his type'. When he looked around The Black Eagle he knew that not everyone sitting there was as innocent as they all made out to be. Apparent benign middle aged men, who ordered the same item every Thursday evening, had been soldiers and had done horrendous things in the name of Germany and they hadn't all just followed orders. Some of them had given those orders and probably did not feel ashamed of it.

The way some Germans were treating the Gastarbeiter now was already reminiscent of those hateful old days. Markus felt that there was something polemic and dangerous in the people around him. Even the Christians, who were supposed to love their neighbour and be nice to each other, were continuously fighting over how to interpret the Bible and in doing so were far from loving and tolerant of people with other opinions, let alone other religions. They ran around as if they were the nicest and holiest of them all, holding their heads up high and trying to stand above everyone else. He was more than disillusioned with what men did in the name of God. He felt no remorse for robbing Anna and Herbert, whose wealth was largely a result of their greed. He could not wait to leave this country and go somewhere with a less depressing history and more tolerance.

Then he looked around him and knew he would miss this beautiful landscape. Having mountain ranges in sight most days and the clear blue skies, the lakes, the forest and the fields: he had come to love all of this.

As he was sitting on the tree stump wallowing in his love for nature he was joined by Marco, the Italian help from Sicily.

"You found my beautiful spot," Marco said. "I come here for beauty."

"Yes, it is a fine place," Markus agreed.

"I cut the tree last year," Marco said proudly. "Now is not so good, not many flowers but in summer is so beautiful. You like the flowers?"

"I do," Markus replied, "but I come here for the stillness. You know, time to think, clear your head."

"I see, you are a big thinker. That is why you are the boss and successful business man."

"No, I think when you come here to nature you realise that money is not everything," Markus said, thoughtfully. "When you run a business you never have enough time to think, there is always something to do."

"I see," Marco said. "Me too, I am always very busy. Always something to do for the little man also. I come here when I miss Italia."

"You must miss it a lot," Markus said warmly. "I was just thinking how much I would miss this land if I ever moved away."

"Is fine but now I like Germany. Good money and good people, also beautiful. I love Italia but I also love here."

"That is nice to hear," Markus said. He felt a bit reassured. If this Italian man could leave his home and not get too upset about it then maybe it would not be so hard to leave Bavaria behind and go somewhere else.

"You need to eat, you need to live," Marco said. "You can make everywhere a good place to be. You already have a good life. You stay here!"

Maybe this Italian boy was right, Markus thought. Was he expecting too much? Did he really have enough reason to complain? Could he not pull him himself together and carry on as before?

"Thank you," he said. "You have helped me a lot. What was your name again?"

Marco smiled kindly. "Marco, same as yours. In Italia you also are Marco!"

"Funny. Well, see you soon, Marco!"

On his way home, Markus was genuinely touched by the naïve kindness the Italian had shown him. They had been talking as equals, not as if one was the master and the other the servant. There had been no hidden agenda, nothing but a meeting of two men in the forest; Markus liked that a lot: no politics and no schemes. Ever since he had met Antoine and had become his lover, life had been full of plans and intrigues. Markus was getting tired of this life even though he was doing so well for himself with it.

It looked as if Markus could learn a lot from this young boy. Marco could not be older than 22. His skin looked as if he was not even shaving regularly, so smooth and soft. He had never given much thought to the Gastarbeiter himself, only in the more political and general sense when people at The Black Eagle had complained about them, then he had always stood up for them and reassured everyone that his Italian helpers were hard working and as good as gold. If he was honest with himself, he had to admit that he had not thought of them as equals either. In his mind they had been a commodity, like machinery and cattle.

On subsequent outings to the clearing in the woods he hoped he would see Marco again but by now it was harvest season and the Italian was probably busy all day long. Almost a week went by until he next saw him out there.

Marco told him about Sicily and its beauty, about his large family and how bad the Italians had been with their own fascist regime in the war.

Markus told him about his dream to sell up and move to South America, or somewhere else where there was no war, no politics and just free living.

"There is no free life like that," Marco claimed. "Problems are everywhere. Maybe a life without fighting is better but life with no work is no good. It is boring, men always want to do something."

"Maybe you are right," Markus agreed. What indeed would he do with himself in South America all day long?

Markus found himself strangely drawn to Marco.

For all the distance between himself and Antoine of late, Markus still thought that he loved Antoine. He had always liked older men and who were more experienced but there was something about this young Italian that fascinated him.

As their meetings became more regular and they grew closer, Markus found it difficult to read the signals the young man was giving him. The Italians were so tactile and physical: he had to be careful not to make a mistake. It was too easy to read the signs incorrectly and easily become the victim of a blackmailer. As soon as he thought about it he immediately felt foolish for thinking such a thing. Marco was so young and naïve, he could only know about love between men if he felt it himself.

Newly inspired by his friendship with Marco, Markus had put all thoughts of leaving Heimkirchen aside and had started to enjoy his life again, rising to the challenges with a new spring in his step. Since Herbert had returned, Antoine was visiting less frequently and almost pushed Markus into the arms of the Italian servant.

The only thing that annoyed him was Herbert and his many requests and complaints, all of which were faithfully registered and acted upon by Anna. She made Markus visit his 'father' almost daily. At least twice a week he had to let the old man win at chess and yet again listen to the old speech about business and money, which he had heard so many times before that he could recite it word for word. Backwards.

The arguments Herbert and Markus had had the day before Herbert was sent to the lunatic asylum seemed to be completely forgotten. Herbert was more benign and peaceful than he ever had been towards his adoptive son, but he was much more outspoken and nasty to his wife and to Helga, which warned Markus always to remain on his guard.

Since Anna was so obedient and patient with her husband's outbursts, Markus wondered how far her new attitude would go and if she might be persuaded to let him make another will. Herbert was unable to walk, was totally isolated in his room and easily ignored but the fact that Anna decided to pay attention and fulfil his every wish was a sign that Markus could not trust her. He decided to speak to Antoine about their future on his next visit.

"If you want to call it a day here and move on I am all for it," Antoine surprised him when Markus finally admitted to his feelings.

"Really? I thought you were quite fond of this place."

"I am fond of you but your family is a lot of hard work. We could make more money much more easily somewhere else. I have got a sample of Herbert's signature and a few spare sheets which he signed himself. We can always use those. Let's strip this place of all the money we can and go somewhere else. Sometime in the future you can come back and claim your inheritance with the 'right will' in hand," he suggested.

"How long will it take before we could leave?" Markus asked.

"A month, maybe two. I have to go to Frankfurt first but then I can make a proper inventory of the possibilities here."

Markus was both excited and anxious: he had never left Bavaria in all of his life. As much as he currently hated the farm and his family, it was also the only world that he had ever known. He liked his meetings in the peace of the woods with Marco. He was not sure if he was ready to give it all up but now that he had spoken about it with Antoine there was almost no way back and the feeling that something unstoppable had been set in motion excited him beyond compare.

It gave him the freedom, however, to be a little more forward in his relationship with Marco. Knowing that he soon would be going away meant that the threat of potential blackmail seemed less dangerous.

During their next meetings Markus was less inhibited in holding eye contact and joined in with all the theatrical hand gestures and tactile behaviour that was customary to the Italian.

Marco always hugged everyone and tried to kiss them on the cheek to which few people responded well. He also liked to put his arm around his friends when walking. Markus stopped shying away from such proximity, to which Marco responded with more touching. Finally, Markus could no longer stand the tension and kissed him.

"We have to be careful," Marco said immediately, "Gustavo has already noticed that I come away more often. He says I am happy now when I get back from the woods, not sad as before."

"Come away with me then." Markus said.

"What do you mean?"

"Like I said when we first met: leave everything here and go somewhere else," Markus said dreamily.

"You really want to give everything up for me?" Marco asked, sounding more concerned than flattered.

"Not just for you, of course. But what kind of life is this fighting and struggling? My business partner, Antoine, taught me how to do it but I don't want to live my entire life like that. If we lived in France our love would not make us criminals. We could be together, live freely and earn an honest and decent living," he said enthusiastically.

"With what money? What would we do?"

"I have some money of my own," Markus said proudly. "I could do anything, work as a waiter, I have some experience in the area. We could run an inn together. If it were not for you, I would not have a reason to leave. You were the one who made me see that it is possible to be happy someplace other than my home town. And now...."

"But your aunt, she loves you."

"She loves no one but herself," Markus said bitterly but then he softened a little. "She never learnt how to. She took a shine to me because I flattered her and entertained her. I could do that because there were already great achievers in the family. Before Otto and Martin were on the scene I was never even noticed. You never met them but they were ten times the men that I will ever be. Honest and hard-working but too naïve to survive in an environment like this farm. I don't want to stay here either."

"What about me? I have a good position here. In France I would have only you and no future. How would we even get in to the country?" Marco said doubtfully.

"Antoine has ways with documents, we won't have to worry about that, so what do you say? Do you think you could like me enough to run away with me?" Markus looked at him with love and optimism.

"Yes" Marco replied quietly and leaned his head against Markus' shoulder.

Over the following weeks the two of them met almost daily, but because of Gustavo and his suspicions they could only meet in the woods during the afternoons. Antoine prepared new passports and working permits for them all in France.

He made no scene when he was told about Marco. Being the dubious character that his ex-lover was, Markus had long suspected him of having other men in different places. Antoine was mainly concerned about the money and how to strip the farm and The Black Eagle Inn of its cash. He and Lorenz worked night and day on it. Finally, Markus went to the bank and collected almost everything that was left in the accounts. That night when the restaurant closed Lorenz, Marco and Markus left together with Antoine in his new car and the next day crossed the border into France.

When Markus did not appear for his breakfast shift the next morning, Luise managed without him, too shy to create a fuss and reluctant to get her boss into trouble. She looked everywhere for him but decided that this was her opportunity to prove herself by dealing with everything on her own. Not until the afternoon did someone tell Helga about Markus' mysterious disappearance.

Marco had already been reported missing that morning, which was a mystery to her. He had been most reliable and loyal. However, once she heard about Markus being gone she knew that all of this was no coincidence.

She hoped against her instant suspicions that the two men had got drunk together and fallen asleep, or, maybe gone away in Antoine's car and had broken down somewhere. Since he had been put in charge of The Black Eagle, Markus had never once forgotten his duties; this had to be something serious.

When there was still no sign of them by the evening, she suddenly remembered Martin's continuous suggestions about Markus' sexuality.

Helga did not have the heart to break the news to Anna and decided to give Markus more time to come back and explain himself. There was no reason to create a scene and cause Anna unnecessary pain just yet.

Then Helga learned that Lorenz had gone as well and there was no more room for doubts. The quiet and almost invisible accountant was rarely noticed by anyone but without Markus present, Luise needed him to lock away the takings from the restaurant and Anna needed to be told because she had the only other key to the safe. The old mistress had the shock of her life when she found it completely emptied. No further explanations were needed.

Anna wanted to believe that this was all a bad mistake but the evidence was too overwhelming. Her golden boy had tricked her after all, just like Hans-Ulrich's children had warned her he would. What a foolish woman she had been to put her trust into someone so dubious. She refused to give any attention to Helga's accusations about Markus and that Italian Gastarbeiter being 'together'. She suspected that the Sicilian man had been involved as the mastermind behind the theft. She had heard the stories about the Mafia and organised crime that had found its way from Sicily to Germany with those darn foreigners: she should never have let those Mediterranean men be hired.

Something needed to be done quickly to prevent damage to the business. People at the restaurant had noticed that Markus was gone and the poorly coordinated cover up had already started the rumour mill about the reasons behind his disappearance.

As much as she hated it, her best bet to re-establish order was to swallow her pride and make up with her brother Hans-Ulrich. If Lukas was allowed to come back to the farm, and bring Maria with him to help out in the restaurant, then she would look less deserted by the family and the scandal around Markus would seem much less dramatic and worthy of gossip.

Chapter 10: Lukas (1958-61)

Magdalena opened the door to her sister–in-law and wordlessly gestured for her to come in. The two women sat down at the kitchen table and Anna told her the dreadful news, which Magdalena had already learnt from women at the church.

Magdalena crossed herself several times while Anna spoke and touched her rosary to gain protection from the evil that had befallen the family.

"I guess you have not come here to ask for forgiveness or to go to church with me to pray for our family. You need Lukas back, am I right?" she said calmly and surprisingly without reproach in her voice.

"No one else can help us right now. I am begging you," Anna said, abashed.

"Well, you know our feelings about church and prayer," Magdalena said surely. "If you are willing to bend to our will then I am prepared to speak to Hans-Ulrich about this. He may not be in favour of it; he sometimes takes Lukas with him to Bonn and is trying to increase his standing in the party and here in town. He will not let him go easily."

"I understand," Anna said humbly, in an attempt to flatter Magdalena. It didn't make any difference what she said to this deluded woman, as long as the result was Lukas coming back. "I know now you were right. If we had been more pious and involved in the church, then Markus would never have left the path of righteousness."

"Amen to that, my dear Anna. Amen to that." Magdalena said. "I pray the Lord will forgive you and take you back in his protective arms."

"Will Lukas even consider coming back to us?" Anna asked. "Maybe his pride is hurt?"

"He would never abandon his family and leave them out in the cold. He has more Christian spirit than that," Magdalena said confidently.

"In that case, do you think you could also spare us Maria to fill in at the restaurant?" Anna probed shyly.

"Of course. Provided Hans-Ulrich gives his blessing. Maria has not done well at her exams at school. I think she is more a practical girl than a clever one, so working would do her good."

Hans-Ulrich took a little longer than Magdalena to come round to the Christian idea of helping his sister. He had loved having Lukas with him and being able to show off his smart and pious son to his party friends and other contacts, both in Bonn and in Heimkirchen.

Lukas had enjoyed this new life. Over the last few months he had learned about politics and people's behaviour. As a mathematical and accountancy genius he had often struggled with interpersonal affairs. He was not a good manipulator and too often took people at face value, leaving himself open to being taken advantage of.

The new world he was experiencing opened his eyes to a completely new way of thinking and approach to life. Once he had learned the basic rules of party politics he became more experienced in reading people and using skilful rhetoric to change their minds.

The thought of returning to the farm stirred up conflicting emotions in him. Maybe it would be a great playground for his new skills. He also felt flattered to be asked back: pleased that Markus had been disgraced. On the other hand, he still felt hurt and resented Anna for casting him out and he was not too keen to work with Herbert living under the same roof.

He decided to stay with his father in Bonn. Initially Hans-Ulrich agreed with him - just to teach his sister a lesson. Magdalena however pointed out how important it was for everyone's salvation to do the right Christian thing and put pressure on everyone until they relented.

Maria was looking forward to be back amongst the people at the restaurant and, compared to her family home, to live in a more relaxed and fun loving environment.

She had grown up with a life revolving around religion and didn't mind it. She didn't have enough obstinacy in her to protest against the harsh regime but she could not help feeling that too much of the gospel was taken too literally in her family.

Even in the sleepy town of Heimkirchen, people started to be more critical and emancipated from dogmatic teachings. Television and films brought the world outside of Heimkirchen closer and began to think for themselves in more areas of their lives than they had done previously under the Nazi regime.

Maria admired her family for their passion and their quests to become better people, but she wished especially her mother would allow herself to trust her own judgement instead of relying on others so much. After the last few months of being locked inside the flat and the church, she was more than ready to go back to a life with more colour.

She arrived at The Black Eagle full of excitement and with great expectations. When she heard the rumours about Markus and Marco and the dire financial situation they had left the restaurant in, she wondered to herself if there was something intrinsically evil in the less regimented and regulated life here. That Markus should have had it in him to become such a deceitful person hit her particularly hard. The grief left her bereft of her naive innocence and blind optimism.

One by one, as the accountancy books and other documents were looked over, Anna found not only the bank accounts emptied, but discovered how much land and machinery Markus and his band of thieves had sold. To cover the running costs for this year alone Anna would have to sell even more land to keep their creditors happy. She had known all along what Markus was capable of but she had fallen for this trickster because he was gentle, handsome and playful. What a fool she had been to think he would not go against her, too; and what a fool she still was, because she missed Markus more than anything and would forgive him everything as long as he returned and promised her to never ever leave her again. She hated herself for her pathetic weakness, her of all people, the harsh and ruthless Anna, mistress of a huge empire which she now saw crumbling to pieces in her hands.

Right here was Lukas, the good and absolutely reliable and honest son of her favourite brother, a man of reason and responsibility and yet, she would trade him at any time for the terrible Markus. What was driving her to such an error of judgement? What was wrong with her and her feelings?

Unable to hear any more of the heinous crimes which her beloved had committed, she put her head in the sand and gave Lukas free reign to sort everything out, the way he believed fit: she knew that at least she could rely on him and his pedantic nature. The less she heard about Markus' betrayal, the better. She hardly listened to what Lukas told her and took to blindly signing any paper he put in front of her.

However, back at home it was hard to find peace too. Herbert had learned to walk small distances with a walking stick, and always asked her hundreds of questions where she had been, leaving her with the constant feeling of being followed and observed.

Once Lukas had realised how ignorant Anna was, he decided on a few schemes of his own. At first, he tried to push Anna into making a will which would disinherit Markus, but it was no use. She refused blankly to do anything against her golden boy. Lukas knew that Markus could come and claim the empire he was busy resurrecting at any time in the future. He would rather burn down the entire estate than see that happen.

So he sold all the land that needed to be sacrificed for the survival of the farm at rather favourable rates to party friends of his father, in return for a generous commission. For every large piece of land he sold, he could buy a small piece for himself in the arrangement. While his actions did save the farm and The Black Eagle he earned himself his own, not insubstantial, portion of the pie.

He kept urging Anna to make a will but she no longer cared. Why shouldn't her Markus get everything once she was dead? She did not care for anyone else. Spurred on by her obviously deliberate ignorance, Lukas ended his previously moderate initiative to 'rescue' the family fortune and became bolder in transferring parts of her empire into his own name.

He got Anna unknowingly to sign large parts of the farm over to him and his sister Maria. Anna did not even know what she was signing, she hardly even looked at the documents he brought her each day. He tried to show and to explain to her what he was doing, but he could tell she was not listening at all. He still talked her through everything regardless, being very careful to monitor her reactions when she was about to sign the transactions in his favour and ready to divert her attention when needed. He justified his actions to himself with the fact that despite having been thrown out previously, he and his sister were currently rescuing the business. He had once been promised parts of the wealth so it was rightfully theirs. God forbid Herbert should leave it all to his useless old sister or some veteran charity – that man was capable of just about anything, and apparently now so was his wife.

Helga decided to solve the problem of Herbert once and for all with the help of nitroglycerine and Pervitin, which despite the worry of finding the bottles in the filling cabinet, she had never managed to get rid of. Since the old tyrant had taken to moving about the house and making unexpected and annoying appearances in the kitchen and the living room, her life had become very awkward again. Lukas had never mentioned anything about the missing pill bottles which she had taken from his office desk that time. Not so much as a dirty or accusing look, nothing that ever suggested his disapproval of her. Quite the opposite. Lukas had been as warm and kind to Helga as he had never been before and why shouldn't he be, she had always been his strongest supporter.

Overnight, Herbert's anxiety attacks and slumps returned leaving Anna severely worried for her husband. She could not bear the thought of him being committed again and as soon as Dr Hofer suggested they do exactly this, she stopped calling for him, even for the heart problems which Herbert experienced, all out of fear her Herbert would be taken away from her. She may not have loved him but he was her husband after all.

The poor man sent Helga to Alice, the gypsy woman, to get more of the onion ointment and the herbal tea that had helped him so well before.

In the anxiety and panic over his returning heart problems Herbert had become very unpredictable but unlike the last time, he was less aggressive. Like a little boy he clung to Anna and Helga, begged them to get the doctor, make him cold compresses and do whatever spur of the moment idea inspired him to think might alleviate his sufferings.

Once again he was talking about changing his will. At first Anna and Helga were able to laugh this off as a childish foible and they diverted his attentions, but gradually their resistance wore down. He, of course, meant to reverse the old will, which favoured his sister. He wanted Anna to have everything now after all.

"If only we had Markus and his Antoine," Anna said, "we could fool him with another false notary and be done with it. I can't really trust him to leave everything to me. What are we going to do?"

"Make promises and put him off as long as you can," Helga suggested. "He might forget about it."

Her stock of drugs was almost depleted and with the current pressure now was as good a time as any, in her eyes, to bring an end to this nuisance of a man once and for all. The next day she prepared his last meal. She gave him all of the leftover nitroglycerine at lunch and when he complained about feeling weak she persuaded him to have another snack to build up his strength. Helga had chosen a good time, the house was empty and she herself could reasonably excuse herself from his presence, so the drugs would have enough time to do their job.

She waited until he had finished his drug-laced snack and then left him to it. She hid the empty pill bottles in her room and then joined Gustavo in the cow shed.

Everyone on the farm could hear Anna's scream when she found her dead husband. In the most hysterical manner the old woman threw herself on her husband and holding his hands she stayed in his bed crying until Helga made her get up and compose herself. Anna was a complete mess, bemoaning how the most precious things in her life had been taken away from her. How much of that grief was for Herbert and how much for Markus was hard to tell.

For the funeral she spared no costs and spent a fortune on flowers, a music band and the coffin. She felt incredibly guilty for assisting Markus in having Herbert committed. She could have intervened or at least tried to do something. Maybe his sufferings were all due to her wickedness, for which she would have to repent and make amends.

Hans-Ulrich and Magdalena stayed with her for the entire ceremony. They were the nicest and kindest support she could have wished for, continuously pushing her to stay strong and to keep herself together. In her weak state she was easy prey to Magdalena's preaching about the trials which the Good Lord sends his children, and how everything would be better if Anna could only give up the struggle and surrender to His will. Her sudden and new found piety mended the rift between her and her brother.

Over their forty years of their marriage, Anna had actually grown to love Herbert, for better and for worse, and no one was more astonished about this realisation than she. For all his faults and all the problems he had caused her, Herbert had been a constant in her life. Despite his many threats, he had never really harmed her. Hans-Ulrich however, her own flesh and blood, had turned against her once and had cut her out of his life. There was no one else in her family who she could count on. Well, maybe Helga, but she was not true family, more an odd mixture of servant and friend.

Markus had betrayed her and she had never been able to rekindle the spark with Maria. Since her return, the young girl had become a bit distant and no longer glowed and radiated the happiness that had been her main appeal. Lukas was ambitious and pushy but too much of a work horse to be good company. There was a hole in her soul since Herbert had died and thanks to Hans-Ulrich and Magdalena's continuous persuasion she opened her heart to let the Good Lord step in to the breach and fill her with meaning, at least temporarily.

In this new 'Christian' spirit Anna started to go to church every day and prayed hard for forgiveness. Lukas, eager to regain his position as her most trusted, accompanied her whenever he could although Anna did not seem to appreciate his efforts either way. He was waiting for another opportune moment to bring up the future of the farm and the little matter of her will, but he knew he had to be careful not to upset her and influence her the wrong way by mentioning it too soon. Anna was terribly tearful these days.

Once, Helga tried to help him by pointing out to her mistress that Markus was still the heir to all of her wealth. Anna responded by admitting that she had considered hiring a private investigator to find Markus and persuade him to come back. Helga was shocked to hear this and passed the information on to Lukas, for whom this news was incentive enough to resume his fraudulent activities to reduce the future inheritance that his arch rival would be able to claim. Almost fifty per cent were now in

Lukas and Maria's possession. If Markus were ever to come back he would not be able to run the farm without Hinterberger help. All he would have left would be The Black Eagle, which in Lukas' view was still too much. He wanted more for himself so that he could make a return to Heimkirchen for Markus an unprofitable venture, and so he continued further with his skilful erosion of Anna's empire.

In 1958 Maria came of age and her sister Klara finally got married. Already an old spinster in the eyes of her family everyone had given up hope for her, including herself. Her future husband Gunter was a widower, whose children were already teenagers. The two betrothed had met at church. Klara's sad and bitter demeanour had strangely enough attracted him as it reflected his own unhappiness. The two shared their miserable attitude towards life and felt relieved to finally be in the company of someone who did not expect them to be grateful or happy about anything.

As a wedding present, Lukas persuaded Anna to give her a small part of the forestry behind the farm land and she agreed to this small gesture. She had no idea that when she signed the document she actually signed away the entire remainder of her wood covered land, taking another huge percentage out of Markus' future inheritance. Encouraged by this success Lukas also suggested a gift for Maria and her coming of age but Anna refused.

"Maybe when she gets married I can help with the dowry," Anna said with noticeable disinterest. "It is time you found a wife yourself, by the way."

In his brief existence as his father's assistant, Lukas had fancied himself as a future politician and had been told by some of the party members how important it was to have a presentable wife. He had set his eyes on many daughters of those wealthy and well-connected politicians and since that time he had found the local girls in Heimkirchen no longer suitable for his needs. He had not been too sure that he should tie himself to a life in Heimkirchen as the son of a famous politician and did not want to choose a wife from the local area. Markus could come back and ruin his life here so Lukas did not want to jeopardise a career in Bonn by marrying the wrong kind of woman.

Those days however were drifting further into the past and the more of Anna's fortune he got under his control, the more he was willing to compromise on this account. He felt he had to make a choice. A smaller but certain fortune in Heimkirchen would be his if he married someone local of an inferior social standing. Or, he could keep his options open for a political career in the future by holding out for a more prestigious match outside of Heimkirchen.

How difficult it would be for him to find any woman was beyond his perception. Lukas had never given much attention to his appearance, nor did he possess charming manners. When it came to women he had always counted on his future wealth as the only asset he needed, and therefore he was perceived as annoyingly arrogant by women.

The interest in him as a husband because of his money and connections in Heimkirchen was far less than he had come to expect. He was aware that his association with the now slightly scandal riddled restaurant probably did not make him look too good and so he came to the conclusion that if a marriage was to be had quickly it would probably have to be with someone like Luise, the waitress in the restaurant. She had always seemed to have a soft spot for him, and as a friend of his sister Maria she was certainly a bit more aware of his many good deeds, which in his sorry view, so few people appreciated properly.

When he mentioned his plans to marry Luise to Anna she was initially far from ecstatic. That simple girl was not much of a catch she thought, pretty enough but not much of a character. Anna wished he would do better, someone richer or with useful connections.

After she had given it further thought however, she realised that Luise had many advantages: she knew the trade and could pull her weight. There was no dowry to expect but also no interfering in the Hinterberger affairs from her family. Since Markus had left under such scandalous circumstances, the reputation of the family had suffered. She too knew that Lukas would only have prospects of a good marriage if he were to cut his ties to her and were to associate himself more with the political friends of his father outside of the farm.

Feeling guilty that she had betrayed him with unfulfilled promises about a will and a large inheritance, she offered Lukas a sizeable piece of land as a wedding gift, large enough to make him go ahead with pursuing Luise, something he had up until then only vaguely considered.

Luise was over the moon when Lukas proposed to her, although it puzzled her that such attentions should come so suddenly. She agreed to marry him without having to think twice. Her boss was an odd and erratic man and totally wrapped up in the business but there was something endearing about him, the way he cared so much about work. He was bound to be as devoted as a husband.

A week before the big day, Anna presented Lukas with his gift, the land she had promised him. She felt a huge relief after she gave him the document, almost as if she had paid off a moral debt and was now free of all guilt and shame. On the same day she hired a private investigator to look for Markus and his whereabouts. She had little information to give to the man apart from the physical description of Antoine and the fact that the man was from the Alsace. She confided in Helga about her intentions to bring the prodigal son back and her servant alerted Lukas to the fact because she could not bear to think that the good and solid, hard-working Lukas should be betrayed so harshly once again. Lukas was meant to go on his honeymoon to Austria for a week. She had no idea how quickly such a detective could achieve results and frowned at the thought of how mean it would be if he should return and find his arch rival back at the helm of the business?

Lukas, already in legal possession of the land, called off the wedding. There was no way that he would go on a honeymoon now and leave his empire undefended. Luise was devastated and left The Black Eagle immediately. Anna never commented on the called off wedding nor did she demand her land back from Lukas. It was almost as if an unspoken agreement existed between her and Lukas in that he had now been compensated for the broken promises of a big inheritance.

The gap that Luise left had to be filled quickly. At first Klara came to help but soon her negative demeanour and unfriendly ways made her a liability. She frequently upset customers and had no patience for the harmless banter and drunken behaviour that some of the regulars exposed her to.

The problems she caused with the punters reached Anna's ears and made her even more desperate to find Markus and bring him back. Under his management such problems had never occurred.

"If only Markus was here, he would know how to solve the problems," she frequently moaned, even in front of Lukas.

"If you promise to make a will and leave some of your money to the rest of the family I will help you get him back," Lukas offered her out of the blue.

"How could you do that? What do you know?" Anna asked excitedly.

"I will tell you when you agree," Lukas said determined. "I can only let you bring him back here if you can guarantee that at least the people that picked up the pieces after him and who dedicated their lives to the farm will be rewarded for their sacrifices. If you give him everything after what he did to us all I am not going to be part to your search, however much I want to help you."

"Markus is family, we need to have him back," Anna said whiningly.

"Maybe you need him but he has run the business in to the ground. For all our sakes I can't bring him back unless I am satisfied that he won't do it again. You used to care about us as well as you did about him but now all you think about is him. You'll have to buy my help now." he said coldly.

"How do I know that you are genuine?" she asked, trying to sound provocative and hide the hope in her voice.

"I promise," Lukas said. "I am sick and tired of the fighting. We all know that you want Markus to return but none of us know if he will ever come back or not. When you are dead he will have his claim. I will always only be running the farm until he comes and takes what it his. My future will always be uncertain unless this issue is resolved once and for all. I would like this to be solved. If you can guarantee us some material security, then I might as well help find him and get this over with."

This did make sense to Anna and it seemed more than desirable to her own battered soul to stop all the tactics and hidden agendas and not pretend any more.

"How big a share are you asking me to give away?" she asked him.

143

"About 15% of your land," he said.

"I will give you ten if you really can bring him back," Anna replied. "What can you do that my private investigator can't?" she added.

"I once saw some documents that Antoine had left on his desk. I have a few names and addresses that should help your detective and speed up his search," Lukas declared. "I thought you would forget about Markus and see us for the kind and helpful people that we are but your heart is set on him. It is the only thing that will make you happy. It hurts but it hurts me more to see you like this."

"Thank you," she replied. "Give me the names. Let's not waste any more time."

The names and addresses that Lukas provided however didn't help to find Markus at all. They were as fake as most things that Antoine had produced but Anna honoured her word. She believed Lukas and thought that by giving him one more part of her fortune she had finally brought peace to the farm. Hans-Ulrich's children now owned most of Anna's empire without her even knowing it.

Despite the scandal and the shame of breaking off an engagement, Lukas' parents were secretly quite relieved about the narrow escape. Magdalena spread the word that Luise had been too liberal a Catholic and Hans-Ulrich emphasised that Luise's father was a Social Democrat and Union member.

Maria, on the on the other hand, was much more outraged when she heard about her brother's behaviour. When he had proposed to Luise, it had seemed to her as if behind his arrogance and harsh business like behaviour there was secretly a shy man with romantic and idealistic notions that just never came to the surface for others to see. How delighted she had felt when she falsely assumed that everything her brother did had been out of love for Luise.

Now it was blatantly obvious that he was just like the rest of the clan here, devoid of feelings and unable to think of anything but material concerns. Maria finally saw him for the manipulator that he was and the fact that he had been capable of hurting an innocent girl like Luise was the biggest disappointment and disillusion in her life so far. After this incident she kept a distance from the rest of the family and planned to get away from this place as soon as she could. Yet when her 21st birthday arrived she had no plan or place to go and so continued to stay at the farm, waiting for her opportunity.

Chapter 11: Bonn (1961-65)

Hans-Ulrich's political career in Bonn had recently gained huge momentum. With the expected retirement of an entire generation of politicians and government officials he was tipped for at least a promotion within the party ranks, if not even for a ministerial position. It was common knowledge that the existing leadership was planning to hand over its power to a new generation after the election of 1961, and so needed to establish the new faces well before they had to brave the public polls themselves in 1965.

The shock over the building of the Berlin Wall had united voters and politicians before the election. The 'unreasonable behaviour' of the Soviet Block and the alleged inexperience of Kennedy made Chancellor Adenauer reluctant to give up his reign. After the election the internal campaigning began. Hans-Ulrich, with his humble demeanour and naïve rural background remained likeable to his fellow party members throughout. He had never posed a threat to any of their blatant ambitions. He was not known to be a fighter or careerist, and any government position would have to be offered to him on a plate by a new chancellor; he would not put himself forward or contest anyone else's candidacy. This trait brought him a lot of good will amongst the power hungry members, many of whom secretly lined him up as a safe addition to their own potential future cabinets and staff plans.

His strong religious colouring had made him an important asset in the election campaign of 1961, where he became a talisman to please the strict Catholic voters in Bavaria. His most valuable contribution to the party was an unexpected rhetorical talent and prodigious biblical knowledge that captured those audiences. Hans-Ulrich knew a bible quote for almost any occasion and could find a scrap piece of Christian ideology to justify virtually any decision the government made.

In the first reshuffling of the government in 1963 it appeared that he was being overlooked. Hans-Ulrich's personal belief in that regard was that the Good Lord would call him when the time was ready and there was no need for him to fight for a position and upset others. This modest attitude consolidated his position even more and in the eyes of other politicians made him a possible ally for the future.

Magdalena's charity work and humble image also contributed to his good standing within the party. A preliminary examination of Hans-Ulrich's family in the area by the campaign leaders for the 1965 elections proved very satisfactory: two children in the clergy, one daughter married, two other children working on the family farm and a brother in-law, who was a war veteran being nursed at home. On paper this appeared just the sort of family life that people could relate to and adore.

Parts of the party were pushing him as a candidate to become the spokesperson for the government, or possibly Agricultural Secretary. He toured the country with tireless energy for he felt that it was his Christian mission to keep the country under the rule of a party committed to God and to save it from the Social Democrats, who were little better than the atheist Communists in the Soviet Union and East Germany.

Many younger members of society had still not come to terms with the collective guilt of the nation and plenty of first time voters were expected to respond with a strong left leaning in their vote. A new layer of society was forming in response to the shameful past of their parents' generation. At the last elections this had already forced the party leaders of the Christian Democrats into a coalition with the Liberal Party. If this trend towards the left continued, it would threaten Hans-Ulrich's party and their Christian inspired government. It was possible that new voters might support the Social Democrats rather than the government parties.

On top of that there was an increasingly serious threat from the far right of the political spectrum. The former German Party, who after the war had been in coalition with the Christian Democrats, had reformed itself with a much more right leaning manifesto, a development that was shocking to politicians and voters alike. Getting into parliament was not easy for smaller parties but it looked as if they might stand a chance of crossing the 5% threshold of votes to do so.

For Hans-Ulrich, the reason behind this threat was the loosening of morals, confirmed in the rise of the Liberal Party at the 1961 elections, and the recent wave of immigration of far too many Muslims to the German nation as Gastarbeiter from

Turkey. He saw it as his duty to the Good Lord to fight the current liberal policy within his party and change this dreadful trend. His was a risky position to take publicly and one that many politicians cowardly shied away from but this brave undertaking to speak up earned him an impressive following amongst the more conservative members of his party.

In the election of 1965, the Christian Democrats held on to power but as suspected, the Social Democrats gained votes and became the largest party in Germany. The far right failed to enter parliament at all because they failed to gain the necessary 5% of votes, which Hans-Ulrich thought was partly his doing by catching the voters from the right with his passionate speeches. Thanks to his popularity amongst the party members and members of parliament, he became the new Secretary for Agriculture and Forestry with an unofficial assurance that this was only a stepping stone to much bigger things for him.

The appointment of a local politician to such a high position made huge waves in Bavaria and Heimkirchen, and was received well by the public, even though Hans-Ulrich had no time to come home and bathe in the glory.

His family was proud of him, although not all reactions were as he had envisaged. Magdalena opted to stay in Heimkirchen so she could act as her husband's ambassador at home, keeping up the family's appearances and continue with her charity work. She was very proud of her husband but the new priest had mentioned how important it was to remain a humble servant in the eyes of God, and not to be corrupted by one's worldly achievements. She knew Hans-Ulrich would be strong enough to remain humble and to resist temptations in the big world of Bonn.

Now that he was in the public eye his apartment needed to be spotless and he would frequently have to entertain guests. He needed a woman by his side but Magdalena was scared of that world. Whenever she had stayed with her husband in Bonn she found herself out of her depth, unsure how to speak to party officials and unwilling to sacrifice the time she wanted to dedicate to worship and her many charitable obligations. It came as a huge relief when Maria offered to fulfil that role in Bonn that traditionally would have fallen to her as the wife. It was the perfect opportunity for the now 25 year old to finally leave the farm without causing too much upset or fall out. No one could find fault with such a decision of a devoted daughter. Maria's offer could not have made her happier.

Anna was too involved in her on-going search for Markus and took little notice of either Hans-Ulrich's success or of Maria leaving The Black Eagle. The private investigator, Thomas Holzapfel, was travelling all over Germany and France at her expense. He had visited Erica in Munich and Gisela in Gottingen but both women claimed not to have heard from Markus.

Anna was so desperate that she even encouraged the detective to break into and search the women's apartments and paid him to travel time and time again to the Alsace in search for Antoine. Every time Herr Holzapfel returned empty handed she fell into bouts of deep depression and when he seemed to have another lead and went on another mission she waited for him impatiently, and could think and speak of little else. Her former 'angel' Maria could not have been further from Anna's mind and this attitude had been more than obvious to the departing young woman.

His father's political career made Lukas somewhat proud. He reckoned however, that his position within the farming community was already strong due to the size of the farm and the many regulars that came to the restaurant out of habit. Initially Lukas felt let down by Maria as she had failed to become the ally and partner he had craved at the farm. He had tried to train her as the inn keeper and wished for her to become more involved in the actual management of the restaurant so that the siblings could run Anna's empire together, but she had shown little interest. The previously cheerful and happy girl had turned into a more serious and withdrawn young woman who hid her head in newspapers and books, and who rarely let on what she thought. Pretty as she was there were many farmers' sons and customers who tried to break the icy exterior and build a good rapport with her, but she never let anyone get close to her. Soon the rejected suitors were talking of her as an arrogant witch; something that Lukas realised was not good for his business. To lose Maria now, who was falling out of favour with the customers, was perfect timing.

Chapter 12: France (1956-65)

Markus and Marco had successfully made it across the French border. They had parted ways with Antoine soon after and had not seen him again since. Their life together in liberal France, however, had not gone as smoothly as they had hoped. Although being gay was not a punishable crime, it was not something that was actively welcome, particularly in the countryside where they initially opted to stay. They first went to Paris out of curiosity to see the big city. Yet both their strict Catholic and conservative upbringing made it impossible for them to enjoy the frivolous and flamboyant gay friendly areas and places at all.

"It is all so sleazy," Marco said in horror. "The men dressed up as women shock me. I don't like that."

"I hate that everyone touches each other and they keep eyeing you up. It is awful," Markus agreed.

"If this is the famous gay life I see why there is so much hate," Marco said, shaking his head. "I want no part in it."

"At least you are Italian," Markus pointed out. "Nobody here even wants to speak to a German. It doesn't matter that I am too young to have been in the war. People treat me with contempt as soon as they hear my accent."

If he had understood half of what they shouted at him he would have left the country right away. Marco, who spoke a little French, never told him what they said about his lover.

Neither of them had ever been much of an admirer of art and architecture and so the time they spent in Paris were a complete disappointment. Markus felt particularly out of place, feeling humbled and lost in those huge alleys. He craved green landscapes and nature in this jungle of stone and concrete.

"Is time to get away from this Babylon?" Marco said after only a short time.

"Yes," Markus agreed. "Let's go. There is sunshine and happiness waiting for us at the Riviera."

After a few years by the beach, Markus became tired of the sea and the tourists. They decided to rent a little hut near the Italian border close to the Alps, hoping that Markus would feel a little more at home there because of the views of the mountains.

With the money that Markus had managed to embezzle, and with their current precautionary and modest rate of spending, Markus was sure they could live without having to work for decades. He had, however, inherited Anna's superstition about currency and its historical tendency towards devaluation. He wanted to create a more lasting fortune and was thinking about investments and other ways of financial security, whereas Marco cherished the romantic notion of a life consisting of nothing but love and leisure.

"I could try and open another restaurant," Markus thought out loud.

"The French will not eat in a place run by a German," Marco pointed out. "And they are very proud of their own cooking."

"You could run the place for me, at least officially. I would be just the stupid waiter as far as the public is concerned, how about that?"

"I don't think that will work," Marco said dismissively. "A German restaurant is bad idea."

"How about an Italian restaurant then? Maybe we could even get some of your family up here?"

"My family will never come. Is cause of you and me, Markus. It is out of question we contact them. Italian restaurant anywhere in the world the Mafia hear and my family find out about me. Not an option."

"Running a restaurant is all I ever learnt. I never worked in another trade."

"Once you speak language and make friends with some local people there come possibilities," Marco consoled him. "Maybe you can work for someone else in restaurant."

Markus had to admit that his lover was right. The ideas Markus had had about his future in France had been mainly led by the thought of leading a life free of prosecution but they had lacked detailed planning and research. It was best to acclimatise to their new environment first, just as Marco had suggested, and to treat their time in France like a holiday, before making any more plans. The two men started to work in their garden, chopped wood for the winter, made minor repairs and improved the look of the cottage they were living in. Being young and in love, the domestic bliss of their new life made them both very happy and content.

During the first few years thoughts of planning ahead were easy to ignore. As long as he did not think about the future, Markus enjoyed the freedom and happiness that their secluded togetherness brought him. Marco took him hiking in the mountains, they went on daytrips down to the seaside and even gambled in the casinos of Monaco. This quiet and modest life was more than enough for Marco but Markus started to feel restless and bored. He was surprised how little he could stand still. The years of slaving away to keep the restaurant afloat had eliminated all of the laziness that he had so frequently been accused of in Heimkirchen. A life without work and its challenges was suddenly unthinkable to him and so was a life as an employee for somebody else; he had been his own boss for too long to work under someone else's direction now.

Marco, on the other hand, was enjoying the freedom from obligations and was getting used to this life of leisure. He was no stranger to hard work and he was happy to pull his weight whenever it should be required, but while there was money enough and suitable work was hard to come by he was happy with wine and good food.

The two men soon discovered just how different they were from each other. Marco drifted into the habit of nurturing long lie-ins in the mornings and gave in to a new found laziness. He ate and drank too much and put on weight, which slowed him down and smothered all further ambition and motivation. He was happy to just lie in the sun and do nothing all day.

Markus, in contrast, became more and more desperate for an outlet for his energy. He spent long hours learning the language, reading the papers and books and kept himself as busy as he could in the little cottage and the garden. Still his frustration grew worse, especially as Marco was becoming lazy and less and less willing to assist him. Aside from feeling useless and redundant Markus started to feel lonely within the relationship.

During the winters, Marco drifted into complete lethargy and only got up to fetch more wine and food. As a Sicilian, he said the temperatures were too cold outside and he spent most of his days wrapped up in a blanket by the fireplace. Markus still went hiking and tried to keep his lover entertained by bringing him books and magazines and cooked new dishes for him, but Marco had lost interest. The only time there was life in the Italian was when he was drunk. Markus started to miss home badly. As much as he had hated his life back in Heimkirchen, he now saw that it had not been all that bad. He had been able to keep his liaison with Antoine more or less secret for years so maybe it would have been possible to do the same with Marco or a different lover. The thought of returning to Germany and Heimkirchen was no longer as unthinkable as it had been when he had first arrived in France.

They had been together for almost ten years but it was already written on the wall that their time was coming to an end. The two of them were increasingly arguing, had nothing in common anymore and often it seemed that there was little love lost between them. If only Markus had not taken so much money when he left, then he might have been able to argue his way out of the situation and back into his old life. Anna had always been easy prey to his charms but he had to face the fact that he had taken it too far and she would not forgive him this time, even if she was still alive.

His mind and heart heavy with all these sad thoughts he was astonished when he saw Hans-Ulrich's photograph in a French newspaper. He could not believe his eyes when he read that his uncle was attending a meeting of European delegates regarding a mutual farming policy and industry standards as head of the German delegation. Seeing the picture made his homesickness worse, even though the face of the grim and serious uncle of his was also a reminder of the strict and harsh way in which the Hinterbergers had led their lives. Could he really go back to that? From that day onwards, Markus bought the newspaper every day and searched for news about his politically successful uncle.

Soon after this he found life with Marco unbearable and when the lease for their cottage came up for renewal Markus announced to his lover that he was not going to extend his stay here, instead he was leaving and moving up north on his own. Marco made an ugly scene at first, accusing Markus for ruining his life and leaving him without a penny but when Markus offered him money the Sicilian just spat in his face and left in a rage, never to be seen again. It hurt Markus to end things like this but Marco was no longer the person he had fallen in love with. There was nothing left of the wise and philosophical man with his amazing sparkle and enthusiasm for life. His lover had become a shadow of his former self and an addict to culinary pleasures with not an interest in anything else. Markus expected and almost hoped for Marco to return and at least accept some kind of monetary compensation for being left stranded in France, but after waiting in the cottage for another two weeks without his lover making an appearance he returned the keys to the landlord and moved to Nancy.

He imagined that he was only likely to find another love in a town or a city that was big enough to have some kind of meeting place for homosexuals, and could only hope that the many negative impressions he had experienced in the big and filthy Paris scene would be absent in a somewhat smaller place. Nancy was one of the places where Antoine used to have business partners and Markus toyed with the idea of trying to contact his old lover. Not to rekindle their spark but to see if he could use his contacts to find work, or a worthwhile occupation. In the end his pride and sense of independence, however, stopped him from doing so.

His new city of residence was not far from Germany and he could easily travel from there to Strasbourg, where the European Union was currently residing. Markus hoped he might be able to see or contact Hans-Ulrich there to test the waters about how the rest of the family had taken his disappearance.

When another Agricultural Conference of the European member states convened in Strasbourg, Markus travelled to the city and tried to work up the courage and speak to his uncle. However, he did not have the guts to contact Hans-Ulrich directly and arrange a meeting with him, so instead he waited outside the conference hall. In the chaos of people coming and going he failed to spot his uncle and he only saw him once from a distance coming out of his hotel. One of the ushers at the parliament building had told Markus where the German delegation usually stayed but on seeing his uncle with his stern and serious manner Markus' stomach clenched. He knew there was no forgiveness from the Hinterbergers and no way back to Heimkirchen for him. It had been a very silly notion to come and speak to his conservative and certainly judgemental uncle, of all people, about returning home. Markus had prepared a long speech about the biblical prodigal son coming home and being welcomed with open arms by his father, but with his own self-doubt he did not believe that even his religious uncle might fall for it. What he had done was unforgivable by any standards, not just Catholic ones. For any kind and loving quote from the Bible that Markus might name he knew his uncle had probably ten to justify strong punishment and unforgiving cruelty.

Full of self-loathing he went into a street cafe near the parliament building. Despite the early hour he drank a beer to build up his courage. Maybe later he would go back to the entrance to the parliament hall and try and attract Hans-Ulrich's attention. He had come this far, at least he could finish what he had set out to do and find out how things stood for him, one way or another.

Lost in his thoughts it took him a while before he realised that the woman in the far corner of the cafe was his cousin, Maria. It had been so many years; he almost did not recognise her. She was writing up some notes from the conference for her father and was too deeply concentrating on her work to notice her surroundings. Markus hurriedly got up and almost fell over a chair on his way over to her table. Her reaction however was much cooler than he had hoped for.

"What on earth are you doing here?" she asked suspiciously.

"I have come to see Uncle Hans-Ulrich but I am having second thoughts," he admitted sheepishly.

"You had better dwell on those," she said testily. "After what you did no one in our family is going to roll out the red carpet for you."

"I guessed as much," he said abashed. "How is everything in Heimkirchen?"

"We all survived your little disappearing act," she continued in her harsh tone. "Lukas had to sell off a lot of the land to save the farm and the restaurant: he is in charge now."

"Good," Markus said. "I am glad he is back, he is a good man."

"He used to be," Maria said full of disdain. "Now he is just like the rest of you. I don't know what it is about the farm but it has corrupted everyone who has ever had anything to do with it."

155

"Why do you speak about your own brother like that? What has he done?" Markus asked full of curiosity.

"Mind your own business!" she dismissed him. "If you really want to know go home and face the music." She was never going to tell him that Anna was looking for him high and low to bring him back. "If it is more money that you are after then rest assured: there is nothing left. Please just go and stay away from us."

"You are right, I deserve your scorn," he said calmly, "Just do me one favour and tell Lukas and Anna that I am truly sorry. For what it's worth, I regret my actions."

"Oh come on, Markus!" She rolled her eyes at his poorly acted humble antics. "I have watched you for years and I know when you are trying to pull the wool over my eyes. You can save yourself the effort. Get out of my sight. You don't have regrets, you probably just ran out of money and want some more. Well guess what: you are not going to get any. If you want to show how sorry you are then go and take back the money you stole."

With that she returned to the papers in front of her and ignored him as well as she could.

"You have become hard," he commented. "You used to be the nicest and most generous woman that I knew."

"Yes, I used to be like that," she took his bait. "I guess one could say that I have matured since you last saw me and you can take some credit for that. I think we have said everything that needs to be said. Please leave now."

"How is Anna?" he asked, trying for his most humble tone of voice.

"Ask her yourself if you have the guts," Maria said coldly. "But be careful, the police are looking for you and the money."

She hoped that last remark had hit its mark. Seeing Markus made her so sad for it reminded her of the greed and pointless fighting at home. She was enjoying her new life in Bonn and found the party politics and tactics sometimes harmless in comparison. At least the arguments were never personal but rational and served to find the best possible solutions for everyone's greater good.

Markus had sat back down at his own table but he was still staring at her. If she wanted to get rid of him she had to be the one to leave, and after a short time that was exactly what she did.

Luckily for her he did not follow. She found another quiet place to carry on with her work and told no one about this odd, chance encounter.

Chapter 13: Maria (1966-68)

The following year brought a breakup of the government coalition over the budget. The Christian Democrats had to form a new coalition, and for lack of alternatives, they were forced to work with the Social Democrats themselves. Because of his right wing politics, Hans-Ulrich was now in the way of the needed political compromise and was one of the first people to be dropped by his party to enable this new unlikely government to function.

After only one year in office he was demoted back to the status of a regular member of parliament. The group of conservative politicians around him became the target of a hateful smear campaign, originated in part by his own camp, who blatantly courted the favour of the Social Democrats. To make the coalition with their former enemies work, controversially minded figures like Hans-Ulrich had to be quietened and pushed into the background. Public image was suddenly everything to prevent a further radicalisation of the political spectrum. Pressure was even mounting on Hans-Ulrich to resign from his seat completely. His eternal commitment to vote only how the Good Lord told him to and not as the party whip dictated had once made him appealing to the marketing strategists, now it made him a wild card in the unstable climate and a danger to the fragile coalition. Newspapers criticised him for staying in a party that was compromising on issues close to his Catholic heart, but he refused to step down on grounds that his seat could fall into the hands of someone less Christian, or to the right wing party. God himself had put him in to this position and to give up would be a neglect of his duties.

Maria noticed much more accurately than he did how insecure Hans-Ulrich's formerly safe standing within the party had become. As his assistant it was her duty to sift through the many invitations to social gatherings and official functions on his behalf and she often made the tough choices for him; now, there were considerably fewer invitations.

Since she was not his official secretary but only a helping hand, her work load decreased so much that she took up reading again. Helping her father with speeches and dry theoretical essays over the last year she had developed an appetite for more entertaining reading and she frequently visited a small and cosy book shop in town, where she would browse through the titles for hours until she decided on a book and took it with her to read in one of the many street cafes.

This was where she finally fell in love, at the age of 26. The place was busy during certain hours of the day and sometimes people were forced to share tables. A Turkish man was trying to get a seat but most guests refused the foreigner. In what was left of her Christian values Maria called him over to sit with her to spare him further humiliation and hostility. There were lots of disapproving noises and looks when she did this but Maria didn't care. The young man thanked her for her kindness and let her carry on reading, without striking up a conversation: he seemed aware that this would have been deemed inappropriate.

Nothing came of this first encounter. Maria eventually took her leave with just a vague, formal hand gesture. She had appreciated his restraint and respect. Knowing her father's view on Muslim men she knew she could not be seen to exchange words with him.

A few days later the same scene played out in the café and she rescued him again. Assured that he would keep his distance, over the next few weeks she let him share her table several times until finally he introduced himself to her.

"My name is Esat," he said. "Thank you for your kindness. I was beginning to give up on ever finding a seat when you so warmly invited me."

"My name is Maria," she replied. "It's nice to meet you. I don't like it when people are so mean to foreigners."

"I heard about these problems for Turks before I came here but I never imagined it to be true. At first I thought it was because I work for the city sewage maintenance. It is a dirty and smelly job but nobody would know that when I am here washed and in my civilian clothes."

"Are you very unhappy living in Germany?" she asked sounding concerned and sad.

"I came to Germany to support my family at home and am grateful to be able to help them. But I also volunteered to escape the restrictive ways of my Muslim family. I would not be allowed to sit with an unmarried woman in public. The constant praying that we have to do every day of our life is so hollow and for appearances only. I really don't feel it is important to my connection with God but I must never say that out loud in public back home. I am frankly quite glad to be here, if only people weren't so afraid or hateful towards me."

"I know exactly what you mean," she said smiling. "I am from a very strict Catholic family and praying every day and taking the gospel literally is something I know all about. If only more of your people knew how we really felt, maybe they would not be so intimidated."

"Who would be intimidated by a young woman like you?" he said dismissively.

"I am working as secretary for a Christian party official," she admitted. "My father is no friend of the Gastarbeiter."

"You seem too sophisticated and modern to me for a position like that. What it is called, an emancipated woman?" he said.

"I think my time here in Bonn has helped me to develop visions of a future beyond what my idyllic and unworldly hometown could make me believe possible. I judge the way in which my devout Catholic family is expressing its beliefs, it is far from Christian and I have begun to distance myself from the organised and dogmatic church. I probably should not stay with the party any longer. What about your conflicts, are they as bad as mine?"

"I am 22 years old, I am meant to get married, probably some woman found for me by my father but I am here for another few years. I am bound to fall in love, I am young. If I fall for a Christian woman, my family is going to disown me but how can I do that if I am not even allowed to meet one of the Muslim women around here either?"

It was refreshing for Maria to exchange views and pleasantries with a man who had so similar experiences but with a totally different religion. She had not expected to find the man so attractive, nor had she thought that she would have anything in common with him, but not only had Esat become irresistibly handsome in her eyes, he also shared her passion for books and he loved the theatre. To continue their friendship innocently he invited Maria to a play the next week. Maria at first declined on the grounds that her father would never approve. Being seen with a Muslim in a place where some of her father's party friends might recognise her was way too offensive for Hans-Ulrich and his friends. Even in the café they were already given strange looks for being together. She had noticed the whispers and thought she had heard some nasty remarks but she chose to ignore them.

A few days later she was typing up a document for her father in which he spoke with venom about the plague of Turkish Gastarbeiters and proposed a hard new party line against them in the next elections. Ever since she had met Esat, she had started to think of him as a friend. Experiencing the way he was treated in public life made the political fight her father was leading more personal for her.

The next time she met Esat she accepted his kind invitation and agreed to visit the theatre with him. She owed it to her own convictions and to her growing feelings for Esat to make a stand and not let herself be intimidated so easily. And she owed it to herself to kiss him in a doorway when he walked her back home. From then on they were dating.

This new 'acquaintance' of hers was noticed by Hans-Ulrich's enemies right away, and was used to undermine his position in a hateful campaign amongst his party members. He was furious with Maria when he found out.

"A Muslim! A Muslim! A Muslim!" he kept screaming over and over again, "how can you go out with a Muslim? Of all the bad choices you could have made, why someone who does not believe in the Good Lord?"

"But he does believe in God, just not in the one that you do!" Maria replied sharply, but to no avail. When it came to religion there was no messing or arguing with her father.

"A heathen, that is what he is. You will end up in a harem, a slave to his every whim. I forbid you to see him again."

"I am old enough, you cannot tell me what to do anymore." she replied.

"You are disowned if you ever set eyes on that man again." he threatened her. "Think of us all, you selfish girl. Your mother will die of a broken heart if she finds out. If your own salvation is of no importance to you as a consequence of your thoughtless actions then please consider how it will affect the rest of us."

"All you think about is your political career and that is sheer vanity," she pointed out to him.

"What I do is not out of vanity, it is my sense of obligation to society and the Good Lord," he tried to justify himself. "My career is the work of God."

"No, it is still vanity. You think that no one but yourself can do the 'Good Lord's' will as good as you? That is unbelievable arrogance," she cried out.

"You know nothing about the Lord's will or else you would not be seen with this Muslim boy," he redirected the conversation and the blame on her.

"Esat does not care about religion, father. He even offered to convert for me," Maria said quietly, for effect.

Hans-Ulrich was dumbfounded and fell silent for a while. He wondered how it would be received amongst the party membership if it became known that his daughter had managed to convert one of those foreign heathens and led him on to the path of Christian righteousness. Such a token conversion might be the front of tolerance and understanding that his party needed and might become his ticket back into the coalition government, redeeming himself in the eyes of his left wing opponents and of the Social Democrats and enabling him to continue his work for God and the nation. He needed to find out just how stubborn and unmoving his more conservative party friends would be on the matter.

In his naïve notion of achievement he made the mistake of telling some of his party fellows, foolishly trusting their sworn silence on the matter. Many of his political allies appeared to be against the Turkish on grounds of religion only but they turned out to be against the integration of anything un-German into society, although they were not prepared to admit that in public.

A converted Turk did not please them at all. A scandal broke loose amongst the party members and calls for his immediate resignation were put forward to the party leadership. Hans-Ulrich received hate letters and abusive comments everywhere. People turned away from him and dropped him like a hot potato; a liability to their good name. Even the announcement that his youngest son Joseph had just been accepted to become a priest was not enough to save him and his reputation. Wherever he went, party members told him that he had become a risk at the next election.

162

"The people in Heimkirchen have voted for me, if it is the Good Lord's will I shall gain their support again," he said at a party meeting when the subject was brought up.

"Hans-Ulrich, you have been an inspiration to us all," the party spokesman said diplomatically. "We must ask you as a favour for us and our joint cause to step down. Huge sections of the nation are concerned about the influx of Gastarbeiter and so our voters are not ready for a member of parliament who has a Turkish son-in-law."

"Not even if we find him a good job and put him in a suit? He will convert to become a Christian, you know," Hans-Ulrich explained once more, hoping that this would turn the tide.

"In a suit he will be even more frightening. It is fine for foreigners to come here and do our dirty work. There will be a hell of a riot if they start taking the good jobs and earn decent wages as well. If we support that then our membership might as well all vote for the Social Democrats and their socialist ideas," the spokesman replied.

"If you stand for parliament again we will lose the seat to the Socialists or the far right," another member claimed. "Do you think your Good Lord would want that?"

Hans-Ulrich couldn't reply to that right away: he had a lot of soul searching to do. He had got used to the life of a responsible politician, almost like a priest shepherding his flock. He could not deny that Maria had been right about his vanity. It would be hard to go back to a trivial job in the city administration. He had enjoyed making decisions and knowing that he would make them with the best of intentions and with a view for the greater Christian good. To give up this responsibility and to entrust it to someone who might not be so pious and conscientious was a big and difficult step. He begged Maria to break off her connection with the man for his sake but his stubborn daughter refused and he saw himself that the damage had already been done, ever since her relationship to Esat had become public knowledge amongst the politicians in Bonn.

His party colleagues were right; there was a lot of controversy and risk in his candidacy now. But if it was the Good Lord's will, then why had He not sent Hans-Ulrich a sign to step down? To do so without permission from Him was to neglect his duties towards the Holy Church and his faith. He felt in a huge dilemma.

Maria did not make his life easier by announcing that she would not return to Heimkirchen with him for the parliamentary election campaign of 1969, she would stay with Esat in Cologne, with a view of moving to Hamburg where the sight of foreigners was more common and acceptable due to the city's long standing trade tradition. When Hans-Ulrich heard that the two of them were going to live in sin he was close to a nervous breakdown.

"Please wait at least until he has converted and you have got married," he begged his daughter. "Have my efforts to make a good Christian out of you been in total vain, then?" he asked tearfully.

"Father if you are going to talk about my salvation one more time..." she started.

"How can you not care about what happens to you in the afterlife?" he interrupted, outraged. "You have always been such a good girl; this can only be a rebellious phase. I should never have exposed your naïve soul to the wicked world here in Bonn. If only I had thought this through then you would still be serving at The Black Eagle and probably be engaged to a normal and good Bavarian man. How can you spit in Jesus' face after he died on the cross for us and move in with a Muslim?"

"I am not spitting in anyone's face and Jesus would not throw the first stone, don't you think?" she replied angrily.

"He won't throw a stone, you got that right, but He will put you in purgatory. I wish I would not have to throw those stones myself but I must," Hans-Ulrich explained. "Your mother will die of heartache if she hears about you and your Turk. God forbid she already has. You have become so incredibly selfish and obstinate my child. Why are you being like this?"

"Father, we are not living in the middle-ages anymore," she replied agitatedly. "The church was wrong then when they burnt the alleged witches and when they said that the Earth was the centre of the universe. They are wrong with their politics of intolerance towards other religions. Try and think for yourself, don't ask the Pope. There is a whole new generation who make up their own minds and they won't vote for you if you are so cloistered and unworldly. Being locked up in Heimkirchen most of your life has done nothing for your understanding of the world

164

and neither have your years in Bonn and Strasbourgh. Have you ever even talked to a Muslim?"

"No, but I can see that you have. Has he put those thoughts and doubts into your mind? Can't you see that this is what they do? Luring good Christian women like you off the path of righteousness."

"Father you are just sad. I have told you already: he is converting. He is already doing you a big favour with this. Neither he nor I are religious but we are willing to compromise for you and your 'career'."

"You think that is generous of you?" he almost screamed at her. "After all I have sacrificed to bring you up. And your mother did, too."

"You and mother overloaded us children with your fanaticism," Maria replied calmly. "I did not mind as long as it made you happy but as I grew older I realised I didn't believe in any of it. If I had stayed in Heimkirchen I would have always believed that something was wrong with me because of it. Now that I have seen more of the world I know that I am not alone. The Hinterbergers, the farm, The Black Eagle and the church in Heimkirchen – all that is not the centre of the universe, it is a self-enclosed cult."

"You devil child!" he shouted at her. "The Holy Church a cult? You are a blasphemous, sinful woman."

"There are so many ways for a human being to be good, it does not have to involve prayer and worship. I don't think you are doing anything good yourself. You spend half a day in judgement of others and tell them arrogantly what to do. The rest of your time you spend with prayer and worship and no one benefits from that waste of time but your over-inflated ego," she said disparagingly.

"Get out of my sight," he fumed. "You have become so evil I don't even recognise you anymore: I shall pray for you."

Maria went to her room and packed her belongings. She was shaking all over because, despite of her strong convictions, there still remained a small kernel of doubt in her heart. She had been surrounded by religious fanatics for so long, some of the things that she had heard continuously throughout her life had got to her and even the most rational of minds could not completely erase the thought patterns and ideas that had been

165

drilled into her for decades. Her father's words had not entirely failed to hit a nerve. What if God was this judgemental and narrow minded? She felt she knew better but a grain of fear remained.

She grabbed her suitcase and took a taxi to Esat's place. His work had rented him a room in a rather run-down apartment block with four other men at the edge of town. She could not stay there but she had nowhere else to go. He took her to a boarding house nearby and promised to meet her the next afternoon to discuss their further plans.

Maria spent a long night awake, worrying about the big step she had just taken. Her family life had been a bit of a cult and leaving it behind made her feel worried and unsure about her ability to survive on her own. Was she making a mistake by going from one dependency to the next?

Esat had been very serious when she arrived at his place and not as happy as she would have hoped. Did he have second thoughts? Would she burn in hell for being so selfish and leaving her family and her father? Alone in this run down place and sharing a room with three other women did not help her feel confident and upbeat about her future.

She was allowed to leave her luggage at the boarding house but had to vacate the room in the morning so that the woman who ran the place could clean up and prepare dinner. Maria walked through the city and decided to look for a room for herself or a flat. There was little to choose from here in Bonn, of course. Since the government had been brought to this unlikely location, the city had flourished and rents were expensive.

She met Esat in the afternoon at their usual cafe place.

"We could never afford a place right here," he told her. "Until you have work and contribute to the rent we cannot get anything else but a room between us. Without being married there won't be many landlords who will have us. And even if we were married it would not be easy either."

"Is that why you were so serious last night?" she asked. "I thought you were displeased with me for making a hasty decision."

"Of course I am pleased with your decision," he said, covering her hands with his. "I am the happiest man alive that

166

you have chosen me. And it is good for you to break free, just as I did. It just came as a big surprise that you did it so quickly."

"I have some money of my own," she told him proudly. "I have some land to my name back in Heimkirchen. I can ask my brother to sell it for me. We won't have to live in the most run down place that there is. I also have an aunt that I could ask for money."

"I don't want that," Esat replied. "We need to keep that money for a rainy day, for when we have children maybe. The price for the land you own might yet go up in value, we should not waste it for our day to day living. We need to find a better solution for those problems. I think you should start looking for work, then we get married and move in together."

"You sound just like my father," she said laughingly but she had to admit that even in the more liberal north there were still some unspoken rules that were the same in the south.

When Esat's work contract came to an end they moved back to Cologne. Maria found a position as a waitress in a busy and renowned restaurant and rented a small room with a socialist couple who had nothing against her dating a Turk, although they would not allow him to stay over.

Maria and Esat visited a Catholic church nearby and spoke to the priest about the process of converting to Christianity so that they could get married. It seemed, however, that the Catholic Church was not very interested in gaining a new member unless he really believed and Esat was turned down by the priest for his half-heartedness. Maria realised that it was no longer necessary for him to convert anyway. She had already left her family circles and was an outlaw in their eyes. She saw no reason for him to exchange one religion for another when he did not believe in either of them and nobody thanked them for the token effort either. Esat might as well stay a Muslim, Maria had already been disowned, at least this way he would not burn all of his bridges to his own family.

She found it very difficult to deal with the open hate and discrimination that she and Esat were so frequently subjected to. Certain restaurants denied them access and abusive comments and dismissive looks became part of their everyday life together. Maria was outraged that such behaviour should be tolerated - in post-Nazi Germany of all countries. She remembered all too well how fast and desperately the young, post war Germany had tried to rid itself of its shameful past and had called for a look forward to the future. Was the dislike of Gastarbeiters part of this better and peaceful future? How many men had sworn that they had not supported Hitler and his racial politics and now they gave her and Esat such hateful looks? Esat seemed much more accepting of this, or maybe he just was more used to it and had become immune. Hoping that their life might be better elsewhere the two of them moved to Hamburg, where they succeeded at least in renting a flat together.

Chapter 14: The Return (1968-70)

Abashed and broken, Hans-Ulrich returned to Heimkirchen to bring the dreadful and devastating news about Maria to his wife. Magdalena however, remained surprisingly calm about her daughter's escapade. As shameful as that kind of behaviour was, Magdalena was not as naïve to the changing times as her husband was. In her charity work she had found herself often dealing with poor families from foreign countries and had learnt to 'tolerate' them. One of her co-workers had been particularly helpful in teaching her to extend her Christian neighbourly sentiments to every child of God, even those heathens.

Magdalena was much more shocked and concerned about the impact this had had on Hans-Ulrich's career. If she was no longer the wife of a parliamentarian she would find it so much harder to raise money and awareness for her good causes. What if a candidate from the Social Democrats was elected in Hans-Ulrich's place? What kind of charity work would his wife do? What would Magdalena do with the rest of her time? Would she still be welcome and useful to the institutions she supported or would she be dropped by them in favour of someone whose husband was more popular and admired?

Now that even her youngest child Joseph had left the family home to become a priest, she was going to be all alone and completely redundant. The thought of a normal and empty life filled her with horror.

She persuaded Hans-Ulrich to fight his corner and during the preparations for the elections to be held in 1969, he managed to win the party's nomination for the seat, despite large opposition to it.

Even so, Hans-Ulrich, and with him the Christian Democrats, lost his seat to the far right party. Although the winning candidate could not take his seat in parliament because the right wing party fell just a little short of the 5% barrier nationwide and so lost all of the seats it had won, the result was the end of Hans-Ulrich's career. He was back in the small world of Heimkirchen in a home devoid of children.

In the meantime at the farm, Anna had started to give up on the thought that Markus would ever return to the farm. The private investigator, Thomas Holzapfel, came back with one report of failure after another and it had cost her a fortune over the decade. She knew he had tried very hard but she grew tired of disappointment and the emotional turmoil every time she sent him away on a mission and he came back empty handed.

During all this time Helga had been pointing out just how selfless and kind Lukas was, tirelessly working for the farm. He was still not married and devoted all of his time to the business. Every other person had abandoned ship and left the farm but Lukas had stood by Anna; she could not deny that Helga was right.

She consoled herself that she had given him enough land as compensation. She would never be able to love him the way she had loved Markus but her estimation and appreciation of Lukas gradually grew the longer her adopted son was missing.

Alone and in her seventies now, she decided to use the little time she had left in life to make a difference and find Lukas a wife. If he was so busy working, maybe she could find some opportunities for him and arrange for him to meet some likely candidates. With Helga in tow she started to visit old friends and farmers whom she had not met for years. In refreshing her connections she put word out about Lukas' faultless character and she implied heavily that he would be the heir to her fortune, now that everyone else was gone. Her tactics worked and suddenly many a farmer appeared in The Black Eagle with his family and eligible daughters, introducing themselves to Lukas and Anna and refreshing their ties.

Unaware of Anna's campaigning, Lukas was thrilled to find himself suddenly so much in demand by the young women of the area. In his youth he had experienced a few phases of high demand and interest in his company followed by periods of abandonment and dismissal by the ladies.

He had never figured out why that had been. As a member of the reputable Hinterberger family and as one of the key players on his aunt's farm he had always expected a lot of female attention. That his arrogant and ego-fuelled ways had driven most of his admirers away was something he had never really comprehended. This wave of renewed interest in him was as unexplainable to him as the long lack of attention that had preceded it. He enjoyed his place in the limelight but in terms of interpersonal skills he was still as helpless and unsuccessful as ever.

"You are putting them all off with endless talking about yourself," Anna told him after one particularly bad evening. "The fathers like to hear about your achievements but they usually already know, else they would not be here. The girl wants to be liked and wants you to be interested in her. These days women want to marry for love much more than they ever did. Of course all the fathers want to have you as a son-in-law but you need to convince the girls that you are a good catch for them as well."

"I want a girl who is interested in what I am interested in. If they want a clown to entertain them then they should go somewhere else. I want to find one that likes to hear about business matters and who shares my ideas about the future," he replied.

"In that case you will live a lonely life," Helga entered the conversation. "Men should be at least a little interested in their wives. They normally want to explore the unknown world that a woman is for them - at least at the beginning. I am amazed you are so disinterested in all of these girls."

"I wish they had something to make me interested," he replied.

During the next few introductions however, he did ask more questions and tried to impress the girls with at least a passing interest in their lives. He didn't consider himself a romantic and as long as the woman was presentable and beautiful enough he did not care much what she was like.

He wanted to marry a woman with a huge dowry or with the prospect of a future inheritance. Although his father was still in Bonn, he had given up the old notion of making a match with the daughter of one of his father's party members. Lukas was getting on in years and set on finding a woman willing to work on the farm with him. With all the land he had managed to get in his name, he could make a good living on his own – away from Anna and Markus – if he wanted.

The sudden socialising with his aunt and her encouraging attitude to find a wife changed the relationship between the two of them for the better. The longer there was no sign from

Markus, the more relaxed and secure Lukas felt. By now it seemed unlikely they would ever see this wastrel of a man again. If the situation stayed like this, Lukas would be very happy.

If he had to choose one of the women it would be the girl from the Rieder Farm. Their farm was huge and he could expect a respectable dowry. Although he would not inherit the farm itself, he would be doing well to have them as allies rather than competitors. Besides, the girl looked pretty enough. He would have to ask her out and make her see what a nice guy he was and how 'interested' he was in her life.

Luckily, there was no rush as far as he was concerned. He read the sudden boom of introductions as a sign that there were no better matches around in the area than him and he could take his time finding the right woman. In his self-delusion of grandeur he saw himself as the object of a bidding war between the farmers' single daughters in the area.

The truth, however, was that most farmers were doing Anna a favour for old times' sake. None of them were expecting much to come of their visits and only a few were even seriously considering Lukas as a son-in-law – whether they thought he would inherit the farm or not.

The scandal around Markus and the restaurant was still putting many of them off and Lukas' obsessive and difficult character was well known amongst both fathers and daughters alike. The alleged suitors were only trying to keep good relations and preferred not to sell their daughters to a life of expected unhappiness.

It was during the end of this period that Maria's engagement announcement from Hamburg arrived on his desk. Hans-Ulrich and Magdalena had kept the scandal to themselves and had not even told Anna about their daughter's wedding plans to a Turk. The news hit Lukas bitterly for in his eyes it was the end of any chance he might ever have had for an advantageous marriage. Why did this have to happen, just as he entertained the idea of making a good match? He was furious with his sister and her inappropriate timing. A year ago he had not even thought about marriage and now that he might marry in as little as a few months' time, Maria had made a disastrous choice of a husband that would impact dramatically on his life. If she was to go ahead with this his life would be ruined. The Rieder family and even

172

much lesser farmers would instantly burn their bridges to the Hinterbergers.

He sat down and wrote an immediate reply, scolding his sister for her selfish and un-thoughtful, if not scandalous, behaviour and he begged her to reconsider before it was too late. Could she not see how her outlandish choice of a husband was ruining his own chances for happiness and were destroying what little was left of the family's reputation? Should she be so stubborn as to go ahead with her misguided plans not only would he not attend her wedding, he would disown her and refuse to see her ever again.

Anna laughed when she heard about the Turkish husband-to-be. She was the only one who saw the irony between this choice and Hans-Ulrich's controversial politics regarding the Gastarbeiter issue. She had given up caring about status and prestige for her family: she no longer worried much about anything. There was no point in struggling, if even her holier than thou brother Hans-Ulrich could not prevent such a catastrophe from happening to his own nuclear family; all this trying to hold the old world order together had done her no good and the rest of the country might as well give up as well. For a scandal like this to hit Hans-Ulrich and Magdalena, of all people, was simply too funny.

She hadn't considered attending the wedding or bestowing the bride with a dowry or a gift but gradually she wondered if maybe she should leave Maria some of the family jewellery in her will, if she were ever to make one. The girl had been a darling and the sweetest thing after all. In her resurfacing and growing affections for Lukas she also began to think more favourably of the rest of the family.

Too often Anna found herself wondering what she had been fighting for all of her life, if at the end of it there was nothing to show for it. No husband, no children and the one boy she had loved as if he was her own, he had disappeared from sight. She had fallen out with all of her siblings but one and he was too busy to see her. Her attempts to make religion and the search for forgiveness the meaning and sole purpose of her life had not worked for her in the same way as it did for many others. She had long abandoned her routine of feverish church

173

attendance and prayer. Humbleness in front of the Good Lord just did not come easy to her when He had denied her children and inflicted so much pain in her life.

With their progressing age, Helga's strength was declining more rapidly than her own. Anna only kept her old servant for the company. Physically, Helga could offer little in the way of farm work but the two women had become dependent on each other after a lifetime of dedication to nothing but the farm.

In this sentimental spirit Anna did send a little note to Maria, inviting her to come and stay at The Black Eagle for her honeymoon. It would outrage her brother, she was aware of that, but she was desperate for company and entertainment and she wondered what this Turk had that had swept Maria off her feet.

Maria was touched that the old battle axe of an aunt had been the kindest of all the Heimkirchen clan. She was in no financial position to decline any money or any other support she was offered and accepted the kind invitation.

At the registry office in Hamburg in spring of 1970, the only guest from Heimkirchen was her brother Joseph, the aspiring priest. In spite of his strong religious orientation, he was the most open to her choice of husband and as the youngest of the family he was closest to her. By the time he was old enough to go to school, the curriculum was full of education about Germany's shameful past and he had fully absorbed those teachings and had found them perfectly in line with how he read the Christian doctrine. Despite the authoritarian regime of his parents, as a teenager in the fifties and sixties he had learnt to think a little bit more for himself than his older siblings. He attended the wedding more for political reasons than anything else. Joseph, however, was not the only member of the family. Anna's brother Paul and her nephew Martin had come all the way from America to witness the wedding.

Paul was also in his seventies and had decided that he would like to see his home country one last time before he was too old to travel and he invited Martin to come along and keep him company on the journey. In America, the two of them had the status of immigrants themselves and had a lot more tolerance and understanding for Maria's husband and his life.

Paul looked older but else he was the spitting image of Lukas – the family resemblance was amazing. Maria was overwhelmed that a distant uncle whom she had never met would be so kind and use her wedding as the occasion for a visit.

She had heard conflicting stories about his departure; some rumours went that he had left due to a broken heart, whereas others claimed that Anna had driven him away.

"I am not sure what drove me to leave in the end, there was so much going on back then," he explained evasively. "All that is such a long time ago. I was lucky I had the wanderlust. I have seen some amazing sights in my life and I escaped all the terrible times in Germany. How are my brothers and sisters? No one ever writes, I am amazed you tracked me down," he said warmly. Paul had a peacefulness and serenity about him that was missing from every other Hinterberger she had ever met. There was no pretence, no falseness and no hidden agenda.

"Did no one ever write to you and tell you?" Joseph asked, astonished at such heartlessness.

"I brought this on myself, really," Paul defended his family. "I moved away and I did not particularly make much of an effort to stay in touch. My younger sisters wrote to me at first but I have never been very good at replying. During the war we were forbidden to have contact with Germany. It would be very unfair for me to complain about it now. Besides, I live so far away, what difference does it make to my life whatever goes on here? Now that I have come of course I need to know. Are all of my siblings still alive?" he asked again.

"I don't want to be the bearer of bad news on such a joyous day," Joseph said. "Maybe we should have this discussion another day."

"You can tell me," he encouraged his young nephew. "At my age most of one's friends are dead already, I am used to it," he assured him. "I know Hans-Ulrich and Anna are alive because you mentioned why they are not coming."

"I am afraid that is it," Joseph said quietly. "You know that the eldest, Gerhard, died in the Great War. Alfons died of tuberculosis after the second war. Barbara died of cancer a few years after him; her husband remarried and moved away. We never see him or the children. Elizabeth became a war widow; she was depressed and killed herself soon after Barbara died. Her children are still in Heimkirchen but they stay clear of the farm. Luise was a nurse during the last war and died in France. "

"Well, I knew I had left it too late to see all of them again," Paul said stoically.

"I am glad I can see at least the future generation," he added, directed at Esat, who had been an outsider in the conversation until now. "You mustn't take this boycott personally, my dear friend. You see, Heimkirchen is very much behind the times. Few people ever find themselves there that have not been born there. Until I moved to America I had never even seen a black person or a Turk or a Chinese man. I had heard about them but they were like figures in a fairy tale or a play. I was ashamed by my ignorance but I had a chance to learn in ways that they never could. Don't get me wrong: This behaviour is despicable and unforgivable but the shame is on them."

"Thank you," Esat replied. "But I do understand. My family disapproves of my marriage, too. People are the same everywhere."

"It is so good to see you as well, Martin." Maria said to her long lost brother. "I was afraid I would never see you again in my life."

"It took a lot of persuasion for me to return," Martin admitted. "For years I was still angry at the injustice at the farm, the favouritism and the fraud that went on. I was eaten up by hatred and I was afraid to come back. If it had not been for Paul and his endless begging I doubt I would have come at all. I came more to keep him company than for my own sake. I am still a little unsure what I am doing here. I doubt that I will go and meet with Anna or Markus."

"Oh, so you don't know about Markus?" Maria said, surprised.

"You have not written to me in years," Martin pointed out. "I know next to nothing. What about him?"

"He is gone. Disappeared. He stole a lot of money and took off with one of the Gastarbeiters. A man! Presumably to live happily ever after," she said with a little smirk, knowing how much schadenfreude he would be feeling over the scandal.

"How has Anna taken it?" Martin asked, sounding surprisingly more concerned than pleased.

"She was heartbroken," Maria told him. "After you left for America and Otto became a monk she became more fixated on him than ever. Anna fell out with father and mother about our church going and prayers. You know how bad they were before you left: it got worse. Lukas and I had to leave the farm and return to Heimkirchen with them. Only when Markus ran off were Lukas and I allowed back to pick up the pieces."

"Oh God," Martin commented. He could just about imagine how all of this would have played out.

"To make matters worse, Anna brought Herbert back from the asylum and nursed him at home until he died. There was so much anxiety about who would get what from which will, it was ridiculous really. The atmosphere was terrible. Even after Markus stole all the money Anna tried to get him back with the help of a private investigator. The last time I saw her she was a changed woman, desperate for her golden boy to return and fill her emptiness. She is a shadow of her former self," she told him.

"Did she ever find him?" Martin asked.

"Thank God, no," she replied hastily but Martin picked up on it and probed further.

"You sound as if there is more to that story," he said. "Has there been no word from him at all? Do you know anything about him?"

"Well, if you promise not to tell," she lowered her voice to a more intimate tone. "I met him once in Strasbourgh. He was following me and father around. We were there on government business and Markus thought of speaking to father. He talked about returning home to ask for forgiveness."

"What a cheek!" Martin exclaimed.

"Exactly what I told him," Maria agreed. "I said he could return any time to Heimkirchen as long as he brought back all the money that he had stolen. He did not like that. He has probably spent it all anyway. Fortunately he never did dare come back. I never told anyone about the meeting because I did not want to open old wounds. I was also afraid that if I had told Anna she might have known where to look and then she would have found him and given him everything that was left of her fortune. I thought hard about it because I was not sure I had the right to interfere and keep it from her but in the end I realised that I would be taking everything away from Lukas that he has still left

177

to hope for, and he, at least, has stayed loyal to Anna and her farm."

"You don't sound too proud of Lukas either," Martin observed.

"He has become bitter and greedy," Maria said. "You'll see when you meet him. Stubborn and principle ridden like our father."

"I thought you were not writing to me because there was nothing new to tell," Martin said laughingly, "I had no idea how much was actually happening."

"I am sorry I kept all this from you," she apologised. "It always makes me so sad to think about how our entire family has fallen apart over money and religion. Writing or speaking about it makes it worse. Every single one of us claims they want the best for everyone but it certainly doesn't feel that way. I have a small photograph of the farm and a portrait of our family after Joseph was born. I used to feel happy when I looked at them, now I only feel sad. The picture doesn't show me my home or my family, it has become a symbol of our private war. If the bombs had destroyed the farm and The Black Eagle we would all have had a chance for a better life than the one we have now, because we would have had to start from scratch. None of those who stayed there are happy. It seems that all of you who have left made a better life for yourselves, especially during the two wars and during the economic crisis. How many people wouldn't have given everything they own to have a life line like this farm and a goldmine like the restaurant for their family. We Hinterbergers had to destroy everything that was good about it out of our greed. Leaving here was the best thing that you ever did, Martin, believe me."

"Now, now," Esat interrupted his bride and held her close to comfort her. "Today is your wedding day, Maria. Don't think about the past any longer. You got away yourself. It is over. Today we start a new chapter and a new family, one that will do better than the old one."

"Amen to that." Joseph agreed.

Chapter 15: Paul (1970)

After the wedding, Martin and Paul stayed with the couple for another day to reacquaint themselves with the language and the country, then they took a series of trains that took them home to Heimkirchen. Paul had promised Martin that they would stay in a neutral lodging and not at The Black Eagle Inn that was linked to the farm. The nephew had worried that old arguments and animosities might resurface and believed it best to have a refuge outside the family boundaries. The old man did not think it was really necessary to be so pessimistic about the reunion but saw no harm in pleasing Martin, if it was so important to him.

Anna was unlikely to see her long lost brother from America as a threat after all those years, and no one could blame a young lad like Martin for seeking his fortune in the wild west of Arizona. The family could only greet them with open arms. Their first visit was to Magdalena and Hans-Ulrich. Martin waited for Magdalena outside the church after the evening mass. She took a while to recognise her own son. She stood still for a few seconds in disbelief, also trying to figure out who was that old man with him, and then she said, somewhat coldly, "You could have told us that you were coming."

Martin stepped a little closer to her, awkward and not sure if he could hug her after this frosty welcome.

"I thought I would surprise you. Aren't you at all happy to see me?" he asked with disappointment.

"You have chosen a bad time. Your father is not well and he doesn't like to have any company when he gets home from work," she almost snapped.

"Why, what is wrong with him?" Paul asked, concerned.

"Who are you?" Magdalena asked abruptly.

"I am Paul, his older brother from America. I came to visit, too," he explained.

"You could have written to us, or at least given us some warning that you were coming. What am I going to do with you two?" she said, seriously displeased.

The two men were taken back by the cold reception. Paul had never met Magdalena and had not quite known what to expect of her but he had not been prepared for such rudeness.

Martin had had a better idea of his mother's character and her foibles, but he had still hoped for at least a little enthusiasm of sorts.

"I am very sorry we are inconveniencing you," Paul said, being the first of the two to recover. "Please don't worry yourself on our behalf. We will return to our guest house. We are staying at the Old Inn. If at some point you or Hans-Ulrich want to see either of us, you know where to find us. Come on Martin," and with that he took hold of his nephew's arm and gently pulled him away.

"Come tomorrow evening," Magdalena finally said in a little more welcoming and friendly manner. "I'll speak to Hans-Ulrich and tell him you are coming. Maybe he will receive you."

"What a hard woman," Paul commented when they were back at their neutral lodgings having dinner.

"I have never known her this bitter: she must have had tough times to be like that." Martin defended his mother. "Under her hard exterior she was always soft and kind and never as harsh as this - unless someone wronged her. I think she has taken Hans-Ulrich's demotion badly. She seems unusually unhappy. "

"She must be upset about Maria's wedding as well," Paul added. "Do you think she knows that this is why we are here?"

"It is hard to tell what is on her mind," Martin replied. "Maria said that she can be very self-involved, especially now with her charity work on top of what she does for the church. I sometimes think she would have been better off in a convent than in a big family where so much can go wrong."

The next morning the two men made their way to Anna's farm, wondering if they would receive a better reception there.

"She will be pleased to see you," Paul said to Martin. "Maria said how lonely Anna has become."

"It is hard for me to imagine her all soft and emotional," Martin replied and shook his head in disbelief. "The woman I remember was a tough cookie and very unforgiving, unless, of course, it concerned Markus."

"I knew her when she was a child," Paul said thoughtfully. "That memory will always stay with me. If you know someone's past you can see underneath a person's rough exterior and you know better why they are the way they are and what good they are capable of. You always experienced her as the strict aunt, to me she will always remain daddy's little girl. Old age often turns us back into the people that we were when we were young. I hope she has lost some of her hardness and found the innocent girl inside of her."

"We will soon find out," Martin observed but he didn't sound optimistic.

At the farm they found Anna in bed. Of late she had become short of breath, even from the smallest exercise, and needed to rest frequently. Her doctor, Dr Hofer, wanted to take more tests but she had refused to undergo any such palaver, as she called it. If her time was up then fine, she had told the rather upset Helga. Besides, the family doctor had not been able to save her Herbert, so why should she believe him now. He had done nothing then, until it was too late and he was only being over cautious now so that he would not wrong the same family twice. She did not think her life was worth the effort of saving.

When Martin and Paul came to her sick bed she was anything but pleased. The unexpected visit got her all excited and agitated. She remembered all too well how she had driven Paul from the farm and how she had talked him into leaving. She sank into a flashback of memories that was far from pleasant.

When she was younger, Anna had always devoted as much attention to the farm as she possibly could and, cleverly scheming, she persuaded the other girls of the family how talented and irreplaceable they were in the kitchen, or in the less prestigious areas of the farm work.

"Nobody can make potato salad as delicious as you, Luise," Anna would say sweetly to her sister. "You go and help out in the kitchen and I will stay here with the boys and keep out of your way."

"Oh, I can't repair socks half as quickly as you do with your sewing talents, Barbara. Imagine how impressed mother will be when she finds out you did it all by yourself."

Having her sisters taking care of the girlie and mundane tasks freed up her time to get involved with those sides of the business that usually were the privilege of men: trading, negotiating and accountancy.

When she had first voiced her interest in these sides of the business her father had humoured her, expecting to find her

181

bored with it quickly or too stupid to understand any of it. Yet Anna turned out to be a fast learner and demonstrated a talent for all sides of the business. In the months leading up to his departure to the Great War, her father dedicated much time in training her so that his wife would have a helpful hand. Proving a tough and skilled business woman, Anna soon played a prominent role in negotiations. Her mother was astonished at how easy it was to rely on the young woman. When Anna's father returned from the war he found, of course, many faults with what she had done, but for a teenage girl she had impressed him beyond his wildest dreams. Wanting the farm desperately over her brother it was her who drove Paul away with a brutal attack on his confidence.

"You are not really planning to become the new farmer around here?" she had asked him outright.

Paul had always been easily intimidated by his older and stronger sister and did not know what to say.

"Why are you asking?" he said, defensively.

"I am not stupid, you know," she replied. "I see you running around with father everywhere. He is treating you as his right hand now and training you up to become his successor. Don't pretend that you don't know that."

"Well, I am the oldest son, if you don't count Alfons," he said, trying to sound confident.

"Can't you see that the farm is rightfully mine?" she asked him angrily.

"You already get to inherit Herbert's family's farm. What happens to the Hinterberger Farm is for father to decide, is it not?" Paul said with little confidence in his voice.

"Father trained me to help him. I have been doing the accounts for years. I even entered into an engagement without love to be able to keep the farm going. I might be a woman but I have Herbert now to help me. Should something happen to father today, only I could step into the breach."

"If you give me more time I will learn everything that you have – and more!" he said defiantly, but he sounded unconvinced.

"You can't deny how much you still have yet to learn," she tried to undermine his confidence further. "How could you risk the survival of the farm and of all the people depending on it? If anything were to happen to father tomorrow and you took over, our future would be in jeopardy."

"That is only what you think." Paul replied angrily.

"No, that is the truth. You don't have the personality to manage a business as big as this. I have been to meetings and negotiated with buyers and sellers for years. You are totally green. The business partners will take you for a ride. The farm needs me." she declared.

"Then stay and help me," he suggested.

"As your deputy and servant?" she said with a sneer.

"Why not?"

"Because the farm is mine," she hissed. "How could you even consider accepting what was meant for me? Do you really fancy yourself capable of all the responsibility? You might have good intentions but you are not made of the right stuff and you know it. Don't fool yourself, Paul, for your sake and for the sake of us all."

She remembered all of this conversation as if it had happened yesterday. How it had broken him and how he had left a few days later in the middle of the night. How could she look him in the eye now?

Besides, Paul knew a lot about her that she wished nobody did: how she had married Herbert without loving him. Paul knew that Anna had cast her eye on a few other farmers' sons at the time, men who would have brought better long term prospects but she had not succeeded to secure their affections in time. Herbert had been a fair compromise, not without flaws, but satisfactory enough. He was good looking with strong cheek bones and wild bushy eyebrows that gave him a raw masculine appearance. He was tall and strong and considered a catch, even though he was a bit of a simpleton and intellectually inferior to Anna and many of his friends. He had only one sister, for whom at some stage a dowry would have to be found. Otherwise, the little family fortune of the Stockmanns was as good as hers. Herbert had admired her for years but she had always dismissed him because his family had comparatively little land and money. He had never given up, even after she had got engaged to Lothar, and she liked his eagerness and dedication, especially as it gave her a feeling of control and superiority.

With Paul coming back to Heimkirchen, her worst sins and first deviations from the path of righteousness came back to haunt her. Was he here to take revenge or lay claim to the farm? What a nuisance, so late in her sickly life. She was getting herself in a state about it even before he had a chance to explain why he was here.

All she could get out was a weak and confused sounding "You?"

"Yes, Anna, your little brother," he said warmly and tried to hug her but she shied away.

"Why are you here?" she asked suspiciously.

"Well for a start I came to see my family and my home one last time. I have been meaning to do this for decades but I just never took the time for it. I am getting too old to leave it too much longer, so I came now. I must say I had a warmer welcome in mind when I set off on this journey. What have I done to upset everybody?" Paul asked.

"You've not been in touch for several decades and now all of a sudden you spring on us unannounced. What do you expect us to do?" Anna replied abruptly. "You could have been dead for all we knew. You went away and never came back. Excuse me, but we did not think you were interested in us anymore."

"You could be happy to see me all the same, or at least pretend a little," he said with a cordial smile. "Tell me about your life, ask me about mine, offer me a cup of coffee," he said with a cheeky grin. "That kind of thing. Nothing dramatic. I am not here to take anything away from you or to settle any old accounts, if you are worried about that. I am an old expatriate that just wanted to stop by and see how life has been without me. I thought when I left it was for the better. It doesn't mean I forgot about you or stopped caring."

Anna was a little sheepish that he had seen through her. She could not help but feel uncomfortable around him and would prefer not having to go through this reunion.

"I am old and ill," she told him abruptly, now deliberately playing up her weakness. "Of course I am pleased that you are here, Paul. As you can see the farm has survived the war and everything else that went on. I don't know what else to tell you. Helga and the others must have told you everything there is to know already."

"I guess they have," Paul admitted. "You have done us proud," he added. "The farm is looking mighty fine. Father would be pleased to see how you kept it all together."

Admittedly he wasn't sure that this was entirely true but he did not want to hurt an old and fragile woman's heart. He could sense how desperate she was for approval and harmony. Why not give her a little warmth as a gift from the returning brother?

"Have I?" she asked, doubtful. "Thank you, Paul," she said, very weakly; then a coughing fit stopped her from saying anything else. When it had passed she closed her glassy eyes, making it difficult to guess if she was still awake or not.

"Maybe you could drop in some other time," Helga suggested. "Anna has been very weak over the last few days. Give her a day or two to digest that you are here and she might be in a better position to receive you."

"Happily." Paul said.

The two men took their leave but Anna hardly noticed. They walked across to The Black Eagle Inn in pursuit of Lukas and here at last they received the welcome they had hoped for.

"Martin, you old fox. Come here." Lukas shouted and hugged and lifted his brother up. "You are looking good. What a great surprise! How typical of you not to announce yourself but to sneak in here like that. I have to say, the food over there can't be all that bad. You have put on weight."

"Thank God I have and you have too. We were all too skinny when I left. The food over there is certainly different from the scraps we used to get here during the war," Martin replied. "Here, this is Uncle Paul, we came together to visit our old home."

"Nice to meet you," Lukas said. "Where is your luggage?"

"At the Old Inn," Martin replied shyly.

"At the Old Inn? Don't tell me that is where you are sleeping. Martin, you can't stay there. You must transfer here immediately. I insist. I won't have my family stay in that old dump," he laughed. "No, I know it is a fine place, but you know me, I don't like the competition."

"I told him you would be displeased," Paul said, "but Martin wouldn't listen. To be honest we did not quite know what kind of reception to expect, after all these years. Your mother actually has not given us a particularly warm welcome and Anna being sick, it has not been too encouraging."

"Oh the only person my mother wants to see these days is the Pope," Lukas joked. "She has been to Italy three times already to go to an Audience in the Vatican. You must take no notice of her."

"She has always been like that," Martin agreed, "but her spirit appeared completely broken when we saw her yesterday," he said towards his brother.

"Oh that," Lukas said knowingly, "yes, she is finding it hard to admit that she is no longer Heimkirchen's first lady. I guess she misses that. Of course, she says it is father who is taking it the worst but that is only because she can't admit to herself how proud she has become.

She wants to pretend that she is still God's humble servant, but in fact she has grown rather presumptuous and full of herself."

"I would have said she is depressed and sad," Martin disagreed.

"Whatever it is, it has little to do with you. Are you going to see her again?"

"I hope so," Paul replied. "We literally only saw her for a few minutes and she was not very happy to see us. We are invited to visit her tonight, after she has warned and prepared Hans-Ulrich. Have you ever heard such a load of nonsense?"

"I am afraid I have," Lukas said with a giggle. "I have known her all my life. Now you better get your luggage. Shall I send someone to fetch it for you?"

"Maybe, well, I am not sure we should stay here," Martin said reluctantly. "Anna is so unwell, I feel we would be in the way here. If we stay put that would save us the travel from Heimkirchen tonight. Maybe we should come back tomorrow."

"Whatever you think best. I have enough beds at the moment. Aunt Anna is probably just shocked you are here," Lukas said in her defence. "Her emotions are up and down, don't take them seriously. Tomorrow she might ask you never to leave her again. She still barks but she doesn't bite anymore."

"If you don't mind we will be staying at the Old Inn then and come here tomorrow, after we had our evening with

Magdalena and Hans-Ulrich," Paul said, unsure whether he even wanted to return.

His life in America had been so easy and carefree he had forgotten how serious and depressing his own family relations were. His thoughts had been warm towards them, and over the years his memory had turned them all into harmless little children who were at most misguided.

Seeing his sister again and experiencing her difficult and self-centred ways, even in this mild form, hit home to him just how lucky he had been to have escaped this life. He had arrived in America long enough before Germany's politics could have affected his own reputation. By the time the war started none of his friends over there really thought of him as German and so they gave him no trouble about it. He was settled in with the community, married and had children, even grandchildren now.

All of his in-laws were kind and genuine people, they lived and worked together without competition and fighting. Maria had been right: the ones who got away were the lucky ones. They might have missed out on the money and the wealth but they all seemed to have made a happy life for themselves.

Lukas invited the two visitors to an early lunch. The three sat together in the still empty restaurant and told each other their stories. Paul and Martin were surprised to find that Lukas hardly knew anything about them. The remaining family members had rarely exchanged news about the ones that had left and 'abandoned' them, it seemed. He wanted to hear everything, from Paul's journey to Hamburg forty years ago, how he had got hold of the visa and saved up for the fare to America.

"I almost stayed in Hamburg," Paul admitted. "For a small town boy like me it was absolutely magical. The big city, the great buildings, the canals and bridges and the harbour. I loved every minute of it."

"Why did you not stay then?" Lukas asked. "It would have been a lot cheaper and easier."

"Yes, certainly, but I had developed a taste for the new and I wanted more of it. I had already made the plans and applied for a US work permit when I first had the idea of staying in Hamburg. I was already set on my course to bigger things. If I had waited until after my first summer in Hamburg, I would never have left; then the visa approval came through and I boarded the ship."

"It must have been quite something to arrive at a new continent." Lukas commented.

"Well, New York was actually terrible for someone as shy and slow as me," Paul admitted. "It was too big and too hard for my liking, nothing like the soft and gentle Hamburg. I struggled badly with the language and I did not find many Germans to cling to, so that I could feel some sense of home. The boarding house I was staying at during the first weeks was full of Jews and Eastern Europeans, none of who wanted much to do with me. I decided to work my way across the country, all the way to California, which I imagined to be paradise."

"Is it paradise?" Lukas asked excited.

"As you know, I never made it beyond Arizona," Paul replied. "The wild, wild west. You have to come and visit us one day. You won't believe your eyes when you see the colours of the sky, the rocks and the earth. It is hot all the time, they have mountains like us but they are completely different. There is desert and the Grand Canyon..."

"Do you like it?" Lukas asked his brother. "I could never imagine leaving Heimkirchen. Wherever I go, once the first excitement is gone, I always long to be home, even just after a few days," he admitted.

"I thought so, too," Martin replied. "You need to see Arizona and some of the places I have been to, then you would know why we are so excited and happy to stay where we are now."

"So you are not planning to stay here?" Lukas said amazed. The men had introduced themselves as visitors and tourists but somehow he had always assumed that they would see their old home and never want to leave again.

"No," Martin said in a slow and stretched manner. "Our home is over there now."

Like his uncle, the young emigrant found it instantly hard to readjust to the subdued and stale atmosphere at the farm. He had brought much more anger and emotional baggage with him to America than Paul ever had and, in turn, he had experienced his new family and the life abroad with a greater sense of relief and liberation. Seeing Lukas still so caught up in this world of

188

family feuds and material struggles made him feel uneasy, for it reminded him of that hard period in his own life when he himself had participated in those stupid power games. He did not wish those times back and if he were to stay here he feared he would turn back into the same manipulative and scheming person that he thought he had left behind. He came to the conclusion that his escape from The Black Eagle had been a successful one. His new life – although from a materialistic point of view far inferior to the one he might have had here – was a true blessing.

He listened with polite patience but with not much praise or comment to Lukas, as the latter described his dealings with Markus and Anna.

"It has been a big roller coaster ride for me and her but we have finally established a good relationship with each other," he claimed.

"What if Markus ever returns?" Paul asked, not letting on what he had learned from Maria about their meeting in Strasbourgh.

"God help us if that should happen," Lukas admitted, "but that is very unlikely, now after so many years. That idiot and his spaghetti must have found a new goldmine somewhere else. He would have come back by now if he had the guts. I think he won't risk it. I am no longer sure that Anna would want him back. She used to miss him but she has not mentioned him in front of me for some time. He can probably guess that she wouldn't sue him for the fraud, but he could not seriously expect that she would forgive him. Time is on my side, my friends."

"You must have had your pick of girls," Paul said playfully, trying to get the young man on to nicer subjects. Why not humour the smug bachelor. All he wanted was to keep the conversation pleasant and lively.

"Anna and I were looking for a bride for me not too long ago," Lukas said, his tone and face darkening, "but then my little sister decided to get engaged to a Turk. Can you believe it? I was just about to make a move on the Rieder daughter, the one with the dark curls. A few months later and it would have been a done deal. Thanks to my inconsiderate sister I don't think any farmer would have me now as his son-in-law, not with such a stigma attached to the family. The town is still laughing about perverted Markus and his Italian."

189

"You can't be serious," Paul said, astonished over the hatred pouring out of his nephew. "Has this country learnt nothing from its past? Are you still condemning Italians and Turks as members of an inferior race? I thought you were a democratic and modern country now, not the fascist Reich!"

"Oh, give it a rest," Lukas said. "No one is killing the foreigners or is making life difficult for them. For all I care they can do as they like as long as they leave us be but marrying them is a completely different matter and you know it. I don't have anything against them but to have a half Turk as my heir or nephew, that is taking modern liberalism a little bit too far. You will find that most people here will agree with me about that. Even if I did not mind, the repercussions in a small place like Heimkirchen for us all would be irreparable. "

"In America everyone is an immigrant," Paul replied sharply. "In our small community there are people from lots of different European countries."

"That just wouldn't work here, believe me," Lukas dismissed the arguments. "Never in a million years."

"Have you even met the guy that Maria has fallen for?" Paul continued.

"I certainly have not," Lukas said loudly. "I wish I had the time to go to Cologne or Hamburg and meet her newest flight of fancy, but someone has to stay at home and look after the family wealth and fortune. When she has enough of being one of many in his harem, then there will still be a seat at the table for her and her bastard child. The damage is done, we will welcome her back as soon as she realises her mistake but I am not going to go and involve myself in their misguided life. I will not shake hands with the Turk and I can only hope that she comes to her senses before she has a little Muslim child to dilute our Bavarian blood line."

"Maybe if you met them you would change your mind and you would be happy for her," Martin finally joined in. "We came for their wedding and we have met the man. Esat is a very solid and respectable man, from what I can tell."

"You went to their wedding? So she really went ahead and did it!" Lukas said, running his hands through his hair in fury.

"She seems very happy," Paul told him, "and the guy is nothing of the things you fear him to be, of that I am certain."

"Of course, he will behave respectably in front of you," Lukas said with a sneer. "He is not going to tell the woman who will provide him with money and a passport that she is going to be one of many, that the gloves come off after the wedding, that he will beat her if she contradicts him and God knows whatever else those Turks do with their wives. You see, we have our share of Gastarbeiter in the country and we can see for ourselves what goes on in their lives."

What Martin and Paul saw was that there was no getting through to Lukas. It seemed pointless to try and make him see how much more actual life-experience the two travellers had accumulated over the years. Lukas was stubborn and closed to reasoning. Put off by his argumentative side neither of the two visitors was planning to return to the farm the next day, or any other day for that matter. It had been a mistake to think that times had changed and the people with them.

"Come to think of it, I am disappointed that you should have crossed the big pond to see their wedding, but you never considered coming here to visit your family before then," Lukas said angrily. "Where is your respect for us?"

"Let's not fight," Paul tried to calm his agitated nephew. "It was just the right time for us when the invitation came. I would have come for your wedding just as easily if you were planning to invite us."

Lukas didn't look at either of them. He stood up from the table and before leaving the room he said quickly: "I need to go back to my work now. I look forward to seeing you tomorrow. Give my regards to my parents when you see them tonight."

"That probably went as well as it could have," Martin informed his uncle, once they were alone. "I knew if we mentioned the wedding he would get upset. This little outburst was actually rather moderate for him. He can't help but feel that we have sided with the enemy now. It is the way he thinks."

"In a way we have sided with his 'enemies'," Paul admitted. "God I had no idea this town could stay so behind the times. Even in our little tucked away backwater in Arizona I feel comparatively cosmopolitan to this."

"Yes Sedona is not Heimkirchen, but maybe it is the Hinterberger family and not necessarily the entire town that has stayed behind the times," Martin said. "Just you wait for tonight.

We are entering the dark middle ages of cloistered life and witch burning. My parents have always been the most blind and radical believers."

The two men made their way back to town. Paul enjoyed rediscovering his old town with the fields and the little wooded areas around it. Away from everyone both of them felt suddenly peaceful and warm again, just as they had hoped they would be when they were imagining their return.

It was strange to rediscover the land that had been the setting for both of their childhoods, and stranger even to do it with each other, when they had never been here at the same time. They found out that they had liked the same beauty spots in the area, used the same hideouts, preferred the same walk ways through the woods and felt equally at home and estranged from the country that had changed so little in its appearance. In the long time since Paul had been here many trees had been felled and a lot more houses had been built. It was amazing how the war with its fighter jets and bombs had missed this area so completely. Compared to most of Germany, the place looked like from a different time. Martin was amazed at how familiar Paul seemed with everything after all those years.

At the Old Inn Paul announced their intention to the receptionist that they would like to extend their stay for another two nights. After those two days they would go hiking together in the mountains, instead of spending their time with the family that did not really want them to be here in the first place.

In the evening they gathered all their courage and braved an evening with the retired parliamentarian and his wife. After the experience at the farm with Anna and Lukas they couldn't have had lower expectations about a successful outcome of this reunion.

Indeed, Magdalena opened the door without much enthusiasm and Martin almost waited in the door to be turned away before daring to step inside. If he was honest with himself, he wouldn't have minded being turned away and spared this. He had never been close to his parents, not in the same way as he was with his new adopted family in America.

What exactly it was he was hoping for from this visit he did not know. A certain longing had always remained within him, even though it was very vague and hard to define rationally.

Besides their praying and preaching, both parents had spent little time with their children. There was little about his life in America that he could tell them that would meet their approval and please them. His life was modest and, even if he was prepared to grossly exaggerate his religious practises, he was unlikely to receive the love and affection he might long for.

Standing on the threshold to the apartment of his childhood so many feelings and thoughts came rushing through his mind. The town of Heimkirchen was and always would be his home, a beautiful setting full of memories but time had not stood still. "No man ever steps in the same river twice, for it's not the same river and he's not the same man" – he remembered those words from Heraclitus. Unlike the countryside and landscape near The Black Eagle, there were lots of new and redecorated buildings in the formerly sleepy town. Seeing it again no longer brought him the same satisfaction or gratification that he had imagined it would.

An even worse alienation was happening with his family. They were his blood but he had no idea how to connect to them, now that he was older and more independent. He was no longer the young boy who would be taking orders, but he had not been there to transform his relationship with them gradually, on to an adult to adult level.

Only now that he had returned and stood outside their door did these thoughts occur to him. He was not sure who or what it was that had beckoned him here. To see the cold woman in the doorway made him feel sad for all the missed opportunities to be part of a loving family, both then and now. His mother invited her visitors in and led them through the long corridor towards the living room.

"Now that Hans-Ulrich is back from Bonn we will have to let out the rooms or move to a smaller apartment," she said, looking at him disapprovingly almost as if it was his fault. "We have fallen on hard times again."

"Won't Lukas help you with the rent? What about father's connections in the administration?" he asked.

"We don't want to live off money that people spent drinking alcohol in The Black Eagle: it would be cursed. Now that the party has dropped Hans-Ulrich his old friends cannot help him either," Magdalena explained.

She stopped before opening the door behind which Hans-Ulrich was waiting for them. "Nobody wants to be associated with him anymore. He has made enemies on both sides of the political spectrum and for most of his supporters he has been away for too long. The time he spent in Bonn has worked against him. People forget their gratitude, and what they owed him after the war," she added bitterly. "I have tried to make him see what a great martyr he has been and how he did the best he possibly could, but he is bitter that he has not succeeded in his ambitions against the Gastarbeiters. He feels he has nothing to show for his efforts, he feels that he has failed us and the Good Lord."

She fought back her tears. "Not a word about politics when you are in there, do you understand? It upsets him too much to talk about it and no one mention that hussy Maria, he is depressed enough."

Martin had to bite his tongue hard not to provoke her. He wanted to ask her why she thought her excessive praying was still not enough to help her husband's predicament and sufferings. For Paul's sake he kept his thoughts to himself. He wanted at least to give his uncle a chance to get past that closed door and have the brotherly reunion with Hans-Ulrich Paul had come here for.

"Of course," Paul reassured her. "We are here to bring you joy, not pain."

They entered the living room together. Hans-Ulrich sat in a large armchair and hardly moved his head when they came in. He stared long and hard at his brother without saying anything. Then, slowly, he got up and spoke.

"You should not have come back," he surprised everyone by saying.

"Hans-Ulrich, why would you say that?" Paul asked as upbeat and cheerfully as he could.

"You would have been better off with your memories unspoilt," Hans-Ulrich said sadly. "Did you really have to come and see how everything is falling to pieces and losing its grace?"

"Hans-Ulrich!" Paul exclaimed happily, ignoring the miserable words of his brother. "Of course I am glad I came. I came to see you. Nothing is deteriorating at all. The farm looks good and Heimkirchen seems to blossom."

"You don't have to try and cheer me up. Did Magdalena tell you to do that? It is no use. The modern buildings have no style, the architects use inferior and cheap materials, the place is overrun by 'Germans' from Czechoslovakia and foreigners from Italy and Turkey. Since you left it has all gone down the drain."

Martin could hardly suppress a giggle at the overly dramatic gloom his father used to portray his perception of the present.

"The farm may look good because they wasted money on painting it and because they use new machinery," Hans-Ulrich continued his lament, "but the soul is gone out of everything. Everything that was good, German and honourable is being diluted and destroyed."

"Oh Hans-Ulrich," Paul laughed heartily and smiled amiably at his brother. "What has happened to you? You sound just like the Nazis in our films? You used to be so full of energy and belief! Where is your faith in God? Does He not send you those trials to grow? You need a good holiday to take your mind off things and you will see that everything is not as bleak as you see it."

"Spending money on a holiday? You think such extravagance will make things better?" Hans-Ulrich asked sarcastically. "Wasting money that could be put to good use? Where is your responsible and charitable streak? I could not justify such an expense for a worldly pleasure."

"I hear you have done a lot of good for everyone," Paul continued with his mission to cheer his brother up. "You have dedicated a lot of time to shape this new nation. You should be proud of yourself for having such a selfless community spirit. Just because it has come to an end there is no need for you to be so upset and pessimistic. I am sure the Good Lord will be more than appreciative that you try so hard every day. Now keep that fighting spirit of yours up and pull yourself together."

Hans-Ulrich just shook his head, not wanting to hear any contradiction.

"It is no use," Magdalena said. "He has been like this for months. Don't think we have not tried the same speeches. The priest, the party friends that he has left and even his work colleagues; all of us have tried to make him see that he is still someone respectable and worthy."

"Do you not want to hear about my travels and my life abroad?" Paul asked, trying to change tactics.

"Why should I care about what you do with your life in America?" Hans-Ulrich said gruffly. "You went away, that is all I need to know. I live here in Heimkirchen and at the city limits that is where my real interest ends these days. Germany does not want me to guide her anymore, so this is all I have now."

"Then there is probably no point in me staying and telling you about my wife and my children either," Martin said curtly.

"Bring them here and we will care." Magdalena said in support of her husband. "Why do run away family members expect those that stay to dedicate their thoughts and prayers to the ones who decided to seek their fortune elsewhere? Anyone who wants to be part of the clan has to stay where the clan is. Those who chose to leave are welcome to their freedom, but they should not come and complain that we have moved on with our own lives without great sentiment and tears."

"You won't be seeing my new family – your relatives - unless you come and visit us," Martin said. "Now father, take that sorry look off your face and do something constructive for a change."

"Leave me alone. I don't need new relatives. I have enough grandchildren already who are here, near me," Hans-Ulrich said abruptly. "Klara and Lukas will carry the Hinterberger tradition and pride forwards. What you do in Arizona with your Indians and cowboys has nothing to do with us."

"Fine, at least now we know where we stand," Martin said and walked to the door. "I should have known that nothing ever matters to you apart from your politics and the church. You love putting everyone else down to make yourself look better but that illusion is only in your head, no one else cares. It is naked pride and the 'Good Lord' doesn't like nor reward that either."

"Oh He will," Hans-Ulrich replied lively, ignoring his son's irony, "if it is used in the name of the greater good. In politics you get to learn that sometimes you have to break the rules to achieve what is for the greater good for everyone."

"You keep telling yourself that. You sound like a Nazi hangman. Come on Paul, we are wasting our time here," he said resigned to the futility of trying to get through to his parents. "You know, father," he said as a parting shot from the living room door frame, "you and this family are the thing that really is deteriorating, not Heimkirchen, not Germany and not the architecture. It is time for a new generation to rebuild the spirit."

"Goodbye, Hans-Ulrich," Paul said. "It was good to see you all the same. I hope you feel better soon. Remember that your family all love you. One day you might come to regret your harsh words from today and then I want you to know that I forgive you."

"Get out you presumptuous fool. Go back to your Uncle Sam, the two of you." Hans-Ulrich shouted. He was feeling dizzy from the anger and the exhaustion which his rage was causing him. He was suffering from high blood pressure these days and was meant to avoid agitation and conflict more than ever.

He had to sit back down in his armchair, overwhelmed with rage and hurt but was well aware that his ego had been flattered by the years of political success and that he was now suffering from the withdrawal of attention. The Good Lord did not like such hubris, his son had been right about that. Lacking control in his private life and seeing his children making such grave mistakes with their lives, such as marrying foreigners and moving abroad, tormented him gravely. He had promised to raise them in the right faith and there they were throwing away all hopes for their salvation and bringing the entire family down with them. Nothing seemed to work or function the way he wanted it to.

The worst thing was that his prayers and worshipping seemed to be completely useless. They no longer provided him with the inner strength and resolve he used to derive from his efforts: this internal crisis was by far the most upsetting development in his life.

He knew his wife suffered from the same symptoms. She still threw herself into her charity work and her obsessive attendance at the church, but when she came back she no longer had the glow of happiness and fulfilment. He could see that she was going through the same hell as he was.

He was sorry he had told Martin that Klara and Lukas were his new pride and joy now: that was not the case at all. He had excluded Otto and Joseph because they would not father any children of their own and so carry the family name in to the future. Because of their commitment to the faith, those two, of course, were the only ones he was most and really proud of.

Klara was simple minded and so was her husband. They probably went to church but they had not the intellectual capacity to truly understand the gospel. Their children would not carry the Hinterberger name and on top of that his daughter rarely looked in on her parents. The only thing that he was remotely proud of was that Klara had given him his first grandchildren – for what it was worth. Not that he was interested in them now, but they were at least some hope for the future and a legacy to leave behind. Lukas might still get married at some point, for men fortunately it was never too late, but he was taking his time and it caused him a lot of concern whether something was wrong with the one son he had left. Deep down he and Magdalena both knew that they were all alone in the world now. The large family from which he came and the many children they had had together had failed to provide them with the social network and support that traditionally came with that territory.

On reflection in his hotel room Paul, agreed with his brother that maybe he should not have come and ruined the perfect memories he had had of his childhood and home. It might have been better to live with the illusion of a distant utopia, rather than knowledge of the sad reality.

Both emigrants had expected to see a booming and proud new Germany but maybe it would take a few more generations before certain elements had grown out of the fabric that made the people.

They were relieved to return to the Old Inn and made immediate plans to depart the next morning on a train towards the Alps. So far both agreed that they had had the best times when they were without relatives in the beautiful Bavarian countryside and decided to see more of it. At the station they sent a postcard to Lukas, saying a quick goodbye without going into further details and explanations for their hasty departure. It was unlikely that either him or Anna were going to be particularly shocked or upset about it.

After a few days of hill walking, the tourists went back to Hamburg to stay with Maria and Esat one last time before boarding their ship home to America.

The newlyweds had plans to travel south themselves to take advantage of the generous honeymoon offer that Anna had made them but on hearing how Lukas had spoken, Esat refused to go.

"I don't care how much money Anna is going to give you for coming," he said agitated. "It would not be right to accept it. The Hinterberger money is cursed with unhappiness. Don't you start and fall in to the same trap. We have managed without them, now let us not get drawn in by greed."

"We are risking nothing," Maria disagreed. "We make a train journey to Heimkirchen. If things get ugly we take the next one back up north. We could do with a little financial help to start us off."

"You stick to your guns," Paul told Esat. "I left without a penny and made my own happiness. It is nice if you do not have to thank anyone for your fortune. If you go down there and it comes to a fight, you will only end up upset and I don't think the money would be worth it."

"Maybe if you left it a while it wouldn't be so awkward," Martin suggested. "Right now they feel very bad about Hans-Ulrich losing his seat in parliament. Give it more time and it might all blow over."

"It bothers me that the money will be left to such greedy and unworthy people," Maria confessed. "We might as well have it instead."

"There is the first green shoot of the Hinterberger greed," Paul warned her. "Leave it be. Who cares what money they have; it hasn't made any of them happy. You have freedom and happiness: you cannot put a price on that."

With that they put the issue to rest and a few days later the American relatives boarded their ship bound back to the States.

Chapter 16: Markus (1966–70)

Ever since Maria had left him that day in the street cafe in Strasbourgh, Markus became disillusioned about his future. It was good that his cousin had refused him so vehemently: this way there was no false hope. Although he had grown up at the farm and at The Black Eagle, and even been adopted to become a Stockmann son, he never felt he fitted in. Too estranged from his own parents over the years, they hadn't given him a sense of belonging. His mother had made that clear when she moved to Munich and 'sold' her son to Anna. In his eyes she was as dead as his father was. For all he knew she probably was.

As far as his sister Gisela was concerned, he regretted that he had never taken the time to get to know her. She had been his sidekick, living his life, joining his causes and never making much of her own existence. She had been the first to know about his love for men and was instantly helpful and encouraging. Yet, when she announced her engagement to Erwin Gahabka Markus had been as surprised as everyone else; that was how quiet she had been about her own affairs. She would probably take him in if he were to contact her in Gottingen but it would not be fair to impose on her after he had used her all of her life. All he could do now was to let her be free and not intrude on her new happiness. In any case, some of his letters to her had been returned so she must have moved and would be difficult to track down.

Markus was still heartbroken and disappointed that things had not worked out with Marco, whose romantic and optimistic character had turned so quickly into alcoholic lethargy and nihilism. In the beginning, the two lovers had seemed so right for each other; he still remembered those happy hours in the woods. They had met without any expectations of each other and discovered shared dreams and ideals, but over the years everything that had bound them together had dissolved. Had their love been merely based on physical attraction and everything else had been an illusion of the mind? Had they really shared a vision? Was their sexual orientation all they had in common? Had the legal situation and the difficulty in finding any other gay man in a small town like Heimkirchen anything to do with it? Meeting a fellow gay man had been hard and dangerous enough, for such a man to be suitable and stay compatible seemed a hopeless battle. By moving to France Markus had taken the worry over legal prosecution out of the equation but in statistical terms, he knew it was still ten or twenty times harder for him to fall in love again.

Nowhere in France seemed to please him particularly. After the disastrous time with Marco in the south he didn't want to return there. The people had been rude and unwelcoming, and solitary walks and hikes in the landscape would only remind him of his estranged former lover. He needed a new location to make a new start. At first he moved to the Alsace, the region by the German border that once had been part of Germany itself and had cultural affinity to both nations. Many people spoke German here and not all of them felt as negative about their neighbouring country as the rest of France. However, he failed to grow roots here, too. He thought about seeing Antoine again but doubted that this would be of any use. His old lover was fixated on youth and Markus was already too old to rekindle the spark that had once been between them, even if Markus had wanted that himself.

He moved to Paris where he hoped that the bigger number of men would improve his chances of meeting someone suitable – despite his dislike of the often sleazy gay scene. He just would have to live with it, he told himself. The country boy inside of him, with the Catholic upbringing and the unspoken sense of propriety, could not feel at ease in the frivolous and flamboyant underground life of the gays here either. He thought it ironic that within the circles of the Hinterberger family of his youth Markus would have been regarded as the most outrageous and colourful character, and yet in the taverns of gay Paris he was by far one of the most conservative characters amongst the clientele. Markus had learnt the language and was used to the local customs but didn't seem to fit in anywhere in France. The few friends that he managed to make in Paris made him feel as if they pitied him more than liked him.

What good would it do him to be in a relationship with a French man? The people here did not understand him; there would always be a cultural gap that he couldn't overcome. Yes, it would be love without fear of legal prosecution but could it be called love? Would it not be just a compromise, a lie, to make him feel better about the misery that his life had become?

While he was wallowing in his indecisiveness, Markus met and became involved with a circle of drama students who were looking for someone to take the part of a German soldier in one of their plays. Temporarily distracted from his personal life he threw himself in to the work for the play. His part was only a very minor one but he attended all rehearsals and surprised his new friends with ideas on how to improve the production. His natural talent for the stage was so apparent that the group asked him to act in and direct the next play they were doing. This next show played to full houses. Over the next two years, even though he only operated in the fringe end of the theatre, he began making a name for himself as a stage director in Paris, working tirelessly on one production after the other.

He went out with a string of actors but as soon as their current project together came to an end, the lovers usually realised that there was little else binding them together. Both moved on to different places, leaving Markus with an empty feeling yet again. Even with a successful and stimulating vocation, he was not made for life in a foreign land.

When the new government in Germany legalised gay relationships in 1969, the gay community in Paris celebrated and he made the decision to move back to his home country. With the name he had made for himself in the Fringe theatre of Paris, he was confident that he could continue with his new occupation someplace in his fatherland. He tried his luck in Berlin but to his dismay he realised that his experience back in Paris had been a unique lucky break. In Berlin no one was impressed with his credentials from France. There was such huge competition, even in the amateur section, and with his southern accent and status as an outsider he failed to make an impression.

The gay scene here was not or him either. He found the same flamboyant and outrageous characters in the bars and cafés. The legislation had only recently been changed, which meant that there was still a big sense of fear and distrust around. He had also been warned off a certain masculine, sadistic type of men that were infamous in parts of the city, who would lure other gays to their home and then brutally beat them, knowing full well that few of the victims would dare report it to the authorities. Markus felt out of his depth and sometimes wished he had never left Heimkirchen, or Antoine, but such fancy ideas were ridiculous and he knew it. The man from the Alsace would not have stayed with him for much longer, Markus had always known that. Could his life with Marco have turned out differently, if only the two had never left Heimkirchen? Would the new legal situation also bring a change in his home town, to an extent that Markus could live there again?

He failed to make a new circle of friends here in the north - it was like being in an entirely different country. People made fun of his accent and treated him as if he was a base idiot. Theatre wise the city was a disappointment, too. Unless he invested his own money into a production no one was prepared to work with him artistically. He produced one play by Sartre, which was well received, but never made him back the money he had put in. Feeling that he had nothing left to lose, he disregarded Maria's warning and made his way back to Bavaria. He had finally learnt the lesson that the grass was not always greener on the other side. Hopefully such a statement might convince Anna of the depth of his regrets, if he dared to face her. He thought it too risky to just turn up at the farm. To see Anna he would have to bypass Lukas and he could think of no other way than to hire a middle man to do that for him. Ironically, he hired the very same man who had been looking for him on behalf of Anna. Despite Markus's new identity as Andreas Fiedrich and the beard that he was wearing these days Thomas Holzapfel, the detective, immediately recognised the run-away man from the pictures Anna had given him. Thomas was delighted: if he played his cards right he could cash in twice for his services.

Thomas told Markus about his long search for the missing son and how heartbroken Anna had been when they had finally given up. The two men agreed that Thomas would first test the waters by paying Anna a visit and telling her that 'new evidence' about Markus and his whereabouts had materialised. Should she still be interested in pursuing those new leads a meeting with Markus would be arranged.

When the detective called the farm to speak to Anna about the 'new developments' regarding Markus he could not speak to her directly. Lukas and Helga were both incredibly protective and would not let him talk to her. Unsure of their agenda, Thomas said nothing but he realised that letters to Anna might also be opened by the two of them. He would have to catch her alone and to do so he had to stake out the farm and watch Lukas and his movements and routines; that way an eventual reunion of Anna with Markus would not be prevented or interrupted by the jealous new manager.

Thomas was pleased to find Lukas to be a man of regular and predictable habits. The man got up with the sun and took to inspecting a different part of the farm every day before breakfast, which he ate every day with Anna in the main house without fail. Then he would spend the day in the office in the restaurant building and only leave it if there was a particular problem outside that needed to be attended to. Lukas never left the farm and he didn't return to Anna's living quarters until the late afternoon, where he sometimes had a cup of coffee and a slice of cake with her. In the evenings Anna would be glued to her new television set and visits from anybody at that time were not welcome.

After he had observed Lukas for a week and had established his patterns, Thomas decided that it was time to focus on the movements around Anna's house. Helga was much more unpredictable and never seemed to be away from Anna for long.

Markus, waiting in his hotel for new developments, was getting impatient. He appreciated and fully supported Thomas' argument that they might only have one shot at getting through to Anna. If it failed, security around the old woman would be tightened and they may not be able to contact her again. But Markus was growing impatient and increasingly desperate for news.

Finally there was a breakthrough. Thomas saw Helga getting into a taxi on a Friday morning and Lukas had already left the building following his daily breakfast with Anna; he did not waste any time and rushed inside the house.

Anna was by herself and asleep in her bedroom. It took the detective a while to find her and wake her up.

"Of course I want you to find my Markus if you can," Anna said, after Thomas had told her about the 'new leads', but she said it with much less enthusiasm than at the beginning of his search for the missing son.

"What are the chances of succeeding?" she asked, business like.

"I would say very high," Thomas said, encouragingly. "My visit here was just a formality to establish that you still want to see him. I remember particularly how opposed some of your family were to your search. In cases like this feelings can change. How would Lukas feel if you brought Markus back here?"

"Oh my," Anna said, sounding tired and confused. "He won't like it but he and I have an agreement."

"Will that agreement hold?" he probed a little more.

"We all resigned ourselves to the fact that Markus was irretrievably lost. I believe Lukas will honour his word. Before we make big waves and upset everyone maybe I should meet with my son alone, without Lukas getting wind of it. There are a few things I would like to discuss with him. Lukas should really not be present then."

"We can arrange that," he said, pleased with the progress.

"Unfortunately, the meeting would have to be here," she said. "I can't move much these days. I can hardly leave my bed, let alone the house."

"How soon would you like to see him?" Thomas carefully asked.

"As soon as you can bring him here," she said, with a cracking voice. All her bitterness and anger dissolved as she allowed herself to hope again but she felt incredibly weak and vulnerable. "I miss him so much."

"He misses you too," Thomas said reassuringly. "Now that I know how you feel I can tell you that he has sent me here to speak with you. He is very concerned that he would cause you more pain than he already has but he can come at any time you suggest."

Anna was becoming tearful. Could her life be complete for one last time with her beloved golden boy back in her arms? She didn't dare let herself trust this new hope just yet. The sadness and the hurt over his betrayal, his abandonment of her, all of it came flooding back to her now. One minute she was angry with him, the next she was happier than ever.

Only a month ago she had received a letter from her niece Maria declining the invitation for her and her Turkish husband to come and stay at The Black Eagle for their honeymoon. The rebuff had hurt Anna and she had resigned herself to the fact that her life was coming to an end. Herbert was dead, her son was gone and that letter had confirmed that any efforts to make something worthwhile from the leftovers of this torn apart family were fruitless.

Having her hopes raised once again was a terrible thing if it were not to come true: she couldn't risk being hurt again.

"Are you quite sure he will want to see his old mother?" she asked fearfully.

"Very certain," he replied. "As a matter of fact, he is waiting for my call in his hotel right now."

"Tell him to come tonight then," she said. "I watch television every night after seven in the evening and I allow no disturbance at that time. Helga and Lukas both do not care for this kind of entertainment." She stopped for a moment then she looked into the detectives eyes with wonder. "Do you really think it would be possible to see Markus tonight?" she asked, fighting her excitement.

"Yes, I can guarantee that: I will bring him personally. He will be here by seven if you wish. I guess you must have a lot to talk about when he comes. I suggest you better rest yourself," Thomas said.

Pleased with the way his mission had succeeded, he stole himself away from the building and walked to his car which he had parked further along the lane and out of sight from the farm.

Unfortunately Markus didn't answer the phone at his hotel. Thomas drove to the hotel but the receptionist told him that the guest in question had been out since the day before. All Thomas could do was to wait for him in the foyer of the hotel. When by midnight Markus had still not appeared, he left an urgent message for his client with the staff and returned to his home.

Markus had found the eternal waiting for news from Heimkirchen very trying. Normally he spent a lot of his spare time reading plays and making notes for possible future theatre productions but his mind just would not settle and focus on any of his current projects. The walls of his hotel room seemed to drive him mad. Despite going for long walks and extended stays in the diner of the hotel, the days would not pass.

Thomas had, of course, kept him informed on a regular basis and from that Markus had assumed it would probably be another week before contact with Anna was made. Bored and impatient he had decided to take a train to Munich and spend some time in the city, where distractions were easier to come by.

He was revisiting the sights of Munich, which he had seen when he was a little boy. His mother had taken him to see an aunt of hers who had lived here. From the station he walked through the old city gates towards the city hall and then he stood in awe outside the Bavarian State Theatre.

For a brief moment Markus considered looking for his real mother Erica but he was still in two minds about it. As he walked up north towards the large English Gardens, he remembered that it was not far from here to the family grave at the Old City Cemetery. It was a macabre but certain way to find out if his mother was still alive and he found that her name was not yet on any of the grave stones. Unsure whether to be pleased about this or not he carried on walking mindlessly, trying to get his head around his ambiguous feelings about his complicated family relations.

During his stroll in the English Gardens he bumped in to an old school friend of his, Balthasar, whom he remembered as a silly and somewhat misguided boy until he - despite his young age - had volunteered for the army during the last days of the war. Balthasar had lost one of his legs because of an American grenade that exploded too close to him and buried a lot of shrapnel in his flesh. By the time he had reached a doctor it had been too late to save the leg. Despite this unlucky turn of his life he seemed a cheerful man.

"I am used to it," Balthasar said, matter of factly. "One can adjust to most things in life if one really wants to. I got lucky: I found myself work and a wife who doesn't mind my ugly stump."

"I am glad to hear it," Markus replied, unsure what to make of his friend's remarks.

"I heard about you running away with the help," Balthasar said, without further preliminaries. "You must be glad they changed the law. Now you can do what you want."

Balthasar smiled with benign friendliness that touched Markus but left him a little confused. What were Balthasar's motives?

"You should not believe everything you hear," Markus replied distantly. He was not going to admit to anything unless he found out more about Balthasar and his reasons for being so forward. Just because the law had changed did not mean that blackmailers had lost all of their incentive for business. Was there a threat from this man? Or had Markus found a kind and caring friend who was not immediately repelled by the thought of a gay man. Markus found that hard to imagine, after all he himself had been disgusted by his sexual urges for large parts of his life and considered himself lucky to have met a man like Antoine when he was so young: a man with confidence, experience, worldly wisdom, who so easily and calmly healed and reassured the shy boy. Without him Markus might never had the confidence to live out his desires and what he now believed to be his destiny.

"Of course, my friend, of course." Balthasar agreed cheerfully. "Don't get all uptight with an old friend. I can see you are getting all worked up about me knowing your secrets. I am sorry, maybe I should never have mentioned it."

"I don't think you can know much about me," Markus said.

"Let me tell you a little about myself then," Balthasar explained. "After the war I moved to Munich to live with my widowed aunt. There was no use for a cripple like me in the countryside so my family hoped that I could make myself useful here. Aunt Margit was quite a character. Amongst her friends were several rather effeminate men, one of whom she had secretly married to give him an alibi, to protect him from the Nazis. That man always reminded me so much of you and your theatrical ways. You were like two peas in a pod, him and you. It was then that I understood about you. My mother always told me the latest gossip about Heimkirchen and of course about the Hinterberger family, the farm and The Black Eagle Inn. She never mentioned once that you had a sweetheart. You were far too good looking and important to not have had the opportunity for a romance or two. So when the rumours about the Italian man reached me I already knew. I wish you had met my aunt while she was still alive, she was a barrel of laughs and could have helped you find somebody suitable."

"Are you....ehm, I mean are you sure that you are not yourself ... you know?" Markus asked awkwardly.

"No, I am afraid I am not that interesting," Balthasar said with a wink. "I do like the bars and the people. I grew up with that kind of life. The sworn secrecy amongst my aunt and her friends, the jolliness and the outrage, I loved it from the beginning. I find it very entertaining."

"Really, you do?" Markus said in disbelief. "I have come to abhor it. The innuendoes, everything being about sex, the sleaziness ... I cannot bear it and I hate myself for being born that way and having to be one of them."

"I don't know which bars you have been visiting to get such an unfavourable impression. My wife and I go to some friendly and open-minded taverns for a laugh and for the company. Let me show you some of those establishments in Munich and let me change your negative views about the gay world."

Reluctantly Markus agreed. He felt both excited and fearful about this excursion. Could it be that there was a little corner of the world right here in Munich where he could fit in, with people who understood him, that he was not destined to be alone and in hiding forever?

The bar that Balthasar had suggested had a red lantern hanging outside the entrance, implying a seedy and disreputable inside. Balthasar had explained that this only served to keep casual and unsuspecting customers from entering an establishment they might disapprove of.

The interior was just like any traditional Bavarian pub: wooden panels, Bavarian blue and white patterns on both the curtains and the table cloths and long tables with benches for the patrons to mingle. None of the people here were obviously camp or effeminate, nothing hinted at the special character of the establishment. So much so that Markus wondered if he had come to the right place. He ordered a beer and sat down by the counter and waited nervously for his friends.

Balthasar and his wife soon joined him. Barbara was beautiful and a much younger woman than Markus had expected. How had Balthasar managed to get her when he only had one leg, Markus wondered. They seemed a very odd couple but then again, with such charm and happiness, it was not a complete surprise that Barbara had succumbed to his charms.

"It gets much busier here on the weekends," Barbara told Markus with an immediate familiarity. "If you are looking for a date you should come back then."

After his disappointing experience in the allegedly tolerant France, Markus didn't dare to dream that far ahead and said nothing in response.

"Balthasar said you would be like this," she said and pushed him encouragingly with her elbow.

"I would be like what?" he asked surprised.

"Serious and worried and God knows what. You know: no one is going to bite you in here. You are amongst friends. So for God's sake try to relax and have a good time. Maybe have another beer. You're a handsome man, you are going to find it easy to make a good match. Just lose that frown my dear. We frown upon that," she said and laughed over her own witticism.

"Herby," she called to the man behind the bar, "turn up the music and play something more cheerful, will you."

"Do you really think the new legislation will make a difference?" Markus asked Barbara a bit later. "I cannot see it changing the country and the people overnight. You know it still doesn't even feel right to me to wink at a man. Even in here, I am sorry, I am just a little bit overwhelmed," he added.

"Oh well, I am sure over time all of it will get easier," Balthasar said optimistically. "For you personally, and for the country. The new law is a big first step. That is important. Now that it is no longer illegal, the stigma will gradually disappear. People need time. The uneducated and inexperienced average person picked up a lot of ideas from newspapers and gossip about the ones who were caught and put in prison. Of course they were led to believe that it was something wrong and they did not think any more about it. Now there won't be lawsuits and court cases in the papers and that will stop the negative associations. Once they see it no longer as something criminal and punishable, hopefully it will become acceptable in their minds. Sometimes the law is ahead of popular opinion; sometimes it is the other way round: for once the law was quicker. It will take a while before this attitude spreads to the countryside, and to old fashioned Bavaria especially, but I am sure over the next few years life will become much easier for you guys."

"How can you be so sure?" Markus asked.

"I feel that the majority of people don't care about the private life of their neighbours," Balthasar stated.

Right then the music changed to an old folk tune with a gripping marching beat that Markus had not heard in years. The song immediately cheered him up, more than the inspirational words of Balthasar.

The bartender Herby dimmed the lights and turned on some revolving glitter lamp. Two men got up and danced together. They were wearing their traditional Bavarian brown leather trousers and Markus was amused by how odd this looked.

"Come on and dance with me," Barbara challenged him. "I never get to dance much," she explained. "You can see why Balthasar can't help me and the other men in here would rather dance with each other."

"I don't know how," Markus said shyly.

"I'll teach you," she said, grabbed him by the arm and dragged him on to the dance floor. Barbara was a good teacher and easily controlled his moves. He found it hard to keep up with her quick steps. He was also distracted by the male couples dancing with each other and the occasional flirtatious wink he got from the onlookers.

Later in the evening Markus described to them in much detail how he had made his escape to France, about the split from Marco, the rebuffing from Maria in Strasbourgh, and his loneliness in Paris and Berlin.

"I am glad you have come home," Barbara said smiling. "The long journey has come to an end and you are back to square one, where you probably should have stayed all along."

"Don't say that, Barbara," Balthasar disagreed. "There were great moments in his adventures and those experiences will always be with him. It sounds to me as if you have learnt to appreciate what you have got at home and you could not have done that without leaving first, could you?"

"I am not home free yet," Markus interjected. "Munich is not my home either, you see. I am a country boy and now that people know about me, how could I return as if nothing ever happened? The Black Eagle was everything to me. I just don't know if I could return there."

"You will soon know," Barbara said.

"Whenever mother talks of your Aunt Anna she says how soft she has become," Balthasar told him. "If she really won't have you back then you can always learn to adjust to life in the city. It is easier than you think, especially with friends like us. You just need to put your mind to it and stop moaning about the past. That is not going to get you anywhere in life, ever. There are restaurants and inns here where you would be able to find work, Herr Andreas Fiedrich," he laughed at the mentioning of Markus' alias.

Markus felt elated by the joyful energy that this couple shared had. They seemed a healthy middle ground between the stern seriousness of his family background and the flamboyant life in Paris and Berlin.

Behind them Herby was setting up a little stage.

"Oh! The cabaret," Barbara said, "I wonder who they have on tonight?"

The answer was a man who had badly dressed up as a woman came on stage and sang a terrible rendition of an old Marlene Dietrich song. Markus was in tears of laughter because in the dress the man looked so butch and masculine, just like Jack Lemmon in 'Some Like It Hot', it was hilarious.

The next act was a man who looked exactly the opposite. It was hard for Markus to tell if it really was a man or a woman. Even the voice only just gave it away; the husky tone could have almost been a contralto.

Markus had seen this kind of thing all before both in Paris and Berlin but the cosiness of the show here made it more fun and less repulsive for him.

"You have a lot to learn," Barbara said as she watched the changing expressions on his face. "I have seen this many times before. Most new comers on the scene have their self-loathing and insecurities to cure. I will help you through this liberation process too."

By the end of the night Markus was a little tipsy. It was too late for him to take the train back to his hotel, so Barbara made up the spare guest bedroom in their apartment and tucked him in before going to bed herself.

"Welcome to your new life," she said before kissing him good night.

Unaware of Thomas' progress with Anna, Markus decided to stay in Munich a little longer. These new friends were exactly the distraction he had needed and longed for and Barbara assured him that even if there had been news about Anna, there was no immediate cause for action. The reunion might just as well take place next week or the week after that.

Since the end of the war Balthasar had worked in the post office in Munich and had loved the job for its simplicity. His good leg had never given him much trouble until a few years ago when it suddenly became painful and stiff. A thorough examination and an x-ray had shown that an overlooked piece of shrapnel from the grenade was close to his spinal cord, too close to remove by surgery. He lived in early retirement now because of it but refused to let the danger of further immobilisation stand in the way of his life.

The reunited school mates spent the next two days strolling through town, looking at the sights and talking about their lives.

"I can put you in touch with some people in the theatre business," Balthasar offered. "Maybe not the top movers and shakers but if you wanted to spend some time in the fringe you could gain experience. You wouldn't have to be a 'nobody', as you were in Berlin. You'd have a decent chance to prove yourself. You know how full of gays and closet gays the show world is."

"Yes, I know about that," Markus said with amusement.

"Let us go and see a few shows while you are staying with us. Barbara and I have not been anywhere for a while ourselves," Balthasar suggested.

That evening the three of them went to see a simple farce, a comedy of errors set on a farm, spoken entirely in dialect. Markus laughed all the way through. Barbara and Balthasar took him to the after-party at the director's house, a close friend of Barbara's and the three of them had a great time. Markus even made some promising new contacts.

The next day they went to see a classic production of Goethe's 'Faust' in one of the more renowned theatre houses in Munich and met with a few of the actors in a bar frequented by show stars, after the performance had finished. Markus felt a little bit out of place. Everyone seemed so educated and intellectual, far from what he thought about himself with his farming background.

"Relax," Barbara said, egging him on. "None of them have studied drama either. Don't be fooled by the big words."

The weekend promised more entertainment and although he meant to go back to his hotel and get fresh clothes and check for news from Thomas, he was too drawn in to this new life to feel any urgency about it.

With his shy and inhibited ways Markus gave a genuinely good first impression, instantly popular with the single men.

He enjoyed the attention but none of the men he had been introduced to had an immediate impact on him. It was good to know that he had options though. It had been a long time since he had enjoyed himself as much as he had these past few days.

When the long weekend was over he decided that it was time to go back to his hotel. Even if Thomas had not missed him so far, the hotel management might wonder where he had gone to.

Drunk on the positive experience of the past few days he arrived cheerfully at his hotel and asked for his keys. The receptionist looked at him with contempt and called her supervisor before handing over the key. Markus had only booked the room until Friday and it was Sunday now. A Thomas Holzapfel had paid an advance and persuaded the management to keep the room for him, he was told. Markus had forgotten about the booking completely. Had it not been for Thomas showing up every day and vouching for Markus, he would have found himself out on the street.

The serious looking receptionist handed him a bundle of letters. Markus fell out of his happy clouds when he saw the series of notes from the detective, all marked as urgent and demanding an immediate reply.

He went up to his room and read through them all in chronological order.

"Contact me immediately. Anna wants to see you tonight. T.H."

"Where are you? Anna was very disappointed last night. Need to re-schedule a.s.a.p. T.H."

"Markus, I hope you have a good excuse. Anna has been waiting for you for two days now. She is very emotional, contact me immediately. T.H."

"New developments. Stay at the hotel, await my call. T.H."

Markus went downstairs to make a call to Thomas but the detective was out. He contemplated making the journey to Heimkirchen to meet Anna on his own accord. There was no reason now why he shouldn't – only the last message from the detective that told him not to move. He wondered what that could be about. If Anna was ready to meet her son then nothing really should stand between them.

Was the caution to do with Lukas? Frankly, Markus could not imagine that this could really be necessary. Anna might be upset with Markus for having gone missing for a few days but if she had been prepared to see him a few days ago then Markus would surely be able to charm his way back into her heart now. These last few days could not possibly have destroyed her love if all those years in France had failed to do so.

He waited by the phone all day until late in the evening and kept calling Thomas frequently, but to no avail: the detective seemed to have disappeared.

Markus was restless and wanted to find out what was going on but managed to control his urge to go out and do something about it. The next day passed very slowly. Surely in the evening he would be able to reach Thomas or to hear from him. The receptionist was starting to tire of his continuous requests to call Thomas for him and so Markus started to use a pay telephone nearby. At eleven o-clock he gave up and went to bed. The next morning he decided to take matters into his own hands and took a train to Heimkirchen and then a taxi to the farm.

He parked the car before it came into viewing distance of the farm and approached the farm slowly on foot until he could just about observe the movements from behind a tree, waiting for an opportune moment to enter the main house without running into Lukas.

Lunch time came and went without Lukas appearing to join his aunt in the main house. Sure that it was safe, he gradually moved closer to the building and finally leapt out of the shadows of a newly built parking garage and ran towards Anna's house. He entered quickly and quietly. Inside he searched for signs of anyone being in the house, all the while worrying that he might run into Lukas instead of his aunt.

There was nobody around at all. The living room, the kitchen and the bedrooms upstairs, all were empty. He was just about to steal himself out of the house when he heard the door fall shut downstairs. The person who had entered the house seemed to be going to the kitchen and then settled in the living room. The steps were too slow to belong to Lukas who always rushed and hurried everywhere.

Markus decided to take a risk and made his way down the stairs as quietly as he could but the creaking noises of the old stairs easily gave him away and by the time he had come down to the ground floor Helga was expecting him with fists rooted at her sides.

"Look what the cat dragged in," she said pointedly. "I didn't think you would have the guts."

"Hello Helga," he replied sheepishly.

"Have you come to take more money or why are you sneaking around the house like a thief?" she said with disdain. "You only need to ask her, she will probably give it to you, that is how much she loves you. Shame on you for breaking her heart you greedy bugger."

"I have not come to take anything," Markus said calmly. "I deserve your scolding, we both know I do, but I am here to mend that heart of hers if it is not too late."

"Oh really, how do you think you are going to do that?" Helga said with distrust in her voice.

"I don't know for sure. I haven't seen her in years," Markus admitted. "Does it not matter that I am here and willing to try?"

"You are not the first vulture to come to the dying bed of a vulnerable old fool and pretend to be the only one who was ever interested in their happiness. What convenient timing for your change of heart, so close to her death. Just how stupid do you think I am?" she asked angrily. "It's one of the oldest tricks I know and I am not going to stand by and watch. Lukas stood by her all those years, even when she favoured you over him. He should reap the benefits for his hard work. Don't you come swooping in here and take it away from him just before the finishing line."

"You may find this hard to believe but I am not the evil person you make me out to be. I have changed. Would you rather she didn't see me? A few days ago she was waiting for me impatiently. I came as soon as I could," he explained.

"You said she was waiting for you? That is the first I have heard of this," Helga said firmly. "I would have known if that were the case, I was here all the time. She would have told me."

"I swear it is true! You remember Herr Holzapfel? He contacted her on my behalf to find out if she even wanted to see me. I was meant to meet her a few days ago, only I was away and didn't receive her invite until yesterday. Where is she?"

"Oh, that was why he suddenly called us," Helga said slowly, taking it all in. "Anna is in hospital," she continued with anger in her voice. "The old fool of a house doctor had diagnosed her with angina. He thought her breathlessness and lung pains were part of it without giving it a second thought. Why she kept insisting on calling the old quack I never understood. What the idiot overlooked was that she had also a tumour in her lung."

"I have to see her!" he said immediately.

"You would like that, wouldn't you," Helga said quietly. "Get to her before she dies to squeeze the last few pennies out of her."

"I don't care about the money, I want her forgiveness. If she really is going to die I want her to do so in peace," he swore.

"You want that for yourself," she corrected him. "Think about it before you do. The last few days she has been very agitated. I am surprised she did not tell me why, if it is true and she was waiting for you. They brought her to the hospital to check her angina and that was when they found out about her lungs. She really is dying, Markus. Do you want to push her over the edge by showing up now? The doctors are trying to keep her calm and still, so the angina won't get worse."

"Of course I want to see her. I know I was a selfish good-for-nothing but I can make up for it now, can't I? She deserves to hear that I did really love her."

"I am not so sure about all that," she contradicted. "You want to ease your guilty conscious but that is just selfish. Do you think that would be in her best interest?"

"She is dying anyway. I would rather have her die happy than upset, don't you agree?" he asked. "Even if it were a lie, it would do her good to hear it."

"You will have to speak to Lukas about it. He is the one who called the ambulance. The doctors treat him as the next of kin. If you want to see her you will have to convince him to let you see her. Good luck with that," she said sarcastically.

"Do you really think she is better off not seeing me?" Markus asked provocatively. "All anger and hurt feelings aside, take a moment and look at the whole picture and what is best for her. She has been searching for me for several years and waiting for me over the last few days. I don't want to disappoint her, do you?"

"I don't know, Markus," she said, her body sagging and the fight receding from her body. "I don't know. I hate you for what you did to her and us, but I admit I don't know what is the lesser of the two evils. You should have come back a long time ago. She waited and waited for you."

Markus was close to tears. "I am so sorry, Helga. If I had known then what I know now..."

"I tell you what," Helga said suddenly straightening up. "If you promise not to ask for money - or even for forgiveness - then I will try and sneak you in. If you love her, then meet her on her own terms and let her say what she wants to say. Can you do that?"

"I promise." Markus replied sternly.

"Swear on your life."

"I swear."

"Lukas will kill me when he finds out but you are right, she would probably want to see you one last time, even if it means she dies from the excitement. Just be very careful not to agitate her, you hear me?"

"Thank you," Markus said with relief.

On the way to the hospital Helga asked him about his sister Gisela.

"You two were always so close I would have thought you would be living with her in Gottingen by now. We were all very surprised when the detective could not find you up there. What happened between you two?"

"A lot of misunderstandings and childish rows," he admitted. "I wrote to her from France once but she was very cold in her reply. I think it was because of a miscarriage. Afterwards, I didn't write to her for a long time and when I did my letter came back undelivered. I have moved myself a lot since then and have not stayed in the same city for very long. I don't know if she ever wrote to me with her new address or whether she meant for me not to know where she lives now. Trying to find her and put things right between us will be my next task."

"It would be a miracle if ever two Hinterbergers should get on with each other," Helga said, shaking her head. "All you lot ever do is fight, even the best allies turn against each other in this family."

"Yes, it seems like that," Markus agreed, "but we also often make up again."

"Yes, when it suits you," she said almost under her breath.

At the hospital a different shift of nurses and doctors were on duty and there was no problem getting Markus access to Anna's room. The receptionist of the warden mistook Markus for Lukas and led Helga and him to the room without asking for credentials.

Anna was awake when the two of them entered her room.

"Mother!" Markus said with a trembling voice and rushed towards her. Immediately the old servant could see how genuine his regret was. Nobody could be that good an actor she thought.

Anna smiled at Markus warmly, clearly happy and relieved to see him.

"My boy has finally come home," she said calmly. "It is about time."

"I know, mother, I know," he said and finally allowed himself to cry.

"Oh, don't be so dramatic," Anna said scolding him but her face was all lit up and betrayed her happiness over his love which showed in his tears.

"Mother I am..." he started but the old woman interrupted him rudely.

"I don't want to hear it, darling. Not a word, you understand?"

"Of course...."

"Markus, I know all about you. I am your mother, remember? There is no need for you to say anything to ease your conscience. A mother always forgives," she said with glassy watering eyes.

"Thank you, but I really..." he started again

"Shush, Markus!" Helga hissed. "Remember your promise."

"There is a lot I should ask you to forgive me as well," Anna told him, ignoring her servant, "but will it do us any good if we both remind each other of our darkest moments?" she asked her son.

"You have nothing to apologise for," he said resolutely.

"Oh, I have," she disagreed. "For crowding a young man who needed his freedom, for clinging to you so unhealthily, to name just a few of my lesser offences. There are many things I do regret but I did not know any better then and neither did you. We are both here now, that is what matters."

"I just wish..." he tried once more.

"I am sure you do," she interrupted him again, "and I wish many things too. But all is well that ends well."

He nodded full of heartfelt agreement.

"Now let us cut to the chase," Anna suddenly said, business like. "We may not have that much time left. Tell me young man, are you just visiting or are you back for good?"

"That depends," Markus said unsure now that he had been put on the spot so quickly. He meant to honour his promise to Helga to not ask for anything or to negotiate any conditions.

"What does it depend on my dear," Anna asked abruptly. "Whether I give you back The Black Eagle or whether I am going to die? What exactly have you come here for?"

After her previously forgiving demeanour there was hurt and anger in her question.

"I have come here to see you," Markus replied. "I know Lukas is running the show now and he is doing a fine job. I don't think I could come back here after the scandals."

"If you want the restaurant back you can have it," Anna said, matter of factly. "I won't let you run the farm. Lukas is better at that. I have already given him a lot of land as reward for his efforts. You coming back won't be much of a blow to him now. When I die everything will fall to you as my legal son anyway and you will have to come to an arrangement with Lukas. If you don't want the farm then please stay for my sake. For the little time I have left I would like you to stay."

"Of course I'll stay if you want me to," he promised tearfully.

"When I go, I want you to look after Maria. She lives in Hamburg now with a Turkish husband. Hans-Ulrich and

Magdalena have disowned her. I was always fond of that lovely, happy girl, promise me you find her and help her out if she needs something, will you?" Anna demanded.

"Of course. In any way I can. I liked her, too."

"I always had a thing for the black sheep in the family, maybe because I myself was one in disguise," Anna said with a wink but then she was struck by a coughing fit.

Helga called the nurse who brought the patient a drink of water and then brought the reunion to an abrupt end by rudely asking the visitors to come back another time.

In the car home, Helga gently touched his shoulder and said: "That went very well. I was worried she might overreact but the drugs they give her must be working."

"I wish she had not been on drugs so that I could be absolutely sure she meant to forgive me," Markus said doubtfully.

"Come on Markus, it is exactly as she said: she has always forgiven you everything you did," Helga said composed. "Without the drugs she might have given you a hard time at first but she would always have come round eventually. You really impressed me in there today. I am relieved to see you have turned your life around."

"I am still working on it," he said evasively.

"Now what has become of that Marco?" Helga asked him pointedly.

"Oh well..." he stammered, "I had better not talk about it."

"Have you got someone new?" she asked him, not letting him off the hook.

"No, and I am not comfortable talking about any of this," he replied resolutely.

"I can tell," Helga replied amused, "but not talking about it is not going to make it go away. We all know so you might as well be upfront about it. You know it is legal now."

"Aren't you shocked or disgusted by it?" he asked her, but Helga just giggled.

"I may be living in the middle of nowhere but that doesn't mean I can't think like a human being. Why would I judge you for that? The stealing I didn't like, or the lying...."

"OK. I get it. How does Anna feel? Lukas? Any of the Hinterberger family?" he asked fearfully.

"I would not try and lodge with Hans-Ulrich and Magdalena," Helga said with a little wink. "I don't think Lukas has an opinion on the issue either way, he is far too busy thinking about money and the farm to have strong and thought-through moral beliefs either way. He will be against it out of tradition, but he might gracefully over-look it if you two are able to patch things up and sort out a deal between you."

"What about you and Anna? How do you feel about it?" he asked when Helga didn't say any more.

"I don't care what you do as long as nobody gets hurt," she replied coolly. "They made us believe all sorts of things, that the Jews murdered people in weird rituals and that they carried diseases. Of course, I had never met any Jews personally here in Heimkirchen, and none of us even trusted the Protestants but, over the last two decades, people have started to talk differently about things and I have learnt about blindly repeating other people's opinions and making hasty judgements. If the government thinks what you do behind closed doors can be made legal, then I will look the other way, but I will always be suspicious about you because of your other sins, I might as well tell you right now."

"Fair enough," Markus said, relieved.

"Anna singled you out because you showed her that there was more to life than the farm. You made her laugh, you charmed her and that thing that you are – I am not sure what to call it – it is part of that special quality that she secretly likes. Now that we all know, you might as well be honest about it. If you hide it, we would still know and be sure that Anna will want to have her say in your choice of … partner, even if it is a man! I think she will surprise us all."

Chapter 17: The Funeral (1970)

Back at the farm, Helga invited Markus to stay in one of the spare bedrooms in the main building. She herself had moved into one of them a few months ago to be closer to Anna during the night, in case she should be needed.

"It will be good to have someone there," Helga confessed. "The house has been terribly empty. With every new farm acquisition Lukas has gained more empty living space that we did not really need. We used to have plenty of people around here with us in the old days but he has moved all staff to the old Filser house. It is part of why Anna is so lonely, I think."

"I am glad to be here. It wouldn't feel right to be staying at The Black Eagle again, not after all I've done," Markus admitted.

"I am sorry but you will have to get over that if you are going to stay," Helga told him.

"What happened to my old room?"

"Lukas turned it in to a luxury guest room; you wouldn't be able to move back in there. Spartan that he is, he sleeps in a small annex to the office. We would have to find you somewhere else."

"I probably should just stay here with you and Anna," Markus suggested.

"She'd like that," Helga said with a warm smile.

"I wonder what Lukas is going to do."

"Surely some gesture of protest."

"I should go over and speak to him right now," he suddenly suggested. "We should bury the hatchet once and for all. I know there are hard feelings but now that Anna is going to die it would be a great parting gift for her to see us getting along at last."

"Markus, you have had years away from all this to get your distance and sort out your own head. Now that you know what you want and have grown up it makes perfect sense to you to cut all the unnecessary pride and stupidity and just come to a sensible solution. Lukas has not had that luxury, he has not had time to take a step back and think. He has had a tough time of it and no one has helped him," Helga explained. "You can't expect him to make that sudden leap forward that took you years to make yourself."

Markus realised that the old woman was right. Seeing things from his cousin's point of view showed there was much more than just the old childish rivalry to consider.

"Has he not grown up yet? He is 34 now, isn't he?" Markus asked.

"Yes, but his life and his childhood were not the same as yours," she pointed out. "You were much older by the time you were given a chance to show what you were made of. You and Gisela had a carefree time of it before you volunteered to work at The Black Eagle. There was no pressure on you. Lukas was much younger when he got dragged into the business. He hadn't had years of childish freedom, not under Hans-Ulrich, and then the war started. All that changed him and made him the stuck up man that he is. Right now is probably the worst possible time for him to speak to you. You will need all of your wits to make that conversation a success."

Markus became quiet and wondered what it would take to turn the rivalry between him and his cousin into a friendship or partnership that would last. He had come here in peace and had no intentions of upsetting Lukas in the least, but as Helga had said, correctly, it would take two to tango and if only Markus was willing to move forward, then living and working together would be very difficult.

While Helga was making dinner he went to the telephone and tried again to get hold of Thomas. At last he was successful.

"Where have you been?" Markus asked the detective reproachfully. "First you give me all this grief for not sitting by the phone in my hotel room and then you go missing yourself. I have been calling you for two days."

"I am sorry, Markus, I had another job to go to," Thomas justified himself. "I tried four long days to get in touch with you. I went back and forth between your hotel and the farm. You can imagine it was little fun to walk in to your mother's life and say I found you, and then to have lost you again. The hotel staff were less than friendly and I had to fork out my own money to keep your room, which was our only hope of finding you at all. I kept putting my other clients off but eventually I had to cut my losses. For all I knew you could have been dead. You have not even paid me, yet. You know she is in hospital, I assume?"

"Yes, I know," Markus started to reply but the detective interrupted him right away.

"Where are you?"

"I am back in Heimkirchen, Thomas. I am staying at the farm. The reunion with my mother has taken place," Markus told him happily.

"How did you manage that? Anna is not supposed to have any visitors. Her weak heart, I have been told. I tried to get in there but Lukas has left strict orders with the staff."

"I sneaked in without any problems. All I need now is your invoice," Markus said.

"Don't worry, that will be in the post soon enough," Thomas said laughing. "Prepare yourself for a big surprise."

"You'll get a good tip, don't you worry, I appreciate everything you have done," Markus said magnanimously. "I have more plans for you by the way. I want to ask you to search for my sister in North Germany," Markus added.

"Oh, Gisela was it?" Thomas said, recalling his encounter with her. "Yes, I remember her. I went to see her. Has she disappeared? What is it with your family and runaways?"

"I don't know," Markus replied. "I think The Black Eagle is like a strong magnet, it either pulls you towards it or it pushes you away. Gisela has moved and I have not found a new address for her yet."

"I am a bit tied up with the current case," Thomas replied. "Cheating husband, classic case but it should not take long. I don't think he is very good at covering his tracks, but my client needs hard evidence for her court case. I will give you a call as soon as I am free."

Markus had hardly put the phone down when he heard the door being opened and hurried feet stomping in the living room.

"Lukas!" he heard Helga call out louder than was necessary.

"Where is he?" Lukas shouted. "I am going to kill him."

"What is the matter with you?" Helga shouted back. "Calm down for a minute and then tell me what you are going on about."

"Do not play naïve with me." he shouted. "I know he is here. When did he show up? Did you tell him, did you call him and ask him to come, warn him that Anna was going to die?"

"Don't take that tone of voice with me young man. Let us talk about this quietly like reasonable people." she suggested.

Lukas, surprisingly, responded to her command. He sat down and took a deep breath before he continued in a calmer voice. "The hospital just called, Helga. Anna is dead."

"What?" Helga said in disbelief.

"She passed away shortly after you and a man who called her mother visited. I guess that could only have been our gold digger Markus. What on earth were you thinking, Helga?"

"What am I going to do without her?" she sobbed quietly. "Oh, that poor soul. Why did they not call us?"

"They only found her this morning. She must have passed away in her sleep, shortly after you two left."

"I am glad she was spared any more pain," she said. "What a way to go."

"Rubbish!" Lukas raised his voice again. "You brought her that bastard son of hers; that is what killed her. Why on earth did you think of doing that?"

"I only did what she would have wanted," she said, tears rolling down her face. "He showed up out of the blue, and you should have seen it, she was so happy to see him. It did not excite or upset her at all. She was calm and so very relieved. Her death can have nothing to do with his visit."

"She had a weak heart, Helga! You two got her excited and tipped her over the edge. You should have known better than that."

"What was I supposed to do?" Helga asked him quite composed and clear in her head. "She didn't have much longer to live in any case, you know that Lukas. I am glad she lived to see him again, that is what she wanted. Maybe that is what she held out for. You know that is true. If that one happy moment has caused her to die a few days sooner than she would have done otherwise then I don't think of it as a loss. I am sure she would have agreed that one happy last day was better than a week of being alive but lonely, miserable and in pain."

"I thought you were on my side," Lukas said angrily, "and there you are smuggling him into her room, after all he did."

"You are not listening to me," she said, with more than a hint of frustration in her voice. "She said it herself, she was so pleased to see him, Lukas, I wish you could have been there, then you would know."

"Oh yes I also wish I had been there," he fumed, "so I could have reminded her of all the heartache that that waste of a man caused her. I could have made sure that she did not falter just as she leaves this world."

"Stop thinking about what you believe is right or wrong; it was her last wish to see him. We could not have denied her that."

"Did he cry and beg her for forgiveness?" Lukas said frostily. "What did he ask for? How much did he ask for? He must be relieved that there is no will that takes care of me and the rest of the family. Did she tell him that everything is his?"

"That is not what it was like, Lukas. You know I have always been on your side. They only had a few minutes with each other: it was beautiful. If you loved her you would have been pleased for her to find this final moment of peace. She was so lonely at the end," Helga said under tears that were starting to stream hopelessly over her face.

"I was always there for her and so were you," he pointed out. "If that were not enough for her I don't know what is."

"Don't be such a martyr." she said, sobbing. "She did appreciate you. One day you will fall in love and then you will know what it can do to your reasoning. The heart can't be ordered to feel one thing or the other. Hers wanted Markus, however wrong that was for her."

"Did he get on his knees and play the humble but reformed sinner?" he asked sarcastically.

"He didn't have to ask her to forgive him; she had done that a long time ago. Stop being so jealous, she was his adopted mother after all. You still have your own mother and father," she pointed out.

"What a god send they are!" Lukas let slip angrily.

"That is not his fault, you know. Don't make him responsible for everything that you have failed to fix in your own life. Why don't you two men try and get on with each other?"

"Get on with that cunning thief, that fraudulent liar and sleazy homosexual? You are having a laugh," he shouted, apoplectic with rage.

"I had just as low an opinion of him when he showed up here," Helga admitted, "but even in the short time since he walked through the door I have noticed how he has changed. Trust my words, just this one time in your life instead of being stubbornly buried in your own judgemental assumptions."

"You are a sentimental old hag and of course you can afford to see the best in everyone now that the end is near. I have a long life ahead of me with Markus in it. I should be damned if I fell for his tearful acting."

"She offered him the restaurant back. Of course it is his now anyway but she expressively said that she wanted you two to bury the hatchet and he had no problem with that. He wants you to stay," she said, hoping this announcement might change the cold hearted Lukas' mind.

"As you said, everything is his now that she is dead. I have nothing but a little land," he said bitterly. "I am at his mercy and I doubt he will stick to his word. Even if he did, it would only be until he knows how to run the farm without me. What long term future would I have?"

"If you have nothing to lose, why can't you try?"

"That is now all up to him, the new Lord of the Manor," he sneered.

"It is not that simple, is it," she said forcefully; she had just about had enough of this boy's ravings. "You know it is really a pity that you should accuse your cousin of being false and manipulative and devoid of decency. Your Aunt Anna is not even cold yet and you are only talking about money and power. It took a lot of guts for him to come back here and try to make things right. He could not have known how ill she was."

"At her age he knew it could not be much longer, maybe someone even told him?" he said, looking suggestively at her.

"Come off your high horse, it isn't becoming with your own skeletons in the closet. You are not remotely as innocent as you make yourself out to be. I know about your own little schemes, my friend. I saw some of the documents that you made Anna sign. Half of the land and forestry is in your name already, is it not? You were planning to bring Markus down the minute he takes over. You actually hope that he will treat you badly and then you will have all the moral justification that you need for your revenge. Stop it right now and we won't have to speak of it again."

Lukas momentarily wilted as he listened to her but then he composed himself.

"Let us see how the golden boy manages all by himself, shall we," he replied obstinately.

"Is that all you have to say?" Helga asked.

Lukas looked to the floor, overwhelmed by his feelings. The last few hours had been such a tear in his heart. He was unbelievably sad that his Aunt Anna had died, far more than he would ever have anticipated. She had become a surrogate mother to him as well, not just to Markus. His own parents had abandoned him, very similar to the way Markus had been deserted by his. That was something the two of them had in common, but luck had rewarded Markus for his pain and left Lukas without the monetary compensation an adoption by Anna would have brought.

Lukas' grief was getting confused with the jealousy and anger over Markus stepping back in, right at the very last minute. He felt betrayed and cheated by fate.

"Her heart just stopped," he said, suddenly quiet and thoughtful. "She was alone, the nurses thought she was asleep."

"You see," Helga said hopeful that this was a sign of Lukas softening, "she died peaceful and happy after all."

"She would not have died if he hadn't come." Lukas screamed out loudly, slamming his fist on the table. "That selfish bastard is going to regret that he ever set foot back on this land," he added threateningly.

"All your shouting is not going to make any of this go away," Helga pointed out. "You will have to face the fact that he owns everything now that was still hers, the things you have not embezzled yourself. If I were you I would try to become friends, that way you two might both get much further ahead; you don't need to be in competition with each other. His head has already shrunk to the size of a normal and reasonable person. It is time that yours did the same."

"I think it is time for you to stop interfering in the family business, Helga," Lukas said again in a threatening manner. "You were a true and loyal friend to Aunt Anna and you have been very supportive to me, too, I won't deny but stop trying to get me to like that perverted freak by singing his praises. It won't wash with me, once bitten twice shy."

"Suit yourself," Helga said. "I see that you have made up your mind. I hope you won't regret it."

Lukas just rolled his eyes at her and stormed off. In the heat of the argument he seemed to have forgotten that he had come to find Markus and only remembered as he left the building. For a moment he stopped and contemplated continuing with his search for Markus but that stupid woman had distracted him and now the moment was gone.

He decided to postpone the big argument with the heir to the throne to a time when he had calmed down and prepared himself more fully for it. There had been a lot of truth in what Helga had said but his pride got the better of him. Markus had had so much time to come back and make amends that it was ironic, and far too suspicious, that this should have occurred right at the end of Anna's life. He could not be expected to work with such a manipulator like that, the idea was preposterous.

After Lukas had left Markus came out of his hiding place.

"I am sorry I didn't join in and defend myself," he apologised. "I didn't think it would be wise to speak with him while he was so angry."

"Oh, I agree," Helga said. "Never mind. Let him calm down. We'll see how he feels tomorrow when he has had time to sleep and think over everything. I am sorry you had to find out about Anna's passing like this," she added.

"What about you? It must hit you harder than it hits any of us," Markus said compassionately. "She was your mistress but you spent all of your time together. She was more your companion than any of ours."

"We will survive it," Helga said evasively. "We all had time to think about this day and prepare for it."

"It is true what he said. I caused her death." Markus said, full of remorse.

"You did nothing of the sort. Lukas is grossly exaggerating," Helga reassured him. "She had a weak heart and she had cancer. Lukas is happy to have something to blame you for. Don't you think there were moments when he drove her mad, too? He could have caused her a heart attack as much as any of us could. You were not responsible for her health problems."

"Thank you," Markus said relieved.

"I am glad you took the chance to see her when you had it, and so was she. You heard her. Remember what she said and don't think about his bitter ramblings."

"I will try," he promised.

"Now think forward and positively, make a plan for the business. That is what Anna would have wanted."

"What do you mean?" he asked.

"Did you not hear that part of the argument? Lukas has conned you out of a lot of the land by having Anna sign it over to him and his siblings," she explained. "You won't be able to run the farm without paying him for the use of the land, if he even lets you use it. You will have to decide whether you want to carry on with the entire business under those circumstances or whether you want to limit yourself to the The Black Eagle and maybe sell the farm."

"How much has he taken?" Markus asked.

"I am not sure, you will have to go through the papers. I have seen a few of the documents but I am not an auditor or a detective. Of course the books are all in the office at The Black Eagle where he sleeps, and only he has the keys to that," she told him.

"Anna wanted him to have the farm, I should just give it to him and be done with it," Markus said suddenly. "I am more than happy with The Black Eagle alone."

"You mean you want to give it to him for free?" Helga asked.

"Yes, that is what I thought," he replied. "It would only be a mill stone around my neck."

"I wouldn't if I were you," she said warningly.

"Why not?"

"He is out to bring you down. He said so himself. I would be very careful about putting him in a position where he has too much power. Why don't you just lease the land from him and give him good conditions that he cannot say no to," Helga suggested. "That way you could show how nice and reliable you have become. Maybe that will make him trust you."

"I am not afraid of him," he said mockingly.

"You need to think of Gisela and Maria and not just about yourself and your own pride," she warned him. "I know it is tempting to throw it all away without a fight but then you would

231

be left with only one part of the business. Anna always said it was better to have two separate incomes to be insured against fluctuations of the economy. Lukas doesn't need to own more than he already does. With more money in your pocket you can help Maria and Gisela. Don't expect him to take care of them. Do you know that he disowned his own sister because of her Turkish husband?" Helga asked him. "Anna specifically asked you to look out for Maria: she must have thought about this. She made the conscious decision not to leave the farm to Lukas, even when we thought we would never see you, otherwise she would have made a will to that effect. Lukas tried to persuade her time and time again to do just that. Think about that before you make up your mind," she implored him.

"I will," he promised. "This is all just so overwhelming. I still have my doubts about staying here. I thought that I would never live in Germany again. Would The Black Eagle even get business with me as its landlord?" he asked doubtfully.

"Yes - as long as you are careful and don't make yourself too obvious," Helga encouraged him, "which I don't think you would."

"How come you are on my side all of a sudden?" he asked.

"I haven't switched sides, I am just able to adapt quickly to the people around me. That is probably why I lasted so long on the farm," she said jokingly. "Ten years ago you were the bad boy and Lukas the good, I had to be on his side. The times where everything was simply black and white are long gone: you have both changed. Right now I trust you more than him to do what Anna would have wanted. You have lost the very streaks that made it hard to trust you. Lukas is still a child and an angry and spoilt one at that. He is losing all of his morals so he can seek revenge and satisfy his growing ego. If he could see sense and behave like a grown up there wouldn't be any more sides."

"I can try but I know so little about running a farm," Markus admitted.

"If Lukas won't stay there are others who would jump at the opportunity. Doubting yourself instead of bragging is often a better starting position. Maybe you can become the first of the Hinterberger/Stockmann clan who looks after everyone, the way that other family farms are run," she said hopefully. "You know what it is like to be cast out. I hope that will make you more kind to others than Lukas is right now. If the roles were reversed you would be out on the street right away."

"It is probably best if I stay out of his way until after the funeral."

"You will have to arrange the funeral with him. You are the son and can't let him make all the decisions and arrangements. We will speak to him together first thing tomorrow, if you like."

"Helga, you should be making these decisions, you knew her the best of all of us."

"Maybe I did. In my opinion, she could not have cared less whether she gets buried in oak or birch, whether there are flowers or not, as long as it was you who did her the honour of choosing."

"Why did you never get married?" he suddenly asked. "I never understood that, you must have had your opportunities."

"Oh …" Helga said thoughtfully. "I often thought about this. You know I had my share of opportunities, I wasn't just left on the shelf, but none of the offers were ever enough to tempt me away from my life as it was."

"That sounds so cold and unfeeling," Markus commented.

"You can't say that. I just never understood how everyone else around me got so carried away by their desires. There were a few handsome men I would have liked to get to know but nothing ever came of it. The ones I could have courted with I didn't really fancy enough. I was in this privileged position at the farm. Anna let me look after you children whenever you were here, that was just like having my own family and children. I regarded that as responsibility enough, getting married and going away would have meant abandoning you. I got stuck in this life but I enjoyed it enough not to feel I needed to change it. Despite all the troubles you caused me, no man could have made me as happy as you all did."

"What a lovely thing to say. I am a little relieved to hear that you are happy with the choices you made," he said with a lump in his throat.

The next morning Lukas did not come to the farm house as usual to have his breakfast but stayed in his office. He had been up since four in the morning and started to prepare all documents and books for a formal and final hand over. His would be moving out of the farm immediately and take up residence

233

somewhere else. Being surrounded by things that were no longer his to have or to command would only add insult to injury.

That he had embezzled parts of the land as compensation did not make him feel any less convinced that he was a wronged party. He could not seriously be expected to stay and put on a brave face on this farce. How vindictive he would be with the leasing of his land to whoever would fill his shoes at the Hinterberger farm would remain to be seen, he would need to do a little more soul searching about that. He would rather sleep on the street than live under the same roof as the gold digger.

By the time Markus had built up the courage to go over to the restaurant and talk things out with Lukas everything had been prepared and was ready for him. The calm professionalism in which Lukas conducted their conversation was a first between them.

"I have made some rough estimates about the current state of moneys and affairs on this sheet for you," he said without the slightest hint of emotion. "Bank accounts, outstanding debts and bills, delivery dates and salaries. Our accountant can give you a hand with that. Everything you need to know to be able to jump in at the deep end is on this piece of paper. Don't lose it.

"Here is also a list of the land that we had to sell off since you have been gone, a lot of which is mine now, as Helga will have told you. My land is still part of the farm land that is being used. After the funeral, we need to discuss the arrangements and conditions for the lease. Good luck and I will be in touch."

"Where are you going?" Markus asked surprised, both at the impending departure of his cousin and at the peaceful manner of this meeting.

"I am not sure. I need to get away from here," he said "You'll be fine."

"Stay." Markus said warmly. "Please!"

"I have been my own boss for too long. How is this going to work?" Lukas said dismissively.

"You'll never know until you try. We are both mature now; it doesn't have to be like this. Anna would not have wanted it."

"Sorry," Lukas said, shaking his head. "I am off."

Lukas left the office and went up to his room. He had already packed a rucksack full of his clothes and documents. He put it on his back, got on his bicycle and cycled towards

Heimkirchen. Initially, he would have to stay with his parents until he found a place of his own. He could not possibly stay at the Old Inn, his competition, and he didn't have any close friends he could have asked to live with for a while.

His parents had taken the news about Anna's passing very stoically. Magdalena immediately went to church to pray for her sister-in-law's troubled soul and for her salvation, and scheduled extra services in commemoration of the deceased.

Hans-Ulrich actually cried a few tears in his armchair, to which he seemed to be glued now when at home. Everyone could tell that the tears were not so much for Anna than for his own misery, a welcome excuse to let out the built up sadness that he otherwise bottled up inside himself.

"Markus was her son, everything is of course now rightfully his," Hans-Ulrich commented, uninvolved in the news that his nephew had returned to The Black Eagle Inn. "You knew this day was coming, son. Better now while you still have options. When you are older it is harder to start all over again."

"You are better off away from the place anyway," Magdalena added. "It's such a money-making machine, it is no good for your soul. Now you have an opportunity to do something good and meaningful with your life."

"Like what?" Lukas asked impatiently, a little irritated at her dismissive comments about what had been the sole focus in his life thus far. "What will make me forget the injustice of it all?"

"When you regret the loss of money it is only greed talking," Hans-Ulrich reprimanded him. "You should be grateful that the Good Lord reminded you of that by taking it away. You have a real chance to learn from this and put your mind to greater things."

"It is never too late to join the clergy," Magdalena suggested, "but I guess you would rather stay in the business world. I am sure you will find something new in that field easily," she assured him. "Your father is right, though: greed and money are only making you unhappy."

The extent of their disinterest was hurtful, even though he had not expected his parents to suddenly become passionate about his life and achievements at the farm or appreciate his choices.

He tried to stay out of their way and went for long walks or rode his bicycle to get out of the subdued atmosphere of his new residence. The days when his mother had other holier-than-thou women over for prayer group or for charitable meetings were unpleasant enough. It was hard to get out of their way and he was continuously put on the spot about his faith. He admired the charitable spirit of these women and their hard efforts for the less privileged but the talk that came with it was very trying.

The evenings were totally different. The moment his father entered the apartment he filled it with the heavy air of depression and disappointment. Even the slightest spark of cheerfulness in himself or his mother was smothered by this grave cloud.

The days until the funeral dragged on unpleasantly. For the first time in years Lukas was without work and he felt rather lost. His problem was a family matter that he could never discuss with outsiders who had no business in finding out the financial and personal parameters of his life but within the family he had no allies he could trust or who would actively listen to him and try and find a solution. He was no closer to making a decision about the lease of his land.

The funeral was scheduled for very early in the morning. The church service began at eight thirty and took place at the Saint Lorenz Chapel, the biggest church in Heimkirchen. Anna may not have had many friends amongst the neighbours but all of them were represented by at least one member of their families to show respect from one farmer's clan to the next. The chapel was packed with people, some of whom even had to stand outside the door and listen to the ceremony from there.

Magdalena was disappointed that a priest of a lesser standing than she had wanted had been allowed to hold the ceremony. If she had been consulted, she would have been able to organise someone with a more prestigious and prominent role in the local clergy, maybe even a bishop. Additionally, there should have been more altar boys and more flower decorations. The modest ornamentation and spending showed the godlessness of Markus and was symbolic of his shameful neglect during Anna's lifetime. Whenever Magdalena could she would voice this opinion to bystanders and her charity friends who had come in large groups to show their support for Magdalena. Few of them even had met Anna in person.

Hans-Ulrich felt that the comparatively low key funeral reflected badly on the status of the Hinterberger family and how they portrayed themselves in public. Here was the sister of a former member of parliament, one of the region's most prestigious politicians; his sister deserved better than this ridiculous little service. He was all too vulnerable to listen to Magdalena's bad mouthing of Markus and came to believe that greed had been the overriding factor in these poorly advised choices.

Lukas had objections of a different nature. By the time the people from Heimkirchen had arrived at the remote location, the front row - which was traditionally reserved for the main mourners – was already filled on both sides. Amongst them were Herbert's sister who had not been seen on the farm since his death.

Among those in the prestigious mourner seats sat Markus, of course, and then Helga and many of the farm workers. The entire Hinterberger family, including Otto and Klara with her husband and children, had to sit further back in the church. Where was Markus' sense of propriety? When he spotted Maria and her Turkish husband next to Helga he had seen enough and could only just control himself not to storm out in a public display of scorn.

The sermon, which acted as a eulogy for Anna, never mentioned any of her faults and shortcomings, her character flaws and her greed, which outraged the Hinterbergers sitting on the back benches. The closest the priest came to a criticism was his mentioning of how long it had taken Anna to find God and the Church again. Only after Herbert had died had she gone to Mass more often and everyone knew that this phase had not lasted particularly long either.

As one of the readings Markus had chosen the story of the prodigal son being welcomed with open arms by his father, now referred to in order to prove the forgiving nature of the deceased. Even Helga had been shocked at the choice and had urged Markus to choose something less controversial. He was shamelessly alluding to his long absence from The Black Eagle Inn and announced to the congregation publicly that Anna had taken him back. He saw Magdalena throwing angry and disapproving looks at the priest as well, probably because this

237

part of the Bible fell short of stressing the need for repentance, punishment and humbleness.

After the service the congregation followed the priest and his altar boys out of the church in a procession towards the cemetery, where the coffin was waiting. The priest blessed the coffin with myrrh and holy water before inviting the mourners to accompany Anna on her last journey.

Once again, the tone of the proceedings was far too positive for some of the Hinterbergers' liking. There was way too little mention of the idleness of the worldly endeavours and too much encouragement of hope for resurrection and heavenly bliss.

The restaurant was holding a mid-morning wake, carefully timed so that the guests of The Black Eagle could still have a late lunch if needed, without causing too many problems for the kitchen staff.

"I am not going to that," Magdalena declared spitefully. "Sharing a table with these godless creatures? I think it is time we cut our ties with that part of the family."

"You are right," Hans-Ulrich agreed. "They have chosen their alliances by inviting Maria and that Muslim."

"What do you expect of a shirt-lifter like him," Lukas added viciously.

"Don't use language like that." Magdalena scolded her son.

"Is that confirmed now?" Hans-Ulrich asked. "I thought it was only rumours."

"I don't know if anyone can vouch for him one way or the other," Lukas replied, "but in my mind there is no doubt."

"It's disgusting what has become of this country," Hans-Ulrich said angrily.

"I am surprised the church was not struck by lightning," Magdalena said.

"If the situation is like this then you can't leave everything without a fight, son," Hans-Ulrich suddenly blurted out. "You need to do whatever you can to bring them down and rescue the family reputation."

"I am not sure there is anything we can do to rescue the reputation after today," Magdalena said resigned. "Neither should we seek revenge. However much we condemn their actions, we must not let our own souls be blackened by hate and greed," she lectured.

238

"We will have to pry the business back out of their unchristian grip," Hans-Ulrich swore. "We owe it to my father and the generations before him who have made it what it is now. The Eagle is our family's pride and joy and an integral part of Heimkirchen. We cannot leave it in the hands of such heathens. The Good Lord would not stand for it."

Magdalena was far from convinced but she was willing to compromise her beliefs if it helped get Hans-Ulrich back his fighting spirit and energy. Having seen him depressed and lethargic for the last few years it was a huge relief to hear him making any plans, even if she couldn't agree with him and his motives.

At the wake Markus served sausages and bread for the mourners. Representatives of the various farms sat together discussing local and national politics. None of them had time for such leisurely get-togethers unless there was an occasion like this and they seemed to enjoy themselves more than might have been deemed appropriate.

Markus tried to speak to most of these guests briefly to give them an opportunity to express their condolences, without breaking up their little parties. He had expected more indifference or distancing from these people because of the rumours around him but they all behaved perfectly normally and were kind towards him. At least on the surface no one seemed to have taken notice of the rumours about him or they had decided to shun him for it.

It was good to know that not everyone was his enemy and none of the people present were seeing him as an enemy.

Little did he know that most of the guests had not seen the Hinterbergers in a long time and would not have been able to tell Lukas from Markus. Many didn't even know that Markus was back. Only gradually during the course of the wake did word get around about the family and the gossip that surrounded them. The sense of security that Markus derived from the atmosphere at the wake was a misunderstanding. However, it served the purpose of seeing him through the ordeal confidently and optimistic for the future.

The workforce had taken Markus back into their hearts immediately. As manager they had always preferred him to Lukas with his rigid and patronising ways. When the farm accountant -

as they had called him - had taken over the restaurant it was the staff themselves who trained him and taught him the ropes and tricks of the trade. Within weeks he had switched roles and had behaved as if he had already surpassed all of them in his knowledge and experience.

His patronising comments and nagging were not just annoying for their own sake, they were unnecessary and out of place. Under Markus there had been something like a soul and a lively spirit and the return of the old master was hailed as a chance to return to those better and happier days.

The staff were aware of the rumours that Markus had taken money and they believed those stories to be true, but that was all water under the bridge now and they were willing to give Markus another chance.

Markus was pleased that Maria and Esat had accepted his invitation to the funeral. He had found her address in Anna's diary and written her a long letter, explaining how he had spent the last few years and how he had come to reconnect with Anna before she died.

He also mentioned his promise to the dying woman to look out for Maria and his intentions to honour his word as well as he could. Maria had not been sure whether she should believe the moving story of the reformed sinner but thought it wrong to miss the opportunity to attend the funeral of her aunt under the circumstances.

It was a good excuse to come to Heimkirchen and show her face so that her parents didn't think she was avoiding them, or 'honouring' their wish never to see her again. She was taken in by the fact that Markus had chosen to collect her personally at the station and she soon began to trust his new, improved character. He seemed seriously improved. It was lovely for her to meet a kindred spirit, someone who had – just like her – tasted the fresh air outside their little nest and who through this had found a fresh perspective on life.

Esat also took an instant liking to the polite and gentle young man at the station. In the liberal city of Hamburg, Esat had come to take respectful conduct, at least towards the more refined and well groomed Turks, for granted. Markus easily surpassed those levels with his natural charm and sleek conduct.

Helga paid little attention to either of the visitors; she saw and immediately fussed over Lorenz, the two months old baby that was Maria's first child.

"He looks so cute," she said adoringly. "Oh my gosh, what a beautiful little boy."

She took the little baby and rocked it in her arms.

"If he stays like this, no one will ever mind that he is a 'mongrel'. He is going to break many hearts."

Maria and Esat rolled their eyes but they recognised the kind intentions of the old woman.

"Why don't you stay here?" Helga suggested to the young couple. We need industrious people like you. There is plenty for you to do."

"Thank you but we are very happy where we are," Maria declined the offer.

"Are you?" Esat asked her, surprised. "It is easy, but are you really happy up north?

"I don't want to be apologising for having a Muslim husband and a mixed race or mongrel baby or whatever names they will find for Lorenz. Have you seen how the people here are staring at us?" she replied.

"People are staring because they haven't seen anything like it in their life," Helga admitted, "Even I can't help it. Give us time to get over it. If you run away again then we will never get used to the modern times."

"I am sorry but we are comfortable where we are now," Maria explained.

"I can see that you are missing your home," Esat said suddenly. "I often wondered if we should not try and see what it would be like to live here. I agree with Helga that maybe after a while it would get better and less of a chore. Someone has to be the first mixed race couple in town. The countryside is beautiful and it would be lovely for Lorenz to have some family."

"Of course I miss my home," Maria admitted. "You must miss yours too. Everyone does in one way or another, but do you really think I would want to move back? Look how most of my family have been treating us. I am not sure I want to live my life fighting or begging to be accepted or at least to be treated respectfully. Maybe I don't feel like I belong in Hamburg yet but I certainly no longer belong here either. When I was young and naïve I didn't know any better but now that I do, I know what I am going to choose."

"My dear girl," interjected Helga, "you have to fight for your corner wherever you live, even in your great liberal city of Hamburg. You can't tell me that no one there gives you two looks or ever says anything unpleasant to you. Each and every one of us is getting abuse and grief but you don't see us moving away. If all of the odd balls move away because of such comments then we will always stay the same. Someone has to stay and fight to be different."

"Helga is right, you know," Markus said. "We can't hide and apologise for not conforming with other people's ideas. You especially are not alone in Heimkirchen. There are many Gastarbeiter here with their families. The days of standing out as much as you think are already over. Like Helga has said, people need to get used to seeing mixed marriages. Don't throw your life away over a few nasty comments. If you feel you belong here than nothing should stop you from staying. If you stay away for too long then Heimkirchen will stop being your home, but Hamburg will never be able to replace it as your home."

"I agree with Markus," Esat said. "There wouldn't be any harm in trying. I know you have a fighting spirit in you, if you are staying in Hamburg for my sake then reconsider. Wherever you decide to live, I will stand by you."

"What about Lorenz?" she asked.

"He is better off here with a family that supports him," Markus said.

"Markus, it is different for you, you are not so obvious in your difference," Maria replied. "No one can see that you are gay, people can get to know you and like or dislike you before they find out about your little secret. Esat and Lorenz look different, they never have the chance for a first impression where their looks and race don't come in to play. Before they open their mouths people will bring their opinion on Gastarbeiter to the table. I don't think I can come back at all."

"Think about it," Helga said. "Keep an open mind while you are here and remember that the door is always open to you."

The wake had been an all-round success for Markus. The farmers that had attended returned to their farmyards and told of the great display of hospitality, the kind and generous tone of the family at the funeral and the restaurant. The news that Markus had returned and taken back control of the business from Lukas was greeted by the ones in the know mostly with approval. He couldn't be gay if he was allowed to march right back in to the family home, said some, others felt it did not matter for business as long as the new boss did not run such a stingy and competitive ship as the last one.

The absence of Hans-Ulrich and his family from the wake had also made the rounds amongst the farming community but ever since he had returned from Bonn, the former politician was renowned for his reclusive behaviour. That he would not come out of his shell on this occasion was nothing peculiar. The 'scandal', as Hans-Ulrich was imagining the news about his Turkish son-in-law, had not even reached those people. Maria and Esat had been taken for workers at the farm and no one was paying any attention to them. Lukas' absence was greeted with cheer.

During the days following the funeral Lukas went to visit some of these farmers himself, offering his farmland to lease to competing farmers in the hope of cutting off Markus' life line. Most of them rejected his offer right away. They objected to any open hostility between the cousins, even when they heard that the rumours about Markus' sexuality were true. Already some of the farmers were no longer as bothered by the issue as they were before. Since the government had legalised homosexuality the behaviour condemning it was more controversial, many didn't really know what to think. Besides, they had more important things to worry about, like the new European Legislations and new trends in dairy farming. Even the gossip mongers amongst them felt that his smear campaign against his own flesh and blood was nothing short of despicable.

As no one seemed willing to lease the land off him Lukas approached the wealthier and more competitive ones to sell the land. Some offers were made but they were far too low for what the land was really worth.

As a measure against his enemy, selling the land that Markus relied upon was not enough for Lukas. Nothing could stop the new owners leasing the land to Markus.

He decided to give up that line of attack and to go back to the drawing board and make a new battle plan with the help of Hans-Ulrich. Since the funeral his father had committed himself to the cause fully and was contacting his remaining party friends for help and advice.

At the same time as father and son were sharpening their knives for an attack on The Black Eagle Inn and the farm, some of Hans-Ulrich's more vindictive political enemies did a little scheming of their own. Some of them sensed a unique opportunity to exploit the current situation and paid Maria a visit at the farm.

Holger Behrens, a trade union leader and one of the most prominent members of the local Social Democrats turned up on their doorstep in person one afternoon and asked for permission to speak to her in private.

She could not think of a reason why he would want to speak to her but she could also not think of a reason to deny him. Esat insisted on sitting in on the discussion to protect her interests.

Holger Behrens was a bear of a man, tall and broad and obviously fond of his food. He had a warm and almost seductive glint in his eyes and the couple took an instant liking to him.

"I hear you and your father don't see eye to eye anymore," he opened the conversation.

"The rumour mill in Heimkirchen is as good as it always was then," Maria said evasively, "although I would consider this old news, really. What is it to you?"

"Frau Hinterberger, you see, the rumour goes that the fall out is based on your marriage to a Turkish man, whose name unfortunately my informants have been unable to find out," he said with a wry smile.

"Mergen," Maria said, "my husband's name is Esat Mergen, and I am also a Mergen now."

"Now I know that a woman of your reputation would not do anything to harm her father in any way," Holger Behrens continued. "I believe you are aware that his political career has been damaged beyond repair. With this in mind I would like you to consider joining our party in the fight for better living conditions for foreigners amongst our midst."

Maria laughed. "Me? What do you think that I could possibly bring to your party that could be of any help? My father's name?"

"In a way," Holger Behrens hesitated a little, "yes, for a start certainly, why not? The political landscape in Heimkirchen is notoriously complicated. Since the arrival of the Gastarbeiter, the conservative vote is starting to split. Nationwide the Social Democrats are gaining popularity, to a point that we believe that the next elections might even be won outright by us alone without a conservative or liberal coalition partner. If that happens we would have free reign to change the many laws that so urgently need adjustment for a fair and worthy society. Imagine the possibilities if only we could swing the pendulum a little further in our favour. You and your husband, your children and everyone in the same shoes as you could be so much better off."

Maria was quite taken in by his persuasive ways.

"What we do not have," he continued, "is a candidate who represents the new Germany. With you on the team we have: a true feminist, a woman who stood up for her love against her conservative father, a woman who knows about foreigners and their worries, a daughter of a politician and a simple waitress, the former secretary of a member of parliament with rural roots. You have so many qualities that make you a great front for our campaign. Your father's political past gives you a certain edge and notoriousness that will get the voter's attention. That is all we need, people to listen to our good arguments, you believe in good for all, don't you?"

"What exactly did you have in mind?" She could not deny that she was intrigued and tempted. Holger Behrens had answered almost all her main concerns right away and made an excellent case. If she were to stay in this little town, then an all-out political battle would be the only way she could imagine living her life; staying here and being a quiet victim and letting other people's behaviour dictate how she felt every day was not an option. This could be the answer to her problems. It would be frightening and exhausting but with a broader purpose than just to survive for the sake of 'belonging'.

"I am so glad you asked," Herr Behrens said with a broad smile. "The exact plan has not been formed yet, but from the top of my head I would say we would like you to come on the

245

committee, maybe become a candidate for the local elections to become a city councillor and join the campaign trail. First of all, of course, you would have to join the party and come to the meetings we have. Not in that order of course. I would like you to join our discussion, contribute and share what you know. We need your input, we welcome it. I am not a dictator, none in our party are. Our membership will still need to elect you to all of those positions that I have in mind for you, so nothing is a foregone conclusion."

"I helped my father during his time in Bonn," Maria replied. "I have some working knowledge of political bodies, even if they were far more conservative than yours."

"I think when you read our manifesto you will find that with your current life circumstances it would be impossible and almost self-destructive if you voted for your father's party. You will have to find out for yourself of course if you felt represented by our values naturally. If you are as blindly conservative as your father is then there wouldn't be any use for you in our party. I think however that you will fit in nicely. "

"Fine," Maria said, "when is the next meeting?"

Chapter 18: The Election (1972)

Markus had always relied on Antoine to deal with the administration of the business. He needed someone professional, trustworthy and reliable to take care of it. Horst Riedl was a retired civil servant who in his youth had once courted Anna. He offered his help at the funeral when he heard about their current predicament from Helga. He was a patient and quiet man who had a talent for explaining everything time and time again, until he was sure that Markus had understood and taken everything in carefully.

With his help Markus felt less vulnerable and capable of taking on the huge tasks ahead of him. Horst Riedl had never married, despite the shortage of eligible bachelors in his generation. He was committed to keeping Anna's legacy alive and worked tirelessly until he could verify the data that Lukas had given them. In his spare time Horst hung around Helga as much as he could to talk about the deceased.

Markus urged Lukas to meet with him so that they could come to a mutually beneficial arrangement about the outstanding matters of the lease and farm equipment but Lukas refused, while still searching for allies amongst the local farmers. Finally, he agreed to meet with Markus and the accountant but then he cancelled and rescheduled several times at the last minute. His plans of leasing the farmland to competitors had failed entirely.

Hans-Ulrich and his party friends had come up with a few minor schemes against the farm and the restaurant business. Certain business partners of Markus said they could be persuaded to boycott him, although it seemed unlikely to bring The Black Eagle down. Customers, suppliers and buyers could not be influenced in high enough numbers to guarantee an end to Markus' business life and exposing him as homosexual would cast a bad light on the entire family, especially Hans-Ulrich, and would not guarantee the desired effect.

All Lukas could do was to enforce harsh lease conditions on Markus. To his surprise Markus offered him very favourable conditions in their dealings anyway when they finally managed to meet up in person. Markus emphasised that he was acting in the spirit of Anna's last wishes for peace and harmony. He even begged his cousin to come back and take over the running of the farm. Markus did not want to admit it to the hostile Lukas but he was desperate to get some time to himself. Since he had been a stage director, he had formed a habit of reading plays and making notes on possible theatre productions. He also longed to get away to see his friends Balthasar and Barbara in Munich again. He could have done with less responsibility than running both strands of the business.

Sadly, the stubborn Lukas walked away from the offer without considering it. Satisfied with the financial benefits he had secured for himself he turned his back on the past. The arrangement that was eventually reached with Markus left him with a steady enough stream of income. With his spartan lifestyle he did not have to work. After years of living for nothing else but the farm he didn't quite know what to do with himself. Lukas remembered how his teachers at school had always predicted that with his genius mind he would become a doctor or scientist. Thinking that he had sacrificed many career opportunities, a wave of bitterness crept over him, and naturally he refused to accept any work that he considered beneath his capabilities and intellectual level.

Magdalena tried to get him involved in church work and his father wanted to recruit him for the party, just to get him out of the house and out of his lethargy. Lukas, good son that he was, tried both of their suggestions for a while but he remained uninspired, mainly because of his own miserly and ungrateful attitude.

He snubbed the charity, which in all seriousness expected him to do the actual leg work of collecting clothes and other minor physical tasks. He was outraged that his managerial talents and experience were not taken into consideration when it came to the allocation of work. The 'stubborn and selfish' people in charge were not prepared to vacate their prestigious positions and make space for him, who in his own estimation could have done a much better job than they did. Before long he excused himself from the charity and accompanied his father to party meetings instead. His appearance there was slightly more appreciated than at the charity. The older party members in particular loved nothing more than the emergence of a conservative family dynasty and to promote the bearer of an already famous and prestigious name. Hans-Ulrich's failure at the last elections could be turned around by the arrival of his son, who could carry the Christian Democrats' Hinterberger tradition on to the next generation of the party.

Lukas, however, was disappointed when he realised that again he was expected to humbly work his way up the hierarchy before shooting to the heights he had in mind for himself. The glowing speeches he held about the economic situation of the country were sound, well prepared and disclosed his educated and capable mind. But this was not appreciated amongst the 'peasants' that were gathered around him, who did not recognise him as a spiritual leader and innovator as much as he would have deemed appropriate. In the local internal elections to appoint party functionaries, the membership did not choose him for the higher and responsible positions, which he had cast his eyes on. One party leader even told him to be more humble and less domineering in his views and start his career on a lower rung of the ladder. Outraged that his talents had been misjudged and underestimated he withdrew from those circles immediately. To avoid his annoyed and embarrassed parents off his back he decided to move out of their home and rent a small room from a widow who lived near the main square of Heimkirchen.

'Misunderstood and cast out' in his own view Lukas became a man of leisure, if one could ever call him that. He rose early every morning, had a constitutional walk along the river to kick-start his digestion, bought the newspaper and read it in one of the street café's. He shied away from all people and avoided contact with the other customers at any cost. He detested and looked down on the empty headed and vain peasants around him but enjoyed being seen snubbing them. The life of a recluse and hermit was enjoyable, as long as enough people could witness it and feel the force of his contempt and his ever so justified snobbery.

Frequently, he took offence at the articles in the local paper or at the news these humble writings contained. As a responsible citizen with lots of time on his hands, he would take it upon himself to compose letters to the editor, company owners or politicians to alert the public, attract their attention and correct their errors.

He would also spend many an afternoon in the reading room of the local library, looking up facts to back up his complaints. The local librarian was distraught about this sudden plague that had so unexpectedly befallen her previously sleepy and harmonious life. He never failed to point out faults in the classification system to her, demanded she ask people to keep the noise down and frequently voiced his opinion to the congregated readership in any way he deemed relevant or necessary.

Without realising it, he rapidly became known and notorious in town as a pedantic and tedious man whom everyone avoided if they could. Charitable organisations like Caritas, The Red Cross and even the Catholic Church politely but determinedly declined his offers of help, which resulted in him writing more of his infamous letters to the head of the respective organisations complaining about the appalling treatment he had received when bestowing the honour of his attention to them.

His parents were frequently embarrassed when stories about his conduct and attention-seeking efforts were related to them. Magdalena responded to such reports with much apology and increased her own efforts in the charities to secure her position there. She included him more than ever in her every prayer.

For Hans-Ulrich, Lukas' behaviour posed a serious threat to his new position within the party. Although he was already reduced from the national level back to the regional, he still considered himself as one of the main players in Heimkirchen and expected to be the main candidate for leader of the City Council elections.

His absence from the local party scene since he had returned from Bonn was being treated by his allies as a short regenerative phase. In the small pond that was the Heimkirchen branch of the Christian Democrats, he was still by far the largest fish. Maria's marital disgrace was by now known around town but it could not reflect too badly on his political influence, he thought.

No one in the party, however, had recently confirmed his assumptions and expectations, not even in his remaining loyal followers. Still, Hans-Ulrich had no doubt that his name alone would bring in a huge number of automatic votes and a top position for him on the list of party members standing for the 24

City Council positions; it was still a few weeks before the city hall demanded all contestant parties to publish the list of chosen candidates.

In this spirit of supremacy and future glory he scrolled through the local paper on his lunch break and saw that the Social Democrats had announced their list of candidates a few weeks early. He could not believe his eyes when he saw that Maria, his own daughter, was on that list. He was fuming. It was a personal attack on him, why else would their leader, Holger Behrens, have made this decision public so soon, long before the Christian Democrats had even held their internal vote.

Well, he told himself, this would make his position more controversial but at least he had a week to prepare himself for the party gathering. He would hold a blazing speech to whip up all the support and fighting spirit amongst the members and take on the challenge that the Social Democrats had thrown at him. In unity, he and his fellow Christians would crush Maria and her pathetic candidacy.

The next day the news was worse: not only had Maria been nominated, she had been chosen for the top spot. In his anger at her cheek to stand against her own father – and for the opposing team – he took the insult but he never paid, what he thought was a minor detail, the attention and gravity it deserved; since this was only a local list he had not considered it newsworthy. However, it was making nationwide headlines as Maria was the first ever woman candidate to top a major party list in Bavaria. Journalists from all over the country swarmed in to the little town of Heimkirchen to report on the impact of the selection and to interview the politicians involved and the local electorate about their views on the matter.

Due to the hugely complex local election system, Maria was practically guaranteed a seat on the council and party spokesmen stressed what a big political statement this was.

The fact that Maria was Hans-Ulrich's daughter, a former government minister, was treated almost as secondary in the news, adding further insult to her father's injury. Maria, Holger Behrens and several big wigs from the Social Democrats in Bonn spoke everywhere about the importance of female participation in politics and how significant this selection was for the entire country. Hans-Ulrich sneered at this lip service to the student

251

movement. He knew his daughter to be a silly girl with a pretty smile. Her foolish and ill-advised associations, first with the Turk and now with the Social Democrats, just showed how naïve and uneducated she was. He was looking forward to exploiting all of this in his own upcoming candidacy. She would be no match for him. Also, he told himself in anticipated schadenfreude, even if the electorate was ready to vote for a woman candidate, they would not choose one with a Turkish husband.

After the first wave of publicity around Maria's selection had died down, the focus of reports turned away from her gender and the press finally refocused on the subject of her famous father, and the fact that she was standing for his rival party. The newspapers studied his sharp rise and fall in Bonn in detail and reminded Hans-Ulrich and all other readers of the most painful moments in his political career and life.

"What on earth does she think she is doing?" he said angrily to his wife. "The Social Democrats in Heimkirchen have no chance to make any difference at all. Why they even bother making a list for the City Council is beyond me. If they get four or five candidates through they will be lucky: we are a good Christian community. Is that what Maria wants, to sit with four other puppets in the same room as us and watch while we, with the majority of votes under our belt, are making all the decisions, regardless of their booing and complaining? She is just doing this out of spite. She obviously wants to harm me because we don't approve of her Muslim husband. There cannot be any other reason."

"I doubt that, Hans-Ulrich," Magdalena contradicted. "Our Maria is not that kind of vengeful and spiteful girl. She probably thinks that she is right in her political views. She has naively been misled by the wrong kind of people. The new generation is different and rebellious for no other reason than that they can. Look at the student revolt, the Bader Meinhof; they act against our generation in general, because our age group followed Hitler. She is not that bad, she had a good heart once. I am sure that she does it with honourable and idealistic intentions, however misguided they are."

"She married a Turk, for crying out loud," he replied loudly. "A Muslim, that was hardly considerate, was it?"

"That was selfish and obstinate of course but she didn't do it to harm you," Magdalena tried to defend her daughter. "I think she really loves him. How that can be possible is beyond my understanding but I am pretty sure of it. I see it so often in my charity work how women of the lower classes fall off the right path and choose a man unworthy of their affections. The heart is difficult to command."

"Oh, save your sentimental tripe for someone else," Hans-Ulrich replied sharply.

"One thing that she is saying in her campaign is correct: there are certain things that a man will never understand," she retorted quickly, but then she sighed and looked at him with tearful eyes. "Were we bad parents to let her slip away? Has our example not helped her to find the correct path at all?"

"It is just another trial sent to test us," Hans-Ulrich said, getting tired of his wife's sense of drama but happy to indulge in his own.

"The vote at our party meeting will be easy now," he informed her confidently. "The Social Democrats have made this a personal vendetta, a fight between father and daughter. They will see how easily we take on that challenge and crush them at the polling stations. The Lord has called upon me to fight my own flesh and blood, like Abraham and his son Isaac. I am ready to shed her blood."

At the party meeting his candidacy was received with surprise and a heated debate took place about his suitability for the top position. Many speakers declared the threat from the far right demanded a less controversial candidate. Hans-Ulrich was confronted not only with the destructive impact that his daughter's arrival on the political scene had made but also with the role Lukas and his eccentric and offensive public behaviour had played in bringing the Hinterberger name in to disrepute in Heimkirchen.

Nevertheless, Hans-Ulrich was stubborn and stood for the top position within the party list, only to be defeated in the showing of hands that followed.

He failed to be selected for the second highest position as well and did not succeed to get the majority of votes until the low rank of 14 was contested. The party membership was amazed at his determination to get the best spot possible, swallowing all of his pride to stand again and again through the humiliation of each defeat. He looked accusingly in to the auditorium to see who was for and who was against him each time, hoping that the moral pressure might turn the tide in his favour.

"What do you expect?" asked one of his former allies in defence of his own voting behaviour. "We need to consider what is best for the party. You will be more use to us if on a lower rank on that list. You are still there and people can vote for you and endorse you if they want. If you had a top position it might offend voters who are put off by your family scandals and that could cost the party their votes. Politics is all about tactics and this is a fair compromise."

"People should judge me by my politics and not by my rotten children," Hans-Ulrich burst out.

"Yes, in an ideal world maybe, but you won't find people being able to separate the two," his friend told him. "If you believe in your politics you won't stand in the way of the party that tries to implement them. If you step aside now then your dreams for Heimkirchen and Germany have much more chance of becoming reality than if you try to fight them by yourself. You have a real opportunity here to do the right thing for the greater good, even if that means you won't be doing it yourself. Just think about the big picture. Don't tell me you have become too proud for that."

"I cannot see how such a cheap trick from the Social Democrats can be validated by the way my Christian Party colleagues have reacted to it," Hans-Ulrich said with grave emphasis. "We are playing into their hands by responding in the way we do."

"You really are just a little naïve farmer's son Hans-Ulrich, aren't you," his friend said, half sarcastically and half affectionately. "I have just given you the lines to read for a graceful retreat so you could save your face. The Social Democrats have enlisted help directly from Bonn for this and have attracted enough attention to drag this affair out for more than it should be worth. I am sorry Hans-Ulrich but they have won already, don't you see? Why someone so simple minded as you ever went into politics with its backstabbing and scheming is surprising, I must say. I always assumed that there was a powerful brain behind your farmer's exterior: that was part of your appeal

254

for us. We have no use for you as an idealistic simpleton, you must understand that."

"I am beginning to," Hans-Ulrich replied bitterly.

He was tempted to withdraw his candidacy entirely and re-open the bidding process but something inside of him still could not let go. Maybe the citizens of Heimkirchen would see behind this stupid power game and hand him an overwhelming mandate. Hans-Ulrich still had a slim chance to shoot to the top of the list if enough people singled him out. He only needed to beat a few of the candidates ahead of him to land a place in the City Council. It would be an uphill struggle but it was worth a try.

Maria's rise to the top of the Social Democrat party in Heimkirchen was as much a surprise to herself as it was to Holger Behrens. Not in his wildest dreams had he thought that the young woman had such rhetorical skills and charm. At a time when the cold war was still bringing any left leaning politics into disrepute, her warm and kind manners brought credibility back to the ideas of sharing and community. At her first party meeting she had been exposed to the first round of awkward questions about her background and her family. It was a relief that for once no one raised an eyelid about her choice of a Muslim partner. Instead she had to defend herself for having such a conservative father, something she was not particularly proud of but she had adjusted quickly and turned everything around in her favour:

"I worked for my father," she justified her time in Bonn, "I never worked with him. I know what he is like and how his party think," or:

"I am not a practising Catholic. I was brought up with the values, so I am no threat to either camp."

Her replies pleased the present members. As with all political bodies there were several factions within the party, some more conservative than others. To speak out against her own father and to distance herself from the church completely was too big a step, even for the Social Democrats. There also were enough of them who didn't look too favourably on the Muslims themselves; the Gastarbeiter issue still divided the left just as much as it did the right.

When finally confronted about Esat she said: "I have married a Muslim, but I have not become one. In the same way,

Germany needs to accept the Gastarbeiter without fearing the loss of her identity."

Her diplomacy earned her a lot of admiration from those present. She was soon chosen for minor positions within the party hierarchy and was quickly promoted through the ranks without much outside help from Holger or Bonn functionaries.

By the time the selection for candidates to the City Council came it had been taken as a given that she would take over the fourth position on the list, which was traditionally the first slot for a woman. The leading woman amongst the local Social Democrats had already announced her retirement. When Maria was nominated for the top spot she narrowly beat her rival who only just managed to hide his surprise and anger over losing his privileged position.

Maria's rise had given the local Social Democrats a new impetus and sense of direction. The Social Democrats were currently in the Federal government but in Bavaria they were in the doldrums. Now there was a feeling that this might change for the first time in history. The success of the Social Democrats at the last nationwide General election of 1969 might finally pay off here in the last bastions of the perennial Conservative vote.

On hearing the news that her father had only secured the pathetic rank of fourteenth in his own party she felt a little pang of guilt and regret but Esat reminded her that if the roles were reversed, her father would be gloating and pointing a condescending finger at her. Besides, she was committed to her political ambition and her plans for a better future. As far as her motives were concerned, her candidacy had nothing to do with her father, although she knew that her political career was inseparable from her name and her roots.

The campaigning was hard work. In addition to discussion forums in Heimkirchen with candidates from other parties, she and her fellow Social Democrats handed out leaflets and information to people on the street and made themselves available for questions. Because of her notoriety, Maria was frequently requested to travel to other towns and support them in their campaigns. Her selection made her something of a symbol of feminism and female voters' associations all across Bavaria wanted her to speak to them about her rise within the party. Organised religious Turks were not too keen on her but most foreigners saw her as a symbol of better times to come and they invited her to social functions and gatherings, too.

Maria tirelessly attended as many of these invitations as she could, continuously telling herself that this was a necessity for her long term goal. She missed being with Esat and Lorenz though and hated having to sleep by herself in guest houses and hotel rooms. However, she knew that 'her boys' were well looked after. Esat had started working in the kitchen of the restaurant and Helga was caring for their son. In that respect everything had worked out well. Maria had all the time in the world to further her career and make a proper go of it. Occasionally she stopped and wondered if she really wanted to lead a life arguing and bickering with manipulative, ignorant and bigoted people. Had she not tried to escape that same world by moving away from her family? Both Markus and Esat were both important moral support for her, spurring her on and reminding her just how important her work was by paving the way for others. Still, sometimes she feared that she had become just like the rest of her family, only being different by standing on the other side of the fence; she dreaded a show down with her father in the political arena.

Fortunately her father had taken a back seat in the lead up to the elections and featured little in the campaign; she had heard this was not due to his lack of trying. The party leadership had carefully orchestrated his campaign trail around her movements. They did not want to lower the tone of their arguments in to that of a family feud. Despite earlier expectations and fears of a mud-slinging contest the run up to the elections was calm and relatively peaceful. Holger Behrens and his camp had done an excellent job of saying what they wanted to by not saying it: the reporters did this work for them. The leading Christian Democrat candidate built his campaign around the fairly safe and uncontroversial issues of child welfare and improvements to the local infrastructure. The rights of foreigners and feminism were not even remotely touched upon as he feared opening a can of worms.

The morning after the elections the city administration gathered all candidates in the town hall and announced the results. Due to the complex system of personal and party votes it had taken the volunteers all night to count and verify the results but finally the end result was in.

Hans-Ulrich's party had lost dramatically both to the far right and to the left. Hans-Ulrich had managed to climb up to twelfth position in the voters' favour but this year the party only achieved eleven seats out of the 23 possible. It was the first time in post war history that they had lost the absolute majority and would need a coalition partner.

Hans-Ulrich was devastated and without waiting to hear how his daughter had fared he left the room and went to his office, behaving as if nothing unusual had happened at all.

Maria dropped to second position on the list; he man who had held the top position at the last elections had climbed back up to the top spot. The Social Democrats had gained two additional seats, totalling a record breaking eight. The noise and commotion in the hall was enormous when the results were read out. Reporters from all of Germany had travelled to Heimkirchen and laid siege to Maria to ask her for comments on the outcome. However hard she tried to make this about her ideas and politics the newspapers could not resist bringing up her father's defeat in every article.

Together with the Liberal Party and an Independent Candidate there was a unique opportunity to form a city council without the Christian Democratic Party. In line with the Nationwide Coalition, the local Liberals offered their cooperation to the Social Democrats and Maria had ousted her father and his party.

Hans-Ulrich Hinterberger rapidly became a national synonym for a failed and old fashioned patriarch, out of sync with modern times. It quickly became a common slang expression to call any fallen and bitter old grouch a 'Hans-Ulrich Hinterberger'. "Who was that?", "No one important, just some Hans-Ulrich Hinterberger."

Lukas made the situation worse by legally challenging the election results since the Conservatives had missed the absolute majority of twelve seats by such a small margin. He demanded a recount, which amounted to no change in the actual seat distribution but stirred up a lot of ridicule for the obsessive streak in the Hinterberger family and the undignified way in which the son of the defeated politician had proved to be nothing but a sore loser. Naturally, the Social Democrats in Bonn took notice of this regional success story that had attracted so much attention and they earmarked Maria as a possible candidate for the next national election, scheduled in 1973.

Chapter 19: Markus (1972)

All the while Markus had been desperate to go back to Munich and see his new friends Balthasar and Barbara. For the first few months after his return to The Black Eagle he had been incredibly busy learning from his accountant. He also started up a personal campaign to mend the many bridges that Lukas seemed to have burned with their neighbours and fellow farmers in the area over the last few years.

Despite the rumours about his sexuality, Markus was able to bring back some of the lost business to the restaurant and establish friendly relations with the neighbouring farmers. After the self-absorbed way in which Lukas had run the show they were relieved to return to more amicable and friendly relations. Access rights, little disputes over fences and boundaries had been a pain for them when dealing with the competitively driven work ethos of Lukas but Markus had a knack for pleasing people and for choosing his battles. By letting the odd conflict go, and by not always insisting on his rights he gained respect and friends, and reaped more benefits in the long term than the small victories would ever have gotten him.

However, this new responsible and intense life demanded long hours every day, a lot of socialising and wining and dining of the local gentry. Only twice were any of his drinking companions ever brave enough to ask him directly about the gay rumours but Markus was sly, and wound his way out of answering them conclusively. To many of the farmers the concept of love between men was so alien that they were inclined to dismiss it as a fabrication anyway.

It was all the more a pleasant surprise to the overworked man to see Balthasar and his wife Barbara come in to the restaurant one evening.

"What a great surprise," Markus said excitedly, and hugged the two warmly. He was over the moon. "Come on, sit down," he said. "Have a look at the menu, choose anything you like. Your meals are on the house."

"Darling, calm down, will you." Barbara said bemused by his agitated state.

"I can't believe you really are here," Markus said happily. "I meant to visit you in Munich. I guess you have heard a little about the situation here."

"Yes, we know all about you," Barbara said, "Gossip travels fast."

"If the prophet won't come to the mountain, it has to be the other way round," Balthasar said cheerfully.

"You must not believe that I didn't want to see you. Not a day has gone by without me thinking of you. Lukas has quit the farm work and left me with both businesses to deal with. I don't know whether I am coming or going some days," Markus explained hastily.

"Don't you worry my dear," she replied. "Balthasar's family mentioned you and the restaurant when we last saw them. You are respected amongst the locals. We thought we would come here and see for ourselves how you are getting on. Looks busy enough, doesn't it?"

"I can't complain," Markus said cheerfully. "Only I never get a minute to myself."

"Better that than losing your business," Balthasar said.

"Of course," Markus agreed, "of course."

"Why exactly are you so busy?" Barbara asked. "Why are you running The Black Eagle and the farm personally? There must be someone else who can do that for you and – if you don't mind me saying this - possibly even better."

"It is a family business, we can't just give it away or hire someone we don't know," Markus replied.

"You could always sell it," she suggested. "Why work yourself into the ground? You have a good thing going in the restaurant. Most people only run one business at a time."

"You don't understand, Barbara," Markus said, "The farm has been the centre of our family for generations. I can't quit it now. I made a promise to my aunt."

"You could easily leave it all behind," Balthasar contradicted. "Who are you going to pass it on to? Everyone else has gone. Lukas has quit and if the rumours about him are true than he is losing his marbles at such a rate it won't be long before he cannot even do simple sums any more. Why fight for a tradition that has nothing to do with you? Does anyone in your family want it? Maria? If so, give it to her but don't burden yourself."

"I can't help feeling that if I let one part go I am destroying the whole," Markus admitted.

"You sentimental old fool," Barbara said warmly, "wasting your life away for something so meaningless. Not all traditions make sense to carry on. You must have your own life or you will end up miserable and odd, like your cousin Lukas."

"You know I even tried to give the farm to the idiot but he would not take it," Markus told her.

"If you sold the farm you would not only have time but you could make The Black Eagle an even bigger success."

"I agree," Balthasar said, "You haven't changed much of the place but the hall already looks much more welcoming than it used to. There is something in the air that is different."

"When are you ever going to get the time to come and see us in Munich?" she asked.

"If only I knew," Markus said melancholically.

"There is your answer," Barbara said quickly.

"Why are you so interested in my welfare?" Markus asked, astonished.

"We have grown rather fond of you," Barbara replied warmly. "There are not many people that Balthasar still sees from his youth, it is nice to have friends you share a common past with, don't you think? It is time that the gay world in Munich becomes less of a ghetto. We want to have friends that are in both of our worlds, here and there."

"We come here quite often to see my family," Balthasar explained.

"I wouldn't dream of persuading you to do anything you do not want to do," she added, "but I have seen many cases like yours. It pains me to see you torn apart and unsure of yourself like this. Some gay men stay in the closet and marry a woman, ending up with a frustrated and sexless marriage of convenience, others throw themselves full throttle into their work, just as you are doing now. You use anything as an excuse not to address the issue of romance and love and avoid the controversy it might attract. If you only were to decide to give your own natural life a chance, I feel that you could achieve great happiness. Maybe that is presumptuous and wrong of me but there you have it. I never learnt to keep my big mouth shut."

Markus laughed. "It is a very nice big mouth."

"It could do with being a little quieter," Balthasar said, rolling his eyes playfully.

"Choose what you want to eat," Markus said, "I have to attend to my other customers, unfortunately. I have neglected them far too long as it is. I will try and sit with you when everything has calmed down."

He sent them a bottle of his finest wine and briefly checked in with them several times over the course of the evening. When it was quiet enough to do so he asked the waitress to finish off the evening by herself, promising her a bonus payment for it.

"I am sorry I had so little time for you until now. I wish I had known you were coming, I would have organised the shifts differently," he said to his friends. "How are you?"

"Not much has happened since we saw you last," Barbara said. "Do you remember Christian, the guitar player? He keeps asking about you."

"How about you hire him and his colleagues one evening to play for your guests?" Balthasar suggested.

"We are not the kind of establishment to have music," Markus said evasively. "I am not sure our patrons would like us to add to the noise they are making themselves. Let alone the guests who try to sleep upstairs."

"Maybe you could use one of the outside buildings, once you have given up the farm?" Barbara wondered suggestively.

"It is worth thinking about, of course," Markus said quickly. He wanted to get the two of them to stop making plans for him and his future; they had made too many suggestions already. He needed time to think them over.

"Just imagine all the time you would have to spare once the farm is gone. You would not have to go to Munich yourself, you could bring Munich here."

"What do you mean?" Markus asked confused.

"Create the kind of meeting place that our community could go to," she explained.

"A gay bar in Heimkirchen? You are out of your mind. Maybe in twenty years, or thirty more likely, that might be thinkable, but now?" Markus said in disbelief at so much naivety.

"No, silly, just a friendly place, how about that?" she asked him.

"I am happy that none of the farmers have taken against me so far," Markus replied. "I am grateful for that and I am not going to alienate them with something they are not ready for yet."

"Perhaps you are right, we are just trying to make you see the long term prospects you have here," Balthasar said diplomatically. "You don't have to worry about your reputation with the farmers, by the way. Lukas has angered a lot of people and he has been going round the farms bad mouthing you and trying to lease his land to them instead of you but that campaign of his has seriously backfired."

"How so?" Markus was amazed.

"Most people here are simple farmers," Balthasar explained. "They have lived here for generations and they plan to do so for the foreseeable future. The ownership of the Hinterberger farm has changed a few times in their lifetime, why would anyone want to get involved in a family conflict that may be resolved in unpredictable ways, and then suffer the consequences if they supported the wrong player? All of that for the lease of a field? No, the people here are no politicians; they want to get on with their lives. They are challenged enough by the new technologies and the modern ways of farming. Their children are losing interest in the family business, their sons can't find brides who would be willing to work in the cow shed and yet they have to stay competitive in a hardening market. They prefer you to Lukas because you have always left them alone. You and Antoine were always good diplomats with your neighbours. Nobody is getting their hands dirty over you."

"What about the rumours?" Markus asked, pleased but also surprised by what he had just heard.

"Amongst all the other gossip that there is about your family that has become old news," Balthasar said with a wink. "Your personal life is not important right now, all eyes are on Maria and how she will fare in the City Council. I know a lot of conservative farmers who have voted for her. That inconspicuous little girl has made a huge impact."

"Even around here?" Markus asked. "I thought people were just polite when they mentioned her to me."

"No, she has done a lot of good with her humble attitude. The way she has handled being a woman candidate and being married to a Turk has broken down a lot of the prejudices around here in one giant step," Balthasar continued. "Not that anyone would want the same for their own children, of course, but they have listened to what she had to say. There are at least some farmers around here that are less threatened by the thought of intermarriage and female politicians now. They know her as such a sweet girl and she is still portraying that image very well in public. Any problems that the people have with your family are only with Lukas and his father for being so obsessive and stubborn."

"That is good to know," Markus said happily, "but I am still not so sure that Heimkirchen will accept me in the long run: me, a lover or a gay restaurant."

"Darling, just think for a minute," Barbara said, "there are quite a few camp characters, I mean really obviously gay men, and they are parading around happily on TV and in the cinema. Nobody is raising an eye brow as long as these characters don't go public and become outspoken or political about it."

"So, there is kind of a gentlemen's agreement to ignore it?" Markus asked.

"Yes, more or less," Balthasar said. "Everyone can pretend that they don't know and no one needs to feel they owe it to the moral standards to act upon it. All the while we get used to the colourful characters and accept them as part of our lives."

"Who is the dreamer now?" Markus asked critically. "You are talking about a society I doubt will ever exist. Accepting gay people? I am not even sure I would feel quite comfortable with that. Can you imagine two men ever holding hands on the street?"

"Sweetheart, there are lots of people around who don't want to see straight couples holding hands, or kissing each other either," Barbara replied. "You know very well that Catholics and any type of sex or body awareness do not go well together. Asking you to keep it out of sight is not a gay issue for them; it is a non sex issue. They won't ask, and you are not meant to tell."

"Do you really think that that is the unwritten deal?" Markus asked.

"Oh yes, especially now that it is legal," Barbara replied. "Maybe in fifty years' time society will be more liberal but for now this is already a giant leap forwards.

"I never imagined that there would be a law legalising what I am," he admitted. "Then I look at Maria marrying her Turk, going into politics and fighting for herself and other women who share her fate and in comparison I feel a little bit like a cop-out."

"Well you already are. You are here without a lover, people can think you are just another bachelor," Barbara pointed out. "You could of course go the other way and, like Maria, become the spokesperson for your people. Nothing is going to stop you if you want that kind of life but in that case I wouldn't recommend for you to be the owner of an inn around here. If you go all political, a lot of people will find they have to cut their ties with you for their own good. Besides, you are too soft for all that."

"Maria is soft," Markus replied, surprised to be rebuffed.

"She is soft on the outside but when she makes up her mind she can be very tough," Balthasar said, "at least that is how I see her."

"I do admire her for her guts," Markus confessed. "Now that I am being known as gay I wonder if I should not fight for the cause for others."

"Take it one step at a time," Balthasar advised him. "First get your own head sorted out and then, if you still feel brave and motivated enough, consider the politics. There are already brave people out there trying to get you the rights and recognition and respect that you deserve. You should only join them when you have your confidence and your views in order. Maria can probably tell you how hard politics can be. You need to convince yourself first that you have civil rights as a gay man before joining a campaign. Maria started to live with the Turk before she decided to make that an issue of her political career."

"Yes, you are right," Markus admitted. "I am still a little hung up about what people used to say about gays."

"Hung up, how?" Barbara asked.

"I worry that maybe they are right and that God hates us and will punish us."

"Even though you know that you never chose to become like this?" Balthasar asked, astonished at his friend's low self-esteem.

"Oh, have a drink," Barbara told him forcefully. "You need to relax and have a laugh once in a while. Being so serious is not good for your health or else you will become like your cousin Lukas. I can see that you have done nothing other than work since we last saw you. You were this reserved on the first day we met and it took a while to get you in a better mood then, too. When you left us you were a changed man."

"Then I was free to be whatever I wanted to be. Now that I am back here I have responsibilities that I cannot deny. That puts some limits on my freedom." Markus said quietly.

Most of the customers had already left. The three of them had sat in a far corner of the restaurant to have some privacy and had not noticed just how the place had emptied. On route from the kitchen to his sleeping quarters, Esat briefly joined the three of them at their table.

"Esat, these are my friends from Munich, Barbara and Balthasar," Markus introduced them. "I went to school with Balthasar, he is from around here. I told you and Maria about him."

"Of course, I remember," Esat said warmly. "The ones who took you to the red light district of Munich?"

"Guilty as charged," Balthasar said with a big grin.

"I can see what Maria saw in you," Barbara told him in a flirtatious manner, "you Turkish men are all so handsome with your dark looks. Very seductive. Thank God I am married already."

"Barbara!" Balthasar scolded her. He turned to Esat. "Forgive my wife, she has had a few drinks and in the circles we normally move she can almost say anything she likes. Because of that, she generally does not know when to shut up in decent company."

Esat smiled uncomfortably but shook his head as if to assure them that it did not matter.

"Where is your wife tonight?" Balthasar asked to change the subject quickly.

"A big party conference in Munich," he said curtly. "She won't be back until Monday."

"Tell her we wish her all the best," Barbara said slurring the words.

"We better get you to bed," Balthasar said to her.

267

"You are such an old bore sometimes," she replied.

"Shall I get you a taxi or do you want to stay here?" Markus asked them. "I have a few spare rooms, if you want."

"No, the walk will do us good," Balthasar declined. "We are here for a few days, so I hope we will get to see you again before leaving."

"It was nice to meet you," Esat said quickly, regretting that he had remained so quiet and even unwelcoming with these friends of Markus.

"Nice to meet you, too," Barbara said with a wink.

"Stop it," Balthasar said, pretending to be angry at her as he playfully pushed her out of the door.

"They seemed nice," Esat said after they had left. "It is good to see you having friends. Since you came back you have spent every day of every month working. You need to look after yourself a bit more," he suggested.

"That is what they said just now. I don't mind it so much," Markus replied. "This time round the work is harder but it is more rewarding, too. I did not appreciate what I had when I first came to be the boss."

"You were lucky to get a second chance."

"Yes, but it is not just that. In those days lots of people were interfering and making life complicated: Herbert, Lukas and even Anna sometimes. Now there are only a few of the family left and we are all pulling in the same direction. Isn't that great?"

"That might be true," Esat admitted, "but only because you are doing everything yourself and delegate the bare minimum. You still need to find time and someone special for yourself. You cannot just live for the restaurant."

"That will come," Markus assured him. "You sound just like those two," he added. "Balthasar and Barbara want me to quit the farm and just focus on the restaurant side of the business."

"That's an excellent idea," Esat said enthusiastically. "You never wanted it in the first place."

"It is a family business. I can't just throw it away," Markus replied.

"You don't want it, Lukas refused it, Maria and I would not know what to do with it. Sell it! If you don't the next owner will. How much longer do you think there will be farms of this size?

The future belongs to much bigger farms where everything is rationalised and modernised. The papers are full of it. The little ones are being edged out. You are lucky you have The Black Eagle to fall back on. You should sell and cut your losses before you start feeding the farm with the money you make here, that is what I believe," Esat said passionately.

"I thought it would be good to keep both businesses," Markus explained. "Anna always warned me that periods of economic health can be followed by years of struggle. If we have another war or another crisis at least I have two chances of surviving."

"That is all just speculation," Esat said. "You know if there is another war it will be nuclear and nobody will survive. The smaller farms are becoming less profitable and you'd do well to get out now, while you still can."

"They would never forgive us if we sold it," Markus said.

"Hans-Ulrich and Lukas you mean? They have already disowned you. There is a lot that they won't forgive you," Esat pointed out.

"Does Maria feel the same about it?" Markus asked.

"She is a politician now," Esat replied, "but even if she wasn't I doubt she would be interested in farm life; she prefers the restaurant. The main thing to remember is that Anna left it all to you; it is yours now, not just a loan from the past. I know it is hard to see something disappear that has existed for a long time but you cannot keep every tradition and every old thing alive. Time cannot be stopped and neither can progress."

"I can see where you got your vocabulary from," Markus joked. "You have been following Maria on her campaign too much, haven't you?"

Esat smiled but remained focused on the main issue. "Think about it: the timing is right," was all he said before going to bed and leaving Markus to ponder about the future and its many possibilities.

Markus felt still obliged to his family and wanted to preserve the farm and the life he had lead as a child but Esat and Balthasar were probably right and he was fighting a losing battle. Times did move on and standing still and doing nothing seemed not an option anymore.

Chapter 20: The End of it All (1975-76)

Lukas stood outside the farm building with a can of petrol. It was two thirty in the morning and he fought against his last hesitation to go ahead with his plan to torch the place down. He had waited for a long time for an opportunity like this and reminded himself of the reasons that he was here.

This weekend all of the occupants were gathered in Munich to celebrate Markus' 45th birthday in an infamous new gay bar. His cousin had even had the audacity of inviting him to the occasion but everyone would have known that he could not possibly be seen setting foot in such a seedy establishment. Surprisingly, he did not find the thought of Markus being gay that bothersome at all. It did not interest him what his cousin was and if he was going to go to purgatory or burn in hell for it. That had nothing to do with him. It was more his own image he was concerned about and if he should associate with that kind of person.

At some point after Markus' return there had been a small scandal about Markus and his lifestyle but it was much less dramatic than one would have thought and the family had weathered the storm easily.

He couldn't believe that a man who had embezzled him out of what was rightfully his had been welcomed back as though nothing had happened: Markus the liar, Markus the cheat, Markus the swindler.

It also bothered him intensely that the elections had ousted his father from active politics and instated Maria as a well-known and even popular regional celebrity; her connection with the farm and Markus were picked up by the newspapers and regarded as something positive. The Christian Democrats had tried to discredit Maria by showing just how 'modern' her views were, and how extremely unconventional 'that woman politician' really was but the shock wave that he had expected and looked forward to was, however, minimal. For the more conservative parts of the population that were following the local politics, this was only a small detail in the continuous decline of the Hinterberger family but he blamed her entirely for his father's fall from grace.

To the more liberal or left leaning voters, apparently such news only demonstrated consistency with the party line and Maria's personal strength to stand up for her convictions. According to some newspapers, during the years that the Social Democrats had been in government, a lot of traditional prejudices in the cold war driven minds of the people of Germany had been broken down. The Social Democrats Party claimed it had proven that it was indeed a centre party with no actual Socialist or Communist hidden agenda.

She was hailed for her progressive yet often also moderate views and this misguided image established her and the local branch of the party as a respectable and valid alternative that no one thought they had to fear. Her apparent likeable, humble and reasonable attitude was said to stand out in the otherwise ego-fuelled and unkind negotiations in the City Council; it was represented as a welcome break from the many rows the citizens of Heimkirchen had been used to from previous politicians. The thought of such false praise made his blood boil.

She had not even been in office for a year when the Bavarian State Social Democrats nominated her as the candidate to represent Heimkirchen in the state parliament in Munich. A campaign by the Christian Democrats to bring her into disrepute for abandoning her new post for higher offices after such a short period in the City Council backfired when she issued a very low key press statement, pointing out that on a higher level she would be able to do even more for her home town than she could do locally. With Maria it was never so much what she said but how she said it that meant that it seemed impossible for anyone to discredit her.

He briefly consoled himself that she did not do so well at state level; she just failed to get elected. However, fate was on her side and two months later she was the automatic replacement for a member who had to retire through ill health. That was when he first decided to take action.

Without thinking how much of an insult to her father this was, she claimed that she would have preferred to stay in Heimkirchen and gather more experience at the local level, but the party leadership in Bonn was determined to send out a strong signal that her rise within their ranks would send out to the entire country, especially since the recent instatement of the first female

271

President of the Parliament in Bonn. Maria's star quality was considered one of their biggest recent assets and the sooner they established her as a leading figure in Bavarian politics, the earlier they could recruit her for federal and governmental positions. From here onwards, in addition to her duties in Bavaria, Maria was frequently ordered to conferences in Bonn.

Lukas had managed to find out that Maria and Esat had left The Black Eagle Inn a few days prior to the birthday party to have a short holiday in the Bavarian capital together; they were accompanied by Helga who was helping with Lorenz. The farm building was empty tonight, the perfect time to bring the mockery that Markus was making of the family name and reputation to a flaming end.

Local slang had branded Hans-Ulrich as the symbol of lost hope and additionally to have the family business be associated with 'Socialists', foreigners and gays, was too shameful to bear. It was crazy that Maria and Markus were making such ignorant and fatal choices in their lives. Hopefully a phoenix would rise from the flames but at the very least there would be an end to this all and the embarrassment that he had to endure as a result of all this nonsense.

The front part of the building consisted of stone with only a wooden balcony and a few wooden planks for decorative purposes on the outside. The back part, however, was mostly wood. Lukas had never seen a house burn down that was not entirely made out of wood and so he was not sure how to proceed. He had to think logically where to use the petrol to inflict the maximum damage to the building and to make sure that all of it burnt down: he did not like the idea of failure, or doing things only by half.

Over the last few days there had been some heavy rain in the area and the wood was probably still damp. He walked towards the hay loft where he had spent so many nights as a child. He poured some petrol around but he wasn't confident that the fire would spread all the way to the main building from here. Hay burnt too quickly to rely on it as a link in a chain reaction. He had to inflict some damage to the main building itself, preferably the roof structure.

He took one of the ladders from the hay loft and carried it to the front of the house. He leaned it against the balcony and got the petrol but using petrol and attacking the front of the house would alert the authorities to foul play and suspicion would immediately fall on him. Was it really worth it?

He took a step back to look at the farm. A brief wave of sentiment came over him during which he considered leaving without accomplishing his mission, but then his anger took hold of him again and slowly climbed up the ladder. He reached the balcony safely, climbed over the railing and opened the can of petrol. What he needed was a cloth to smear the petrol on to the planks so the fire would engulf the roof. As he looked around the balcony floor in the dark he fell over some boots and tipped the petrol can over the edge. By the time he had climbed down and found the can there was hardly any liquid left inside.

He could not believe his bad luck. He took the almost empty can and smashed one of the front windows with it, soaked one of the curtains with the last drops of petrol and then lit it with a match. Without hesitation he ran towards the hay loft and dropped another few matches in there then he made a dash to his bicycle and cycled away as fast as he could.

Before long he heard the sirens of the fire brigade, assuring him that his mission had been successful. With this one swift action the Hinterberger Empire would come to its deserved and melodramatic end. Unfortunately, the noise of the sirens had woken up half of Heimkirchen and when he got to his home his widowed landlady was standing outside their building to find out what the commotion was all about. Now she would be able to tell the investigating police that he had been up at the time that the crime had been committed and she might even be able to smell the petrol on him.

Markus and his friends in the meantime had a fantastic time, oblivious to the dramas unfolding back home. Balthasar and Barbara had put on a great celebration with cabaret acts and a live band to play old favourites. Barbara's neighbour had offered to keep an eye on little Lorenz so that Helga could attend the party too. If the young boy should wake up and cause problems she promised to call the bar immediately.

"One part of me thinks that this is all disgusting," Helga confessed when she saw the men dressed as women, "and the other can't get enough of staring at them. I never thought I would live to see something like this."

"Oh darling," Barbara replied, "this is nothing new, you know. In the twenties and thirties there was plenty of it in the big cities. Everyone here who is old enough can tell you that. It is not your age that has spared you the sight, it is your location."

"Oh well, it certainly makes for good entertainment," Helga commented. "That guy over there looks so funny, not like a woman at all."

"You better not tell him that," Balthasar said quickly. "He wouldn't like to know."

"I am very grateful that you came," Markus told her. "It is like you are standing in for Anna."

"What about your own mother?" Helga asked. "Did you invite Erica?"

"She can't walk anymore and she really isn't interested in me or Gisela. When I speak to her she doesn't seem to listen or care, she might as well speak to a stranger from the street," he said sorrowfully. "I guess I have myself to blame for that, I never made enough effort with her either. Life at the The Black Eagle was always so much more fun than being at home with her and my father. It's what I deserve. I would have liked to make it up to her but there is no getting through to her now. At least she is with her own family now, who look after her."

"As your mother she could have made different choices. Don't take the blame. What about Gisela? Has Thomas found her yet?" Helga asked.

"Still no success. The insurance company that Erwin worked for went into bankruptcy. Thomas has been contacting other companies in the area but we are not having much luck. It is such a shame. Finding her should be so easy."

"Thomas has a habit of suddenly striking gold, just when you think there is no hope," Helga reminded him.

"Let's drink to that." Barbara said.

"Of all these men there is not one that could take your fancy?" Helga asked him. "I find that hard to believe."

"Tell me about it," Barbara agreed. "All of these men are so beautiful, so gentle and handsome. If I were a gay man I

274

would not know where to look first: our Markus cannot pick even one."

"There are enough attractive men here," Markus admitted, "but falling in love is a different matter."

"Markus, I was lucky to have had a substitute for a marriage or family of my own," Helga said sharply, "but at any moment Herbert or Anna could have sent me packing and I would have been all by myself. Don't turn your back on a chance of happiness for yourself. Go over there and speak to the men. You are not getting any younger. You won't fall in love by standing her doing nothing. Find someone who can keep you company when you get old."

"Please, enough now," Markus said jokingly. "It is my birthday and I don't want any lectures today."

"Fine, be like that," Helga replied sulkily and turned to Maria. "What are you working on at the moment in 'Socialist' headquarters?" she asked.

"Social housing is our main concern at the moment. We need to build more affordable homes," the young mother replied.

"With what money?" Balthasar asked her.

"There are a lot of good schemes in discussion," Maria explained. "One option is for the future tenants to become owners, part owners or depending on their income and capabilities, simply rent at affordable rates. The state can borrow temporarily and make it back over time without losses for the nation, only without the huge profit margin that private companies would demand if they did the same."

"A fragile concept if there is no profit margin for the tax payer," Balthasar claimed.

"Stop your politics," Barbara intervened. "Maria, my husband is very conservative. Don't be fooled by his nice appearance and his tolerant presence in here. When it comes to economics he has no soft streak."

"The gay issue is a liberal issue," Balthasar protested. "I am a Liberal voter."

"Remember how you told me to sell the farm?" Markus reminded his friend. "Well, I am considering closing the farm and selling the land to one of the companies that are planning the national social housing scheme for the government."

"You are mad if you do that," Balthasar said curtly. "I guess they won't be paying you the top market price?"

"Maybe not as much as I could sell it for but enough for what I need," Markus replied.

"There must be a law against such a conflict of interest," Helga said. "If Maria is part of the political movement behind it then it can't be legal for her family to make a profit from the scheme."

"I am not directly involved in it," Maria argued. "The party and the government are."

"Mark my words, that will drag your name through the dirt," Balthasar told her. "The people of Heimkirchen won't be able to distinguish between the politicians in Bonn and yourself."

"I hope the people of Heimkirchen will be happy that there will be affordable housing," Maria said.

"They have a point," Esat addressed his wife. "The mob here will only see that your cousin is selling his land in a scheme that your party initiated. That will be regarded as profiteering and underhand dealing."

"Most of the land belongs to Lukas anyway," Maria pointed out. "Everyone knows that he and I don't see eye to eye."

"We will see how sophisticated people will respond to the news," Balthasar said self-assured.

"Enough of this political talk," Barbara said angrily. "Esat, is this your first time in a gay bar? How does it feel for a Muslim?"

"You tactless cow," Balthasar scolded her. "How can you bring up something like this?"

"It is fine," Esat reassured him but he could not hold back a little smirk about it. "I am used to people seeing me as the representative of all things Turkish and Muslim. It is my first time, Barbara, and I find it also very entertaining. I am not a strict Muslim at all. I don't think that Allah really has anything against the people here."

"Do you fancy any of the men dressed up as women?" she asked. "Balthasar has admitted he likes some of them."

"It is time to get you sobered up," Balthasar said to his wife.

"No," Esat said with a shy laugh, "I don't fancy any of them. Too much make up, they look like tarts."

Barbara gave him a suspicious look, worrying he was alluding to her own generous helping of foundation that evening. She liked to dress elegantly and put a lot of effort in her looks.

"It is time we had a dance," Markus said quickly rescuing the situation and he took Barbara by the arm and dragged her on the dance floor.

"Don't listen to Balthasar," Barbara said. "I think it is a great idea to sell and an even better one to do so with a view to charity."

When the band took a break he returned to their table and took Helga aside.

"You have been very quiet about me selling the farm. What do you make of the idea of selling up?" he asked her.

"I don't understand much about the legal aspects of selling it like this," she said evasively. "I can't give you a lot of advice on it."

"I don't mean it in a legal sense," Markus replied. "I am talking about tradition and what Anna would have wanted."

"Anna would have said no to a sale," Helga replied, "but for all the wrong reasons. She did not grow up in the same times as you have. She lived in a bit of a dream world for the last years of her life. She couldn't see that farming was undergoing a change. She just about acknowledged that life was not as it was before but I doubt she would ever have taken it as far as giving up the farm entirely. If she were your age now maybe she would know better. If you want to sell it then go ahead and do it. She gave the farm to you, at some point it became yours and yours to keep or to pass on yourself. She can't have a hold over it for ever and beyond the grave."

"What would you do?" Markus put her on the spot.

"I would check the legality of that sale," she said, "but if it is all kosher then why not? You would be doing a good thing. Anna is not getting anything out of it if you keep the business for her. She is dead, if you hadn't noticed. No one is reaping any benefits from it at all. The Rieder family is buying up a lot of the farm land around here, they can pocket whatever the government doesn't want, so the tradition can be served that way.

The next morning Helga and Markus returned to Heimkirchen to find their home seriously damaged by fire. A guest at the restaurant had called the fire brigade almost immediately. The flames from the hay loft had been so bright that he woke from the light even before the smoke could be smelt.

The loft building had completely burnt down to the ground but the house had taken far less damage thanks to the quick response by the fire brigade, who was still securing the property when the two residents arrived.

The police had found evidence of foul play easily. The fact that the fire had started at two different locations and that there were traces of petrol around the building were more than enough evidence.

Helga and Markus were taken to the office in the restaurant building to give their statements to the investigators. Although both of them had a hunch who might be behind the fire, they did not point the police in the direction of Lukas. Without concrete evidence Markus thought it unjust to make such an accusation and Helga could not make herself say what she knew in her heart to be true. There was still some of the admiration and love in her for the young man that she had once known as honourable and worthy of her affections. If she were to tell the police her suspicions, she would kill the last part of an illusion that her former favourite might turn his life around.

Other staff at the farm and the restaurant were a little more outspoken about the possible arsonist. Lukas was questioned several times but fortunately for him the widow gave him an alibi. She did not believe for a second that this honourable, if somewhat eccentric, man could have been capable of such a horrible crime. She declared that she had heard Lukas leave the flat only seconds after the siren had started and that he had been in her house all day until then. Lukas claimed the same without knowing that she had backed up his story.

The crime remained unsolved and became subject to much speculation. The insurance footed a separate investigation but also came to no official conclusion. In view of the devastation of the farm building, Markus found it easy to come to his final decision of selling the farm and the land that he owned around it. Maria added what was left in her name to it and after a brief negotiation with the social housing holding the sale was made public.

Naturally, the news was received with a lot of controversy and more speculations linking the fire and the sale.

Lukas instigated an investigation about what he called a conflict of interest between Maria's party politics and her profit in the sale. Maria replied with a public statement that she would donate the money she made from the sale, should a court find her guilty of profiteering.

Both her and Markus' names however were cleared by the investigative team who found that no violation had taken place and the sale was allowed to proceed.

The holding group approached Lukas to buy some of his land but he refused to sell at the low prices they were offering and approached the Rieder Farm to sell to them instead. The farmers were prepared to buy for even less. They felt unsure about tending to fields that were located next to a massive future building site and were not looking to expand anyway.

Too proud to go back to the holding company, he left his lands unattended and started to live off his savings.

Markus used the proceeds of the sale to renovate the Inn and he also bought a small tavern in Munich, which he asked Barbara and Balthasar to run for him. They were over the moon to be given such a great opportunity. As more gay people came out of the closet, there was increased demand for social venues. Barbara was very careful not to alienate the owners of existing pubs. She had been a regular at those places for such a long time that none of them wanted to see her as competition. Her outrageous and over the top style complemented the current scene perfectly. Thus far, the gay establishments had all been very traditional and careful not to stray too far from the mainstream and so Barbara decided on going in a completely different direction and open a glamorous and glittery place which she named Flamingo. She decorated the place almost entirely by herself to make sure that no straight laced handymen cramped her style: gold, red and purple featured heavy in her designs. When she opened the pub for business it became an immediate success for the more flamboyant men on the scene, which left the already established bars more room for the novices and the less adventurous men.

Helga was pestering Markus not to invest too much money in the refurbishment of The Black Eagle Inn. She predicted that the building site that was not too far away, and the future occupants of the social housing estate, would have a bad impact on the business but he remained optimistic. The construction did not affect the business negatively over the coming years. The Inn was still located idyllically enough and was well sheltered from view of the site. Some of the workers even came for lunch to the restaurant and Markus added a little pub area and bowling lanes to the premises where they could gather after work for a beer before going home.

Lukas, meanwhile, was starting to fall behind in his rent. The widow was so besotted with him that for several months she allowed him to fall in arrears but eventually she could not afford to do so and broached the subject with him.

He had to bite the bullet and approach the holding group to sell at least a small part of his land. By now, the construction had gone so far ahead that his land was no longer as useful as it would have been at an earlier stage of the planning. The price for it was now much lower than he had anticipated. Forced by his new monetary situation, he sold the most awkward strip of land which was virtually surrounded by newly erected buildings anyway and was of no use to anyone else. As the company now only wanted to convert the area into a playground, he was offered a pittance for it.

Esat, tired of waiting for his wife to return to The Black Eagle on the weekends, decided to give up his position there and joined Maria in Munich, where the busy politician had bought a flat with the money she had made from selling the land. While Maria was getting drawn into a nationwide campaign for the next Federal Election in 1976, he decided to ask Barbara for a job at her new tavern. The older woman was beside herself to have such a good looking man working in her establishment. Her customers adored Esat and fell over themselves for this lovely man. He enjoyed the attention and found he preferred the colourful ambience at the tavern to the hard work and often unfriendly atmosphere in the kitchen of The Black Eagle, or at the docks in Hamburg. Had it not been for Barbara and her natural authority with some of the more difficult and bitchy customers, he might have taken longer to get used to the flamboyant and outrageous characters but after a while this became his new home. His association with the gay scene of Munich had caused some internal controversy at the Maria's Party. The more conservative of its leaders were concerned that Maria and her husband were taking their extravagance a little too far and feared that should the Christian Democrats single her out as a target in the election campaign, the voters might respond in a negative way; she could be used as a scary example of how far the Social Democrats were going in their progressive and modern ways.

When Maria got wind of the brewing storm against her she contacted the Liberal party, who was the current federal coalition partner of the Social Democrats and who was expected to continue this partnership after the elections. The Liberal Party had been the actual mastermind behind the legalisation of homosexuality in Germany back in 1969 and their party leaders were appalled at the possibility of an internal attack on Maria by her fellow Socialists on grounds of her husband's workplace.

The following month the federal party leaders met to agree on a joint election manifesto and to have preliminary talks about possible candidates for ministerial positions. The Liberal delegates at the meeting insisted that the Socialists nominate Maria for one of the important posts. The inconspicuous little girl of Catholic parents had risen to the top of German politics and was unstoppable.

Feeling superfluous in Heimkirchen since her home had burnt down, Helga had been staying in one of the staff rooms at The Black Eagle and had begun to dedicate her time to Lorenz, so that his father Esat could work in the restaurant. When the young couple moved to Munich for good they asked her to move with them as their child minder, an opportunity that Helga jumped at. Once again the old woman considered herself lucky to have gone from one great opportunity to the next. She could have been cast out many times over the years from the farm, especially after Anna died, but she had always found a way to make herself useful and be needed in a way that pleased her too.

In the last few days leading up to the federal election, Esat had to join his wife on the campaign trail and left her all alone with Lorenz. It seemed the perfect opportunity for her to take the boy on a trip to Heimkirchen and introduce him to his grandparents. Hans-Ulrich and Magdalena were old and stubborn but whose heart would not melt at the sight of this beautiful and charming boy?

Lorenz was six years old now and had inherited his mother's charm. Everyone who got to meet him fell in love with this cheerful and loving young boy and so would his grandparents, she was sure of it.

She took an early morning train and arrived in Heimkirchen around 10am. She walked from the station to the main square, showing the young boy around a children's playground and a little park area where swans were fed by generous feeling pedestrians. When she treated him to a buttered Pretzel and a hot chocolate in one of the street cafes, she saw Lukas sitting alone at a table and reading the papers. He flinched when he recognised her but had nowhere to run; pretending that he had not seen her he buried his head in the paper and turned his back towards her as far as he could in his seat.

Helga hesitated a little. Seeing the odd miser behaving in such a distant and rude manner made her think twice whether her plan to introduce Lorenz to his estranged family was such a good idea after all. She had been so certain that the mere sight of the child would transform those bitter people and melt their frozen hearts. She just had not thought about the hurt and the damage that a possible rejection might do to the boy himself.

She told Lorenz to stay in his seat and walked over to Lukas by herself.

"What are you doing here?" he asked her rudely. "I thought you lived with Maria in the Socialist Palace in Bonn?"

"Don't be like that Lukas," she said calmly and warmly. "You and I go back practically all of your life. There is no need to be snappy with me. How are you?"

"How am I?" Lukas called out loudly. "You have a cheek to ask me such a question, Helga. Didn't you help that wastrel Markus to get back in to the saddle? When he decided he had seen enough of the world and had spent enough of the stolen money he came and took what I had resurrected from the ashes. And then he sold everything to social housing, making the little land that I had left utterly worthless. I am not great, thanks to you. I think I have every right in the world to be snappy to you."

"Oh, let go off your pathetic self-pity, Lukas," she replied angrily. "No one forced you to leave the farm. It was legally his,

282

you know that. Blame Anna for that but at least she was honest with you all the time. You could have looked for a life elsewhere. Your stubbornness has taken you to where you are. You have been almost like a son to me, much more so than Markus but you make it so incredibly difficult to like you these days. You cling to your anger and bitterness when there are outstretched hands everywhere. Look at what you have become and even now you spit in my face? What for? When you go back to your bed tonight are you going to be proud that you told me to go away? What is it like to be so cold and lonely? Over there is your nephew. I would have thought that without children of your own you might be happy to at least have a look at the boy and see the new generation of Hinterberger family, even if he is half Turk."

"You see Helga," he said with a sneering laughter, "I am not as desperate as you just yet. The next thing you will be telling me is that I should be proud of Maria's political career and be godfather to that little Muslim boy. Being a politician for those 'Socialists' is worse than being no one at all and the same goes for that damn child."

"You are good at putting everyone down Lukas," Helga said sharply. "I would like you to tell me what you are living for? Is there anything constructive or good that you are achieving with your own life? I hear that you are good at writing letters and criticising the ones who actually do something but you yourself, what is the last thing you have done that has had any positive impact on anyone?"

"Believe it or not, but my criticism is very important to better our society," he replied arrogantly. "I am making a difference continuously by correcting the people around me."

"You are deluded if you think that anyone is taking any notice of you," Helga told him coldly. "Half of the world laughs about you and the other humours you so that you go away and leave them alone. Stop being so hardened and reach out to your family while you still can. It doesn't seem like you are leading a happy life. You are not fooling anyone."

"Happiness is overrated," he said quickly.

"I know, the Good Lord and his rules of suffering," Helga said. "So you are taking after your father now. Do you really not want to say hello to little Lorenz? He is such a darling."

"No, I will not, thank you very much," he said. "If you excuse me I have some reading to do. While the rest of the world is wasting their time with adoring half cast babies and voting for the Reds, some of us will not stick our heads into the sand and watch that happen without a proper fight."

"I used to believe in the good in you," Helga said. "So much that when the police were investigating the arson at the farm I could never tell them that I feared it was you. Looking at you and your obsessive delusions I could not be more certain of your guilt. Just wait and see what the Good Lord will tell you about that on Judgement Day. Just because you judge everyone else around you for the smallest mistake they make won't deter Him from seeing all the terrible sins you have committed yourself. If someone used the Bible and its maxims against you in the same harsh way as you do for others, you wouldn't come out looking good. Trust me."

"Oh what do you know about these things?" he said disparagingly.

"I am twice your age," she said confidently. "I have seen a few things you haven't seen yet."

She left him to his reading and returned to her little boy. Lorenz had finished his Pretzel and hot chocolate already.

"Who was that man and why was he so angry?" he asked her.

"He was angry because he is sad," she explained. "The poor man has made a few mistakes in his life and now he is too proud to admit it and change his ways. Inside he is crying but he does not want me to see it, so that is why he is so angry."

"Can't I go and try and cheer him up?" Lorenz suggested full of sympathy.

"I wish you could, but he won't let us," she told him.

"What a sad man," Lorenz said.

"Yes," she agreed. "It is sad."

The two left the cafe and went for a stroll through the city before turning towards the main square and the church opposite Hans-Ulrich and Magdalena's apartment. The church bells were ringing, inviting the faithful to join the priest for the late-morning prayer service.

Disappointed by Lukas and his hard stance, Helga was wondering whether to risk another sad encounter or just to go home with her mission unaccomplished.

She sat down on a bench outside the church while considering her options. Hans-Ulrich had retired from his office and was at home all day long. She had heard from Maria that he was also no longer active for the Christian Democrats. Helga could not imagine that he would not want to see his grandchild now that he was out of the public limelight. Had he not at one point considered endorsing Maria and her husband as a moderate and conservative mixed race couple? He could not be all stubborn there had to be some hope for a change of heart, especially since the child had not been made a Muslim in any way.

Magdalena also could not possibly be as hard and mean spirited as she once had been about Maria and her Turk. An ageing woman who used to have such a big and loving heart simply had to succumb to the sight of her grandchild, especially one as cute and sweet as Lorenz.

As she sat there contemplating what to do Magdalena was crossing the street towards the church and recognised the two on the bench immediately. There was plenty of time for her to get away without being seen, Helga was clearly deep in thought and unaware of her surroundings. However, Magdalena felt a surge of curiosity and could not stop staring at them until it was too late. The boy had noticed her fixed gaze towards him and alerted his nanny to the woman across the street. Well, there was nothing else to do than come closer and greet the two civilly, Magdalena decided and did just that.

"This is Lorenz, Maria's son," Helga introduced the little boy, "and this is Magdalena, an old friend of mine." She did not want to put pressure on the child's grandmother to act in a particularly friendly or motherly way.

"Handsome," Magdalena said kindly, "very handsome."

"Isn't he just, "Helga said proudly. "I wanted to show the young man where his mother grew up."

"What a lovely idea," Magdalena replied. "I would invite you to come to prayer with me, which is what I did with his mother every day, but I must assume he has not been christened?"

"I am afraid he is not, but if it is any consolation he is no Muslim either," Helga said with a smile. She was very impressed with Magdalena's accepting and warm demeanour.

"I would love to invite you to our apartment but this week is not very good for that," Magdalena explained. "Hans-Ulrich has been following the election campaign closely on television and he is not a happy man at all. I think the timing for an introduction is very bad. How about we go to the lake and feed the swans?"

"Yes, we can do that again, can't we Lorenz?" Helga asked.

"Yes, please!" the little boy said excitedly.

"I am surprised you have a TV," Helga said.

"I don't think much of it," Magdalena explained, "If it was not for the transmission of the Pope's Easter and Christmas Messages and the Blessing live from The Vatican we would have never considered it. Now that Hans-Ulrich is at home all day and does not want to leave the house due to shame and bitterness it is a very good thing. Now Lorenz tell me, how old are you?"

"Six!"

"So you are going to school already. How do you like it?"

"So so," the little man replied. "It means I am gone for half of the day and won't see Helga."

"Yes but you see me before and after school," his nanny pointed out. "That still is plenty."

"At least at school you get to meet lots of other children your age, that must be so much more fun than hanging around with an old woman like her or like me," Magdalena said and smiled at Helga. She was immensely grateful for the chance to meet and spend time with Lorenz. Her experience with Turkish families in her charity work and her growing loneliness had helped her to lose some of the harshness that had been more an acquired part of her character, rather than an innate part of her. She saw so little of her children these days and of her few friends too many had died already. She often felt isolated in her life. Even at church and at the charities there were young and modern women who had different beliefs, and ventured less rigid and literal interpretations of the Bible and the scripture. While she was unable to answer those open ended questions by herself, she had let in a little doubt and taken to the possibility that maybe, just maybe, there were things that she had been wrong about. In her growing lack of certainty about what was right and wrong she thought it would do no harm to talk and play with her grandchild. It was not Lorenz's fault that his parents had been such ignorant fools. Of course, Hans-Ulrich must not find out about it or she would never hear the end of it. The Good Lord had let it happen that this child had been brought in to the World; it could not be in his interest that the poor thing should be abandoned and ignored by his own flesh and blood.

Was she a good Christian for forgiving her daughter or would it have been better to force her daughter to come to her senses by continuously shunning her? The new priest at the church was taking a much more lenient and sympathetic line in his preaching, whereas Hans-Ulrich became harder and more judgemental by the day. Quite frequently when Magdalena confessed to views, deeds or feelings that she had, and Hans-Ulrich considered a transgression on the scripture, the man in the confession box would assure her that she had done nothing wrong in the eyes of the Good Lord. The widening gap between the two worlds confused her no end and left her without proper guidance. Since it was impossible to please both the priest and her husband at the same time, or find a way to establish for sure which one of them had a better connection to the Good Lord, for the first time in decades she started to listen to her own feelings. She walked back home to spend the rest of the day listening to Hans-Ulrich's doom and gloom about the elections on Sunday and the sure disaster that was to befall the country upon the implementation of its results.

Helga and Lorenz decided to have some lunch of their own and what better place to have it than The Black Eagle? The two took a public bus to the restaurant. Markus was not working today and Helga had to ask one of the waitresses to tell the busy manager that she and Lorenz had come for a visit. They took a seat in the packed restaurant and looked at the menu. Since she had been here last a lot of things had changed. The food on offer seemed much simpler and cheaper. The customers too were not the same regulars that she could have recognised.

"The farmers and the local gentry don't come here anymore," Markus explained after he had joined them and she asked him about it. "Ever since the social housing estate was completed, we had more of the new residents coming in for a few pints in the evening. The established snobs around here didn't like to mix with the new lot and started to stay away. I had to change the menu because our new clients couldn't afford what we used to offer. It has all changed so quickly."

"Has the business suffered from it?" she asked concerned.

"Oh, not to worry," he reassured her. "We still make enough. The food we serve now costs us less to make so we are still doing all right. The Rieder Farm has sold some of their land to the holding group so there will be even more new buildings in the future. Heimkirchen needs a new sewage plant and that is probably coming our way too, near where the Wimmer Farm used to be, which also means more business from the construction site and the workforce there. The Black Eagle is no longer what it used to be. The city is growing and we are being swallowed up by it. We have a different kind of business now, but that is fine."

"You don't mind?" she asked surprised.

"Not really," Markus replied. "I liked it the way it was but nothing ever stays the same. Getting sentimental about it is not going to help me; besides, the new customers are not such hard work and so I have more time for my theatre group."

"Is that why we never see you in Munich?" she asked.

"Yes, I am sorry. I should have come to see you," Markus apologised. "I spend a lot of my time in rehearsals. That, and I didn't want to look over Barbara's shoulder while she is establishing herself. I thought she might want to get going without feeling she is being checked upon. She knows how to reach me if she needs to ask me anything and I prefer her to run the business the way she thinks fit. I am actually desperate for a good night out. Next month the play has its premiere. After that I should have more time to come and see you all in Munich."

"What play are you putting on?" Helga asked.

"No Exit by Sartre," he replied. "We are rehearsing in the barn at the back of The Black Eagle. The Grammar School is letting out their assembly hall on the weekends. You will have to come and watch."

"We will see about that," she said evasively. "Sartre sounds awfully serious and exhausting. Maybe when you do a comedy I will come to see it."

"Tell Maria that the Social Democrats are having some of their party meetings in my restaurant now that it is no longer so posh," he requested. "I hope she is as pleased as I am about it. Of course, in the social housing estate there are more members of the Social Democrats party than there were amongst the farmers."

"Oh dear, if the old generation were still alive to witness that fall from grace," Helga said, half smiling half mourning.

"Some of them still are," he pointed out.

"Yes, at least in body, if not in mind," she said, thinking of Hans-Ulrich.

"Tell Maria good luck and that she is always welcome here." Markus said before going back to his theatre production.

"I will. I am sure that this time next week you will have a relative in the government," Helga predicted.

"I am looking forward to it."

That Sunday at the polling station the Social Democrats received enough votes to remain in office, and, as agreed between the coalition partners beforehand, Maria was offered a ministerial position. She became head of the newly created portfolio of Secretary for Women and Integration of Gastarbeiter.

Epilogue

Maria remained in government until the breakdown of the coalition in 1983, after which she returned to Munich and Bavarian politics full time to be able to spend more time with her husband and son, instead of the constant commute between Bonn and her home. Although shunned by both of their families, the couple lived to enjoy a popular and happy life together in Munich and never regretted their role as pioneers for mixed marriages.

Esat succeeded Barbara and Balthasar as the manager of The Flamingo Bar in Munich after the former landlady suffered a stroke in 1981. In the same year, Helga started to lose her eye sight due to an aggressive case of glaucoma and became housebound for the rest of her days. She still kept Lorenz and Esat company in the apartment, even though she was no longer able to be of any assistance for the two and was more being looked after than the other way round.

The gay bar continued to be an excellent business under Esat - even when the panic around AIDS hit the scene viciously and many gay men stayed at home in fear of contact with each other. The Flamingo had always attracted the more loud mouthed, noticeable and political parts of the gay community, who would not allow themselves to be defeated and fade into the dark corners of society where they had spent the years before 1969.

Twice the bar was attacked by Neo Nazis and once Esat was even beaten up by some anti-gay 'Christian' demonstrators on his way to work. The pub stayed in business regardless and witnessed and celebrated the further liberalisation of gay rights that were to follow in the decades to come.

Despite his progressive upbringing, Lorenz did not follow in his mother's footsteps. He was not interested in politics. His goal in life as teenager of the 1980s was to become rich and be cool. He studied economics and became a leading executive for an import/export firm which predominantly traded with Turkey and Syria.

He preferred his friends not to know that his mother was the bohemian and left wing politician and when he was asked about his famous surname he usually just replied that it was a very popular Turkish name.

Hans-Ulrich lived a long and miserable life during which he was forced to see his daughter almost weekly on television, walking from political triumph to triumph, while his own name remained an often used insult. His daughter's popularity was a constant reminder of his own failure on every level: as a father, as her instructor in matters of faith, as a politician and as a good Christian who could not make himself forgive and turn the other cheek, however desperately he wished he could reach out to her.

His wife Magdalena died in 1977, very suddenly of heart failure, and left him alone in his apartment disgruntled and isolated. Even the return of the Christian Democrats to government in 1983 could not make him happy.

Still mortified to hear his name being used in such a derogative fashion as a symbol for a 'has-been', he stayed indoors as much as he could and never even answered the door bell. His body was found by concerned neighbours two weeks after he died of a brain haemorrhage.

The legacy of which he was proud was only some of his children:

Firstly, there was Otto, the monk that – like his father – had not left his 'home', a monastery, in decades and devoted his entire life to worship and abstinence of all sins. Hans-Ulrich would have liked to see more of this fine example of a Christian upbringing but had reason enough to be proud, even from a distance.

Secondly, there was Klara, the only child of his that had married well and produced grandchildren he was proud of. Even if he never got to see them, he could still think about them and be content.

Martin sent him the occasional letter from America with family pictures of his wife and children. These were the only bearers of the Hinterberger name but the fact that his wife was not German and that this all was taking part in a distant land was enough to make him upset instead of proud.

Hans-Ulrich was blessed to be spared the truth about his youngest son, Joseph, whose controversial and modern views led him to be extricated from the Catholic Clergy and who went on to become a priest for the progressive Old Catholic Church, a group of formerly faithful, who allowed women to become priests and who did not recognise the authority of the Pope. If he had known about that he might have died much sooner.

Lukas lived off the sales of his land until his money ran out. Unable to find 'suitable' employment he was eventually evicted from the apartment that he had shared with the widow. He lived on the streets until a cold winter night claimed his life.

Markus never seriously got involved with another man. However, he found his own kind of happiness with the amateur theatre group that he successfully led until his death in 1998.

Sadly he never found his sister Gisela. After her husband Erwin had lost his job at the insurance company the two of them moved to several cities, each time following short term employment opportunities that did not work out. They ended up not far from Hamburg and could have been easily located if Thomas Holzapfel, the detective instructed to locate them, had spoken to the right person in an insurance company that had temporarily taken Erwin on.

Gisela had sent several changes of address cards to her brother but the timing was so unfortunate that none of them reached him. Until her death, she believed that her brother was no longer interested in speaking to her.

When Erica, their mother, died of pneumonia Markus put the announcement in several national newspapers, but this huge investment did not pay off. The week it was published she and her husband were on a holiday in Denmark.

Despite this tragic end to the relationship between brother and sister the silver lining for Gisela was that – since the last attempt to contact her brother in 1970 – she truly moved forward with her own life, without regrets or looking back. Her marriage, which up until then had been a means to her escaping from the farm, became a proper home and source of lasting happiness, something that might not have happened if her thoughts had still been fixated on Markus and The Black Eagle Inn.

After Markus' death The Black Eagle Inn was sold to new owners who kept the name but refurbished it in a modern yet traditional Bavarian style.

The End

Did you like the book?

Let everyone know by posting a review on Goodreads, Amazon.com or Amazon.co.uk to tell others about it.

More books by Christoph Fischer:

The Luck of the Weissensteiners (Three Nations Trilogy Book 1)

In the sleepy town of Bratislava in 1933 the daughter of a Jewish weaver falls for a bookseller from Berlin, Wilhelm Winkelmeier. Greta Weissensteiner seemingly settles in with her in-laws but the developments in Germany start to make waves in Europe and re-draw the visible and invisible borders. The political climate, the multi-cultural jigsaw puzzle of the disintegrating Czechoslovakian state and personal conflicts make relations between the couple and the families more and more complex. The story follows the families through the war with its predictable and also its unexpected turns and events and the equally hard times after. What makes The Luck of the Weissensteiners so extraordinary is the chance to consider the many different people who were never in concentration camps, never in the military, yet who nonetheless had their own indelible Holocaust experiences. This is a wide-ranging, historically accurate exploration of the connections between social status, personal integrity and, as the title says, luck.

Praise for The Luck of the Weissensteiners: "...powerful, engaging, you cannot remain untouched..." "Fischer deftly weaves his tapestry of history and fiction, with a grace..."

On Amazon: http://bookshow.me/B00AFQC4QC
On Goodreads: http://bit.ly/12Rnup8
On Facebook: http://on.fb.me/1bua395

Sebastian
(Three Nations Trilogy Book 2)

Sebastian is the story of a young man who has his leg amputated before World War I. When his father is drafted to the war it falls on to him to run the family grocery store in Vienna, to grow into his responsibilities, bear loss and uncertainty and hopefully find love. Sebastian Schreiber, his extended family, their friends and the store employees experience the 'golden days' of pre-war Vienna, the times of the war and the end of the Monarchy while trying to make a living and to preserve what they hold dear. Fischer convincingly describes life in Vienna during the war, how it affected the people in an otherwise safe and prosperous location, the beginning of the end for the Monarchy, the arrival of modern thoughts and trends, the Viennese class system and the end of an era. As in the first part of the trilogy, "The Luck of The Weissensteiners" we are confronted again with themes of identity, Nationality and borders. The step back in time made from Book 1 and the change of location from Slovakia to Austria enables the reader to see the parallels and the differences deliberately out of the sequential order. This helps to see one not as the consequence of the other, but to experience them as the momentary reality as it must have felt for the people at the time.

Praise for Sebastian: "I fell in love with Sebastian…a truly inspiring read for anyone!!!!" – "This is a MUST read, INTELLIGENT, SENSITIVE, ENGAGING, PERFECT."

On Amazon: http://bookshow.me/B00CLL1UY6
On Goodreads: http://ow.ly/pthHZ
On Facebook: http://ow.ly/pthNy

Historical Note and Disclaimer

This book is a work of fiction. All characters apart from the obvious historical figures mentioned, such as Hitler or Elvis Presley, are the result of my imagination. No regional or local politicians are based on actual people. Official dates and the outcomes of all mentioned elections however are real - apart from the Heimkirchen City Council elections.

Although there are some outer similarities with my hometown and the social environment I grew up in, my fictional characters are not meant to reflect on any actual people.

The politicians of the Hinterberger family and their portfolios are entirely made up.

This book is also no assessment of current party politics. Given the political landscape and party lines in Germany after the war, I could not have chosen different party affiliations for my characters. My book does not reflect political ideas of my own, only humanitarian ideas maybe.

I wanted however to portray and pay tribute to a new generation of Germans which probably first became visible to the outside world in 1970 when the Chancellor of Germany, Willy Brandt famously sank to his knees in front of the monument for the Warsaw ghetto uprising.

The book is also not intended to offend religiously devoted readers: no religion is being criticised.

A Short Biography

Christoph Fischer was brought up near the Austrian border in Bavaria and has since lived in Hamburg, London, Brighton and Bath. He always loved books and one of his first jobs was in a library.

'The Black Eagle Inn' is the third and final book of the 'Three Nations Trilogy'. 'The Luck of The Weissensteiners' was published in November 2012 and 'Sebastian' was published in May 2013. The trilogy has a thematic connection but no direct link in the plots.

Since becoming an author, Christoph has begun to support other authors and has joined several internet author groups.

For further information you can follow him on:

http://writerchristophfischer.wordpress.com

www.christophfischerbooks.com

www.facebook.com/WriterChristophFischer

@CFFBooks

5890942R00165

Printed in Great Britain
by Amazon.co.uk, Ltd.,
Marston Gate.